London, 1950. Opera singer Luci[...] concert. But she has no intention of going onstage. A terrible secret from the First World War has finally caught up with her.

London, 1917. Lucia, a young Jamaican exile, hopes to make it as a musician. But her past haunts her, and when she meets Lilian, an old woman damaged by war, she agrees to a pact that could destroy everything she has striven for.

From the Western Front and Glasgow, to black society in London, Lucia's story tells a tale of music, motherhood, loss and redemption.

LUCIA'S WAR

SUSAN LANIGAN

To Luca, of course

The intellect of man is forced to choose
    Perfection of the life, or of the work,
    And if it take the second must refuse
    A heavenly mansion, raging in the dark.

-W.B. Yeats, 'The Choice'

PROLOGUE

1
GLASGOW, 5 APRIL 1917, 8 P.M.

The wind on the Firth of Clyde was getting up and it was time to go home. All month it had been like that – choppy too. Kenneth Reid, captain of the tugboat *Mariette*, had not eaten anything since his usual cheese and pickle sandwich five hours ago, but still his stomach was jumping upwards. It was no fun being a sailor prone to seasickness. He'd hardly had time to stop for even that bite of lunch, and Maudie had promised him a steak and kidney pie when he got in that night. He was more than ready to release his charge, the unoriginally named HMS *Endeavour*, into the wild and go home to his two-up two-down in Hutchesontown.

It was nearly summer, but a freak blast of poor weather had overcome the British Isles that week, and by sunset the heavy low sky had little colour. There was a plume on the sea, a persistent drizzle felt rather than seen, only showing itself in the glow of the starboard lamp as the boat continued towards harbour. It settled on his face and hands. Maudie had rubbed tallow over them that morning, but he'd not had time to replenish it, and his skin had little protection from the elements. He could only hope that please God it wouldn't snow again.

The *Mariette* had been busy that day, towing newborn ships out of the massive Inverclyde complex that stretched all the way from Govan out past Linthouse and Port Glasgow as far as Greenock. West of there, free of the exigencies of navigating through a busy port, they powered south, a mighty flotilla. They needed to be. Since the Jerries had started up unrestricted submarine warfare again, British merchant ships were going down like flies. Many of them had been personally seen out of harbour by the *Mariette*, and Kenneth Reid felt the loss of those ones particularly keenly.

The names of the new convoy ships were all of a type – variations of *Endeavour* and *Endurance* and *Victory* and *Britannia* and the Lord knows what. It seemed that the more anxious the British Empire became about losing the war, the more they put on a bold front with their ship names. Fast as they were let out, another row waited their turn in the shipyards, the welders putting the last touches on the armourplate for each one before it was cut loose to slide down to the sea.

On the south bank, that was all there was to see for miles and miles: shipyards and yet more shipyards. Twenty-two miles of them, full to the brim of men toiling away for the war effort. And women . . . girls! That was another change, one among so many these days.

Dan Rickards, the first mate, was steering them back to the depot at Govan, and as the *Mariette* made its way between the navigation markers, Reid could smell the city of Glasgow around him: a sulphurous bite, a warning that hung in the salty air, putting dirt into God's good rain. Still, no matter. It was home.

It was only a matter of luck that he saw her.

At first it was just a momentary flip on the river's surface that caught his attention. Like a fin, or perhaps a seal, though it was rare for them to be seen this far inland, too busy these days with all the steamers and warships – not to mention the filth. He dismissed it from his mind. But then Rickards changed course slightly so that the light shone out over the murky water where before it had been in gloom – and now he could see a pair of arms that jerked and flailed before submerging once more; then, again, flipping upwards, then, again, vanishing.

He knew what that meant. Had seen it for the first time back in '98 when he was on a fishing boat entering Stornoway harbour and a sudden wave had knocked one of them overboard. Peters. That had been the man's name. *Help, help*, he had called out while Reid struggled for the lifebelt, then he stopped shouting, and all Reid could see were those arms, jerking up and down. Then nothing. Then going under.

Reid leapt up the steps to the cabin, holding on to the railings as the boat swayed. 'Dan!' he shouted over the roar of the engine. 'Dan, I think there's somebody in the water.'

'Did you throw them the lifebelt?'

'No time,' Reid panted. 'He'll drown soon. Need to get him out. Turn around towards Greenock and go about five yards.'

Rickards swore and brought the wheel hard to starboard. Slowly, slowly the boat turned, the bow cutting a trail through the water. Merely feet away, Rickards cut the engine. It was a good drop, but with the third crewman MacFarlane behind him shining the torch, Reid took a breath and jumped into the Clyde.

The shock of its cold and filth hit him all at once. He had not thought to take off his coat and it was weighing him down. Christ, he had seconds to spare. He executed a quick front crawl and was soon right up behind the drowning person, whose arms were still jerking up and down like a puppet's. Leaning back, treading the water to balance himself, Reid got a hold under both arms, squeezed them hard, and gave an almighty tug until the head was out of the water. He pulled it closer to his chin and smelled the salt of a tidal river and the bits of green sea-moss that had got entangled in the hair. Loosened from all its grips and ties, it flowed over his arms, and he realised that the drowning person was, in fact, a woman.

Reid struck out back towards the boat, briefly twisting his head around to see MacFarlane tie a rope around a winching post and fasten it before climbing over the edge. Rickards hovered anxiously at the gunwale. Reid struggled in the water, the weight of the unconscious girl weighing him down as her head lolled back against his shoulder. 'Here! Here!' MacFarlane shouted, and Reid swam towards the voice. Shortly after, he saw MacFarlane's feet in his eyeline then his legs descending into the murk, and before he knew it his aching arms were released of the weight they had been dragging.

MacFarlane called to Rickards to winch him back up, and as he and the woman were pulled up on board, Reid heard him exclaim in surprise. He waited, treading water until the rope was tossed over once more and he grasped it. The sky was inky dark with a show of stars – but no more than a show: the clouds would gather overhead soon enough. His teeth chattered. It was no night to be out in the cold river.

He heard shouts and commands as he hung on to the rope, his hands beginning to tire. They were working on the girl. 'We have a pulse! A bit fluttery but definitely there.'

'She's no' breathin' though.'

'Lungs full of water. We need to give her mouth-to-mouth, to help clear her airway.'

Reid kept his feet firmly in the lower groove of the *Mariette's* hull, wedging his boots in so hard his toes hurt. Presently he felt a tug on the rope: Rickards was pulling him back up.

'Good job, cap'n,' he said, and went back to restart the engine.

'What about the girl—?' Reid began, but was interrupted by a loud bout of coughing, followed by a slow, horrible creak of inhalation that sounded more like the hinge of death than consciousness re-emerging. The woman was rising to her hands and knees, her head slumped forward, her breathing noisy and stertorous. Then, after a small hiccup, a torrent of river water gushed from her mouth, soaking the deckboards and merging with the spray and rain, followed by more coughing, then something akin to normal breath.

'Thank God we didn't need the chest compressions,' MacFarlane commented. 'A few breaths was all it took.'

To his horror, Reid could now see that the girl was heavily pregnant, possibly about to give birth. Surely no bairn would have survived the near-drowning of its mother. Her hair, entangled with riverweed and other flotsam, hung forward over her head. With a gesture of strength, she flung it back. For a moment, her eyes gazed in a lost place, and she knew nothing of where she was. Then they focused, and she straightened. Her face turned to the harbour searchlight, and once again Reid was shocked. *Heavens above*, he thought. *She's black!*

At that moment she swooned, and he had to move quickly to catch her in his arms. The light allowed him a view of her face close to his: long lashes, generous lips and a nose that was wide and flat. Yes, definitely a coloured girl. Young, too, maybe a few years on his eldest at most. Had she been walking by the banks and fallen in? Seemed unlikely – the walls were too high. Had somebody pushed her? Had she got on the wrong side of some nasty folk? Again, Reid thought of his own daughter, with a stab of tenderness and fear. Vigilance always, when you had daughters. What could you do, save locking them up, to keep them safe? *Better get the lassie below deck*, he thought, *warm her up a little.*

With some difficulty, given the list and sway of the boat, he got her in a fireman's lift and brought her below deck, having to swing his shoulder downward on occasion so as not to bump her against the low ceiling. The place smelled of bilge, and trying to keep the surfaces dry and clear of slick was a near impossible task.

There was precious little space in the tug to put her, but finally he was able to offload her onto a bunk and pull her up to a sitting position, all the while trying not to stare at her pregnant belly and the terrible future it must be about to foretell. He pulled off his gloves and attempted to dry her knotted hair at the roots with a scrap of a towel, as if she were one of his own babies in the tin bath by the kitchen fire. At this she sighed some more but did not open her eyes. It was only when he felt the gunwale bounce against the pier edge and heard the splash of the anchor descend overboard that she opened her eyes again. 'Well, luvvie,' he greeted her. 'What brought you here?'

When she finally spoke, he could hear that the life had nearly gone from her voice, but there was still the trace of a Caribbean lilt, a homeland thousands of miles away. 'A mistake, sir.'

'A mistake?' Reid repeated, staring down at the face of the woman he had just rescued. Then, with some compassion, 'Well it must have been one big mistake, because you look very lost.'

To that, she nodded, adding in the same melodious cadence, 'Yes, I am. I'm lost to God and to my fellow man. I have lost everything.'

'Have you really?' Reid persisted. 'You nearly lost your life, but we found you. By the finest hair of chance, but find you we did. So perhaps God isn't finished with you yet.' At that a weariness spread over her features, and she did not speak for almost a minute.

Then – 'Surely He wouldn't be so cruel?' But before Reid could ask the girl what she meant, her head fell back once more, and he was calling for MacFarlane to get the doctor the moment they came ashore.

2

LONDON, 1950

I've been singing all day so don't really need to warm up tonight, but I shall. Because tonight will be special. I have done the same warm-up routine for thirty-seven years. It will fit for this occasion too, even though I won't sing one solitary note. First, relax the throat. Yes, like that. Make a yawn, with no sound. And again. And again. Open your mouth as if you're thirsty beyond belief, longing for the cool, fresh, sweet-bitter tang of orange juice. Then relax the throat again.

Take all tension out of your shoulders. Release the neck muscles. Shake your head from side to side. But don't say no when you shake your head, just blow through your lips, making a rude noise, like blowing bubbles on a baby's tiny round belly, inhaling the smell of his skin like you know in your heart you'll never see him again.

Try a few arpeggios of that blowing-raspberries exercise. Start on C. Don't force it, don't worry if it sound like you a poppy show, a fool spitting all over folk. Appearance never matters. Then drop the jaw, loosen the tongue. Keep them relaxed and open, as if you are letting the river water flow into your mouth and lungs and letting your mind disengage from the worry of breathing. Never mind that your body struggles for air. Relax into the water. Relax into the darkness.

Your jaw should not move as you sing from C to G. Your tongue should hang out, as if you are gasping for one last piece of air before you sink. Then – are you ready? – this time start on D. You know the note. And you sing in a major arpeggio up, then a scale down, stretched all ways like an enormous umbrella: *Bel-la – señ-ooooooooo-ra*. And up to E flat. And then to E. And so on. *Bella señora, bella señora*. And breathe. Not from the head. Or the chest. But from the belly. Support the note. No note should be forced. It should float.

The warm-up is done. And I see, below me, the music critic is crossing the street. I cannot see his face, but I know him from his sense of purpose. And there! he has gone in. He will ring for me soon, and I must meet him downstairs.

Begin. After all, you have done this so many times before. In good times, sing. In bad times, sing. In the most terrible times of all, yes, then too you must sing.

3

LONDON, 1950, THE HOTEL BAR

S ir. I know you as well as you know me. I've read your reviews; I've seen how they make seasoned bass-baritones cry into their drinks. I have learned the grace notes and *rubato* of your prose style, as you have listened to mine in song. Even the drink you bring to my table is no surprise to me: I guessed a neat whisky with ice, and here it is. Two? You're wasting your time, man. Plain cold water is the only thing that shall pass my lips tonight. What, you don't believe me? I'll show you!

I know everything relevant about you, except why you are here. You wrote me while I was in New York, requesting an interview, but I do not understand why a music critic would wish to meet me before the performance. Are you planning on criticising my shoes? That I look a little old for these roles? I'm on the wrong side of middle age, I freely admit. But you! You carry the sallow, tired look of a survivor, with your thin-framed spectacles and over-sized shirt. The way you fiddle with the knot of your tie like a schoolboy. I don't mean to be rude, but even feet away your breath smells of metal. And here we both are, freezing in this hotel bar, in the middle of this skeleton city. Five years after the war, and half of London still not rebuilt! I passed the Alexandra Hotel when I arrived here, and its roof was only part complete.

All you will say in reply to my question, with a dipped head and a half-smile, is that you are a connoisseur of the work of Lucia Percival. I'm flattered, I admit. You must be a very sensitive man. Tactful too. Not a mention of the heavy rings around my eyes, the wrung-out flattened cheeks of a woman worn out from crying. Look here, I've had some bad news – news of interest to no one but myself, about a person of no significance to anyone but me. Just an everyday sadness, told to me by a sorry vagrant. Which means I hate to disappoint you in two days' time when I don't turn up. There you'll be, in your box in the Royal Albert Hall, all curtains and plush red velvet, poised with your little pen-light, and the conductor – that old Nazi! – will come out and say, 'I regret to tell you that Miss Percival . . .' Oh, don't shake your head! Everyone knows. Did you know I once sang Wagner to a roomful of Nazis? They attended a recording session, and I sang in a curtained booth. They didn't see me, nor I them, so they never knew I was not the Aryan goddess they hoped I would be . . . Unless they bought the record. But it was a very limited edition. What? You have it? Oh, you *are* a devotee.

There is one important thing people forget about Isolde, you know. That she was Irish. Not German. Cu yuh, I had an Irish friend once who nearly threw herself off Beachy Head. For love. I talked her back from the cliff edge. Whenever I sing the Wagner, I imagine that I am she, and make a run, run, run – each phrase like the waves building up – and then, right on that last G sharp, I throw myself into the big blue air and float for a second, before falling, falling . . . Except now there's nobody to call her back to life.

Oh, it is a pity. My last performance before retiring for good, ruined. Gone the vision of myself standing in front of the orchestra, wearing a Christian Dior dress of blood-red silk with ivory satin roses at the bust – no lie: it's hanging in the wardrobe upstairs right now – looking Herr Dirigent inna him yeye, the orchestra surging and swelling behind me. But it won't be. There will be no *Evening Standard* review, no ovation in the Albert Hall, no red dress, no Last Song of Richard Strauss, no flirting with the conductor. Because I am wild with grief, wilder than poor Isolde. I have no heart to sing, now or ever again.

You ask what is my story. Oh, my young friend. I surely cannot tell you. It is too brutal for the readers of the *Evening Standard*. If it were an opera, no one would swallow the plot, and the censors would be out like they were with poor Mr Shostakovich and his Lady Macbeth. He was writing film scores for a long time after that, poor man. And yet. You have taken up your notebook and pen. You say, tell anyway. Your eyes, through those spectacles, bore into mine like drills. Before you write anything more, let me get something from my bag. See this crocheted blanket, tiny and worn? I have kept it since 1919. It is so dirty now, but I shall never wash it, and it will go with me to heaven or to hell, whichever destination it pleases the Lord to take me. Probably the latter, but blood fiah, there will surely be a queue, and I will recognise a lot of them!

And so, seeing as you're still here, my opportunistic friend, I might as well unburden myself. Lean in, let me whisper it: I, Lucia Percival, have committed a great crime. I have seen the worst of war. I have loved and lost. I have sung, yes, but that was not all I did. I am glad you ordered that second whisky after all. Yes, yes, I know what I said about water, but seeing the golden glow of the whisky in those glasses, and bearing in mind what you ask of me . . . Let me drink it now, quickly. Down in one! The way I did with the absinthe that night all those years ago with poor Arthur at the Dorchester.

Since you want to know, let me distract myself from grief. Let me tell you about the time when the first war was raging, and my life took that wrong turning from which I have never recovered. Where to begin? Ah, it is not easy to sing it straight: I must do it in false codas and grace notes.

See, if you will, a rainy evening in August 1917, and a down-at-heel chamber in Soho. A girl of twenty-one, black, though there is Irish in my family tree, two years out of Jamaica, altogether jaded with life. Three years into the first great *bangarang* and no sign of an end. Pleasant weather, fresh fruit, courtesy from strangers – all lost dreams. Rain, all the time. Skin with a bloom of grey on the surface. Mind shrunk down. An open heart turned surly as the weather.

We were all sick of war by then, fed up to the back teeth of it: the lying headlines, the obituaries taking up half the paper, the men it chewed up and left dead or half alive, the endless posters and rules and rationing and by-laws and DORA . . . Everything mash up. That was the evening I began the search for my dear sweet one in earnest and the night Arthur Rosewell entered my life. That evening is as good a place to start as any.

PART I

PART I

4

13 AUGUST 1917

'Are you sure this is what you want, Miss Percival?'

I was in the office of Mr Edgar Manning, a coloured gentleman and private investigator from Jamaica whose pure cockney accent had surprised me on my first hearing it. A mounted boar on the wall stared down at me, as did the man himself. The room, a first-floor walk-up in Soho Square, was such a riot of colour and disorder that it reminded me of Chipperfield's Circus: chocolate-brown wallpaper with columns of white fleur-de-lys; Aubrey Beardsley prints hanging unevenly, all grotesque – the severed head of John the Baptist and the exposed breasts of some winged duppy creature being the highlights – the whole ensemble unseasonably dark, lit by one table lamp on Mr Manning's desk. By the door lolled an elegant white cane, which I suspected was hollow, with a handsome gold handle.

'Yes,' I said. 'Quite sure.'

I had come from work at the war hospital in Roehampton, with the sweat drying on the armpits of my shirt and the unexpected rain drenching my sleeves. On my way through Soho, I passed chophouses with Chinamen at the windows and narrow doors opening to downward flights of stairs through which soldiers on leave would disappear. In one such door a woman lingered, pink-lipped, her leg drawn up so that her suspenders were visible, thigh pale as milk. I could see the stretch marks on her skin. I hastened my step: this was not a neighbourhood where I wanted to linger.

I found the house and rang the bell. A dead-eyed girl with a sprinkling of white powder on her upper lip slowly dragged the door open. When I asked her about Mr Manning's whereabouts, she looked at me languid as you please, then beckoned me to follow her upstairs, where I encountered Mr Manning himself, leaving his office.

He was better presented than his surroundings: not exactly handsome, his mouth being rather too wide and his cheeks too low, but in possession of a defiance that charged the air about him. He was just about to go out, he told me, but he would hear me a few moments.

Prior to that, I had never met Edgar Manning. All I knew was that he had left Jamaica the year before and had worked in the munitions factory in Dartford. I'd heard of him while doing similar work in Enfield and made note of his name. He was what you might now call a wide boy, occasionally doing private investigation and occasionally dodging the law himself. When I related to him the particulars of my case, he seemed cautious, and tapped a silver-topped pencil on his jotting pad. 'Miss Percival, people in your situation generally don't request information unless they are prepared to act on it.'

'That's my decision, sir. All I ask is the information. I have the money. Look.'

He waved it away. 'That's not the point. Such stories rarely have happy endings. I guarantee you will not get what you want out of this.'

'Let me be the judge of that.' I stayed calm, betrayed no emotion. What I needed Mr Manning for was my business and nobody else's.

He tutted in the Jamaican style, making a kiss-teeth sound. 'You already in too far. Wanti wanti kyaan getti. I'm warning you, girl. Have sense and walk 'way, nuh.'

Anger flared in me. 'You are too presumptuous, sir. Here is my money, as honest as anyone's. Do you want my custom or not?' Although I tried to stay businesslike, I could feel my cheeks burn and had to blink several times. Edgar Manning was my last chance. I could not let him refuse me.

'Hush!' he said, seeing my face, and I knew he meant it in the Jamaican way: *I am sorry*. 'Usually I'd say nothing, but you . . . you come like mi sista. And it's a brother's job to protect.'

'Mr Manning, I already have a brother.' I was determined to keep it formal. 'And believe me, I've made sure that I'm protected.'

'Then you are very fortunate.' His shoulders slumped. 'I was supposed to read for the Bar. That's what my parents wanted. But they don't know the reality of being a black man in London. Now I keep a Colt .38 by my bedside at night, in a coromandel box I was given after a fight.' Hearing me suck my teeth in turn, he shook his head. 'This is where I am now, but it's not where I wanted to be when I started. And I am a man in my prime. But you – a woman wandering alone in London, black as I am? If you were truly protected, Miss Percival, you would not be in my office right now, would you?'

The clock on the mantelpiece chimed six-thirty. The room felt constricting: the slightly musty smell that lingered around everything, the shouting on the floor below, the draught that pervaded the walls even in August – why was this sorrowful country so cold all the time? – and the intermittent assaults of rain on the window-panes. Even in late summer, Mr Manning had felt it necessary to keep the lamp switched on. Which said it all.

I still held a ten-shilling note. Silently, I passed it across the desk. With a meaningful look, Manning left it untouched. For a moment, I feared that some scruple was preventing him from taking on my case. But no – his look was taut and expectant. He just wanted more money. With a sigh of relief mingled with irrita-tion, I put another five shillings' worth of coins on top of the note. Only then did he accept my offer, secreting the money into a desk drawer which he then locked. He rose and put the key in his coat pocket. Our meeting was over. 'Since you insist. I will write to you in three weeks' time. It is doubtful I will have news for you before then.'

'Take your time,' I said, 'but not too much of it.'

He nodded. 'Now, I'm already late to meet a gentleman who does not approve of lateness. May I see you out?'

'Yes. Thank you, Mr Manning.'

'You are welcome.' Then he added, as we made our way together down the stairs, 'Walk good, Miss Percival. Try to stay out of trouble.' Now that, as my friend Eva would say, was the very definition of shutting the stable door after the horse had bolted.

I waited until I was fully outside before opening my umbrella, and by the time I had it up, he was gone. He carried my hopes on his shoulders, so I hoped that he walked good too. As for me, I ducked and dived through the crowded streets, dodging puddles and automobiles and hurrying Englishmen until I could get to a safe street and catch the bus home.

After my dishonourable discharge from the Voluntary Aid Detachment – an auxiliary nursing body set up during the war – and my subsequent ordeal, I had managed to find my feet in London once more. I worked at the hospital and lived with a girl just about my own age called Eva Downey in a large but dingy street-facing room just off Fulham Road, down a dutty little lane with no lighting or protection from ne'er-do-wells, in a building where they once kept horses and straw and which seemed barely improved since then.

Eva was the Irish Isolde who had almost thrown herself off Beachy Head a few months before. Now she submitted to the business of living with such grim resignation that I sometimes wondered if it had been wrong to save her. We had met through circumstances so insalubrious that we both kept a silent pact not to discuss them. To make it brief, when I first clapped eyes on her in November 1915, I had already been informed that she was in trouble and needed to procure an abortion. I knew a Haitian ex-priestess then carrying on a backstreet practice in Beak Street and arranged an appointment for her.

At the time, I was working for the VAD at Mile End, having done some small training at the fever hospital back home in Mandeville that qualified me to join. The VAD work brought in next to no money, so I needed to supplement it with tasks to which I would have otherwise held a strict moral aversion. (I hold up my hands: when conflicted between God and Mammon, I sometimes let the latter win. God is good, but He has never paid my rent.) The place I worked for might have been illegal, but to my surprise I found it was not unprofessional. Doctors and midwives were employed there, and even with men out at war, business was, unfortunately, brisk. Women of all classes took their business there; for all that abortion was illegal, in reality people were quite matter-of-fact about it. Someone willing to play go-between could earn a decent cut. I made a choice between morality and money, reasoning with myself that I could settle with God in the next life. But this reasoning sat badly with me, like a nagging tooth.

Eva, one of my 'referrals', was almost pathetically grateful for my help. She had fallen pregnant for a man she had been forced to marry by her family, who had since died. We stayed in and out of communication over the years, and I followed her war story at a distance. Suffice it to say it was as ugly and painful as mine, and by August 1917, when we shared a home, ours was a house of grief that took turns to express itself.

She was sometimes difficult company, but for a woman like me, living alone in London was not an option. I tried it briefly, just after my arrival in England in the late summer of 1915, all fresh and green from the boat that had docked in Southampton, and thinking I might meet at worst some mild insult or injury to my person on account of being of another race. I even convinced the port official who questioned my status under the new Alien Status Act that I was indeed a full (if not legitimate) citizen of the British Empire, smiling at him, tilting my head to one side, a carefully preserved gardenia under my hatband. *Am I not the prettiest alien you ever did see, Mr Guard?* I thought if I used the full force of my charm that I could somehow get by every time.

I was soon proved wrong. It wasn't the casual insults, the slights or the cuts that did for me, though I endured them day in, day out. Not the click of the door shutting in my face when I responded to any advertisement for rooms or employment. Not even the time when, one blustery day, trembling with nerves and dolled up in my best winter dress – grey merino with double buttons and a crossover bodice – I presented myself at the Royal Academy of Music and timidly asked if there was any way of earning a scholarship for singing lessons. My request was greeted by a hoot of laughter by a jaded-looking receptionist. Then, 'Are you a cleaner? Oh wait, you couldn't be: we have no vacancies for cleaning staff right now. Run along there with your *frock*!' I fled out into the traffic and noise of Marylebone Road, burning with humiliation and barely swallowing back my tears.

It wasn't even the weather, or the food. And let me tell you, both were awful. Made me feel bad for Mrs Rochester Number One whose husband had her locked up while he rhapsodised to Jane Eyre about how he loathed the warm, tropical climate of our shared native land. No. It was the men. All day, every day. *How much? Come on love. Give us a smile. We know you lot all love it.* Grabbed on the street in plain view, hands sneaking around my backside on the trolley buses, chased down the street after buying groceries so half the eggs were cracked by the time I got home. The smell of one commercial traveller who put down his briefcase and pressed me up against a wet brick wall; the thick beery-tasting meat of his tongue forced into my mouth before I managed to elbow my way out with some force.

Of course their queries about price were pro forma; their kind was used to sampling my people for free, just like that. My late, much-loved father had warned me of this. I should have listened to him. Especially when he told me that I didn't listen to him enough.

After my great fall in 1917, after I was rescued and I returned to London, well near destitute, I realised that if I were to raise myself again and reclaim that which was rightfully mine, I would need the protection of a white person – even one who considered herself of no importance and whose accent revealed her Irishness during times of high emotion more often than she would like. Someone who might feel some duty to me because of my help in her time of trouble. To be frank, a talking tub of lard would have done fine, as long as it looked European.

So in the spring of 1917, I deliberately sought Eva out and found her about to throw herself off Beachy Head. I managed to talk her out of it, for a mixture of selfish and selfless reasons, and back to London we went. Eva could never have imagined how much easier my life flowed when my living standards were raised, relatively speaking, from my destitution to hers. It was she who secured the ground-floor room for us, on a rolling six-month lease, visiting our future landlady, a widow called Mrs Baxter, on her own to agree the details. Our rent was two pounds fifty a month, a price that kept Eva and me scrabbling for every spare farthing when rent day came around. Most of the money was mine, since my work in Roehampton, though tedious, paid well.

I had made it clear to Eva from the outset that she must respond to all 'Room to Let' advertisements alone. One afternoon trailing around Highbury making door-to-door enquiries *à deux*, and having the door slammed in our faces before Eva could finish explaining 'We've come about the—' was enough to convince her I was right.

On Mrs Baxter's inevitable discovery that Eva's companion Miss Lucia Percival was rather darker in appearance than expected, it was Eva who managed to talk her out of evicting us both onto the street. I don't know what she said exactly, but being forced to live in Ireland for several years had toughened Eva up considerably, and when she was in one of her angry fugues her cornflower-blue eyes acquired a cast of absence that would frighten anyone out of their resolution, even a cockney landlady.

Approaching our building, I saw the grim glow of the electric light behind the drawn calico curtains. Eva must already be home. That was unusual. Still with the VAD, she was doing donkey work at St Thomas's, working all the hours God sent. To take her mind off things, she said. It was unusual for them to let her out early.

I could hear a strange, repetitive noise: thud, thud, thud. Did Mrs Baxter have a tradesman in? It seemed like an odd time for it. I would keep my head low, my face shielded by my headscarf when I went in. Just in case. As I approached the door, the noise grew louder. I tried to ignore it, thinking instead whether there might be something to eat. Eva was a good cook, having learned

that year she lived in Ireland, before her husband enlisted and got
shot for desertion at Saint-Omer. 'RIP,' she used to say whenever
she mentioned his name, her eyes shut piously, pausing a few
dramatic seconds before hissing, 'Rot In Perpetuity, you bastard!'
and laughing like a demon, her cheeks flushing as red as English
apples. I knew too well that her hatred for him was only love for
someone else, someone who had left this earth more recently. It
was a love that had nowhere to go so congealed into anger instead.

After the rain outside, the hall was cool and dry, and that's the
nicest thing I could say about it. The wine-red and green terracotta
tiles were covered in muddy footprints because nobody bothered
wiping their feet, and the top of the tallboy was all covered with
dust, including its solitary chrysanthemum wilting in a nondescript vase. Even on the rare occasion when Mrs Baxter did hire a
cleaner, it never rid the place of cooking odours: cabbage, pota-
toes, oxtail soup. And they were the nicest fragrances on offer,
believe me.

There was no sign of any tradesmen, but still the noise continued: the slow thump of something heavy hitting a surface,
reminding me of the sluggish march tempo of the tenor aria 'Cre-
deasi, misera!' So rhythmic was it that I could nearly have sung the
doomed cavalier's song to its accompaniment – but I had got in
trouble with the landlady before for singing in the hallway.
Besides, I had the distinct impression that it was coming from the
other side of our door.

Cautiously I turned the key in the lock, uncertain of what I
would find. Nothing could have prepared me for what I did
witness. Eva was standing at the table, the Belfast sink beside her
piled with dirty dishes. Her cheeks were flushed red, her eyes
wild, her fair hair hanging thick but limp by her side. Her arms,
raised above her head, held a frozen leg of lamb, entombed in ice –
Eva had a gift for scavenging food from all sorts of surprising

sources – then *thump!* She brought it down on the deal table's much-abused surface. I feared not only that she would splinter the wood but that the whole table would collapse.

'Eva!'

She took no notice of me, bringing the lamb down again and again, her teeth showing, her eyes gleaming but blank, her dress splattered with melting ice. As she lifted the thing once more, her eyes caught mine but did not see me: she had gone into another one of those fugue states of hers. Since I had talked her back from the cliff edge, just five months before, Eva would from time to time withdraw into a strange world and become utterly mute for minutes at a time. I had come home from a late shift once or twice to find her at the table, surrounded by sheets of paper, fingers stained with ink, staring into the middle distance.

She was writing an article for *Blackwood's* magazine which was intended, she said, to confess her grievous sin under her own name. I thought, at first, that she was talking about her abortion, and strenuously advised her not to continue. She looked at me like I had two heads. 'That? Oh, I'd forgotten. No. I meant the white feather.'

Her reply shocked me. Giving the man you loved a white feather, even when you were forced to, like Eva – cha, it would be a distasteful deed, but surely abortion would be the graver sin, many times over! Of course, I should have known she would not feel that way. For Eva, morality was never objective. No, it depended entirely on the character of the person she directed it to. She hadn't loved the man who got her pregnant, and had not consented to his advances, so her abortion was no great offence, but the man she sent out to war . . . Ah, that was another story, one that had come to a sad and horrible end a year ago. That story was the main reason I kept my shock to myself. She was suffering enough and could not get out the other side of it; even with the article, she'd been writing it for months, with no sign of finishing. Now here she was, beating an inanimate object with an uneatable weapon. And no sign of any dinner.

It was only when I grasped her forearms hard and looked her straight inna har eye that she recovered true consciousness, jumping back as if I had electrocuted her, the leg of lamb hitting the ground with a clatter.

'Wha 'appen tu yuh? Why you a beat the leg a lamb so?'

Eva looked at it herself and shook her head in wonder, as if she'd never seen it before. 'My God,' she breathed in dismay, before turning to me, her straw-coloured hair plastered to her temples, her expression as shocked as mine. 'I think . . . I meant to defrost it.'

'You a joke! Fi how lang?'

Eva looked at her watch. 'Half an hour, an hour maybe?'

'Looks pretty frosted still.' *Mi Gad, the neighbours must love us.* Aloud, I said, 'Where did you get it anyway? I've never seen frozen meat for sale in any butcher's.'

'I was walking down by Victoria Station by chance and saw it roll off the back of a truck. It was intended for the troops, I think – that's why it was frozen. The truck hit a mule, the back door burst open, and this piece of meat rolled out, right in front of me. I made off with it while all was chaos.'

It was clear to me she had not thought this through. 'So you brought dis *ting* all the way home?' The icy shinbone had only melted very slightly, so Eva's palms were covered with the stinky meat water while the joint itself was intact.

'I . . . suppose I did. I must have fallen into a dream,' Eva said in a small voice. 'I remember now. I thought it would be nice to boil it for dinner, but then I realised I couldn't fit the whole joint in the saucepan and I'd have to melt it. And then . . . I just got frustrated.' She trailed off.

She didn't have to finish. I knew how it would have progressed. She would have gone on hammering that leg of lamb until either the table broke or she fell on top of it. Her frustration would have started out with the direct object in her path, then broadened out to everything that had happened to her in this rotten war. She couldn't write it down, but she could hammer it onto a table. If I, or someone less friendly, had not intervened, the hammering might never have ended.

I guided her to the one, sagging, armchair in the corner of the room and fetched her a tumbler of water. She thanked me in that same small abstract voice, as if she were a machine. Then a muttered, 'Sorry about all this.'

'Forget about it,' I said gently. 'We're going out soon anyway, remember? You promised Sybil you'd go to this séance tonight and' – I checked my watch – 'we're running out of time.'

At the mention of her titled friend, Eva looked a little livelier. Sybil could get quite peremptory if her demands were not fulfilled. 'I wish I'd never agreed to it. I hate the theatrics, and Sybil gets so maudlin at these things. She always hits the gin beforehand.'

'Her brother died, sweetheart. It's understandable.'

I imagined how I would feel if my brother Reginald, across the Channel in Dunkirk, met a similar fate at the end of the enemy's bayonet. Perhaps not sad enough to drink myself silly, but mighty sad all the same. And guilty too, for all the stress I had caused him of late, when I had been spirited away and he had no idea where to find me. Thankfully he was doing nothing more hazardous than guarding stationary aircraft.

'She reeked of it the last time.' Eva was still quite distrait, but she had lost that dreadful pallor and had begun moving about, washing her hands at the sink with the bar of Lifebuoy soap, then splashing her face, dampening her hair and sleeves as she did so.

'Eva,' I said, 'you sure you're able for this?'

She laughed shortly. 'Lucia, you know I never relate that sort of tommyrot to my own life. I don't believe in spirits, even though you do. Haven't we had this conversation already? I'm only going to humour Sybil.'

'All right,' I said, not wanting to get into yet another debate, 'but what do we do about the . . .' I gestured at the leg of lamb where it lay on the floor. The poor creature – it had died for this?

She shrugged, 'Leave it. Who knows, it might have defrosted a little by the time we get back.'

'All right, but why don't I put it pon di table—'

'*Leave it.*' Eva was so vehement that I snatched back my outstretched hand and left the grotesque object where it lay.

We both changed. I pulled out my outfit from where it had been neatly packed under my bedstead and shook it out: a wide-necked oriental blouse with red stitching and chiffon sleeves and a rayon and velvet skirt that rippled in the lifeless air. This I paired with light suede gloves and a broad-brimmed soft hat. Eva gave the ensemble an approving nod – though her own judgement on what was fashionable was, to put it mildly, weak. 'Looks nice.'

'Thanks.' I admit I was looking forward to wearing it. Those penitential days during the Great War had few enough opportunities for socialising, and for coloured people like me, that 'few' shrank to 'nearly none'. Eva might think such events creepy and morbid, but I maintained it was worth it for the chance to dress up and go out somewhere that wasn't work or church.

Eva stared at me mockingly, the blue and white checked cotton day dress she had chosen half draped over her shoulders. 'Church? I've never seen you darken the door of one.' It was my turn to give *her* a look. 'Figure of speech,' she amended hastily, shrugging her remaining arm through.

'Had better be,' I said, glad to be off the subject of church.

The knocker on the outer door banged loudly three times.

'Syb's here,' Eva said flatly.

'Eva!' Shouted like a company commander. 'We need to be at Euston Square on the dot of half eight! C'mon!'

Sybil was not a woman to be trifled with, even in her current sad state. Earlier in the war she had volunteered as an ambulance driver, and she and her friend Roma Feilding were awarded a Military Medal for taking over a delivery of pigeons when their male commander was killed by shrapnel.

'Oh God,' Eva sighed, 'definitely the gin. I can tell.'

I hung back while Eva went to the door and let Sybil in, or, rather, cleared all obstructions so she could burst in like a storm on a hot day.

She was a tall woman, five foot nine at least, pale-featured with a head of magnificent red-gold hair. Once or twice I had seen it fall free down her shoulders, and, cu yuh, it burned like the sunset. This evening it was wrestled into a hairnet and covered by a blue serge faille hat – a few vermilion strands escaped from her bun and glinted in the sunlight filtering through the window. She wore a light-brown wool belted coat and a pair of crocodile-skin boots.

She looked us both up and down. 'Well, you're ready at any rate,' she declared. 'Nice outfit.' This was directed at me. 'Car's outside. Let's go.'

I thanked her with little more than a stiff nod. We did not get on, for a multitude of reasons. I found it hard to be natural around her; something about her made me clam up and feel resentful. It could have been because of what she said to me once, outside the National Gallery, when she looked me up and down and declared, drunkenly, 'The thing with you is you're not at the top or the bottom of society. You're outside it entirely, and that's why I don't know where to place you.' *Blouse and skirt!* How was I supposed to respond to that?

Or it could have been that disastrous visit to her home, when the maid glared at me when tea was served, and where I learned how Sybil, a divorced viscountess, lived unashamedly with Roma Feilding, carrying on a liaison which at the time I could not regard as Christian. She was inordinately protective of her friend and could not tolerate even the slightest criticism. I had been about to challenge the morality of her position when Eva broke in nervously and mentioned that she would like some whisky, which was a sure sign to both of us to back down, since it was not three in the afternoon and we both knew Eva hated the stuff.

Or it could have been because Sybil had been the one who telephoned the Mile End exchange to arrange the fixing of Eva's little problem. The price of Eva's freedom turned out to be high, and Sybil questioned me repeatedly about it, until it became clear that she thought I was creaming off too much. This insinuation vexed me, and I asked her outright if she were accusing me of impropriety. Her response was to set her mouth in a thin line and hand over the notes.

For all these reasons, and perhaps others I didn't know about, Lady Sybil Faugharne and I didn't trust one another. But as I clung to Eva, Eva clung to her. So whatever my reservations were about the evening ahead, I would keep my mouth firmly shut.

'Righto, what are we waiting for then?' Sybil said, tapping her watch. 'We'll need to hurry if we want to get a seat . . .' She trailed off, gazing at the floor, her eyes fixed on the one object we had all been trying to ignore. 'What,' she said, pointing at the leg of lamb, 'on earth is that?'

I SLID into the back of the Wolseley after Eva, feeling the soft give of the black leather against the backs of my calves and thighs. The rain had cleared, and white light gleamed from behind the remaining clouds. This light also glared from the puddles on the road, and the cobblestones too, which were slick from the rain. Sybil sat next to the driver, a solid, broad-shouldered man, who took a left, then a right, driving on past Holland Park.

'I hope this one's good,' she remarked, twisting her head around to face us. 'The last one was very ropey. Ectoplasms, spitting and the like – quite revolting. I say,' she continued, noticing Eva's pallor for the first time, 'you look like you walked into a truck.' Sybil didn't tend to mince her words.

'I'm fine.'

Sybil didn't believe her. 'Is it anything to do with that . . . *object* I saw on the floor just now? Honestly, Eva, I know things are bad, but there's no need to live in filth.'

'There was no time,' I cut in, not wanting Eva to upset herself by talking about it again, 'so we decided to leave it.' I hunted around for some way of letting Sybil know that it was not a good idea to probe further, but she must have divined as much from my expression because she backed away. I'll say one thing for Sybil Faugharne: unlike a lot of her titled cohort, she wasn't stupid.

'And what about you, then, ah . . . ?' Sybil could never quite bring herself to say my name. 'Are you expecting to hear from anyone?'

'Sybil,' Eva said wearily. 'That's private business.'

I stared right back at her. 'No. I have no deceased relatives except for my father, and he never approved of idolatrous practices. I'm here for the company.'

'Oh, hoity-toity. I was only asking.'

'And I am telling you.'

Ten minutes later, we were at Euston Square. To my surprise, a small crowd was milling on the path outside the address. This was going to be a big one. The house itself was not as grand as it looked from the outside. The ceiling cornices in the foyer were peeling paint, the Turkish patterned carpet was shabby and stained, and the mirrors were so smoke-worn and convex that everyone, even a reed like Sybil, looked mampsy in reflection. Poor Eva disregarded the mirrors entirely so was spared their withering criticism.

'They're taking their time about letting us in,' Sybil said. 'Setting up the room I suppose.'

'"Setting up the room,"' Eva repeated, mockingly. 'What a farce. What frauds.' Nobody paid attention to her. I scanned the crowd: nearly all of them women. Their interest was focused on the far corner of the hall, where a very tall and tanned man in late middle age held forth to his followers in a high-pitched reedy tone. He was bespectacled and wore a red neckerchief, and had a look I'd often seen on older, white men: an air of scattered absent-mindedness that barely concealed a proprietorial, controlling presence. I could tell he was used to being recognised, too.

Beside him stood a girl the same age as ourselves, fashionably dressed in an outfit – an olive-green wool drop-waist dress – that made her look a bit too old for her years. Her hair was auburn, like Sybil's, though duller, and she had a square jaw and piercing eyes that never left the man.

'Who are they?' I asked Eva.

'That is Mr Yeats, the famous poet. The woman is Miss Hyde-Lees. She's supposed to have designs upon him. She follows him to every séance in London.'

'Him? Her?' I exclaimed. 'But he's old enough to be her father.'

'Perhaps she would have found a younger man,' Eva said, 'were they not all dead.'

'True-true,' I murmured automatically, sensing another of Eva's rants about the Horrors of War coming on and flapping my hand at her in warning. But then I stopped mid-gesture and promptly forgot about Mr Yeats, the would-be Mrs Yeats, and everybody else. Because behind the poet hovered a handsome man, Mr Yeats's equal in height, with broad shoulders and close-cropped hair. He wore a wool jacket with a pink handkerchief peeking out of the breast pocket. His mouth was serious, but his eyes smiled and turned slightly downward, as if sharing a confidence about something ridiculous. When my eyes met his, the smiling look suddenly dimmed, and he looked down and away, cut yeye, interlacing his fingers and bending them back.

Oh, and did I mention he was black?

'They're opening the doors,' Sybil hissed, gesturing to the pair of floor-to-ceiling French doors, panelled and grey-blue, which were now being pulled open from the other side. We filed into a larger room that was almost completely dark and fumbled around in the gloom, trying to find seats. There was a lot of shushing and fussing and making sure the shutters were bolted. The smell of perfume, sweat, starched clothes and cigar smoke mixed in the still air. I had a few people bump into me and murmur apologies. For a moment I was surprised they were so pleasant – and then I remembered: it was too dark for them to see me.

As my eyes accustomed themselves to the dim light, I discerned a toy trumpet standing mouthpiece-up on a small table covered with a green baize cloth. It was detectable partly due to the luminous rings set around it, which glowed a garish lime green. It was the kind of instrument one might buy a child in a department store. I turned to Sybil, who I could hear unscrewing that little magic bottle that solves all life's ills beside me. 'What is that?' I whispered.

'It's for the voices of the dead,' Sybil replied. 'The woman's a trumpet medium.'

'A *what*?' Eva cried out with disdain.

Then movement: the medium stepped forward. I could not

make out her face, though her voice sounded old. 'The spirit controls cannot be heard unless there is utter silence in the room. So can I have your cooperation please?' After a bout of coughing and shushing, the room fell into a collective pause that lengthened, lengthened into dramatic intensity. Sybil was cracking her fingers – *cha, it was irritating!* – when somebody gasped. 'Look!' Fizzing orange lights darted through the air and towards the ceiling before fading and disappearing. My heart leapt upwards like a fish in a boat, pounding right in my throat, and I stifled a scream.

Eva was unmoved. 'Phosphorus: I recognise it. The Germans light 'em up and throw 'em in the sky.'

'Shhhhh!' hissed the entire room, enraged.

The warmth of the room, the cloying lack of oxygen, was getting pon mi nerves, and I had to flex my own fingers not to start biting my nails. Eva could call it phosphorus if she wanted; I called it spirits, and truly I was afraid. Although I was not a medium, thank God, my inner ear, already pitch-sensitive, had of late become so refined I could sometimes hear voices that did not even belong to this world. Clairaudience, they called it. I called it a curse, and I'm mighty glad I haven't experienced it for decades since. The Bangarang did not help this at all, and I began to regret attending this event. I folded my arms across my chest, to protect myself against the malevolent ones. The air was close and tight, sour-smelling. I reached for the small silver cross around my neck, forgetting it had been taken off last November.

Then the trumpet lifted clean off the table and started flying around the air! I yelped in shock. *Lard a mercy!* I was spooked. I felt a jab in my side. Eva. 'For God's sake, pull yourself together,' she hissed. 'You don't think that thing's actually flying, do you? Ask yourself why they do it in the dark.'

I was about to tell Eva she had no right to say 'pull yourself together' when she'd just had a nervous breakdown over a piece of frozen meat, but then, out through that trumpet, a voice spoke, and my mood changed. It fell like a cold blade on my heart. 'Mama!' It sounded like a child. 'Mama!'

Somewhere in the crowd a woman gave a sobbed exclamation of grief and joy.

'I'm happy, Mama. I'm wearing my nice dress with the stripes.'

'Oh yes,' the woman cried out, 'the starched cotton – and your little blue shoes! When they put you in the coffin I polished them up special and sent you out with 'em.'

'This is cruel,' I heard Eva mutter, but I remained mute. My throat was closing over: I could not speak. A tiny child was dead, from who knew what malady or injury, and her mother, grieving and raw, was wandering from spiritualist to spiritualist seeking the little ghost. My imagination ran wild as I reconstructed the short, sad story: the pickney who had barely started out in life, who played on kitchen floors and in parks, laughing happily, and who was now rotting in a cemetery along with her favourite summer dress. A small, sad, innocent death, which, among all the slaughter and bloodshed, would be forgotten in the years to come, the gravestone covered in moss until even the little name was obscured. I could see it all. A horrible, horrible sadness over-whelmed me, as dark as the room. I felt it deep down inside, a physical rebounding ache in my belly and my heart. Her mother could grieve, but I . . . I could not! I felt Eva's arm on my shoulders, lightly and briefly. She knew my story. She understood. Bless her Irish heart.

The trumpet voice moved on to an approximation of a male. 'He' had a gruff accent – I would say north of England. He intro-duced himself as David, later modifying it to Donald, and for a moment I wondered if Eva had a point about it all being a charade. Killed in Passchendaele . . . or was it Messines? A recent battle, anyway, but three years in, it was hard to keep track. At the beginning of the war we had regarded the long death columns in *The Times* with horror and awe. Now? We used the pages to wrap fish.

The medium's credentials now established, a long line of requests followed from the audience. Battlefields were recited in a litany, as far back as Mons and Festubert. Eva was yawning. Then, unprompted, a woman's voice emerged from the trumpet horn, singing something Celtic and guttural. At that I smelled a sudden waft of a man's cologne, a violet fragrance. Mr Yeats had leaned forward, his attention engaged. 'Who have I?' he said in a shrill weebly-warbly tenor.

'Susan,' the voice answered.

'By God,' the poet murmured, ''tis my mother. She would sing that song to me when I was a little boy.'

Whispers rustled around the room. It was one thing for ordinary men and women to hear their dead speak to them, but famous poets – another thing altogether. Surely the authority of the medium was beyond doubt! Then a loud noise came through the horn, so deafening it nearly made my ears bleed. 'Frustrators! Frustrators!' a different voice called out. 'Everybody grab hands and sing!'

'Frustrators,' Mr Yeats informed us in his high-pitched, melodious tones, barely audible above the trumpet, 'are daemonic agents that try to interfere with the medium's channel. We must do as she asks.'

'We' didn't, at first. We just sat there, stunned into silence while the horn roared and roared like a bull. The airlessness of the room weighed on me, and I wished I had never come. I could not shake the feeling of the dead child's trapped spirit beating on my heart with little wings. *Oh, please let somebody open the window!* A rattle, then a chink of late evening light. My prayers were answered! Cool air, God's gift even in this filthy city, came trickling into the room. Still the weight was not dispersing; still I felt that a stone had been placed on the small of my back. The evil energy was still present.

'Sing!' Mr Yeats urged, and all of a sudden one particular voice broke into a tremulous 'Abide with Me' that became stronger, swelling and rolling as it grew in power. To the glad astonishment of my conscious mind, I discovered that the voice was my own.

A few bars later, some elderly quavering vocals joined in, then some younger ones, and then everyone, even – alas for anyone with sensitive ears! – the discordant Mr Yeats himself, whose relationship with musical notes was flexible to the point of being nonexistent. The room filled with song. This felt better. This was familiar territory.

On the last day of my dear father's nine-night wake, two years before, I had led the singers outside our home with this very song, and then again in the small tin-roofed church in Mandeville at his interment. It felt easy and natural to lead them now, these lost Englishwomen, all the grieving widows and high-society Henriettas with their hopes and dreams wrecked around them like shards of glass. I heard a steady baritone, a sure note, accompany my soprano. With a leap of joy in my heart, I knew, just knew, that it was the handsome stranger I had seen earlier.

After the hymn, the medium instructed everyone to recite a prayer, and then the lights were brought back up. We all looked at each other in stupefied amazement, as if we had just been through a rite of passage together. I was astonished to see tears on Eva's cheeks, she the non-believer! Sybil, who had heard nothing from her brother George, or 'Bo' as she called him, appeared dry-eyed, cold and withdrawn. The brash light from the nine-bulbed chandelier showed her beautiful features badly, making her nose look too sharp and her lips drawn in.

The stranger had not yet left. Now that the séance was over, I saw my chance. I was all set to cross the room, had identified a clear path through the crowd, when he moved off. Then I saw him in a corner talking to Mr Yeats. I approached the men using a discreetly diagonal route, but cu yuh, Mr Yeats was now hallooing and waving at me, beckoning me to approach. Miss Hyde-Lees was looking daggers at me. I could only marvel at her obsession and how it eclipsed all common sense. How on earth could she think *Mr Yeats* was the party I was interested in?

The ladies who previously blocked my way now parted for me as if I were Moses himself and they the Red Sea. Alas, to my crushing disappointment, just as I reached the two men, Mr Yeats smilingly shook the stranger's hand and said, 'Would you excuse me, Mr Rosewell?' *Bax cova!* He wanted to cut the other man out of the conversation and have me all to himself! For a moment Mr Handsome looked confused, but he nodded and took his leave. Did I imagine he looked just a little disappointed?

Mr Yeats, eyeing me like a crocodile might his prey, broke into a plump-lipped, pretty smile and put his hand on my arm. Then he declared that I had the voice of . . . oh, *mi Gad*, some Irish princess of yore, I can't remember. He praised me on my 'dusky complexion' and started wittering on about Arab ladies and whatnot.

'I deserve no praise for it,' I retorted. 'I was born that way, and I'm no Arab—'

Mr Yeats was not listening. His watery eyes dissolved in on me as he started quoting poetry. His breath smelled of humbugs and something stale, like old newspaper. *Help*, I silently prayed to the Almighty, though what right I had to trouble Him further is anybody's guess.

Just at the corner of my eye, I caught a flash of dark skin and grey cufflinks. The stranger was leaving, and, cha, I was left to stand and nod and smile while this pompous windbag wasted my time! But then I felt a light tap on my arm, and looked up, straight into the eyes of my stranger. This time, they were smiling. 'Excuse me, ma'am. You dropped something.' I noted his American accent immediately. Baritone, too, nice and deep. I had been right.

'Did I? No, I'm sure—'

He bent down and retrieved something from the carpet. 'Ah, here it is.' He inclined his head to stop me talking and handed me a card. I got the hint, grinned back and immediately stuffed the card into my purse. 'How kind. Thank you.'

'No trouble. You sang well.' Before I could ask him how he guessed it was me, he turned away and headed for the door.

Eva was now at my elbow, and Sybil had managed to pull herself off her chair, staggering a little as we headed towards the door. But Eva's hopes had been confounded: Sybil was drunk again, and Eva ushered her off into a corner, whispering furiously.

The weather had cooled a little, so I retrieved my hat and gloves and went out ahead of them. Sybil's sleek black Wolseley was parked across the road next to the railings on the green. I would wait nearby. But I had barely reached the steps before the front door of a neighbouring house was flung open, and a man in uniform strode out onto the street. I got the quickest glimpse of a face all made up of rage and a bristling blond moustache and a brocaded parade cap pushed back from the forehead. Cologne, nauseatingly sweet and strong, floated across the railings. That was what I first recognised about him, that smell.

Before I could get over the shock of realising who it was, and just as the door was about to close, another figure slipped out like a quick wind. It was a woman, elderly, with a sharp profile, wearing a too-long grey ensemble softened only by flounces at the sleeves. Her headscarf was patterned with silver birds, her boots short and heeled.

Her I had seen before too – more recently. Again, I felt fear, but this time it was the familiar tightening in my stomach. She was one of the Mackenzies' goons – I was sure of it! – and had been following me for a while now. I had seen her silhouette on street corners too often for it to be a coincidence. She did not look my way, but she surely had caught sight of me. In London, in 1917, I was hard to miss.

Her name I did not know. His I knew well.

Lionel Anthony McCrum, Brigadier.

I had encountered him almost a year ago, on a warm, cloudy September day in a field hospital in France, towards the slow end of the Somme offensive. I was with one of the surgeons, Robin Mackenzie. I was a volunteer nurse then, assigned to work with him in Operating Theatre No. 3, a prefabricated hut. Our second patient that morning was a young boy of ten or eleven, a civilian. He had been sitting on top of a grain cart – even during wartime the barley harvest had to be brought in – and had met with a mishap on the road. Falling to the hard ground, he had broken his leg, as well as suffering concussion and cuts to his head.

The accident happened within a mile of the field hospital, so the farmhand driving the truck decided to bring him to us. We ensured the skull had not been fractured, the spine was unaffected, and there was no internal bleeding. Then, and only then, even though the pickney was howling his head off, could we get him ready for surgery. Although it was a compound fracture, the operation itself went well.

Robin was, as always, a masterclass in concentration. His shirtsleeves were rolled up to his elbows, and I remember the blush of sunburn on his pale, freckled forearms as beads of sweat gathered on his sparse russet moustache. His thin lips folded inwards as he calculated the next move. 'Hmmmm,' he said, and again, 'Hmmmm.' Then he gestured towards the long, low table behind me where we kept the instruments. 'Pin. Nine-inch.' I passed him the implement, along with the T-handle he hadn't asked for but which I knew he would need.

Knowing well what Robin intended to do, I put a cushion under the boy's thigh, and Robin carefully made a small incision and set the T-handle through the bone and the long pin in place. Then he instructed me to call on Mr Bird, one of the orthopaedic specialists, to transfer the boy to a medical ward. I was preparing to leave on that very errand when I was blocked at the door by the imposing frame of the man I had just now seen bounding down the steps of No. 26 Euston Square.

Seeing his high rank, both Robin and I saluted him immediately. He briefly introduced himself, then gestured at the supine boy, who was beginning to come around. 'He is coming with me.' The voice was harsh and high-toned, the kind of tenor that would wear out your throat professionally if used too long.

'Sir,' Robin responded, his Scottish accent deepening, 'he's no' ready. We just have him lined up for traction.'

McCrum's eyes darkened with truculent rage. 'That was not a request, man. This boy is an orphan and has nobody to claim him. He comes with me. Now.'

'The village will know whose he is. Why not ask them?' I piped up, only to have McCrum stride over and flick his fingers against my cheek. It stung like the blazes! 'You don't ever speak to me,' he hissed. His cologne drifted all over the small hut like a malodorous cloud.

Robin stepped forward. 'You cannae hit her like that,' he said quietly.

'I can do what I like, Captain.' McCrum's use of Robin's rank was not a mark of respect. 'This boy is under my command. There's a place up in Rouen ready for him. Release him now, and I will see to his treatment.' See to his treatment? Did he not understand what traction was?

'Sir,' Robin said, 'as long as he is in my theatre, army regulations mean he is under *my* command. I cannae release him yet. Not without going through the proper channels.'

'How dare you, man? I *am* the proper channels!' McCrum roared, spittle flying from his mouth. At that the boy stirred, blinked. Robin rushed to his side, putting himself between him and the brigadier. The boy murmured something in French. Robin, half turning, never once giving McCrum his back, replied in the same language. Even though it was heavily inflected with his Glaswegian accent, the boy understood, and gave quiet answers.

As for the other officer, he was breathing noisily, like a bull getting ready to charge. Instinctively I crouched a little, like a coiled spring, ready to let loose and fly if he moved forward. But he did not. Robin had won this battle. 'I'll be back to check later,' McCrum muttered under his moustache. 'And when I do, I expect no obstruction, Captain. Understood?'

'Yes, sir!' Robin stood smartly to attention and his right hand nearly hit his forehead he was so ready with the salute. I quickly followed suit. The brigadier turned without a word and strode out, his cologne lingering behind him the way a foul wind lingers after a Tube train goes into a tunnel.

I sighed and put my head in my hands. What a to-do! The boy was wide awake now, chattering, and me unable to understand much. It was only when he kept going on about *Monsieur le médecin* that I realised he was asking for Robin, who was standing over by the table where I had so recently arrayed the surgical implements. His back was to me and his shoulders were heaving. I went over and tapped him gently. 'Robin, yu deh?'

When he turned to me, I was shocked. His cheeks were blotchy, his eyes wild, his mouth twisted. He looked as if he were drunk. I grasped his wrists. 'Robin,' I said, a little more urgently.

He wrenched his hands from my grip and set them on the table, breathing hard. 'That man. That McCrum. "A place in Rouen" – You know what he meant, don't you?' I shook my head. Robin did not elaborate, just spread out his fingers and said through his teeth, 'He's a cunt.'

Robin swore all the time, and I used to upbraid him for it. But I had never heard him use that word before. It made me jump.

The next time I saw the boy was a day later, in the orthopaedic ward. He was surrounded by a gaggle of people talking in French. Even with my limited command of the language, it was clear to me that these people were parents, grandparents, siblings. *You lying toad, McCrum*, I thought to myself, *claiming he was an orphan*. While I shall have a great deal to say against Robin Mackenzie as this story continues, I will always acknowledge that he saved that boy from a very uncertain fate.

My reverie was broken by Eva joining me. 'I say, are you all right? You look like you've seen a ghost.'

'I'm all right. Had something in mi eye.' She looked dissatisfied with my answer, but there was no way on earth I could tell her the truth. Lionel McCrum's impact on *my* life had been unpleasant and brief, but he had *destroyed* Eva's. He had taken away the one joy of her life, the one man she had lived for, all out of spite and rage. She could not know I had seen him. Her equilibrium was fragile enough; the leg-of-lamb incident testified to that. The thought of *him* might send her stone mad. Mind you, I was not thrilled to see him myself either. Not here in the heart of London, where there were plenty of young boys around.

'We're going home,' Eva announced. 'Sybil's off to some shindig with Roma, and we're not invited. So we'll have to walk.'

'Pity we couldn't go with her part of the way.' I was not entirely unsympathetic to Sybil in this case, even if she didn't like me much. I guessed she was embarrassed at being caught drunk and wanted to slink off without being subject to Eva's wrath.

'She offered. I declined.'

Well, thank you very much! For a moment I wanted to protest aloud – the Wolseley had been exceedingly comfortable. Then I remembered the last time we had left a séance in Sybil's car; she had insisted we come into her apartment on Moscow Road and proceeded to ramble at us, or rather at Eva, for hours while I sat there mute as a wooden doll. It had not been an entertaining evening.

'What about the curfew?'

'Hang the curfew! I've had enough of it.'

We wandered through Fitzrovia for a while without exchanging a word. I welcomed the lack of conversation since my heart was full. I was thinking of the séance, the child, the handsome stranger, the memory of Robin and me together as we protected that helpless boy against a powerful man's desirous anger.

Eva barrelled ahead, her small dumpy figure almost comical in its resolve. I had to quicken my step to follow her. She had her arms folded while she walked so that she looked like a small tank making her way down an avenue of enemy fire rather than a young woman ambling past Hamley's toy shop.

'Eva,' I panted, 'slow down, nuh.'

She did, but cut her eye at me, glancing sidelong. Then she started on another subject altogether. 'Why were you flirting with Mr Yeats? He's a rotten fellow.'

For a second I had to recall whom she was talking about. Then I laughed aloud. 'Him? Mi Gad, I was doing no such thing, I promise you!'

Eva was having none of my denials. 'Honestly, how could you? He's a parasite, him and his generation. Happy to let the young men die so they can move in on the women. Did you know he was asked to write a war poem, and he wrote one saying better leave it to the politicians and go to bed with young girls instead?' For a moment the thought flickered in me that maybe the old man had a point, but going by Eva's heavy frown I didn't dare mention it. 'He's an utter fraud. Him and his ghost mother and that trumpet.'

I shook my head. 'He may be a bore, but he seems genuine enough.'

'Christopher couldn't abide him.' There it was. 'Hated his early stuff. Said he was the worst kind of maudlin verse machine. Kept quoting from the "tread softly" poem and said he hoped he'd tread on a banana skin.'

She was talking about her dead fiancé, who had also been her tutor. In November 1916, Christopher Shandlin was killed at Salonika, where he should never have been in the first place given that he had been crippled with shell shock. His death had been nasty and improper, impossible for Eva to move on from. Most pertinently, it was a death that would never have happened if Brigadier McCrum, the man I had just seen exiting No. 26 Euston Square, had not forced Christopher back into action.

'Maybe he would have changed his mind about Mr Yeats's poetry . . .' I began gently. *If he had lived* hung in the cooling, damp air. Unspoken.

'I daresay,' was all Eva would answer, and to my relief we lapsed into silence once more. I pulled my shawl around my shoulders, then tightened my headscarf. My stomach taunted me with thoughts of the perfect supper: the sweet clove spices of ackee and saltfish, nestling with a generous helping of rice and plantain, then *just* a little portion of buttery fried dumplings on the side, all washed down with June plum juice and ginger beer . . . oh, had I only been in Jamaica! Not in England, the world centre of awful food.

This led me to wonder about the handsome stranger who had given me his card and what sort of food Americans might eat. I wanted to ask Eva what she thought of him – surely she'd noted his presence? – but didn't want to sound insensitive when it was clear she was sad. 'When Sybil drags you to these things,' I said, trying to keep my mind off food and handsome men as we crossed over to Maddox Street with all its paipsey buildings and fancy shopfronts, 'do you ever think, or hope . . . ?'

'That Christopher might show up?' Eva's laugh was short and bitter. 'No. He's gone. I shall never see him again, I'm sure of it. And even if he did have a spirit, and it could make contact, how on earth would I be satisfied with just a voice? I would want all of him back, physically. How could the spiritualists give me that? They'd have to find some way of sticking him together piece by piece.' Eva's tone was flat, but I couldn't stop myself sucking in my breath and wincing. The poor fellow, on stretcher-bearing duty for the British Salonika Army, had stepped on a landmine and . . .

'Dreadful,' was all I could say, tut-tutting as we made our long tramp down the King's Road.

'But why ask me?' Eva cut into my thoughts. 'You know my opinion on all this stuff. Are *you* hoping someone will show up? Or fearing, maybe? I felt you flinch when that poor woman thought she was talking to her dead child. When I heard that, I honestly wanted to go find that charlatan and beat her to death with her blasted trumpet.'

I said nothing. Partly because I thought it foolish of Eva to discuss spirits in such a cavalier manner, but mostly because emotion had seized me, and I found myself quite unable to respond. But she was not for stopping. 'I've noticed you've started buying books on . . . subjects that are dangerous for you, let's put it that way. And there was a look in your eyes earlier when you told me you might be late coming back.' I shook my head, but Eva pressed on. 'You kept saying it was a business meeting. People like you and me don't have business meetings. Business doesn't care about us.'

'Speak for yourself,' I began indignantly, hastening my step as we passed Parson's Green, but Eva stopped dead in the middle of the footpath and blocked my way. 'Look, it's clear you're up to something, and I'm worried it's about the . . . the other matter.' She looked away. 'Lucia, you must leave the past alone. I know you want to do something about it, but honestly? You can't. Be realistic.' Her message delivered, she turned away, directed her gaze resolutely forward, and quickened her pace.

The evening had already darkened into night, and the indigo sky allowed itself a scattering of stars. The book. Yes, I had been careless. I would have been better off going to the library to read Dr Holt's volume on *The Care and Feeding of Children* rather than buying it. But long-haired, bearded Mr Rubinstein who ran the second-hand bookshop on The Strand was quiet and friendly and did not scorn me for my colour, being an immigrant himself.

I must have left it out on the bed, or perhaps on the night-stand, and Eva must have spotted it. I presumed that led her to guess the purpose of my meeting with Mr Manning – which was why she was chiding me. I was not in the mood for it. 'You're telling me not to hope, because it makes *your* despair easier if I'm feeling the same. I'm not falling for that.'

Eva, to her credit, did not curse me out on the doorstep for being so rude. She didn't even look that upset, though she was quiet. Her only answer was, 'Well, it's your funeral.' Then, abruptly, 'There's little in the way of food, I'm afraid. That lamb will be useless, I'd say. We'll have to manage with bread and cheese tonight. I'm not even sure about the bread. It's been out a week.' That message delivered, she barged in ahead of me.

Oh Eva! Two years ago, in the field hospital, she was showing me her letters from Christopher with nervous hope in her eyes, begging me to interpret his intentions. (They were obvious.) We were both so free, so full of joy and hope. What had war done to us?

THE NECESSARY WAS a tiny lean-to at the bottom of the garden. Every evening, armed with a towel and washbag under one arm, a rolled-up sheaf of scores under the other, while a trench torch that had belonged to Eva's late husband dangled from my hand, I would make my way outside. First, I would leave my scores in the small shed in the other corner of the yard, to return to later, then I would start breathing through my mouth so that I could tolerate the necessary, watching for rats around my feet.

When I got there it was, thankfully, unoccupied, the wooden door gaping open, the top hinge almost falling away from its joint. I pulled the door to, and it scraped off the floor softly and awkwardly as it closed.

The rain danced and pinged on the corrugated tin roof as I switched on the torch, shut the seat of the water closet and sat down on it. Then I took out the card:

ARTHUR J. ROSEWELL, ESQ.
CHAIRMAN
THE COTERIE OF FRIENDS
Exclusive Society for Negroes of Excellence
Meets Every Tuesday at 7.30 p.m.

AT THE BOTTOM, in cursive, was an address. Harrow Road. Quite a

journey, and it would be straight from work, but I was eager to go.
I used the WC – and, believe me, I stayed standing up the whole
time, there was no chance in hell I would sit on that! – before
cleaning myself with the greaseproof paper provided in a small
box to the side – a lovely touch from Mrs Baxter. Heaven knows
what it did to the local plumbing. Then a quick dash to the garden
tap to wash my hands, followed by scales.

The other shed was not much larger than the necessary and
was filled with rusting garden tools which, to look at the grass in
the yard, you could tell had not been used for some time. My
scores were waiting on a small shelf just at my eye level which also
held three screwdrivers and a spirit level that I used to keep the
pages straight. The walls were thin timber ply and the acoustic
was deplorable, but it was a suitable enough distance from the
house that people generally left me alone. I never needed a tuning
fork. I have 'perfect pitch', you know what that is? You're nodding
your head, oh yes! 'The ability to detect a note without external
reference.'

I would start on a – yes, that's it, that's my Middle C you're
humming, you facety man! So, I would start from there, and climb
up, up, up until I hit that crazy E flat of my namesake, Lucia di
Lammermoor, when she goes totally mad. You're no soprano, you
can leave that alone.

Chromatic scales, arpeggios and melodic minors were my diet
for the next half hour, and I set to dining on them with relish. I
managed to finish before I heard someone approaching on the
garden path. I stiffened. Usually these people were only intending
the use the necessary but sometimes they objected to my singing.
They would bang on the shed door, shouting at me to stop that
flaming racket or they'd complain to Mrs Baxter and get me
thrown out.

Thankfully this person only wanted to relieve themselves and cared nothing for any accompaniment. Just in case, since I was nearly finished anyway, I sang the last few scales at double speed, then went back inside.

Eva was already in bed and asleep, having left a light on so I could find my own way to bed, even though she'd already lent me her torch. I swung the light around to see if the leg of lamb was still where Eva had demanded I leave it hours before. But no! it had vanished. I was a little disappointed.

Eva was not twitching or calling out yet, for which I was thankful. One time she had mimed dancing in her sleep. Cha, that had been disturbing! As for me, I lay flat on my back and stared at the high discoloured ceiling, tracking the patterns made by leaks and cobwebs and damp stains. What with the meeting with Mr Manning and the unplanned encounter with the handsome Mr Rosewell, things were really beginning to get moving for me now. I could not afford to let poor Eva pull me down, and so I had been a little short with her, but I wanted that forward movement for her too. I wanted her to have both feet in this world rather than one still dangling over the edge of the cliff from which I'd gone to the trouble of rescuing her.

Pulling the blankets around me, I thought of Mr Rosewell, his suave smile, his self-assuredness. Then Mr Manning, shaking his head: 'Are you sure this is what you want?' I was excited and a little afraid of what was to come, and it was a long time before I was able to drift off to sleep.

When I did, as luck would have it, I had that dream again. It starts with Operating Theatre No. 3, but this time there is so much blood – a bright red fountain of it. Its sweet coppery smell hovers in the unmoving air, festering under the canvas roof. Robin throws off his gloves into a dirty bowl, the blood on them staining the already contaminated water. I must empty that, sterilise everything. 'There is too much blood,' I try to protest. He leans in close.

When he speaks, I hear the steady *wahh-wahh-wahh* of a tiny, hungry baby and see that baby's open mouth instead of his.

At that point, I am catapulted past the torpor of the operating room straight into cold, muck-black, treacly water. It slowly fills my lungs as I sink into its velvety depths. My arms jerk like a marionette. My body is being pulled under. And then I am aware I am holding on to something. *Wahh . . . wahh . . . wahh.* The awareness happens just before whatever it is is torn from my arms. My chest, full of water, hurts like nothing else. *Weh yu gwaan, baby?* My nose is full of the stink of tidal river water. I know I am done for. The swell of brown washes in my eyes, the little specks in the opaque water dance around me.

Baby had a little feed . . . baby had a little feed . . . Then I realise, with shuddering shock, that the current has taken the baby out of my arms . . . he will surely drown. I cannot call his name because my mouth and nose and lungs are full of water. It make me voiceless. It make me breathless. Finally, I emerge violently upwards – only to wake with a shuddering start in a chilly dark room off Fulham Road.

Dominic, I had tried to say. But the dream had not allowed me to. It never did.

Across from me, her fair hair just visible by virtue of the streetlight pouring through a gap in the curtains, Eva stirred, gently murmuring something. I watched her, hand on my chest as my heart thudded and knocked like a derailing train, the unshed tears already shrinking from my eyes. She, by contrast, so peaceful. At least one of us spared our usual torments as the night deepened.

BY THE TIME I woke up, Eva was long gone, her sparse bedding pulled up. Alone in the room, I yawned and blinked as light streamed in. Sleep had not been good that night, and I feared another nightmare if I dropped off again. My mouth tasted like tin, and my stomach felt a little sick.

I winced when I saw the hour. Not much time to wash, fix my hair, sing a circle of fifths to wake up my voice and manage the Tube change and the long walk to the war hospital at Roehampton. I smoothed my hair with peanut oil – I preferred olive or jojoba but in wartime England neither was available – ran a comb through it and tied it down so roughly with bow clips, pins and slides that my scalp hurt. Then C major: doh-re-mi-fa-sol-la-ti-do! Same in G major, then D, then A, and so on, until all twelve keys were done. Then twice tempo. Then the same with the minors. The whole thing only took six minutes, but on a bad day it was the difference between catching the right train or missing it.

At Parson's Green station I reached into my handbag for my season ticket – every day I thanked God for it because the stress of buying a separate one each day would be high for me. I had not forgotten the ticket clerk's incredulous look when I asked to purchase it first. He seemed unable to comprehend that a coloured person would like to travel somewhere. Though I suppose even he would have got used to me after a while.

The station was above ground, and the day was bright and warm. A flock of pigeons fussed along the edge of the roof, and splodges of their whitish-grey droppings lined the platform's edge. I was tired but told myself that a dream is just a dream.

And then I saw the old woman again: the one who had followed McCrum out of the building the evening before. She was on the platform, wearing the same coat and scarf as yesterday. She was not looking my way, but she must have known I was there. It would have been too much of a coincidence otherwise. The sight of her gave me the creeps. I had always thought the Mackenzies were behind the fact of her following me. Even though they were in Scotland, their tentacles reached everywhere, like poison ivy. But now, knowing she was involved with McCrum ...

I got on the train when it pulled in. She did not because as the white and red paddle was raised for the train to go, I could still see her profile as we moved off and the sparks hit the rails.

Mi Gad, I was a wreck. It was not even nine o'clock in the morning, and my nerves were as rattled as the carriages screeching through the shallow tunnels of the London Underground. My fellow passengers were like automatons: key workers in double-breasted suits sweating through tweedy armpits, their exemption badges prominently displayed to put off the white-feather brigade; a few women too, in staid pinafores and thick cotton blousons.

None of them took any notice of me. We all took the same journey every day, and the novelty of staring at me had long worn off for them. Still, I worried that one or more of them had been sent down by Glasgow to secretly take notes about me. Cu yu, it was melodramatic, but I had my reasons to be jittery. I knew all too well how the Mackenzies operated, how they bribed, terrorised, and controlled. If that woman had been sent by them, I was in trouble and no two ways about it.

I had a long walk after my second Tube journey to the war hospital in the basement of Roehampton University, which was fortunate because nothing else would have cleared my head. By the time I walked through the university's double gates and past the park and rugby fields, undisturbed by any members of the public, I was just about ready for the day's work. In five minutes' time, I would be seated at a long trestle table with three other women and one man, where we would whittle away at prosthetic limbs, roughly carved by a lathe from balsa wood. We used penknives and, occasionally, a blue-handled hacksaw. Neither suited me very well since I am left-handed, but I made do the best

I could. We worked for eight hours a day with a half hour for lunch. It was boring and unpleasant but paid twenty-one shillings a week – almost unheard of for a woman's wage.

I clocked in five minutes late, and the supervisor, Major Carroll, greeted me with a snarl. Carroll was plagued by an internal ulcer, and during its flare-ups he would march around our tables, bent forward with his hand on his side, so convulsed by pain he could not speak. Other times he would lean against the door to the stairs, skin yellow as old paper, lips liverish-white, smoking like a chimney. If they ever cut open his veins, pure nicotine would flow out.

'Whyever doesn't he go to hospital?' I once asked Audrey Partridge. Audrey was all right. She always nodded at me when I came in and said 'Good morning', and although I generally sat alone at lunchtime and she with her group, she would always signal a discreet hello when I passed by.

'I think he's scared,' she answered, applying the sandpaper carefully to a splintered edge, smoothing it out as she rubbed the paper up and down. 'He's ex-army. Worried he'll lose his pension or summat.'

'He won't live to get it the rate he's going.'

'Ah, he's all right when that ulcer ain't playin' up.'

I tried to imagine a life that had fitful, sporadic periods of 'all right' interspersed with constant, radiating, brutal pain. My own life was bad enough, but I had my health and my teeth. 'Here,' I said. 'You missed a bit on the index finger.'

'Oh, I'll fix that now. Be right as rain.'

I don't know why we bothered to work so diligently. Half the limbs we made were discarded because they were unsuitable. They were largely deployed for cosmetic purposes, to fill a sleeve or trouser leg, and were not so much for the invalid as for the public so they wouldn't be frightened or repulsed. As functional limbs, though, they were not just useless but actual hindrances. Wait, I lie. I do know why we worked so hard: it was pride. Audrey in particular cared about every item she fashioned. Sometimes she would flex out her own fingers and line up her hand and arm to the one she was working on to compare. She treated her work like art, and she worked honestly. For that, too, I liked her.

That morning, when I slid into my allotted seat with my late time marked on my punch card, she nodded at me. 'All right, Percival.' The women usually addressed each other by surname, though I rarely returned the same, simply responding 'Good morning.' Centuries of fear made me reluctant to address any white person by surname only. Had my ancestors done it, being shot to death would have been the luckiest outcome.

Even though my work demanded attention, my thoughts did not stop racing immediately. I was worried about that woman and what her appearance might mean, especially now when I had finally decided to do something about the injustice of my situation and about Domi . . . I was so preoccupied with worry that the morning sped by, and I did my two hours at the lathe operator's station without thinking much about what I was doing or where my hands were. Thankfully, nobody was injured.

At lunchtime, as I ate my soup, a girl with small eyes and thick hair tied back in loose plaits sidled up to me and said in a loud voice, 'Not being funny like, but why aren't you in your own country?'

My soup was cooling rapidly. I tasted it and weighed up the ingredients carefully, concentrating on nothing else. It was oversalted, and its main ingredient was leek, a vegetable I'd never heard of before arriving in Britain and have never eaten since leaving it.

'Cat got your tongue, then?' She rocked back and forth on the bench until it thumped the floor.

'Leave it out, Cath,' Audrey chimed in. 'Percival's all right. She covered that time my mother was sick.'

I knew her as Spicer, but she and Audrey were friendly outside work so often addressed each other by their first names.

'I was just saying,' the girl protested. 'What's wrong with asking a question?'

'It weren't nice, Cath, and you know it. People all over the world are fighting for our country. Percival here's on our side.'

Cath made a sort of huff, and air escaped from her lips. 'I just think the least she can do is speak up and have some respect. Our own are starving on the streets, and them savages cutting them down in the Mesopotamia and the like.'

'Don't pay her any mind,' Audrey told me. 'She's just mean, she is.'

But I turned in my chair to look at Cath full on. 'My brother is in the British West Indies Regiment. He's seen action. Thousands of us enlisted for *your* war. Hundreds of them got frostbite and had limbs amputated before ever setting foot in England. Five of them froze to death because nobody could be bothered providing them with proper clothing.'

Cath narrowed her eyes. 'Fairy stories. Never happened. Weren't never no darkies going soldierin' with our boys.'

'Leave it *out,* I said.' Audrey put her hand on my arm. 'Percival. It's all right.'

All right? That was not for her to say. The young troops in the SS *Verdala* were left in their tropical fatigues and froze in the hold off the coast of Canada, and now this girl here had the cheek to say it never happened!

Cath curled her lip and sniffed. 'You'd want to watch the company you keep, Audrey Partridge.' She walked off.

'Cath's best boy lost his job,' Audrey explained. 'Came back from the front with a blighty and couldn't handle civvy life. Found a coloured fella who got him some morphine for a price. He was meant to start at the boot-blacking place in Chiswick last month but never showed, so they've lost that income. War's the reason, but it's easier for her to blame the coloured fella.'

'I don't care.' I took up my bowl and spoon and headed for the queue at the left-plates trolley.

'Don't be like that.' To my surprise, Audrey followed me. 'I'm on your side.'

'Nobody's on my side.' I set the tray into the trolley with an almighty crash, and several people looked up. I fixed on them such a stare that they immediately looked down again.

'Tell you what,' Audrey said. 'Me and a few of the girls are going out tonight. To a show in the Vaudeville. A revue.' She pronounced it 'ree-view'. 'The Egyptian Enigma's going to be there. He's a rum fellow. D'you know he swallows a load of petrol down his gullet and then breathes out fire? And turns into a water fountain when he spits out water?' Seeing the look on my face, she added, 'Don't worry, Cath ain't comin'.'

For a moment I dithered, not wanting to refuse Audrey's kindness but not wanting to spend my evening cheering on a man for spitting out fire and water. Then, with relief, I remembered. Tuesday evening: the Coterie of Friends! I would have to give the Egyptian Enigma a miss and meet an enigma of my own. I smiled at Audrey as we walked back to our stations. 'Thanks. That's mighty kind of you. But I have another engagement tonight.'

Audrey clapped her hands. 'Oooooh! Is it a beau?'

'Not quite.' *Not yet*, I was thinking.

Audrey slid into her seat and took up the next right foot in her basket with a cheerful grin. 'You're a right woman of mystery, you are.' At least she didn't call me a dark horse.

THE ADDRESS on Mr Rosewell's card was Harrow Road, near Paddington Station, which entailed a long journey on the District Line. Given that it would take forty-five minutes and I had two hours to spare, I decided to return to Fulham to freshen up, then made my way back to Paddington.

When I got there, emerging from the tunnel and surveying my surroundings, I noticed it was not an ugly neighbourhood. The weather had turned again, and the street was washed in sunlight after days of rain. The smell of ozone made me dizzy in a pleasant way. I found the door, by the side of a shuttered shop, and knocked loudly, wondering if I should use a secret rhythm. But when the door opened wide and I came face to face with Mr Rosewell himself, rather than a servant, I was glad I hadn't.

On seeing me, his slightly severe features broke into an immediate smile. 'I am so glad you could come. Please, let me take your hat and coat, Miss . . . Oh.' He looked at me with mock sadness. 'You have me at a disadvantage.'

I extended my gloved hand. 'Lucia Percival. I already know your name, Mr Rosewell. I read it on the card you accidentally dropped.'

''Deed you do.' He shook my hand and gave me a wink. 'Follow me up.'

We went upstairs, and I followed him through an open doorway on the left of the small landing. Before I even entered the room, I could smell cigars and woodsmoke. Then I heard laughter and the unobtrusive sound of a record player – some orchestra playing gentle ragtime. Proper order! I couldn't care less about soldier songs or ditties concerning Lloyd George and his rhaatid beer. Inside was a complement of twenty people or so, and, the best bit, all of them were black. Furthermore, the men all rose to their feet when I entered. These two facts were most cheering. I find that the constant company of white people gets pon mi nerves and forces me to suppress parts of myself, and the strain is only noticeable when I get a break from it.

The room was far better appointed than the exterior would have had me expect: its wallpaper was a rich wine-red with white stripes all the way up to the high corniced ceiling, and a burnished oval mirror hung over a large black-marble fireplace. In its grate was a roaring fire – not out of place in such a rainy August. On the mantelpiece were several skinny silver figurines, with exaggeratedly huge heads and long legs.

'Miss Percival, welcome to the Coterie of Friends. This is Dr Alcindor,' Mr Rosewell indicated the gentleman standing by a sideboard near the window, moustached and with a fuzz of hair, well into middle age but wearing it well. 'He has a medical practice just down the road.'

Dr Alcindor replied with a nod of the head and the slightest of smiles. 'Pleased to meet you,' he said. I noticed that his accent sounded Trinidadian, and commented on it.

'Dr Alcindor is indeed from Trinidad but has lived here for twenty-three years,' Mr Rosewell explained.

'I most certainly am,' Dr Alcindor smiled, 'and I am guessing you are . . . not too far away from there? Jamaica, I think?'

I told the good doctor he had guessed right, while Mr Rosewell gestured for me to sit by the fire. 'You will find that many of us here have our origins in the Caribbean. I guessed that you, Miss Percival, had a similar background to Dr Alcindor's.'

'How soon could you tell, Mr Rosewell?' I asked him, amused.

'From the first note,' he affirmed, then explained to the rest of the assembled group, 'I heard this lady sing to break up malign spirits at a séance. I'd been invited by Lady Daunt to meet the poet Yeats; otherwise I never would have gone. The event was mediocre, but Miss Percival's pure clear voice saved the day. From two bars in,' he continued, 'I was assessing you for suitability for membership of the Coterie of Friends. I knew Eddie would approve.' He gestured at a man in a mint-green jacket, sitting by the far window, his hat on his knee. He raised it to acknowledge me. 'Mr Edmund Thornton Jenkins, the greatest living American composer,' Mr Rosewell announced.

'Hey, Artie, you ain't bad yourself,' Mr Jenkins responded amiably.

'You flatter me,' Mr Rosewell smiled – I sensed a motivating rivalry between the two men – 'but your *Charlestonia* is sublime. I cannot match it.'

Mr Jenkins nodded, taking the praise as his due. I noticed Mr Rosewell frown slightly at that, much to my private amusement. He continued, addressing me, 'Naturally I wanted to speak to you personally, but the ambience of the room was a little unfavourable.'

'You said you were assessing me . . . ?'

'You observe, Miss Percival, that the entire company in this room is made up of coloured folk?'

'It didn't escape my notice.' Laughter rippled across the gathering.

Mr Rosewell cleared his throat. It was then I noticed how young he was, not more than twenty-five at a guess. And yet he bore himself with precocious self-possession, even with the transatlantic twang of his accent. 'You are here because, to put it bluntly, you are a talented musician and a person of intelligence and good breeding—'

'Sir, I am not a racehorse—'

'I am not finished!' he said, laughing. 'We – that is, Mr Jenkins and I – founded this little coterie just a year or two ago because, let's be honest my dear Miss Percival, haven't we had enough of being brushed aside and insulted by white folk?' A murmur of assent went through the room. 'Can coloured men and women of distinction not form a good society of their own?' Another 'yes' from his listeners.

'Eddie,' he said to Mr Jenkins, 'would you care to tell us about the day you made the decision to found our club?'

'Sure,' Mr Jenkins said with a smile. I felt the audience settle and realised they had probably heard his story before. 'I was walking down Oxford Street, fashionably dressed—'

'You're never *not* fashionably dressed!' another man interrupted, to more laughter.

'Let him continue,' Mr Rosewell admonished.

'It's no problem,' said Mr Jenkins. 'Anyhow, I was with a friend, minding my own, when a group of white "gentlemen" started looking my way. Then one of them addressed the other two, pointing at me, saying, "Look at that *thing*."' His easy-going manner had vanished, and his face was altogether stern. 'And then they banned me and my friend Mr Tandoh here' – he gestured at a shorter, darker-skinned man with a bare head who nodded at me – 'from the London University Club.'

'Shame! Shame!' chorused the room.

'They will let any drunk or fool or even prime minister in there—'

'Especially if all three are present in the same person,' Mr Tandoh chimed in, to bitter laughter.

'But they saw fit to leave Mr Jenkins and Mr Tandoh off the list,' Mr Rosewell took up the story, 'for no other reason than the colour of their skin. Now, Miss Percival' – he turned to me once more – 'having heard Mr Jenkins' tale, can you honestly say you have no knowledge of these sufferings?'

'Honestly?' I cried. 'I know all about it, sir!' The room broke out into applause. Still sitting apart by the window, Mr Jenkins waved his hat.

'Then you will understand the need for our little club.' Mr

Rosewell clasped his hands and bent forward. 'Eddie and I wanted to gather together people of distinction, people of talent and culture. So what if we're not allowed in their little cliques? We'll have our own!'

'For sure,' a woman declared in agreement, and a few others nodded along with her.

'There are so few of us here in London, you see, Miss Percival. You will understand that when I saw you I became quite excited, but I did not want to betray myself until I knew more of you.'

I wasn't sure I liked his flattery. I was beginning to feel like a butterfly firmly pinned on a wall by a rather single-minded collector. Mr Rosewell knotted his fingers together and rocked forward slightly. 'It's more subtle than that, I hope. It's more . . . we need our own nobility, do you understand? I don't want to dismiss anyone's background or culture. We've all had enough of that nonsense in our lives. It's just that you sang so prettily, so cultured.' His brow furrowed. He was worried he had put his foot in it.

'You can relax, sir,' I laughed, 'for I am delighted to join your club.'

'That's wonderful! We would love to have you,' Dr Alcindor said.

We were interrupted by a wan-looking maid with a hod of coal in one hand and some logs in the crook of her elbow. Mr Rosewell leapt to his feet, and it pleased me to see his quiet, efficient courtesy as he assisted with logs, stacking them a safe distance nearby, while the rest of us talked and circulated. On a table near Dr Alcindor were several large china plates full of savoury pastries in little doilies. Some guests were already loading side plates with them. I tried one: the fish paste was a bit strong, but for wartime food it wasn't bad. Mr Jenkins filled a plate and brought it to his seat. He smiled at me but did not approach. *He has a musician's temperament*, I thought, *and solitude suits him best.*

The maid emptied more coal on the fire, Mr Rosewell threw logs on top, and the whole thing hissed and crackled. The heat flared and nearly burnt my cheek. Bald-headed Mr Tandoh offered me some wine, which I declined, explaining that my father, being a church elder, was strict about alcohol when we were growing up. Nothing was ever brought into the house, except the few bottles of aged dark rum stored in the cellar and only taken out for guests at Christmas time. My sister Meredith and I had never taken to it as a result; Reginald, our brother, had perhaps gone too far in the opposite direction.

Mr Rosewell turned from the conversation he had been having with another lady (whom I later learned was Gwen Coleridge-Taylor, daughter of the English composer) and regarded me with further interest. His upbringing had been somewhat similar, he said, though he had conquered his resistance to alcohol since arriving in London.

Mr Tandoh then enquired where I had been educated, and I explained that for a while I had attended Manchester High School but that I had been withdrawn when my father judged the standard inadequate. He had then educated me himself – an undertaking that had mixed results. I knew my Shakespeare, but my ability at foreign languages was poor, and as for my arithmetic, the less said the better. He allowed one exception: Home Economics, taught to white and upper-middle-class black girls all over Jamaica. Cleanliness and order were values every parent on the island desperately wished to instil in their daughters, so he allowed us to attend Manchester High School for two hours every Friday for this purpose. (Eva once remarked that sampling my cups of tea, you wouldn't be able to tell, but Irish people are odd about tea. Scottish people too, but that's a whole other story.)

This interested the listening Mr Rosewell very much, as his father was also a reverend (though not a magistrate like mine) and had founded an orphanage in Charleston, South Carolina, which had its own brass band he personally oversaw. We laughingly agreed that both our fathers had possessed a managing nature. With less laughter, we learned from each other that both were deceased.

Mr Rosewell later moved to Atlanta, before crossing the seas to London on a scholarship with the Royal Academy of Music, which both he and Mr Jenkins had been awarded. They met on the ship over and became fast friends. 'My own father was not a musician,' I said, 'but when I was very young, he once travelled to London to hear Nellie Melba sing "Regnava nel silenzio," the song about the ghost girl from *Lucia di Lammermoor*. He loved that opera so much he named me after the heroine.'

And then I stopped, because of a sudden memory, of an evening in the summer of 1908. My father and I were in the kitchen, sitting on stools, a gas lamp hanging from the white wooden joist above us as the twilight quickly deepened into tropical darkness. Rose and Athaliah, the two servants, had long gone home. Outside, the frogs in the rotting tree trunks were making their night call: *gleep-gleep-gleep.*

I remembered how the yellow stone tiles kept the day's heat, and how they were now warming the bare soles of my feet. Ours was an old clapboard plantation house of modest size, called Cinnamon Hill. The family who built it and who profited from the labour had left the island seventy years before, and the plantation, on the edge of Mandeville, was now largely overgrown and built over with new housing. The house itself had gone derelict when, just after my sister Meredith was born, my father saw an opportunity and bought it.

I was twelve and just beginning to show the first signs of womanhood, so I was awkward around my father then.

He was whittling down a block of wood with a pearl-handled army knife, and I watched the pile of shavings mount at his soft-shoed feet. There was no great domestic need for him to reshape the block, nor was it his task to do so, but he was the kind of man who always needed something to occupy his mind. I had said something to him – some half-baked idea about marriage. Meredith was just a year older than me, and even at that early age our mother was keeping an eye out for prospective future partners.

It would not be a difficult search for Meredith, who had light skin and delicate features. I consider myself attractive, but at home in Jamaica I did not possess the right sort of attractiveness, not being light enough. That was all my mother cared about. In time I was to flee the prospect of marriage and end up in England, but in 1908, all that was far in the future.

My father's reply that night will never leave me. He said, 'The trouble with you, Lucia, is that you can do anything you want.'

I had not been expecting that reply. He must have seen the questioning look on my face, because he answered, 'I am only a lover of music, but you are a born musician. You're not made for domestic life. For you it would be like taking back up the chains your grandparents were allowed relinquish.' He put his fist to his mouth and coughed. 'Your mother's people are Maroon, and your grandmother upped and left her plantation at Salt Spring and went to live in the Cockpit Country. She wanted more, and she wanted better. Your mother pretends to forget what *her* mother did, but I see it in you. You'll do the same, Lucia, and that's why I worry. The world isn't ready for you yet. I fear for you, more than I do for the others. Be careful, gyal.'

Fresh tears filled my eyes at the thought of him being gone. He had been my guiding light, and without him I had felt lost for a long time. And he'd been right; I *had* fled. I scrambled for my handkerchief, dusty and crumpled, at the bottom of my purse. 'Are you all right, Miss Percival?' Mr Rosewell hovered at a discreet distance. Upon my shaky *yes*, he passed me the most beautiful blue silk handkerchief, gently scented with citrus cologne, the initials A.J.R. embroidered in the corner with gold-coloured thread. All without words, to spare embarrassment. The material was so lovely I could not in all justice start blowing my nose on it, so I used my own instead, shabby as it was.

At length I composed myself and engaged in the discussion, which covered the topics of musical composition and the difficulty of finding fresh fruit (many of us Caribbeaners shared that complaint). I cannot tell you what a pleasant change it was, spending the evening with such like-minded folk as Dr Alcindor, who did great work with the poor, often for free, though he had a private practice and was well respected in the community. As Miss Coleridge-Taylor, who had inherited her father's talent for musicianship. She, I soon established, was quite precocious for her age, particularly when she spoke of her composition 'Goodbye Butterfly' and her interest in wielding the conductor's baton. As Mr Tandoh, who turned out to be a prince from Ghana but happily laughed off my shock at discovering this fact.

Everything was wonderful, and though I was sober there were champagne bubbles in my heart. That was until Mr Rosewell proposed that I sing, with Miss Coleridge-Taylor accompanying on the piano. Normally, in such safe company, I would have been delighted to oblige, but then Mr Rosewell, professing a love for Scottish ballads, asked if I were familiar with 'Loch Lomond'. Mi Gad, if it had been any other song . . .

'Mr Rosewell,' I said, after a long pause, 'I cannot.'

Immediately he was solicitous. 'I would ask why, but one look at you and I feel it would be imprudent.'

'The bangarang – I mean, the war . . .' I couldn't continue. An awkward silence fell over the room. Miss Coleridge-Taylor was still sitting at the piano, her fingers dancing on top of the keys but not touching them. I hated depriving her of the opportunity of performing, but Mr Rosewell's request had brought me up short. A log fell on the fire with a massive crackle, making the assembled company jump.

'Let me tell you a story, sir,' I said. 'After I arrived in England, I saw how war fever was in full swing and signed up for nursing service in the VAD. I had some training already back in Jamaica, so after a few weeks they sent me to the base hospital in France. I sang a lot while I worked – I like singing, as you have already guessed, Mr Rosewell.' I could not resist giving him a coy smile, which he reflected back with his eyes. 'Well, one day another VAD told me that the Matron wanted to see me. An officer, Captain Bryant from the Royal Scots, had heard me sing and wanted me to go to a dying major in his company. I said, "Surely a priest would be better?" but Captain Bryant replied, "A priest brings them to the next life. Major Loder needs to be guided out of this one."

'So I followed him to one of the medical wards, where he handed me a sheet of paper with lyrics about purple heather and Scottish lakes. Thankfully I knew the tune: "Loch Lomond". Major Loder was truly suffering; he had been shot and patched up in the field as best as could be done, but in spite of all the good work, by the time he got to us he was septicaemic. I sang all the verses, and by the last one his people had come for him. They—' I stopped. How could I describe what had happened with the dying sergeant? Even now, it filled me with wonder. 'When I held his hands, I knew everything, in a flash. His men had been in an ambush. They had all died, except him. Now I felt them all in that stuffy hut with its corrugated iron roof; they were waiting for him to join them. And when I sang that last chorus, they sang with me. I heard them, and I felt his soul leave the room. So, forgive me, but I will not sing that song tonight.'

'My gosh,' said Miss Coleridge-Taylor, inadvertently hitting a loud discord on the piano.

A heavyset woman in duck-egg-blue linen with hair set in a mid-length weave crossed herself and murmured, 'Heavens!'

'Heavens, indeed. What a story,' Dr Alcindor concurred. Mr Rosewell took my refusal to sing in good humour, and the gathering recovered its spirits, only for the little clock to chime half past nine and people to start looking at their watches. The meeting was over.

Mr Rosewell insisted on calling me a cab but had some difficulty getting a driver to stop for us; drivers slowed down, made out his skin colour, and rapidly sped up again, cantering or motoring off into the London fog with barely a pause. Mr Rosewell muttered something under his breath.

'See, nuh? It's easier to take the Tube,' I said gently.

'I won't hear of it.' He was fierce. 'I'll get you a cab if we have to stay here all goddamned night – excuse my language.' No excuse required: I liked the way he swore. I liked the way he did everything.

At that moment the road was empty. A little way off, I heard the call of a bird, maybe a heron from the Brent river that flowed nearby. Mr Rosewell too was quiet a while but then enquired, in a low, confidential tone: 'What did you think of Mr Yeats, anyway?'

I grinned. 'You want my honest opinion?'

'Absolutely nothing less.'

'A bore of the first order. And completely in love with himself. Why is it that the people who think they are the most interesting are always the most dull? I could not wait to get away from him.'

'I had precisely the same impression!' He laughed.

'Were you trapped in conversation? Imprisoned by his tenor drone?'

'Yes! I wanted to talk to *you*—' He stopped abruptly and looked away. Was he shy? I was about to reassure him that the desire had been mutual when another cab appeared, put-putting down the road with irritating slowness.

Mr Rosewell immediately leapt into the road to hail it, and thankfully this time the car stopped. He ushered me in with studied disinterest. Then: 'Miss Percival, are you currently under formal voice tuition?'

I said I was not.

'Well, I am good friends with Freddie Corder. He took over teaching me clarinet for two years at the Royal Academy of Music. He's also instructed a lot of singers and would help you out in a jiffy. Have I spoken out of turn?' He must have noticed my agitation at the mention of the Royal Academy, which I could not conceal.

'You haven't, sir,' I reassured him. 'You're very kind. I had a bad experience there two years ago, that's all.'

'Please tell me,' Mr Rosewell said, 'if I can be of any help.'

The driver coughed discreetly, but did not seem to mind our conversation, presumably because he had it on the meter. 'I went there to enquire after a scholarship. But I never got past the door. They laughed at me.' The humiliation rose in me once again, and I felt my cheeks burn with remembered shame. 'They told me they didn't need any cleaners and turned me away before I could even start explaining.'

'Oh.' He breathed out slowly. 'I understand, Miss Percival. I completely understand.' There was such emotion in his voice that I could not help hoping he would take my hand and leap into the car with me. But he stayed exactly where he was. In a very controlled tone, he said, 'That will not happen again. I'll make sure of it.'

I believed him. There is a quality about some men that when they enter the room you are compelled to pay attention. It is something that *should* transcend race or birth or any other divide you can think of. Mr Yeats, irritating as he was, possessed this quality. So did Arthur Rosewell. The difference being that, qualities or no, Mr Yeats could command transport any time he wished, and Mr Rosewell could not.

'Will you think about it?' he asked.

My response was swift. 'I don't need to. This is the chance I have been looking for since I arrived in Britain. Pass Mr Corder my details, please.'

'Why you are a peach!' He grinned broadly, then apologised profusely for the informality, calling me 'Miss' three times in the one sentence. I didn't mind in the slightest. 'I'm fixing to meet him next week, so it will be then sometime.'

I dimpled. 'Thank you, Arthur. I appreciate it mightily.'

'Arthur, eh? That is very familiar, ma'am!' But he sounded amused rather than offended as he pushed the door of the cab shut. If it was familiar of me, I wasn't sorry. I sung it in my head: *Arthur, Arthur* . . . hmmm, not quite right for opera, a bit prosaic. *Arturo*, though, with heavy emphasis on the second syllable, sounded quite heroic. The black knight of the round table . . .

As the cab moved off, he stood all alone in the middle of the road, holding his fedora in one hand as if he were a British subject and the king himself had passed by, and he waited there until my cab took the turn at the end of the street.

IN BED THAT NIGHT, scales and ablutions all done, my mind still

fizzed from my encounter with Arthur Rosewell: his urbanity, his
solicitude, his fine looks and demeanour. Eva, already asleep, was
a twitching lump under her blue felt blanket. I longed to wake her
up and tell her about the fine gentleman I had met at the séance,
but I realised this was just impatience. Let the poor girl sleep,
when dreams were all she had.

Then that book caught my eye. Eva must have left it at the foot
of the bed, to make a point. I should put it away. I should ignore it
. . . But I soon had it open, had borrowed Eva's torch and had
forgotten Mr Rosewell altogether.

At what age may a child be given a full tub bath?

Usually when ten days old; it should not be given before the
cord has come off.

How should the bath be given?

It should not be given sooner than one hour after feeding. The
room should be warm; if possible there should be an open fire.
The head and face should first be washed and dried, then the
body should be soaped and the infant placed in the tub with its
body well supported by the hand of the nurse. The bath should be
given quickly and the body dried rapidly with a soft towel but with
very little rubbing.

Simple things I could never do. These hands were useless
because they could not test water temperature, or hold an infant
having its bath, or towel him softly dry (no rubbing.) I closed the
book. Too much anguish to continue. Eva was right. I shouldn't
have bought the rhaatid thing in the first place. And now emotion
got to me. Grief is like a sniper: he waits patiently for hours while
you try and live your normal life. He keeps his sights trained on
you while you move about, waiting for the moment when you
pause . . . then *im finish*! He gets you in the heart, and you are
down.

My excitement about Arthur Rosewell had entirely ebbed

away. I felt as if the little candle I had lit against the overwhelming dark of war and loss had been snuffed out. It agitated me that I had heard nothing yet from Edgar Manning, even though mounting such an investigation in Scotland would take time – and resources. As for Mr Rosewell, even if this introduction came to something, even if I were at last able to start my career as a musician after all those wrong turns, I could never tell him about the greatest loss of my life. Where could I start? How?

I had already started along the path of finessing the truth. When I told the gathering at the Coterie of Friends about singing the dead major on his way, I left out what would seem to be a trivial detail: after I released Major Loder's cold hands, and washed my own at the small basin beside the nurses' station, on my way out I passed someone. Someone I certainly noticed but didn't think anything of at the time. Listening that night outside the ward was a Royal Army Medical Corps man and friend of the major who heard the singing but kept his distance – a pale freckled man with clipped red hair and intelligent eyes.

5

3 JUNE 1916

A fortnight after my VAD unit was deployed to France, I was visited by Ward Sister Hedley, whom I knew well from Mile End Hospital. Hedley was a no-nonsense Liverpudlian who had a soft spot for me, probably because, unlike most of the VAD nurses, I wasn't a complete bumblepuppy. My time at the Mandeville fever hospital back in Jamaica stood me well, and it was clear I was not indulging in nursing as a hobby to look good in the society columns – and not only because I was not a part of that society. No, I worked hard, learned fast, and she liked me for it. That she interrupted me cleaning bedpans was typical.

She bustled in from the pleasant June heat and barked at me: 'Percival! You're needed for a gas-gangrene case.'

'Sister, I know nothing 'bout treating gas gangrene.'

'That's what I told him. But he insisted.'

'Who?'

'Mr Mackenzie – the surgeon in Theatre No. 3.' She said his name in the same tone of hushed admiration she might have used to describe the Archangel Michael. 'He's Scottish. They say a bit aloof. Very good though.'

I was not unwilling to obey. After all, I was cleaning bedpans. But the request seemed strange.

'He called for you specifically, and it's urgent,' Sister Hedley said, 'so you'd better look sharp about it.'

Oh dear. When I said I knew nothing about treating gas gangrene, I was not being modest. Only a few weeks before I had learned that the condition had nothing to do with mustard or chlorine gas. No: to put it elegantly, the source of gas gangrene was cowshit. Undisturbed for centuries, cattle excrement was being churned up in the mud of battle, and occasionally the released gas infected the soldiers' open wounds. It settled beneath the skin, expanding in inky black lumps that rippled and crackled angrily to the touch. It was a horrible affliction and could kill a man stone dead in minutes. That much, but little more, did I know.

'Right, then,' Sister Hedley said. 'If you just go past hut A9, then take two blocks to the left past the RAMC mess—'

Something struck me. 'Do I not get an escort?' While the RAMC doctors and orderlies interacted with the VADs all the time during working hours, any socialisation, even to eat together or sit on the same bench, was strictly forbidden. When Captain Bryant requested I sing for poor Major Loder, the matron kicked up a bit of a stink, and only when the captain persuaded her that singing was work was I allowed to go. I was glad then that the standards had been applied as strictly with me as with any other girl.

Sister Hedley's sigh was sufficiently heavy to create subsidence in the chalky earth and sink us both. 'Percival. If you can't manage a hundred yards' walk keeping your ruddy virtue intact, then there's no hope for you.'

'Yes, Sister.' Once dismissed, I set off for Operating Theatre No.

3 with some trepidation. Who was this man, and why had he asked for me?

In the two weeks since we arrived from Boulogne, I had come to enjoy the place, if not the company. For a military headquarters in wartime, it was, at first, peaceful. The sea air was pleasant and reminded me of the temperate coast of my own island. Not the misery of England! I loved how you could sit in the middle of a meadow and look straight out over the railway line to the sea, and watch a flock of oystercatchers fly overhead, making their way inland. Their black and white zigzag wings, their coordination in flight. Unlike man they were preparing to breed not fight. Sensible birds, nah.

As I pushed through the flap of tarpaulin that substituted for a door, an orderly slipped past me, pulling a gurney backwards down the ramp onto the grass. The creak of the wheels went into a slow decrescendo as he vanished into the distance. Operating Theatre No. 3 was another hut hastily thrown up to meet the requirements of battle. Its low pitch-pine roof was supported by a series of splintered-looking planks that looked as if they had been fished out of the nearby coast and briefly dried out. But the black and white tiles were new and smelled of borax, light streamed in the small windowpanes, and the instruments were all lined up, not chaka-chaka and dumped in sterilising jars with blood still on them, as I had seen elsewhere. The one oddity was a small chess-board, on the same shelf as the dressings, whose squares echoed the pattern on the tiles. It was a foldable magnetic set, open at the hinge, with the pieces set out as if starting a game. The board and pieces were yellow boxwood, but I knew from my father's set that a sheet of iron underneath the wood bound the pieces to the squares.

A man I presumed was Robin Mackenzie had his back to me and was bent over his patient on the table. His shoulders were tight, back narrow, auburn hair cropped above the neck, cap nowhere to be seen. He turned around, and instantly I recognised the officer who had been listening outside the ward while I sang to Major Loder. He had the lightest of beards and a mere suggestion of a moustache, a neat parting to one side, freckles and small grey-blue eyes.

'So here's the Dark Angel of Mons,' was his greeting, delivered in a strong Scottish accent.

I saluted him with extremely bad grace, reported for duty, and said not a word more. Dark angel, indeed! Mr Mackenzie did seem a bit embarrassed. 'You sang for poor Willie Loder.'

'I was asked to.' I was not going to give him an inch.

'You did a good job of it.' No response. He sighed. 'He was a friend of mine. From university in Glasgow. Now, any chance you can help a fellow out and do a half-decent job on this as well?' He gestured at the patient's wound, which was on his left inner thigh, lightly covered by a thin gauze. I held my breath and lifted it.

There is no nice way of saying this. My friend, it was disgusting. The skin was swollen and black-purple, with huge, dark, shiny blisters filled with blood. Mr Mackenzie pointed at the patches of skin between blisters. 'I wouldn't advise you touch it, but when you do, it crackles. Crepitation, it's called.'

And that was just the *sight* of it. I cannot describe the *smell* of what came out of those blisters.

I looked at the man's white face and shaking fingers and nodded. 'I can see the problem, sir,' I told Mr Mackenzie. 'He's already in shock. The Casualty Clearing Station didn't do their job properly, and this wound was not sterilised. We need thicker dressings.' I ran to the low shelf on the far wall where extra supplies were kept, only to be rudely halted.

'Ach, I thought you'd be different. For God's sake, you no' put bandages on a gas-gangrene wound, you fule. Where did you learn that rubbish? You keep it wide open.'

'I've never done a gas-gangrene case before,' I snapped back. 'What do I need to do?'

'Oh, hoity-toity, what do you need to do?' He mocked my well-inflected English. 'What you are told to do, for God's sake! I'm fed up of these gerruls who turn up with no training and no idea. I was told you had a bit of experience.' He was almost on top of me he stood so close. I could smell his hair tonic and the tobacco he used for his cigarettes. I moved back a little, to make it clear he was in my space.

He gestured me over to the table. There, a set of tools were laid out, shiny and sharp: a curved scissors, a forceps with similarly curved blades, a silver probe with an eye and a newly sharpened scalpel. 'Have you ever heard of debridement?'

'Yes, but . . . wasn't that used back in Napoleon's day?'

'Well,' Mr Mackenzie said, taking up the probe and scalpel, 'debridement is back. We are going to scrape that wound, Miss Percival, and get all the little nasties out.'

'What about the anti-gas-gangrene serum? We could order some.'

'Don't have me wet my trousers laughing! Serum, aye! That stuff is French piss. Oh, what now?' He looked at me with exasperation. 'You don't like my language, is that it? Well, if I put that serum on his wound he'll die for sure. But if we do it my way, we might just have the ghost of a chance. How does that sound?'

I spent the next half hour watching him scrape away all the rotted tissue, while stanching the occasional flow of blood when he pressed on adjoining living material and called me to help out. As he worked, his wrist flicking very slightly with each cut, I feared the injured man would feel pain, but when I asked about it, Mr Mackenzie shook his head. 'All the nerves are gone – it's eaten right through 'em. Sorry!' He lifted his head and addressed the patient.

'That's all right, guv,' he replied, faint but still conscious, 'just spare the family jewels?'

'I'll do my best,' said Mr Mackenzie, cutting away. When he finished, I was asked to put the lightest of coverings on the work, and Mr Pierce the orderly was instructed to bring a tissue sample to the field laboratory. 'So that we can find out which bacterium we're dealing with,' Mr Mackenzie explained. 'My money is on Madam Clostridia.'

A second orderly returned with the same gurney – I could pitch that squeak, it was a high B – and wheeled the man away to the medical ward. He already looked a little better, and I realised with great humility that Robin Mackenzie had probably saved his life. The gentleman in question turned to me. 'You did better than I expected.'

'Me? I was wrong from the beginning.'

'You were willing to change your strategy rather than just standing there. Flexibility is important, aye.'

At the mention of strategy, my eyes flicked to the chessboard. Mackenzie sighed aloud. 'Ack, chess. Going against the officers is no fun anymore: they're too easy to beat. Then they say it's a trivial pastime. Because there's no connection between war and chess, is there? The chumps.' His eyes darkened with contempt.

'I play, Mr Mackenzie.'

At that, he looked genuinely surprised. He put down a bottle of saline solution without fastening the stopper and stared at me. 'Any good?'

'Yes. I'm good.'

It was true. My father had loved chess and enjoyed playing with me on his huge rosewood set, up to the point where I started to beat him. Then he would frown and eventually concede with a laugh and a sad smile.

'Fancy a game?' Robin Mackenzie said. The dinner bell rang, and he grinned at me. 'Saved by the proverbial, eh?' Then he added, 'That "Loch Lomond" you came out with broke me up, you know.' I was about to thank him for the compliment but he waved me away. 'Now run along and take your break. I've other things to do.'

'One more thing, Mr Mackenzie.' My heart was fluttering a little fast, but if I didn't nip this in the bud now . . .

'Yes?'

'I found your "dark angel" comment unamusing.'

He looked at me with some thought, brushing his upper lip with his finger. Then, 'In that case, I'll mend my ways and not make such comments in future. Good evening to you. Oh, and Percival?'

'Yes, Mr Mackenzie?'

'Come back tomorrow. That's a direct order, and you can tell your matron so.'

'Sir.'

After he dismissed me, I headed out into the sweet evening air for an indifferent mess dinner with a gaggle of VADs, who, I discovered, all had a 'pash' for Robin Mackenzie and resented me greatly for winning his attention. Even when I reassured them it was a gas-gangrene case, not conducive to romance (and, I added to myself, I was not seeking such attentions from white men), their jealousy was not assuaged, and they gave me the silent treatment all night.

6

SATURDAY, 2 SEPTEMBER 1917

r Rosewell said it would be the following week when
he next met with Mr Corder, so it was at my third
meeting with the Coterie of Friends he told me my
appointment was fixed for the following Saturday, at eleven so I
wouldn't have to miss work. I shared this good news with my new
friends, who expressed their delight and wished me luck. Gwen –
Miss Coleridge-Taylor – swore that Mr Rosewell was sweet on me,
which I coyly denied even while wishing it were true.

I had good reason to be hopeful. Mr Rosewell observed particular details about my appearance and complimented them: on
one evening the pillbox hat with its small veil; the next, an artifi-
cial peony pinned to a cloche and set behind my ear; the white
lace detail on the organdy collar I was wearing that night. I spent a
great deal of my money jar on trinkets that would draw his attention while fooling him into thinking they were casual after-
thoughts with no calculation behind them. For his part, he
flattered me by showing me – tentatively – the first page of his next
symphony. Within fifteen seconds, humming the melody as I

followed the strings line, I was deeply impressed by his virtuosity. 'This is so deep and rich,' I said. 'It's better than Beethoven!'

'I wouldn't say that,' he demurred with an embarrassed smile. 'Dvořák, perhaps. A bit of the "New World".'

When he made remarks like that it reminded me that he was a scholarly man, a fellow musician, and if I wanted to achieve his respect – and more – I would need to apply myself to my studies. And nobody loved a challenge more than I.

I arrived outside the Royal Academy on the Marylebone Road, for the *second* time, a little early and clutching my satchel of sheet music. I won't deny I was nervous. After my first disastrous foray, would they even let me in the door? And nobody had mentioned how much this thing would cost. I had done some scribbling on the back of an envelope: five shillings fifteen pence an hour, multiplied over eleven weeks on average for a single term. That would be a large sum indeed, one I would struggle to meet along with rent, expenses and the other little fripperies I liked to enjoy, to keep the misery of war at bay.

Fortunately, I was not left waiting and fretting very long: a car pulled in, and Mr Rosewell leapt out and bounded over to me. He wore a light-blue velvet blazer that looked rather well on him. 'C'mon, let's go in.'

As we entered, I heard the sounds of practice: a flute's chromatic scale rising rapidly as if travelling in a spiral into the sky; the slow thud of a Chopin piano prelude; the sweetest rendition of the Gran Partita wind serenade; then the barking puffs of a low-register brass instrument, probably a tuba, playing the same repeating interval of a fifth. Soh – dohhhhh – soh – dohhhhh – and so on.

'That tuba player is a bit much,' I commented.

Mr Rosewell frowned. 'Oh, that's Ernie Cuthbert. He's a veteran. Signed up with all the other boys in the local brass band to one of the Pals battalions and lost both legs at Festubert. First thing he wanted when he woke up from surgery was his tuba. Well, I declare, the nurses had to help him hold it, and he couldn't get any air down at all. But he was determined. I've played brass instruments, and I've no idea how he manages it. Admirable.' Admirable indeed; audible too. But Mr Rosewell was right. Keeping going like that took guts.

Just as we reached the stairs, a portly man in a loud green check jacket with a clarinet case under his arm collided with me, and my bag nearly fell from my hand. 'So terribly sorry,' he exclaimed. 'I'm in a hurry . . . I'm supposed to meet a Miss . . . Percival?' He blinked like an emerging hibernating animal.

'With me,' Mr Rosewell answered smilingly. 'This is she.'

'Really? Oh my goodness. So terribly sorry. Absent-minded.' He extended his hand. 'I'm Freddie Corder. Artie's told you about me?' His shake was strong but loose-boned, as if indeed he had half his mind on something else.

We went with him through a light-filled lobby that had marble pillars, a wrought-iron staircase, stained-glass windows and strange linear patterns on the mosaic floor. To my surprise, several people said hello to Mr Rosewell, who cheerily returned their greetings.

'We're very keen on having more Negro musicians,' Mr Corder said to me as we headed upstairs. 'Composers too. Eddie Jenkins is supreme, but Arthur here's not bad either. I don't suppose you've heard his work?'

'Oh, come now,' said Mr Rosewell with a modest smile that did not quite manage to hide his irritation at once again being ranked second to Mr Jenkins. I couldn't blame him; it would have annoyed me too had I been in his position.

'I'd love to hear Mr Rosewell's work,' I answered. 'Are there any plans to perform it?'

'There certainly are. We're putting on a premiere in the Duke Room in a month's time, and his First Symphony will feature. You must come.'

'Wild horses couldn't keep me away!'

Arthur gave me a look.

We entered a room with white walls and two tall sashed windows that were dressed with green velvet curtains. In the centre was a piano; to my right and along the back wall, stringed instruments of all shapes and sizes dangled from hooks or leaned against the wall, in and out of their cases. The whole place gave me a deep tug just below the solar plexus. Give me a room furnished with instruments, anywhere in the world, and I am home.

The piano was beautiful: a marbleised walnut Bechstein. Mr Corder lifted the lid and removed a soft green cloth from the keys. When he ran his fingers over them, the notes ran mellow and clear. Then he started getting distracted and played bits of Brahms, while Arthur rolled his eyes at me. Just as you did with me, I gave Mr Corder a Middle C arpeggio to call him to account. He stopped immediately, then played the chord to make sure I had it right.

'Clever party trick, that.' But he got down to business. I could tell he directed choirs as often as singers, as he started with the one, one-two-*one*, one-two-*three*-two-one exercise my father dragged us through when I was in the Methodist church choir at Mandeville. Oh, how that motley group had disappointed him! I was determined not to give Mr Corder any cause for disappointment, even if it were only *Bella señoras* and arpeggios and my intercostal muscles were barely stretched.

Not long afterwards, Mr Corder closed the lid again and wiped his forehead with a puce handkerchief. 'I'm satisfied, Arthur.' Then, to me, 'Who were you with before?'

'Mr Oswin Garfield of Mandeville, Jamaica.' That broiling room, shadowed by eucalyptus trees, on the King Edward Road. The descending quavers of 'Who Is Sylvia?' sung again and again until they gave me a headache. The sweat gathering in my armpits. The piano out of tune. The clamminess and unexpected cold of Mr Garfield's hand on mine, his sudden, unwelcome declaration of passion as his wedding ring ground into my finger . . . I came back to the present and the wan London light as Mr Corder made notes.

'Did this Mr Garfield enrol you in the Associated Board of the Royal Schools of Music examinations?'

'He showed me some of the set pieces.' That he had done. Credit where credit was due.

'Good! We'll put your name forward for the exams next June, probably at Grade 8.' Mr Corder got up and put his scores in his bag. Wait . . . was that it? We had hardly been there ten minutes. And nobody had addressed the one question that had been preoccupying me since I had grabbed that envelope and started scribbling.

'How much will this cost?' I blurted out, my face on fire.

Mr Corder looked puzzled. 'My understanding was that this was already taken care of.' He looked questioningly at Mr Rosewell, who nodded, without looking at me.

'Oh I couldn't—' I began, then stopped. Someone who knew my circumstances was helping me. Possibly Mr Rosewell himself, though he didn't seem keen to acknowledge it. I corrected myself. 'I'm very grateful.'

'Excellent. Now, let's go next door.' Mr Corder rose and guided me through a door into another room, one with bare walls and floorboards and a dust-covered bust of Beethoven on the windowsill. The piano in *this* room, an upright spruce, looked like it had seen better days.

In the middle of the room stood a tall, long-necked woman in a long, plain cotton dress and brown cardigan. Her hair was pulled back in a bun so severe that her scalp was visible, pale as chalk like the rest of her face. I guessed she was somewhere in her mid-thirties. Her spectacles were very thick, so much so that I could hardly see her eyes, but I could see the anger in them, glinting like shooting stars. The worst of it was, I recognised her.

She had been there that awful day two years before when I had summoned every spare ounce of courage I had and entered the building for the first time only to be mocked and dismissed. When the receptionist had sniggered and told me to run along, I had looked upwards in despair, and there that woman had been, on the stairs. She had paused, staring at me in that way English people sometimes do, as if I were some sort of specimen they wanted to exhibit in a museum. What I recall most about her was her stillness: how she watched as I was degraded, humiliated and laughed at. How she watched, and said not a word.

Mr Corder introduced us. 'Miss Percival, Miss Slade.'

Miss Slade did not so much nod to me as inhale, as if I had said something incredibly stupid and she was restraining herself from correcting me. 'Miss Slade is one of our most distinguished instructors. She will conduct a short lesson with you now, and you will return next Wednesday evening and every week after that for ten weeks until the end of term.'

'I'll be back for you at half-past,' Mr Rosewell reassured me, seeing my alarm at being left with this woman. 'Wait for me inside the hall.' He closed the door quietly, Mr Corder having departed with him, leaving Miss Slade and me alone. She looked at me through those glasses for what seemed like an age. Then she thrust a score in my hand. Mozart, in Latin: 'Exsultate, jubilate'. That language held a peculiar private pain for me, one I could not explain to this wordless, hostile woman. She sat down on the piano stool, which squeaked and creaked, and while I was wrestling with the battered-looking music stand, trying to get it to my height – it was set a good foot too low – she launched into the piano part.

'Wait!' I cried, but she ignored me and played on. Thankfully the preamble was long, and, with the stand almost at the right height, I was able to join in at the correct point. She played so fast I was constantly on the back foot. And that *aethera cum me*, sight-reading those semiquavers . . . blouse and skirt, what a piece to start me on!

But the angrier I became the more I put into my vocal; rather than break down, I got more controlled and put some steel in my spine. I would beat this woman. Mi Gad, it was thirty years ago, and yet I still remember each phrase, each inflection. I eyeballed those notes! When we got to the cadenza, the bit where I solo just before the end . . . well, let's just say I took my sweet time and made that fine Miss wait until I was done. I slowed it down so comically in places she could not have mistaken my intent.

By the time I hit the last note, I was sweating hard, with anger as much as exertion. The piano stopped too. And then . . . silence. Miss Slade looked the same as she had done at the beginning: like a bulldog chewing a wasp. Still saying nothing.

'I sight-read that entire piece, Miss Slade.'

She looked at me over her glasses, her eyes an odd sort of hazel and blue. And cut me down with one word. 'Marvellous.'

What a bitch!

I said nothing more, and eventually she opened her mouth. 'Miss Percival.' Another pause. She let it lengthen. Then: 'You need to work on your breath support in the higher register. Several of those fast notes had no base to them. From now on, I don't want to hear one more unsupported note. You can choose to be lazy or you can choose to be a musician. You can't be both.'

'I *am* a musician.'

'Time will tell.' She clicked her fingers. 'You may go!' she shouted, and I went, running as if she had set dogs after me. I barrelled down the stairs, nearly knocking over Mr Rosewell, who was waiting for me as promised, leaning jauntily against a pillar.

'Whoa!' he exclaimed, catching my arms as I ran at him.

'That . . . was . . . awful!' I cried. 'That woman! She made me . . . I had to sight-read . . . didn't even say hello . . .' I couldn't finish my sentences, my outrage had me so out of breath.

Mr Rosewell smiled wryly. 'Oh, yes. The Venetia Slade experience. Tell you what,' he said, 'we're not too far from Regent's Park. Since it's a fine day, I wondered if you fancied a picnic? I packed some food.'

That he had prepared for this scheme disarmed me, and I gave him a grin that might have been described as flirty. 'Lead on, sir.'

Mr Rosewell gestured me to follow with his arm in such a way that I wondered if he might draw me close to his side. But no, once I matched his stride, we walked parallel, a decorous three feet apart. I continued to rant and rave about Miss Slade, finishing up saying, 'I'm not sure I want to go through that again.' He stopped and regarded me tenderly. His eyes were the softest brown.

'Come now. You've crossed the Atlantic, you've travelled thousands of miles, for this chance. You're hardly going to let one bitter woman stop you.'

'But she hate me, nuh. Maybe she prefers her own kind. She was there when I got thrown out the last time, after all, and did she do anything? Nat a ting!'

'Maybe so, but given the amount of ladies in tears after a session with Venetia Slade, I suspect that ain't the problem. She's notorious for it.'

'But why is that tolerable? Why should she be allowed bully people like that?'

Mr Rosewell laughed and put a hand on my arm. 'Because she's good, frankly. She can find your weak spot and strengthen it.' I thought about that for a moment. Her comment about my unsupported vocal had been correct. My voice did lack solidity up at the highest point. That would be fine for a mezzo but not for the soprano I wanted to be. If I had practised the diaphragmatic exercises, this would not have been a problem. If I had not lost six months of practice last year to my imprisonment and then losing Domi . . .

'Fine,' I conceded. 'She's a good critic. But why her face have to be all push up an' sour about it?'

'Because she's not the woman she used to be.'

'Huh?' I forgot my manners, I was that curious. The sun came out, and an omnibus clattered past. Two pigeons flew up at the noise of it.

'Before the war, she had a very promising career ahead of her as a woman pianist. And she had a fiancé, who had a brilliant political future ahead of *him*. Then the war came, and he went off to Egypt with his regiment. When news came of his death, Venetia fell to pieces. Probably just about the time you saw her first, now I come to think of it. If it hadn't been for Freddie and the rest of the fellows, she would have lost her job. They kept her on even when she was a shambles. She recovered in a fashion, but she will never be the great musician she once hoped she'd be. That day, when she snubbed you? She probably didn't even see you.' He sighed. 'Honey . . . Miss Percival' – he quickly corrected himself – 'I know it hurt you, but I doubt it was personal.'

I shook my head. She had seen me well enough. And that story struck me as a poor excuse. Cu yuh, I might criticise Eva, but look at her all the same, still showing up for her work, day in, day out, after going through sheer hell. 'Shame for her, a true dat, but still no reason to be abusive. Plenty of women are losing their sweet-hearts in the war. Your hat's crooked, by the way.'

Mr Rosewell adjusted the brim immediately, before resuming: 'I think the way it happened was the issue. Freddie did say she never came to terms with it.' And with that he quickened his step again, until I was nearly run off my feet.

As we rounded a corner, the wind suddenly turned ill-tempered and the light got sucked out of everything. I nearly tripped over a man who was sitting at the bottom of a flight of grey marble steps, his head slumped over a notice. He reeked of cider. On the shoulder of his frayed military uniform was stitched one yellow chevron: corporal. Stooping a little, I read the note he held in his hands:

HOMELESS WAR VETERAN
WIFE AND CHILDREN TO SUPPORT

Without thinking much about it, I took a penny out of my purse and was preparing to drop it in when the man lifted his head and cast me a look of such sullen rage that I straightened up right quick. His face was ferret-like, cheeks hollow. 'What're you lookin' at me like that for?' I knew that look from base camp. He was in war mode. Just then my hand loosened, and I dropped the coin on the man's face in fright. He threw down his sign and sprang to his feet, the change in his cup scattering everywhere.

'Please leave me alone!' I cried, attempting to run, but then he grabbed me. I tried to pull away, but he was too strong. A firm hand prised us apart, and Mr Rosewell led me away by the elbow the way I'd led Eva away from the cliff edge. I was so shaken up I nearly collapsed on his shoulder. 'Are you all right?' he enquired when we were clear of danger.

'I – I think so, yes.'

'I'm sorry you had to go through that. And I'm sorry I didn't punch the guy's lights out.' I could feel him swallow back his anger.

'You had to protect yourself, too.' Things could have escalated very quickly, and the sight of a black man in a fine suit throwing a punch at a war veteran . . . He had made the right call.

But he looked anguished. 'I should have been protecting you.' He draped his arm loosely around my shoulders, as carefully as if my body were made of tissue paper. I wanted him to keep it there, but he did not. 'Let's sit down for a while. Get our breath back. Have that picnic.'

We went through the gates of Regent's Park, where I counted maybe one man to every twenty-five women and children picnicking on the grass. And babies in prams. I tried not to look too closely at them, or imagine their cries and coos. Or approximate their ages. I was walking with Mr Rosewell now; I could not think of such things. My mind did briefly wander onto the continuing silence from Mr Manning. Although he was a crook, by his own tacit admission, I had hoped he would be honest with me.

A woman in a maroon knitted shawl walked past speaking English with a heavy Italian accent. She had her arm around a man in civilian clothing whose blank eyes told the same story as all shell-shocked soldiers. She was trying to bring him back, to ground him in each detail of grass and tree and path – but was failing. I thought of the bullets Eva had caught, and the ones she had dodged. How long could romantic love last when you had to be a shell-shocked man's eyes, ears and guide, day in, day out? Another girl with a black armband on her sleeve sat under a spreading catalpa tree while her two small boys ran around it in circles. My heart tightened. So much damage. So much harm.

'Do you know those children?' Mr Rosewell's question startled me out of my reverie. 'You seem curious about them.'

'No, I don't. I just feel sad for them. They've lost their daddies, and they're so little.' I tried to keep my voice steady. Because I had lost my own father, of course. As well as the other, secret reason.

'It's a darn shame,' he agreed. 'At least they can play in the sunshine. Life goes on, doesn't it?'

Life goes on. Except for me it stopped six months ago, and I was having trouble getting it started again. Why, even being accepted at last by the Royal Academy had not satisfied me. Rather than thank Arthur Rosewell for his kindness, I had gone on and on about Miss Slade's behaviour. Whatever had happened to me? I used to be grateful for God's blessings, but now I took joy in very little.

'The kiosk looks open,' Mr Rosewell said. 'Shall we have cordial?' He had to ask twice before I heard him, and then I shook my head. 'I'm sorry, but no. I don't have it in me to have any more interactions today.'

'I understand. I feel a bit the same way myself.' His voice was deep and sad. 'I used to think it would be easier over here. In the States you get told very clearly how it is. The buses, the restrooms, the water fountains – all segregated. Stay at the back, give up your seat. Here you sit where you like. But then you relax, and once you do, and forget your place, you're in trouble.'

'Exactly.' How right he was in my case he could never imagine.

He changed the subject. 'Shall we take a turn up Primrose Hill? There are some beautiful views, if the weather clears.'

'Yes, I'd like that.'

We left the path. My boots were good strong leather, and I walked easily through the long grass. Below us lay all of London in a sulphurous haze. I realised that everyone who saw us would presume we were a couple. Mr Rosewell seemed struck by the same thought because he suddenly stiffened and moved away until there were a good two feet between us again.

At the top of the hill we stood watching the city go about its business. The hum of the omnibuses and motors and factories seemed distant. A stillness gathered about us. Then Arthur said, 'Sometimes I forget myself and draw castles in the sky.' He looked at me with such concentration in his brown eyes that my heart filliped a little. 'If I were to start composing a melody right now, about all this' – he swept his hand at the dull, misty city below – 'would you sing it?'

'If it were in my range.'

'Well then.' He opened his briefcase, pulled out a blank manuscript and pencil and drew a huge ornamental treble clef and four flats. Before he could start with the notes, I stopped him.

'Arthur, no score. You sing it to me, and I'll sing it back.'

He flashed me a winsome smile. 'As you wish.' He started humming a melody simple enough to memorise; I took up the line, he sang a counter-tune, and then we both went into a fugue in the manner of a Bach two-parter. We were having so much fun that we carried on for what seemed like a long time, shifting keys, trying discords, syncopating the rhythm a little, as you do. When we stopped, we were greeted with applause. I hadn't noticed an audience creep up.

'Lovely,' a middle-aged woman sighed, a broad smile wreathing her plain face. From the simple cut of her skirt, I guessed she was a servant on her day off. A small man with a round head and a striped suit too long for his legs clapped his hands in the manner of an instruction. 'Encore!' he shouted, but Mr Rosewell shook his head.

'We're not performing seals. Ain't nobody paying us.' His tone was jovial but carried a clear note of warning. The man backed away.

We rambled on and found a seat, but there was a tension between us now that neither of us could dispel. Mr Rosewell opened his bag again and took out a small vacuum lunch box which turned out to contain plain ham sandwiches cut neatly in quarters. He gestured at me to take one, then linked his fingers and looked at the ground, where a pigeon strutted about, searching for stray crumbs. Arthur took one of the sandwiches, tore off a crust and threw it at the bird; it jammed the whole thing in its beak, swallowing greedily until the entire thing had gone down its fat neck. The breeze was cold, an easterly fresh off the Thames, and I could feel my skin prickle underneath my blouse as I drew my scarf around my neck and shivered.

'I'm surprised that bird doesn't choke,' I said.

'Flying rats, my daddy used to call 'em. Still, I like watching the little buddy eat.' He threw a crumb a few feet away. The bird fly-waddled after it.

'I enjoyed today. Even with all the drama.'

He grinned, and all of a sudden the atmosphere felt a little lighter. 'Me too. A bit like a minor opera. Maybe a farce like *The Marriage of Figaro*. Or *Carmen*.'

'Oh, please.'

'We can give that nasty fellow a tiny line or two of recitative, but you, my dear, will get a whole aria in response. And I shall be Arturo, the *toreador*, flying to your aid with my trusty red cloak.'

'Escamillo,' I corrected him. Then, smiling prettily, 'And are you calling *me* a bull, Mr Rosewell?'

'Gosh darn it, I know it's Escamillo. And I am most certainly *not* calling you a bull. I'm trying to get the bull away from you, that's the whole point.'

I liked this scheme. 'I know who Miss Slade could be! Mistress Quickly in *Falstaff*.'

Mr Rosewell raised an eyebrow. 'Or, y'know, she could just turn the pages while you sing.' I quite forgot myself in the midst of this enjoyable fantasy and threw my fist up at the clouds at the thought of that miserable bakra slavishly turning the pages at my leisure. 'Yesss!' I cried, prompting a smiling reproof from Mr Rosewell.

When the last morsel of my last sandwich was gone, he said, 'I enjoyed our little picnic. And you were very poised during that ... provocation. I meant to say earlier, but I didn't want to misspeak.'

Now it was my turn to be shy under his affectionate gaze. 'Me too. It's nice not to think of serious things all the time.'

'It's nice to spend time with people who take your mind off the serious things.' He had sneaked in a little closer to me, and I could see the fine profile of his jaw. When I had first met him, he had been clean-shaven, but since then had allowed a small, fine crop of stubble to grow on his chin, like Robin Mackenzie had done. But Robin's had grown in an established small beard, while Mr Rosewell's was new and a little boyish. If I traced his jaw with my finger, I would feel just the slightest presence of fine hair. It suited him, though.

'You will keep coming to our meetings?' His breath was warm and near.

'Of course,' I said, then wished I hadn't. A woman does well to maintain *some* mystery. At least that's what my mother always told me, in between trying to flog my sister and me on the meat market. Since my father had once been violently in love with her, and my father was a man of calibre, I did listen to her advice on matters of the heart.

'That would be swell,' he beamed. 'I should certainly like to see you again, if my company doesn't bore you senseless. I'm told – I fear – sometimes I go on about music too much.'

I smirked at him, tilting my head sideways. 'Really? Can't imagine why.' The conversation continued in this vein until we parted company half an hour later.

Heading home, I was in high spirits. That September afternoon, we were transformed from Mr Rosewell and Miss Percival, cordial acquaintances, to Arthur and Lucia, friends who duetted together. Vocally, anyway. For a brief moment, I forgot the Bangarang and all my troubles. Arthur Rosewell gave me the chance to be someone else, a chance I was willing to grasp with both hands.

At the gate I bumped into a telegraph boy in a hurry, a slip of paper in his hand. He angrily told me to get out of the way, since he had an urgent message for a Miss Percival. After several minutes of my pleading that I was indeed that person, he finally, reluctantly surrendered his document. I perused the one-line message and handed it back. 'Tell him I'll be there. Thank you.' The message was from my brother Reginald. He was on leave, would shortly be in England, and wished to meet me.

SATURDAY, 8 SEPTEMBER 1917

'S o,' Eva said, as I bent low in front of the mirror, brushing on tiny amounts of electric-blue eyeshadow, 'where are you meeting your brother?' She, too, was dressing to go out that afternoon, which in Eva terms meant putting on a coat.

'Waterloo,' I replied. 'And before you ask why, I have no idea. Place is a building site right now. Hammering and chiselling, morning, noon and night. Not to mention the rhaatid trains. I've no idea why he picked there when there are plenty of nice places to go.' Though perhaps, I did not add, all that noise would not be unwelcome. It might fill up dangerous gaps in the conversation as and when they arose. Our relationship was rocky at the base, and events in my life had only piled more rocks on top of that. He had stayed silent so long that I considered getting him one of those pre-made greetings cards from J. Beagles & Co. starting 'To My Dear Brother on Active Service'. I thought he might get the joke. But on the off chance he might take offence I had decided against it.

'What about you?' I asked Eva. 'You going to meet Sybil and ...

them?' I still couldn't bring myself to utter the name of Sybil's paramour.

'Oh no,' she laughed. 'I fancy going to Liberty's and buying myself a cloche. Sybil would only insist she knew what best suited me and try to direct everything. I'm better off doing it myself.'

What? Eva, buying a hat? I put the eyeshadow brush down. This was a big deal. As far as I could tell, it was the first time she had bought herself something new since . . . well, since her fiancé got blown to bits and she nearly threw herself off Beachy Head to follow him. 'Oh, sweetheart,' I said, 'what's the occasion?'

'I just wanted to celebrate,' Eva said shyly. 'I finished writing a draft of that article I want to submit to *Blackwood's*.'

Finally! I gave her a spontaneous hug. 'I thought you never would. I'm so pleased for you.'

'I used that day off I took yesterday to power on through and tell the whole story. It was very hard – I cried a lot – but it was such a relief to get it done. Oh Lucia, I wrote about everything – well, almost everything.' From the smile that played around her features, I guessed the material she withheld concerned matters of passion between Christopher and herself. 'I feel the need for a little celebration. Even if this never sees the light of day, at least I've done it. All I need to do is to type it up.'

'It will be published, I am sure,' I said. 'I hope you find the perfect hat, I really do.'

Eva laughed. 'I'm not really a hat person, but it's never too late for a change.'

'Maybe you'd like some of this?' I waved the eyeshadow palette at her. She shook her head. 'Oh no, I can't carry those bold colours you put on.'

'You don't carry *any* colours,' I said, in mock disapproval. 'How you know if you don't try?'

Eva waved a hand. 'One step at a time, all right? I hope all goes well with Reginald,' she added in a more serious tone. 'I know it's been a while since you've seen him.' She was tactful enough not to add why.

'Yes,' I sighed, 'and he is sometimeish around me most of the time, so my expectations are low.' With Eva, I used the expressions from home often enough that she understood them. 'Sometimeish' meant moody, volatile and somewhat cranky. It was an adjective whose meaning Eva could easily understand; she was sometimeish enough her own self, and by all accounts her late fiancé had been even more so.

'At least you have the chance to talk to him, though. Not like me with Imelda.'

I kissed my teeth in dismay and sympathy. Imelda, Eva's older sister, had died in Switzerland, officially of tuberculosis, but Eva told me in confidence one day that she had gone out in the snow in her nightdress until the cold put an end to her. Their father and stepmother decided to have the funeral without Eva and notified her of Imelda's demise by typed letter. He even *date-stamped* it, the pathetic, miserable . . . ah, I have no words for them!

Eva's family were really something else. If you think us Percivals had problems, they were in the ha'penny place in comparison to Eva and her relatives. She no longer spoke to any of them, and, honestly, I couldn't blame her. They had what we at home call bad mind, and I was glad she had the good-good sense to avoid them.

When we said goodbye, I kissed her on the cheek. 'Have a nice time. Buy the most colourful hat you can think of. For Imelda.'

Her smile was soft and genuine. 'What a lovely idea. I think I'll do exactly that. And do tell Reginald about your new beau. I think it might be time. You've been walking out – what, a month now? And I haven't even met him yet.'

'Not exactly walking out, I would say,' I demurred, but she

wasn't paying attention. When I left her, she was even humming a tune under her breath. Cha, that was *my* department!

Waterloo was a long way from Fulham Road, and getting there involved a good deal of walking and a convoluted combination of the District and Northern Tube lines. I had ample time to contemplate my relationship with Reginald and how we could go about mending fences. The problem went back a long way. Relations with Meredith had always been easier, always warmly distant. She, the more beautiful of us sisters, was gentle and compliant, and, unlike me, tended to rein in her thoughts. Reginald, on the other hand, often argued with our late father; as a result, our relations had always been a little fractious because my father had been devoted to me and hard on him, to the point of paddling him for minor infractions. No surprise then that Reginald had always been surly and self-contained around me, so I usually had to drag a 'good morning' out of him.

He did not take to authority from anyone, and during the war I did worry about how he would accept non-stop orders from Englishmen. Since the previous November these worries had preyed on my mind even more. Reginald, to give him his due, was worried about me too, though that was not surprising given that I had, well, disappeared for six months.

Now, seeing him rise stiffly and remove his hat to greet me, hair strictly cropped, awkward in his military uniform with its silver BWIR badge on his belt, something caught in my throat. He too had a lighter complexion than I, and, even though the weather was better in Dunkirk than in London, he looked a little pale.

Like Robin and Mr Rosewell, he had managed to grow a moustache, but in his case it was a ridiculous little thing. When he was thirteen and had tried to let it grow out for the first time, I had mocked him so ceaselessly that he ended up shaving it off in a fit of rage. This time, I said nothing. Let him have his moustache;

he'd earned it. For all that he was my brother, he looked fine and handsome.

We shook hands. Ours was not an embracing family, especially not in public, and particularly not in a busy railway station swarming with soldiers and nosy passers-by. I would hug Eva sooner than my own brother! 'I ordered you some tea,' he said. 'I hope you don't mind. They're serving free food over there at a buffet' – he gestured – 'but I think it's just for the soldiers.' I wouldn't have taken a chance on it either. My maxim was: presume everything nice was for whites only until otherwise indicated. Taking a seat, I complimented him on his belt.

'They made me an officer.'

I clapped my hands. 'Reggie! That is wonderful news. But I thought—'

It was a sore subject for both Reginald and me that the rules disqualified him from being a commissioned officer. That, too, was 'whites only'. For a crazy moment, I wondered if Reginald had so far exceeded expectations that the authorities had decided to bend the rules, like they did with the black fellow in the Football Battalion who got made second lieutenant earlier in the year. But the way Reginald's face fell soon disabused me of that notion.

'Just a sergeant,' he said dispiritedly, 'and even then, my only job is to carry out their orders on my men.'

'Still,' I said, trying to hide my disappointment, 'a sergeant is not nothing, Reggie. They've obviously noticed you.'

Reginald slurped down half his tea in one go. 'And you think being noticed is a good thing, Lucia? By these people dem?' Looking around, seeing people at other tables either staring or looking pointedly away from us, shushing their curious children with disapproving shakes of the head . . . he had a point. I, after all, had spent the past two years being noticed by all the wrong people, and look what I had to show for it.

'Well, your belt, it a luk nice, see? Be easy.' But now I saw it as he did: a bauble to pacify someone considered to be no better than an infant, or a troublesome pet. I was about to change the subject when we heard a sudden crash. Turning, we saw fragments of gold and green stained glass in smithereens all over the tiled station floor. A man in black, presumably the foreman, was shouting at a group of labourers using language that could best be described as Billingsgate.

When I had entered the station, I had seen a large open space above the main hallway that was obviously meant to host a stained-glass window in honour of the London and South Western Railway company whose trains ran through Waterloo. As the men scurried about scooping up fragments of glass, it was clear that this gap would remain unfilled today.

'Oops,' I commented, allowing myself a giggle. But Reginald did not join in. His eyes were dreamy, the colour of the cloudy tea he had just drunk. He sat with his chin resting on the heel of his hand, his gaze far away. I decided not to nag him or tell him to snap out of it.

Our father, the Reverend Selvin William Percival, district magistrate, leader of the Mandeville Wesleyan Church and son of freed slaves, did not have much patience for dreamers. I'd joined in with his disapproval too often in the past, often enough that Reginald had quit us all in a fury to go enlist, missing saying goodbye to his own father on his deathbed.

'Remember,' he was saying now, his murmur almost inaudible amid the fuss-fuss at the station, 'that time when I didn't do my homework, and the teacher made me stand in the hall until I was ready to apologise, and I stood for hours and never did? And then they got Papa to come and pull me off the stage and im lick mi good and proper?' His voice was becoming less dreamy now, heavier with resentment. Our father had indeed thrashed him, and Reginald had never forgiven him for it. 'That's rather like what I'd like to do now. I hate their orders. You know Dale, the fellow I talked about in my last letter?'

My face fell a little. His last letter had been quite some time ago. 'I think I remember.'

'He served alongside me as a private. But then they said he smiled at an officer. *Smiled.* And for that Captain Irwin gave him Field Punishment No. 1. Tied him to a gun wheel, put him upside down and left him for a day and a half without food or water. *A day and a half.* It's only meant to be for two hours maximum.'

I clapped my hand to my mouth. 'Bax cova! How dreadful!'

'He hates us all. Treats us like dogs then says we're unmanageable. All I want is someday not to salute Captain Irwin. Just to stand there and not return his salute. Like I did on that stage. That's what I'm doing to do. Oh yes, Lucy, I'll—'

'You'll do no such thing.' My tone was unexpectedly sharp, and his eyes were all focus now, staring into mine. The sun came out and hit off the shards of glass on the station floor. A jackdaw fussed in the gods, unbothered by the commotion below.

'I'm the head of the household. I'll do what I want.'

'Mek me tell you about my friend Eva, then, and see if this changes your mind.' I took a great gulp of tea. Scalded my throat, but I needed it. 'She an Irish gyal who fell in love with a Henglishman. He was made go to the Bangarang, and after the Somme im did go twis' up ina im head, so they put him in the soldier madhouse to recover. But this bakra of an officer was wandering around, skinnin' teeth at all the poor buoy dem with the shell shock. So Eva's man was a facety type, and he did say to himself, mi nuh gwaan salute this fella if I see him. So when he came into the room looking for his salute, Christopher – that was his name – im did siddung pon di table and fold his arms! like so!' I folded my arms tightly across my chest. 'And everyone else in the room did like *this*' – putting my hand to my forehead in a salute gesture. 'A im do what you waan do. And wha did 'appen to im? Mr Officer was head of the Medical Board, and he did brindle so much at the insult that he called Christopher to a tribunal the next day and sen' him off to Salonika. Now he was unfit, remember? He had the shell shock, bad-bad. So then in the battle with the Bulgarians he step on a mine and' – I flung my hands in the air and fluttered my fingers to mimic how Christopher's body shattered on impact. 'That's what happened to him for not saluting the officer, Reggie. And he was white, do you hear me? He – was – *white!*'

I banged the table so hard that several other diners gave me looks. Reginald meantime said nothing, but I could see his upper lip tremble. 'Keep your voice down,' he muttered. But I was resolute. Even if I must lower my volume, I would not dilute my sentiment. This was too important.

'If that's how they treat one of their own, what do you think they will do to you? Do you think they gwaan bother with tribunal and dem tings before sending you off somewhere? Egypt maybe? No, sah! They go shoot you inna de back a yuh head and dump you in that trench you just dug the same mornin'. Mark my words.' With that, I gulped down the rest of my tea, my hand flying to my neck from the heat of it going down my gullet.

I hoped Reginald would heed my warning, but the signs were not good. He was slouching in his chair, looking every inch the boy with the push-up face who had lingered on that stage. 'A you gwaan lecture me, sis? From your position of moral authority. With your jacket you couldn't even keep.' There was a sneer in his voice I couldn't ignore. My brother knew exactly how to nettle me. He'd had over a decade of practice, after all. And to speak that way about little Domi . . .

'Reggie.' I tried not to lose my temper again. 'I'm not telling you this to be superior. You know how far I have sunk. I'm telling you because I love you. Mi nah waan lose you like that. If you fell in battle' – I could see his face change, and I had to swallow down my emotion – 'at least that would be an honourable way to go. But to go so nasty, to have your good name ruined, because of some officer's whim?' I reached across the table and took both his hands in mine. They were cold and clammy. 'Don't do that to the people you love, Reggie. Or yourself. Don't let them win.'

He was looking pon mi a little softer now, a thoughtful look in his eyes. 'A yuh dat let them win, though? Came over here after me with all sorts of dreams and ideas – and look pon you now, with nattin'. Nah even 'ave yuh dignity.'

'Dat I can't deny,' I agreed dejectedly. He was absolutely right.

'At least you didn't marry that Mr Dakins,' Reginald added kindly. Very kindly, under the circumstances.

I laughed. 'A true dat, brother. Thank you.'

Our mother, at the height of her Mrs Bennet phase, had for me fixed on Paul Dakins, a clerk in the import/export department of the United Fruit Company in Kingston, as light-skinned a man as a man could be while not being white. This last aspect, far more than his profession or suitability, endeared him to my mother. After two weeks of correspondence between the families – Mr Dakins Senior had been an elder in my father's church – Paul had finally visited us in our home in Mandeville.

To an uninvolved stranger, his presence might have seemed an imposing one, walking along the road, freshly ironed shirt and linen suit, straw boater set high enough to allow for visible traces of sunburn, and an unfortunate porter several feet behind him carrying two large brown leather suitcases. But he repelled me on sight, standing there in my father's house, his head bent as if the ceiling were too low. Cha, he didn't even bother offering a small gift!

If his arrogance had been earned, I would have resented it less.

But it was lazy and assumed. He spoke little, largely because he could not be bothered to complete a sentence, and when Athaliah brought him a tonic and lime he took it without thanks, sipping at it in a half-hearted manner that I suspected extended to every single interaction he made. If a fly crawled on his cheek he wouldn't have brushed it off, he was that lazy.

Reginald had met him once before his departure in the May of 1915 and could not hide his disdain for the man. Shortly after Paul Dakins left, he came to me in my room. I was attempting to follow a pattern for a pair of socks as part of Mrs Briscoe's island-wide wartime sewing and knitting club. Reginald had hung in the doorway and muttered, 'Lucia, I wish I could get you out of this.' We had both witnessed Meredith's marriage to Mr Willis, a shop-keeper my father's age who won a settlement from the government after his premises were blown down in the 1912 hurricane.

I hoped that he might, in the end, get me out of it. But a week later he got himself out of Jamaica instead, signing up with the First Battalion of the British West Indies Regiment without telling anyone beforehand, including our ailing father. Two months later, fatherless, I followed him, leaving my wedding dress hanging in the wardrobe. It was a beautiful ivory charmeuse with chiffon sleeves and a lace detail around the bodice – so soft to the touch, like a wave of fresh, cool water on my skin when I held it close. I was glad to be free of Mr Dakins but regretful that I never wore that dress. Given everything that had happened since, it was unlikely I would ever wear anything like it again.

Reginald broke the uncomfortable silence, shifting in his seat. 'Mi sarry. For dem tings I said.'

'I know it.' I was gentle.

'I'm glad you've got yourself together, gyal. When I heard nothing since last November, I thought you – well, you know.' I saw for the first time the small ring on his pinky as he fiddled with it. An absurd elegance, but his fingers had always been long and delicate. 'Thought maybe Fritz took you.'

I burst out laughing. 'Fritz never saw the back of me never mind the front!'

'I know that now,' Reginald said crossly, 'but at the time, hearing nothing, I thought the worst. Then, at the end of April, that you were sent off to Scotland, and had a . . .' He trailed off, only mouthing the word 'baby' as if it were so disgraceful it could not be spoken in common tone. At least he wasn't saying 'jacket' any more.

'Dominic,' I said firmly. 'That was his name.'

Reginald leaned over the table. 'Now Lucy. You've been straight with me, so I'll be the same with you. That pickney have no name, and you know it.'

'Reginald—'

'No, girl, a your turn to list'n.' His voice was cold with anger. 'You had no business doing what you did. It all went wrong, and you lost the baby. Sad, yes, but you should thank God for it. You need to forget that ever happened.'

'I can't. And I won't.' I had planned to lie about my intentions, but the way he patronised me drove me mad enough that I started telling him about my meeting with Mr Manning. He cut me short. 'I know all about that foolishness.'

'What? How?'

'He done write and tell me everyting a'ready. Care of the regiment.' He patted his pocket, making a crumpling sound.

That rhaatid wasteman Edgar Manning! I had told him not to interfere. 'You need to hold your corner,' I snapped at Reginald, meaning he should mind his own business, but Reginald was now cornering *me*, leaning in with a glare. 'Manning wrote to me because he understands family. He knows women need protection. If this gets out, no man will touch you. And you will bring disgrace on us all.' Protection for whom, I wondered, for me or for the family name?

He stood up and fastened his coat. 'Why else would I have paid all my wage to get leave here? I came to tell you that if you don't forget about this, you won't be part of our family anymore. I'm not going to have our mother find out.' His English was stiff and formal. It was as if he were writing me a letter of severance.

'Reginald, what are you—? You can't just walk away from me!'

He paused, and I could tell he was relishing it. 'Perhaps I was wrong,' he said, cold and petulant. 'Perhaps you should have married Mr Dakins and stayed in Mandeville after all.' Without shaking my hand, he went directly to the counter to pay. Then he walked off without saying goodbye.

I put my head in my hands. What a to-do! Everyone who knew my story was against me in this matter. Eva, Reginald, even Mr Manning, who I was paying to help. They seemed all to misunderstand – wilfully – what Domi meant to me. They thought it was a secondary matter, something to move on from, like all the other flotsam and jetsam cast aside by this bloody war. While my dreams, nearly every night now . . .

Standing there in Waterloo concourse, surrounded by pigeons and soldiers and men in black picking up glass, and the hooting of departing trains, I recalled one ally: that tiresome, warbling, Irish poet Mr Yeats.

During the weebly-warbly monologue he had directed at me at the séance, he had gestured at Miss Hyde-Lees and said, his voice low, 'I believe the time will come when I must obey an astrological imperative.' I must have pretended to be curious, because he elaborated, 'I am a barren man, my dear, with nothing at fifty-four years but books and memories.' His horoscope had told him he must marry that October, never mind who. 'It is not a question of desire or lack,' he sighed. 'It is the stars that drive us to fulfil our destiny, no matter that spiteful commoners may take us for fools. I see that in you too. That same restlessness.'

For all that he made me cringe with his married-man sophistry before he was even married, that Irishman understood the nature of my dilemma. Perhaps finding Domi was *my* astrological imperative. (And, I had to admit, I liked the 'spiteful commoners' comment.) It wasn't much, but it was all I had in my defence.

I got home a little late that evening, after all the toing and froing with trains, to find that Eva had returned before me and was darning a hole in one of her skirts. She was sitting on the stool with the uneven leg, rocking slightly. When she looked up, her expression wasn't happy. 'Did Reginald not escort you back?' she asked, and I shook my head.

'We had a to-do and he vex me,' was all I would say, not wanting to go over our quarrel once more. Eva's demeanour had changed completely from earlier. The joy had gone from her eyes, her lips were sucked in, and her face looked sharp and sallow. When I asked her about the hat, she just frowned and said, 'Oh, none of them suited. Besides, I've lost the humour for hats,' then turned back to her darning needle.

Wh'happen? I wondered, but I hardly had the energy to ask. I had so many problems of my own I could hardly worry about hers. 'Was there any post?' I asked. Until Mr Manning's letter *to me* arrived, I couldn't move forward. He had said three weeks, and it was now almost a month since that meeting in Soho. He had time to write to Reggie, for God's sake, why not me? And a note from Mr Rosewell would have been nice too. I would see him in two days, but still. I would have liked to know he was thinking of me in the meantime.

'I'm afraid not.' Eva allowed a little amusement back in her tone. I had asked her the same question several days in a row, after all. For my part, I hoped whatever was bothering her would pass. I was feeling a bit fretful. My quarrel with Reginald had put me out of temper, too much to be able to sing, even. There is a complex relationship between my emotional stability and my singing energy – exerting the power of my voice can bring me to a more level place, but if I am too far out of centre to begin with I cannot sing myself back to normal; it is necessary to find other ways of righting myself first. Then, and only then, can I reserve sufficient energy to even get started.

Some other activity would have to ease my nerves. The last tenant (who, I gathered, had to leave in a hurry) had left behind a draughtboard which was gathering dust on the shelf above Eva's bed. I knew better than to ask her if she were interested in playing. Even when she was in a good mood Eva had little interest in board games. Whereas I . . . now, that was a different matter altogether.

I stretched up and pulled down the dusty box, taking out the pieces and setting them in their rows. Then I proceeded to play myself, flipping the black pieces over the white, and vice versa, and not really getting anywhere. You need a twelve-by-twelve board to play a decent solitaire, and this one was only ten by ten. I did my best, but a game against oneself has a certain emptiness. As I mindlessly flipped the pieces hither and yon, I could not help but recall another game, in another place, where I had a worthy opponent.

8

30 JUNE 1916

After our first encounter over the gas-gangrene case, I was posted to work with Mr Mackenzie – he refused to allow me address him as 'Captain' – nearly every day. I learned a little more about him and how he came to be in France, doing his bit.

'My people are in trade,' he declared.

'So are mine.' Short pause. 'I mean, they were traded.' I was deadpan.

'Oh,' said he, laughing with embarrassment. 'Touché.' He went on to explain that his maternal grandfather, Stuart Ingram Henderson, endured a childhood in a three-up two-down in a Govan slum before founding a confectionery empire called Barker & Henderson. That man's daughter, Laura-Jane, married Professor Norman Mackenzie, an eminent psychiatrist with a distinguished career and a tendency to splash around the money. Her fierce obsession with reputation, and her constant bullying scrutiny, had driven Robin away from home, even though he had just qualified.

The circular from the Scottish Medical Service Emergency

Committee had arrived just in time, in the autumn of 1915. 'I couldnae take it any more. I needed to get right away from her,' he admitted. As he took his leave of her, Robin told me matter-of-factly, his mother gave him one last warning: any inappropriate relationships and she would cut him off and make sure all of Glasgow's well-to-do did likewise.

This information neither applied to me, nor could offend me, since I had no notion of any romance with any white fellow, let alone Mr Mackenzie. So I merely made sympathetic noises at appropriate intervals. What I did not realise at the time was that his explanation was a disclaimer: he was marking his territory before the game began.

The game – that is, the long tussle between Robin Mackenzie and me – began with little ceremony the night before the Somme offensive started. This time we were in Surgical Hut No. 1. Everything was quiet: the air was hot, taut with waiting. The smell of iodine was almost suffocating.

We were sitting opposite each other on folded stools. Robin had rolled up his shirtsleeves to expose the mottled freckles on his forearms. He leaned forward until his head nearly touched mine, and I could see the pattern of the red hairs on his forehead. Then he lifted the white king's pawn and put it on the fourth square. 'Your move, Percival.'

I put my finger on the black king's pawn, feeling its smooth bakelite surface. My heart began to beat a little faster as a thought came into my mind. 'Put that pawn back, Mr Mackenzie,' I said very quietly. 'Today, black moves first.'

He looked at me as if I were mad. Then he put the pawn back to its starting square. 'I would have given you white if you'd asked.'

'I don't want white. I want black to move first.'

He leaned back and folded his arms. 'Well. Go on then.'

For a camp full of thousands of people on the move, with

troops heading north and south, trains disgorging them almost every hour, it was very quiet that night. I could hear the long slow buzz of a nightjar from a clear-felled wood on the other side of the road, as well as the drone of a lorry turning into the camp. When I lifted the pawn and set it down on the K4 square, Robin responded in kind.

'What do you plan to do after that unusual start?' he said in a hoarse whisper.

'Cha, no need to get so excited,' said I. 'We only one move in.'

But something in me had stirred, and him too, I could see it. We knew a big bit of the Bangarang was coming, but we were having a nice little bangarang all our own self. Time to goad him into a capture. I put my pawn on the king's bishop square.

'Och aye, I'm not sure it's proper to accept a gambit from a lady.' But he picked up my pawn nevertheless; in response, I moved my bishop. It was still quiet. I could feel the evening deepen slowly, inexorably, into true night.

I should have been in my Alwyn hut with my room-mate, a pretty, freckled, gap-toothed girl called Amelia Hall, who had exclaimed to a group of us at lunchtime, as she fixed her wide-brimmed sunhat, 'My! We shall all be as brown as berries soon.' Then, with a sidelong glance at me, 'Well . . .' It had not been the first time she tossed such asides my way, and wouldn't be the last.

She made a big deal out of ignoring me but had become obsessed with a lock of my hair that wandered its way out of my cap. She had tugged at it, commenting in a level, Home Counties accent, 'That bit sticking out there is so irritating. It doesn't even feel like hair. Cut it off, please.' Times like that I would repeat one of my favourite vocal exercises to calm myself down: 'Tip of the tongue, teeth and the lips, tip of the tongue, teeth and the lips,' only with my Yaad accent I would occasionally lapse into 'teet' an' da lips,' at which point she would smirk and say, 'Pretending to ignore me is so immature.'

There was something relentless about her. I knew she would never let up – and I would never surrender either. So can you blame me that I would rather stay and play chess than go and subject myself to more of that foolery? I set out my queen's bishop, then Robin put his pawn in harm's way, for some reason best known to himself and several dozen chess books.

After I took his pawn with my bishop, he paused, hand hovering above his queen. Would he make such an audacious move? But no, he let his hand flop down by his side. Then he got up and started to walk in a small, obsessive circle. 'You've heard what's coming?'

I nodded. He was talking about the forthcoming attack.

'There's talk all over base. If it's anything like the last one, it's going to be brutal. We'll have a bloody campaign, and I'm not lord-mayoring this time.' 'Lord mayor' was rhyming slang for 'swear', though in Robin's Scottish accent it didn't really rhyme. 'I mean literally bloody. Those fules back at base couldn't add two and two let alone make this work. I'm scared, Percival. Anyone with half a brain should be.'

'Maybe we should stop the game then?'

'No.' He whirled around on his heel, giving me an intense, blue-eyed stare. 'Let's continue tomorrow. There's no better time.' He lifted the chessboard back onto the shelf. The pieces, held to the board by magnetic force, did not fall off.

Unfortunately our troops were not held on by magnets. The following morning, at seven-thirty, the British forces all around the Somme region went over the fire-step and through no man's land towards the German wire, which, as far as they knew, had been cut for them to break through. It had not been cut, and word soon buzzed around: casualties would be brutal. When I heard, I escaped to our makeshift chapel and prayed for their souls, and ours. Robin Mackenzie was right to be scared.

We were sent to Operating Theatre No. 5, where the stretchers started lining up late that night – and it went on like that for weeks. I was constantly scouting for supplies: bandages, iodoform, morphine, scalpels. I remember running so hard my belly hurt and I got a stitch, all to corner a passing quartermaster and beg him for more. When I was in theatre, I cleaned and sterilised and wiped and scrubbed, but it was never enough. Both Mr Mackenzie and I were permanently tired, and could not wash off the smell. It was as if we had set up camp in a slaughterhouse. The heat was relentless too.

Our exchanges became something like this.

SPOKEN: 'Percival! Please sterilise these forceps immediately.'

SUNG: 'With wha-at, dear Henry, dear Henry, dear Henry? With what?'

SPOKEN: 'With dishwater fer all I care, ye cheeky bint! Jest get aun wi'it! Oh and . . . check.'

No matter where we set up shop, that chessboard came with us. That time, he had checked me with his queen. Meanwhile, the patient of the hour, a private in the Sherwood Foresters, was screaming blue murder, bits of his jacket sticking to his chest, as I struggled to pull down his trousers and inject him with morphine. Cha, he was strong! And in such pain, we could hardly hear ourselves think with his yelling. I was at such a hallucinating stage of exhaustion that all I could see on the table was a big screaming white pawn with a mouth. Not an inaccurate assessment, mind you.

'You leave my king alone, Mr Mackenzie.' I moved His Majesty back to safety as the drug finally kicked in and the Sherwood Foresters man quietened down into bubbling, stertorous snores.

Thank God! We might save this one. His humanity came back to me; he was chess piece no more.

For the next week, as casualties continued to pour in, the two of us bickered, jested, bounced off each other – and continued playing. Robin gambled his queen's knight's pawn. And I? I chased his queen. I chased her with my knights, pawns and bishops. Every time he tried to develop his game, I attacked her.

Like all men, his head was turned. If he had only let her go, realised all her powers were useless in a close, tight game . . . but he could not. My mind was clear and cold, even when upside down with exhaustion. I gave up my bishop without a moment's thought, then both rooks, then my own queen. And when I let him take that black queen, he groaned, put down his instruments and threw his hands in the air. He was too good a player not to know what was next.

So that is how, at the end of the first week of the Somme offensive, on a rare five-minute breather after nearly one hundred and fifty men saved and forty lost on that one operating table, I checkmated Robin Mackenzie with a bishop and two knights.

An hour later, when things had calmed down a little, he cocked his head to one side, a lit Player's Navy Cut in his hand. 'Jesus. You're something else, you know that?'

'What do you mean?'

'You come all the way from the West Indies to England on your own. You walk in singing about the wee birdies on Loch Lomond, and you play chess like a man who'll hang tomorrow. I've never met anyone like you in all my damn life, excuse my French.'

'I do not excuse it. Clean up your language, sir.'

He ignored me, sucking deeper at the cigarette. 'Y'know, I knew I was losing a while back, and I couldn't stop myself going further down the wrong road. That's human nature isn't it, not to know when to stop? Like this fu— this shambles.'

I blinked at him. My eyelids felt heavy-heavy.

'Percival,' he went on, 'you ever hear of *Zugzwang*?'

'Nah,' I yawned. 'He some German general?'

'It's when you have no move available that won't lose you the game. So naturally you don't want to make a move. But chess doesn't allow that: you *must* move. And therefore, you must lose.' He blew out a large cloud of smoke that hovered a moment then dispersed out the door into the warm night. 'I shoulda just not moved.'

He looked at me in a slow, lazy-lidded way, and in the greenish glow of the bulb hanging from the roof he looked almost reptilian. 'But I had to see how the game would go, you know? I had to play it out. We are risk-takers, we two. And some day, Lucia Percival, you'll play a game, and the same thing will happen to you, and you won't even see it.'

I laughed lightly. 'Nah, I don't believe you. You just sore loser.'

He mock-waggled his finger. 'Just you wait, girl. Just you wait.'

9

6 JULY 1916

Our next game ended up as a draw by perpetual check. Knight to king's rook five, check; king to king one. Knight to queen square three, king to queen one; knight to king's rook five, and so on. It was about as interesting and productive as the battle that was raging seventy miles away. The slaughter of the Somme was beginning to take its toll on the hospital staff as much as its fighting men. We heard tales of fights in the RAMC mess, of men smashing glasses and running up and down the hall screaming, just from the pressure of what they had to deal with.

Mr Mackenzie was not immune to that mental distress. That blank look, the hysterical laughter . . . every now and then in the middle of an operation he would stop and lose himself. I would have to gently guide him back, just as I did with Eva a year later. Things came to a head when Mr Russell, another surgeon whom Mr Mackenzie particularly disliked, reprimanded him for performing a ghostly waltz with a severed arm. Don't look at me; I did try to stop him.

'Have some respect for the dead, man!' Russell shouted at Mackenzie, who answered with a cracked laugh, 'Och, don't worry yer head, Russell. He's no' dead. We amputated him this morning and sent him to Blighty.'

'For God's sake, man! Dead or alive . . . It's not done.' Russell's disapproval was nearly as deep as the sunburn on his forehead and cheeks.

Robin Mackenzie took his time answering. 'I wonder where in the Buke on Gentlemanly Etiquette,' he said with heavy sarcasm, 'ye might find the wee section on "What a Gentleman Should Do to Pass the Time During Mass Slaughter"? Would it be after "Fish Knives" or before "The Correct Way to Wear Gloves"? You arrogant piece of cod!' And before Russell could answer him, he stormed out of the room, throwing the amputated limb on the floor.

'He's under a lot of pressure, Mr Russell,' I said. 'Try and go easy on him.'

Mr Russell huffed and puffed. 'I don't take advice from the likes of you—'

I was already halfway out the door, along with the disembodied arm, in search of Robin Mackenzie. Under my fingers, the cold stiff skin felt weird, like the skin of a gourd. Where was Mr Mackenzie? Was he all right? I found him behind the mess block, smoking hard.

'Is that the hand of God on Judgement Day?' he enquired, with a slight smile. Blood fiah! I had forgotten to throw the blasted arm in a medical waste bin. I threw it on the grass instead, in disgust.

Mr Mackenzie sucked on his cigarette. 'I'd pick that back up if I were you.'

Catching his eye, I started to giggle, just a little at first, then louder, until the laughter caught in my belly and came so hard it hurt. I didn't know why, for I was no longer amused, and some-

thing in my hysteria must have alerted him because he threw
down his cigarette and gave me a very gentle shake. 'You need to
pull yourself together, Lucy-loo,' he said. 'I know it's hard when
the whole world is stone mad.'

He let me go, and I swayed forward; he caught and righted me.
I felt the tension in my own limbs, as stiff as that dead arm, relax.
Somewhere the rest of that man's body would recover, live, drink,
laugh. I couldn't imagine it at all.

'Come on, let's go get some water. I've got a wee bottle in the
theatre. Or something stronger, if you like? I'm not like that
reformed pisshead Doyle.' He was referring to an Irish surgeon
who worked alongside Eva. 'I'm not going to throw a fit if I so
much as catch sight of a medicinal brandy.'

'Water will do. I should wash my hands too.'

'You can do both. It's quiet now.'

We reached the operating theatre. Mr Russell had long since
left and the place was empty. Finally there was time to take stock
of the chaos: filthy tiles smeared with blood, instruments all
dumped in containers or simply left lying around, cigarette butts
where the orderlies hadn't bothered to sweep them up. I blinked.
Would I have to tidy all that up? I was fagged out, as the English
VADs would have put it.

'Forget it,' Robin Mackenzie instructed, to my relief. 'Just get
your hands washed and come on outside.'

Behind the block was a small field where sacks used for
bayonet training swung idly in the slight breeze. Beyond that was
a bank of trees, and after that the railway lines and the gentle,
receding hiss of the sea. I heard the soft call of a wood pigeon.
Prrr-oooo-oooo-oo-oo. Although there were thousands in this camp
– Australian troops, Canadian doctors, Turcoman cooks, Indian
labourers, Scottish doctors, Londoners doing everything – still I
felt the quietness and solitude of somewhere sweet and remote. I

leaned against the hut's wooden wall and felt its warmth on my shoulders. The thought crossed my mind that the severed arm still lay where I had flung it. I was too tired and indifferent to bring it up, though.

Mr Mackenzie and I were close enough that our shoulders almost touched. He struck a match – it roared softly in the warm dark – and let it burn for several seconds before lighting his cigarette. Then he spoke, so quietly I had to lean in to hear him. 'When I was in medical school, I read a book called *King Solomon's Mines*. You know it?' I said I didn't. 'Probably just as well. I'm guessing you wouldn't like it.' He took another drag. 'Anyway, there was a passage there that got my attention. Two African tribes were having a fierce battle, and they had medicine men dealing with their casualties. If the injured man was a hopeless case, they would just cut open a major artery and let him pass away, quickly and with mercy.'

He took up the cigarette again, then exhaled deeply, a stream of smoke unwinding in the still air. 'I couldn't get that passage out of my mind. I checked my textbook to see which artery the author might be talking about and concluded the easiest option was the left carotid, cut just below the sinus bulb.'

'You thought about this?' I shivered, in spite of the warm night.

'I did. I had the strange feeling I might find the need to use it some day. Now, I'd no idea what was going to happen. No special psychic powers.' He laughed hollowly. 'I just kept it in the back of my mind. Then we got out here' – he gestured around him – 'and I've refrained so far, but I swear sometimes I've been tempted.'

I tried not to sound shocked. 'Mr Mackenzie, that would be murder.'

'Och, how though? When the poor chavie is already half dead? It's the decent thing, to spare him pain. But with your gimlet eye on me, I didnae dare.'

'Mr Mackenzie, there's nothing gimlet about my eyes.'

He laughed softly. 'Aye, Lucia, I'm sure there's not. But sometimes it was the only check I had to stop myself.'

His using my name took the tension out the conversation. I felt for him, seeing so many of his friends and associates die, and could understand how he was tempted to violate his oath. What use was long-dead Mr Hippocrates when men were screaming and dying in their thousands in front of you?

The tension had gone from him too; I could feel it. For a while, neither of us spoke. The cigarette smell eased out of the air and was replaced by summer and wild garlic. It cleansed me, and I fell into a standing doze. During that brief minute, I dreamed of when I was with my mother's people in the Accompong region. Her mother's brothers, my 'big uncles', had killed a wild boar and roasted the meat. I salivated at the memory.

'Lucia.' I jerked and twitched awake, wiping my chin, to Mr Mackenzie's amusement. 'What were you dreaming about?'

'Pulled pork.'

The next thing a pair of khaki-sleeved arms were around me, and that short Scottish fellow had planted his lips on my cheek! Just for a little minute, but the skin he touched burned. 'You know, if you'd said something else, some rubbish like "war" or "the meaning of life," I wouldn't have done that, but pulled pork! Pulled fuckin' pork! Oh look, that would be the lord mayor again. Sorry.' He stamped one of his discarded cigarette butts into the grass, then scrubbed it in even further with the toe edge of his boot. 'You're really something else.'

'Mr Mackenzie, I don't know who I am. I feel lost,' I said, in a sudden burst of truth.

'Would you call me Robin, for Chri—' He put his arms around me again, pulling me in tighter. His body was intensely warm, but bony, so it felt as if there was no space between my cheek and his heart. Yes, he was a short man, but all his energy was fiercely compacted, ready to blow like a pressure cooker.

'I'll tell you what you are, sweetheart,' he murmured. 'You're Jesus in human form. You're proof rum. You're the only person who can get me through this mess. I need you, Lucia. I need you like a drowning man needs air.' My friend, why do you shake your head? I cannot stop now. I need to explain what I did, or the rest of it makes no sense.

When he kissed me again, I was so light-headed with the soft taste of him, cigarettes and Fry's Peppermint rations, that I let him pull me against the wall. Then he slipped in a bit of tongue, just a teasing tip. Oh my friend, let me tell you, it was nothing like that commercial traveller! On the contrary, to my surprise, I liked it very much. Then he knelt down on the grass, beckoning me towards him.

And we did what people do, and for a while everything else went blank.

10

5 SEPTEMBER 1917

oyal Academy of Music – For Practice Notes Only –
Notes by VS
Date: 5 September 1917
Student Name: Miss L. Percival

SCALES: Chromatics, in solfeggio (doh-re-mi). All major and minor keys, ascending and descending. Do not repeat top note on descent.

PIECES:

Gilbert and Sullivan, 'Poor Wand'ring One'. Staccato – LIFT ALL MUSCLES. Ribcage open. Breathing – steady. Avoid excessive throat.

Mozart, 'Exsultate, jubilate'. Good light touch, be careful to relax face and neck on high notes.

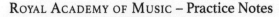

ROYAL ACADEMY OF MUSIC – Practice Notes
    Date: 12 September 1917
    Student Name: Miss L. Percival

SCALES: As previous. Add dim. 7ths

PIECES:
    'Poor Wand'ring One'. Staccato v. effective.
    Mozart, 'Exsultate, jubilate'. Again good. But high notes must be sustained.
    PRACTISE!
    New piece??

ROYAL ACADEMY OF MUSIC – Practice Notes
    Date: 19 September 1917
    Student Name: Miss L. Percival
    Scales: As previous.
    Pieces: 'Poor Wand'ring One'. Continue to work on staccato and breathing.
    'Ex. Jub.' High notes MUCH BETTER this week. Well done.
    New piece: 'In solitaria stanza' (Verdi). NB: Speak lyrics first, to master pronunciation.
    Very good progress made this week on quite challenging work – V. Slade.

SOMEWHERE IN ITALY
18-19 September 1917

MY DEAR SISTER LUCIA,

I'm sorry it took me so long to write after our Meeting. We just recently arrived at _____ and we have spent all the time getting set up. But now we have a nice long time to write as our duties are a bit Boring. We guard the _____ in the _____ at ___ but nothing ever happens. The Weather is better than our previous posting, if anything it is a little Hot, even for us Island Boys.

The march here was very Tough as the English officers who command the B.W.I.R. are Strict indeed. Captain Irwin as always is very Particular about standards and Discipline. My dear Sister, although we might have Quarrelled, as we often do, I can reassure you that after a while I took your words to heart. I don't want what happened to that other Fellow to happen to me, and I don't want you or Merry weeping after receiving a Telegram about me. My Mission from here on in will be Staying in one Piece, and I will bite large Holes in my tongue if necessary to make sure that happens!

Anyway, I am glad you are keeping well and staying out of trouble after your perilous Mistake last year. It worries me that I cannot keep more of an Eye on you, being the man of the House in our dear Father's absence. If I expressed that badly, I am sorry once more. I have not heard anything from Meredith and not much from our Mother. She thinks I am Crazy to get myself involved in this Bangarang, and who knows, maybe she is right.

Your Affectionate Brother
Reginald S. Percival

11

WEDNESDAY, 19 SEPTEMBER 1917

I t had been a long, hard day at work – Major Carroll's ulcer was playing up like a symphony orchestra, and the unlovely Cath nearly lost a thumb when she didn't spot the lathe (sadly only *nearly*), but when I left the Academy that evening, it was in high spirits. Miss Slade had written such kind remarks on my notes that I read that evening's summary again and again.

Arthur Rosewell, who was 'just passing by' in the corridor, insisted on knowing why I was smiling so much, and when I passed the paper to him, his grin was even broader. He got so giddy he threw his hat in the air. 'I've never heard her speak that way about anybody! You must be special.'

'She's talking about my doing Grade 8 next summer,' I said happily. 'It was going to be November, but she thinks I'll be ready sooner.'

'That's good news,' Mr Rosewell concurred. 'Sooner you pass that exam, sooner you'll be on a stage. War permitting, of course.'

I felt buoyed by his belief in me, excited too that he and I could be composers and performers in this new world order when in previous times we would have been shut out. He was right: excluded from traditional society we had truly made our own! Our shared mood was so infectious that instead of seeing me off at the Tube he ended up accompanying me to my door, walking all the way.

The September evenings were drawing in, the days getting shorter and colder, but as we traversed the footpaths, well past curfew and our hats and shoulders spattered with rain, neither of us, for once, complained about the weather. When we reached the small pathway to my door, he made so bold as to take my hand loosely in his and brush my knuckles with a light yet lingering kiss before loping off into the darkness, turning back once to wave. I was underdressed for autumn, but that wasn't the reason why I shivered as the wind whipped my skirts against my calves.

It was late, so I presumed Eva would have long since gone to bed, but the moment I shoved that big hall door open I heard voices coming from behind our door. Hers, complaining in a pronounced Irish accent that she was entitled to go where she wanted and when, and that nobody would be the boss of her. Then, slightly more muted, Sybil's, declaring with cut-glass disgust that Eva was the most selfish creature in Christendom. Mi Gad, if Sybil was there in the middle of the night and Eva's accent was slipping, it must be serious.

I was tempted to turn tail. Quarrels are not to my taste unless I happen to have started them. But since I had nowhere else to go, and was cold, I put my key in the lock and rattled it about a little to give everyone fair warning, then entered the room.

I walked in on two very pale and angry girls. Sybil was leaning on the counter. She'd had a haircut since our last meeting: a smart bob in the new style. I didn't like it. Eva was slumped in the armchair, mutinous, examining the worn horsehair fabric as if it held the secrets of Solomon.

Sybil spoke first. 'She didn't even tell me. Had to find out from a doctor friend at St Thomas's.'

Eva barely lifted her head. 'Because I knew you'd respond like this.'

'She didn't tell you . . . what? What's going on?'

I noticed then that Sybil's eyes were red-rimmed, her hair wet and uncombed, her dark-blue ruffled blouse jacket buttoned up wrong. I'd never seen her that upset and dishevelled, even in her cups.

'I see you've even kept your best girl in the dark. Are you going to tell her? Or shall I?'

'Sybil's mad at me because I'm going back to France.' Eva was still staring at the chair.

When I heard that I nearly had to sit down myself. 'You're going where?'

'Étaples again,' Eva told me, her voice a little hoarse. 'Tomorrow. Lucia, I meant to tell you and give you more notice, but the words kept drying up in my mouth.'

'I'll bet they did,' hissed an outraged Sybil.

'I applied for the transfer a few weeks ago. I will be working on the German ward, assisting with the prisoners of war. That's all.'

That's all? Helping Huns? No wonder Sybil was angry. But my horror was, if anything, greater than hers. After all the effort I had gone to in order to make my world safe, Eva was abandoning me. I would have to live alone in this hostile house, in this hostile country – all so she could go off and help a hostile people? It was lucky for Eva that Sybil was in full flow because if I'd the chance to open my mouth . . .

'You *volunteered*,' Sybil spat. 'You actually *asked* to look after . . . those people. After the things they've done. To our boys. To Bo. How could you, Eva? They're not even human.'

'That's a ridiculous thing to say. Of course they are,' Eva shot back, but Sybil was having none of it.

'You're a fine one to talk about being ridiculous, when you're about to waltz off and patch up those killers, and all because you ran into Lilian Shandlin at the third-floor checkout at Liberty's nearly two weeks ago now, and you *still* can't get over your self-pity!'

Bax cova! Christopher's mother? No wonder Eva had returned hatless that evening, and in a bad mood. And just when she was beginning to come back to life a little, after almost a year of misery.

'Did you speak to her?' I said, curious. A little hurt, too, that Eva had not told me at the time, but I wasn't going to mention that.

'Lucia.' Eva looked at me despairingly. 'You know what she said about me to Gabriel Hunter. After she found out about the white feather.'

'Here we go again.' Sybil mimed playing a violin. I didn't smell alcohol, but she must have been drunk to have been that insensitive. I shivered, my hands on my sleeves, very sober indeed. I knew what Lilian Shandlin had said about Eva all right. Eva had told me on the train back from Eastbourne, after I'd talked her off the cliff.

God would be unjust if she died a quiet death.

Where I come from, a statement like that is bad magic, a curse even. Even recalling it in my mind made me want to throw salt over my shoulder, the way superstitious people did back at home to ward off evil. I'd never come across a white person – never mind an Englishwoman – versed in obeah, but I had a horrible suspicion that Lilian Shandlin might have been quite good at it. The woman was a crassis, pure and simple. Bad luck.

I realised that it was from that time onwards Eva had become secretive, not answering my questions about whether she had sent on the article to *Blackwood's*, evasive about forms she was filling out and purchases she was making. All of it must have been for her journey back to France. She must have made up her mind there and then, at that third-floor checkout in Liberty's.

'I'm finished with you, Eva.' Sybil stood up and put on her gloves. 'Finished with this whole situation. It's like pouring all my energy and concern down a black hole.'

I expected Eva to retaliate. Sybil had a nerve complaining about pouring energy anywhere, when all she seemed to pour those days was booze down her own gullet. But she just bowed her head and took it. I too said nothing, even as Sybil shouted a few more unpleasantries before exiting the room, banging both inner and outer doors with such violence I thought the building would fall down.

When we were alone, I gave Eva what for. 'What on earth did that woman say to you? Because I'm telling you, it had better be good after the mess you have put me in now. Or bad. Whichever.'

Eva sat down on the bed with a heavy sigh. 'I've mucked this up completely, Lu, I'm sorry.'

'Sorry won't pay my rent at the end of the month. Sorry won't help me do the things I can't manage alone.' I did not bother hiding my anger. 'We had an agreement, Eva. We support each other. We help each other. Until we make it out of here.'

She spread her hands over her knees. 'Don't worry about the rent. I'll leave my share and send over postal orders.'

'That's not what I'm talking about, and you know it.' To that, I got only silence, so I tried a different tack, sitting down beside her. The bed groaned under our combined weight till the springs nearly kissed the floor. 'Reggie had some experience with the Germans, you know. They saw him and his fellow West Indian troops from their prison wagons as they passed in opposite directions. Eva, these men don't even speak English, but the names they called his battalion . . . it's not easy for coloured troops, but at least they don't get insults like that from the British. And Reginald only had words to deal with. Not bayonets, like poor Bo Destouches.' That was Sybil's brother. 'And Belgium . . . the women and children? How can you justify that?' Tales and rumours had flown about what the Germans had done in Belgium. I had been at home in Jamaica at the time. Reginald had read the articles too, in the *Gleaner*, provoking his first argument with my father about going abroad to serve the Empire.

In response, Eva sounded like a truculent child. 'It's all government lies, that Belgium stuff. The Germans are no worse than we are. It's not their fault.'

'Blouse and skirt! It *is* their fault! They invaded Belgium and started the whole Bangarang all by themself.' Eva just shook her head. It was as if her mind was made up already on the subject. 'I want to know what that woman said to you,' I said again, 'to turn you traitor so sudden.'

Eva's responding laugh was as harsh as untampered steel. 'Turned traitor? I've been a traitor these past three years.'

'You mean the white-feather thing?' I said wearily. In the back of the room, the sink tap was going drip, drip, drip. Why had I not noticed it before? Eva's rhaatid family had taken offence at Christopher's refusal to enlist when the war first broke out. Her sister had been ill with tuberculosis, and they'd hung the price of her treatment over Eva's head as a way of blackmailing her, demanding that she gave him a white feather of cowardice in the street.

I'd never heard of the custom before arriving in England. Not that there wasn't war fever in Mandeville, but the men who wanted to enlist did so willingly enough, black and white alike. There was no need for shaming. Eva and Christopher had been walking out at the time, but, not surprisingly, they didn't speak for two years after that, until a chance encounter (and some encour-

agement from yours truly) brought them back together. And then
. . . well, you see why I had warned Reginald not to try any kind of
mutiny?

'Of course I mean "the white-feather thing," as you call it. Why
else do you think his mother won't speak to me? You ask me what
she said that day in Liberty's. The answer is: nothing. It was the
way she looked.' Hugging her knees, her eyes wide as a child's, Eva
looked small and vulnerable. 'I saw the face of someone I loved,
the same features, the same intensity, but with such a look of
horror, shock, disdain, disappointment, all focused on me.' Seeing
my scepticism, she became animated. 'I realised all in an instant
that I couldn't send off my article. I had no right to stir up such
pain, all for my own selfish interest, just to try and redeem myself.
My papa once told me I was shot through with irredeemable flaws
from the start. He was a horrible man, but he was right. Oh Lucia,
I felt so ashamed of myself.' She put a finger to her cheek, but not
quickly enough to stop a solitary tear rolling down it.

In spite of my anger, I felt a terrible pity for her. How wretched,
to walk this earth with such a burden on one's shoulders. And so
unnecessarily! I put an arm around her. 'I am not as widely read as
you are in the classics,' I said, 'but you know that line, "Other
men's crosses are not mine"?'

'Yes, it's Donne.'

'Well, whoever it's by, it's true. Not to be cruel, sweetness, but
who cares what she thinks? You wrote to her, you tried to mend
fences with her, didn't you? And she cursed you out for it. Not in
your hearing, but the words were said, and she knew they'd get
back to you. She a witch, nuh?'

'Well,' Eva said, 'I can't complain. She lost her surviving son,
didn't she?' And after *that* remark, a chasm of silence, as she
realised through the fog of her despair that she might have put her
foot in it. I withdrew my arm and sat quite still.

'Sorry,' she said, after a moment. Then, 'I hesitated before applying. Because of, well, that. Quite frankly, I was worried that without me here you'd go off and do something stupid. But I can't think about that any more, Lucia. As you said yourself . . . '

'Other men's crosses are not mine, a true dat.' *But a mother's cross is different.* I glanced over at my bed, where the baby book lay, spine up, and felt a brief pang of sympathy for Lilian the Witch. If losing Christopher had been terrible for Eva, it must surely have been very nasty indeed for the woman who had given birth to him. But I had to get back to my objective, which was to talk Eva out of this fool-fool idea of hers. 'All right. What if I say I will do nothing unwise as long as you stay here rather than looking after Germans?'

Eva shook her head then got up and poured herself a glass of water, turning the tap off tightly. It was a relief not to hear the drip for a few seconds before it resumed its tiresome rhythm. 'Lucia, you'll be fine without me. I've spoken to Mrs Baxter, and she reassures me she won't bother you. Why, you go around town with Mr Rosewell and do all sorts of things and nobody causes you any trouble!' I had not told her about the angry beggar, and she still didn't understand the effort it took to get out of the house. 'I'm hardly the social connection you need. You're well on the way to the success you always wanted. All you have to do is avoid dwelling on the past.' Coming from her, that was rich! 'And avoid running into the past's mother in haberdashery stores,' she added, with a rueful grin.

'What about Sybil, though?' I moved on to try another tender spot. 'You saw how upset she was. Chances are she won't speak to you again.' I knew it would hurt Eva to be estranged from her friend.

'The pieces will fall where they may,' Eva said harshly. 'She prefers the bottom of a bottle over me these days. I think even over Roma.'

I had one last argument to use, and I used it with all my might. 'Weren't you always going to go to that ... Summerplace? How can you do that if you're over the Channel nursing Huns?'

'Somerville College in Oxford. Yes. That's what Christopher hoped I would do. But even starting to study again would bring back too many memories of when I was still able to tell him all about it.' She drank down the water then ran her finger along the rim of the glass, which was too dry to sing a note. I could occasionally manage a D if I wet it enough and applied a light enough pressure. But Eva was not bothered about musical notes. 'You do know that every day since you talked me out of killing myself I've regretted allowing you persuade me? Just waking up in the morning and realising I've another day to get through seems a cruel joke. I can suppress my feelings most of the time, but at the slightest provocation they overpower me. No, don't say anything.' She put the glass down on her nightstand. 'I know what I owe you. You ask too much to try and make me stay here, that's all.'

My friend, I was quite dumbstruck. I knew that things were not right with Eva, but I'd hoped she was making some progress away from the horrible fog that had enveloped her earlier in the year. Even in this creaky shabby room with its one gas ring and its draughts and its leaky tap and our small monthly pay, I thought that she might be able to take on the world the way she had always wanted to. Because I had managed, here and there, to live with my sorrow, I thought she was managing hers. Cha, I felt a bit guilty.

'I should tell you,' she said abruptly, rising once more, 'that a letter came for you yesterday. Postmarked Soho. I admit I was suspicious about it, so I hid it. That was wrong of me, not to mention against the law. If I'm going to leave you in the lurch, I don't get to dictate what you do.' She went to her bureau and handed me a small, sealed envelope, not looking me inna mi heye, a small courtesy that relieved me since I feared my emotions would be written all over my face. 'Here you go. Now, I'd better finish packing. I have an early start tomorrow. Whatever you do, I don't want to know about it.'

'All right.' I could barely get the words out as I held the enve- lope. That wretched little room suddenly seemed very far away. The universe was me and that letter – and nothing else.

SOHO SQUARE, London
17 September 1917

DEAR MISS PERCIVAL,

I know it has been over a month since we last spoke; please accept my apologies for the delay. I was detained on unavoidable business and was only recently able to begin making enquiries. I have a man, Duncan, for requests involving Scotland, so sent him up to make plausible enquiries with the Sisters of Morpethswade regarding your query.

He posed as a War Office official wishing to order soaps on the cheap from the fallen women who are forced to make them. This might have worked as the women who wear the wimples in Morpethswade are Sisters in Mammon rather than in Christ. However, the moment Duncan mentioned the name 'Mackenzie', he immediately hit a brick wall – with the Sisters, and everybody else. Miss Percival, you do realise that you are a scandal that must not get out? And that your opponents in this matter are the most powerful and well-connected in-trade dynasty in Glasgow?

In spite of this, Duncan managed to access the file and follow up: the named person is alive and well, currently residing at the

Pullman residence at 45 Park Circus Avenue off the Great Western Road.

Again, speaking to you as a brother or father might – as your own brother surely already has after I wrote to him – Miss Percival, I beg you: leave this alone. You put yourself in mortal danger if you cross these people. I would also advise you to destroy this letter after noting its contents. If you are thinking of taking that train, I strongly advise against it.

Yours sincerely,

Edgar Manning

12

SUNDAY, 23 SEPTEMBER 1917

I took that train.

Just to look. Just to see the little one safe. Surely not too much to ask? I had promised Eva that I would not do anything rash. I would stay in control of the situation, that much I was sure of. But obey Mr Manning's recommendation to abandon my quest? That I was not willing to countenance, not in a million years.

Oh, that letter. Mi Gad, I could barely keep my fingers still long enough to open the envelope, trying not to harm its contents. Even so, my fingers were shaking so hard I tore the letter in several places. When I read 'the named person is alive and well, currently residing at', I put my fist in my mouth and wept. Tears ran down my knuckles and wrists. I was quite a streaming lump of nose naat.

'Alive and well': such a relief but almost an insult too. How could little Domi be 'well' when he was separated from me? My tears were superseded by anger once more. Anger at the people who had made this happen. Who had decided my future for me, and his for him.

Eva had been so quiet, I'd forgotten she was there. Then I heard her ask me, in a deeper and more Irish accent than usual, 'Major or minor key?' That made me smile. It was a refrain between us that I had started and she had unexpectedly taken up. I took a clean hanky to wipe my eyes and blow my nose. 'Major, I think. Here, read it.'

'No,' she said, 'I'd rather not. Then there's no having to condone anything I might disapprove of. Just . . . be careful, will you?'

'I could give you the same message,' I laughed.

She shrugged. 'I'm never safer than when I'm in the middle of war. It means there's only one thing to worry about. Worst thing can happen is that I'll be killed.' *Which I would welcome*, I suspect she was thinking. With the blood hot in my veins, all I could feel for her was pity: she had no one to long to see again, and no sustaining belief in the Lord to carry her through.

She left for France the following morning, long before I rose myself, and I was quite alone from then on.

Left to myself, I would have secured a ticket for the Glasgow express the following day, but unfortunately I had work, and work was not amenable, even though I tried to impress on Major Carroll the great personal urgency involved.

'We're at full demand here,' he barked, gripping his side. I guessed his ulcer was troubling him. 'Passchendaele is the battle that won't end. Lots of legs needed, Percival. Arms too. Conveyor belts of 'em, more 'n Henry Ford needs car parts. I can't give anyone leave, for any reason.'

We were in his office, situated high over the factory floor like a church organ. He could pace the length of the mezzanine and survey his workers below. I could see Audrey, her hair unsecured, her goggles huge on her tiny nose. Major Carroll did not look at me. He had this habit of running his fingers through his hair, one he should have abandoned long ago since most of his hair had abandoned him. Perhaps it distracted him from the pain.

'It's force majeure, sir,' I protested. That cut no ice with Major Carroll, who, bent almost double with pain, still managed to waggle a crooked, yellowing finger at me. 'You would want to be careful about causing trouble.'

'Why? Have I given you reason to worry?'

He tapped his watch. 'Punctuality. You've clocked in late several times these past weeks. Plenty of local men would kill for work, and you here, you're slacking.' So that was it. I wasn't a man, and I wasn't 'local'. Never mind that I'd hardly had a day's leave since I'd started in that rhaatid dunghill.

'And there's the singing.'

The singing. Ah, yes. He might have been referring to my occasional tendency to hum under my breath to distract myself from that intractable bloody right-handed saw. I never knew I was actually vocalising until someone turned around to say, 'Percival, pipe down that bloody racket, will you?' That is, if they were in the mood to be polite. I thought it rather unfair. A bit of Mozart never harmed anyone, surely?

But I was in no position to take offence. I needed that time off, so I deployed charm. 'Major, I am so sorry. I promise I will do better in future.' He looked unimpressed. I would have to make my buttering up a little more personal. 'And, sir, I am so sorry you have been ill lately. You must have suffered a great deal and endured it in heroic silence. You never complain, but your stoicism and bravery do not go unnoticed.'

I felt I'd over-egged the pudding by mentioning stoicism, a word I doubted the major understood never mind employed, but to my surprise the gambit appeared to work. He straightened up and stroked his chin. 'Will Monday do?'

'Tomorrow would be better, sir.' Having the Friday off would give me the weekend to return, not that I would need that long.

'You'll have Monday and be grateful for it,' he snapped. 'And don't make it any more than that one day. I need you back here.'

What, even though I'm so useless some local man could easily take my place?

'Yes, sir. Thank you, sir.' I got a dirty look for my troubles, but I had the leave, and that was all that mattered to me.

I secured a ticket for the Sunday morning express to Glasgow, which gave me the Monday to return. It was to be a long journey – the timetable said eight hours, and from the very start I was agitated at the thought of what might be ahead. As I made my way to the station, my hands and fingers sweated and felt swollen in tight heavy gloves. My throat was caught in my neck, as if a fly were buzzing there. But I dared not clear it. Frightened of discovery, I thought that even the tone of my cough might give me away. Because, you see, I was in disguise.

No longer Miss Lucia Percival, late of Manchester Parish, Jamaica, I had transformed myself into Mrs Herminia Cuthbert, war widow of Ernest, who in another universe had failed to return to Blighty and torment us with his tuba but had died nobly, not to mention quietly, in battle. I had discarded my own blue suede travelling gloves for ones of heavy leather, shrouded my face with a veil and wore a heavy mourning cloak made of black bombazine, which smelled of camphor and mothballs. All these items I had borrowed from Audrey Partridge. Bless her: she was quick and asked no questions, even though as far as she knew I was alone in England and had no family who might require my presence at a funeral.

The two other travellers in the train compartment – by their conversation I inferred they were in the furniture trade – glanced at me briefly and oddly from underneath their homburgs before returning to their newspapers. I looked out the window through the netting of my veil. A few well-wishers dotted the platform and porters wheeled vans stacked with luggage into the guards van. We were ready to go. And then, I saw her again, standing alone on the platform. The old woman who had been following me all this time.

My hand flew to my chest. *Bax cova!* How had she found me?

A long shriek tore along the platform. The engine agitated, and smoke drifted down past our compartment window. A whistle blew, the windows closed up, and the train moved off. Too late to go back now. The old woman did not move away, as I thought she might, nor did she look in the train's direction. As the train rounded a corner, her profile faded from view. I turned back to my compartment. Through a jalousie of lace, I watched the two busi-nessmen remove their hats and put them into identically sized hatboxes: one maroon, one gunmetal grey. These were stowed neatly on the shelf above my head – both begged my pardon as they reached over me.

After that, they took little notice of me, and I tried to relax, or at least appear relaxed. I had feared all along that the Mackenzies were watching my every move, and the old woman's presence seemed to confirm it. Logically, this made no sense; they would have had to put a man on me day and night to track me down like that.

My thoughts began to spiral into deep worry. I feared that Mr Manning's letter, the closest to a written record of my hopes and designs as ever existed, could somehow have been intercepted and read en route, even though the envelope bore no evidence of tampering. I believed, too, Mr Manning's warning about being in mortal danger. He had underscored those words so deeply the paper was nearly torn.

A wha' mi kyaan do? A wha' mi kyaan do? I wondered, to the rhythm of the train. Only one thing to do: I vowed that if they did find me, I would fight like a tigress. I would claw and scratch and . . . *This is only an exploratory journey*, I reminded myself. *Just to make sure the little one is safe. No need fi vex up, nuh? This not one of your threepenny operas.*

The clacking of the wheels, the train's accelerating rhythm, and the autumn sunshine warming the stuffy black bombazine caused me to drift into a half sleep that deepened when we passed Watford Junction. I woke after an hour, when I took out my book. I had trouble turning the pages, because of the heavy gloves, but the plot was unobjectionable and kept my mind off the old woman and the Mackenzies.

When I got out at Glasgow Central, the platform was almost deserted apart from the few other passengers who were also alighting the train. A shabbily dressed man held up a notice saying OVERTON SOFA COMPANY, to which the two businessmen made quick haste. I left the station by the Gordon Street exit, stopping under the wrought-iron porch outside the Grand Central Hotel, where I leaned against a pillar and breathed deeply as I looked around me. It was clear that no one was watching or in my pursuit, and any terror I felt on my return to Glasgow subsided.

I needed refreshment and decided to take full advantage of my new identity and enjoy tea and cake in the hotel. For a station inn, it was impossibly extravagant, with a compass motif on the marble floor. The vaulted ceiling was supported by pillars, and behind them were dotted tables and chairs. Large sashed windows looked out onto the Glasgow night. I sat down in a plush maroon seat and decided I would order something ridiculous. How about a plate of those little petits fours?

The waiter hurried off and soon returned with three of the

delicacies, on a lovely silver saucer with a doily, and hot tea with a porcelain jug of milk. Mrs Cuthbert was getting much better treatment than Lucia Percival had ever enjoyed, as long I took care to keep my gloves on when I picked up one of the dainty little things.

Then the waiter's face changed, fast as a cloud eclipsing the sun. His look was filled first with hostile surprise, then open revulsion. Damn! Without waiting for him to leave, I had pushed the veil aside to eat my cake, and had revealed my face.

'Is everything all right?'

I didn't address him as 'sir,' which I normally did for all white men. He must have noticed that, because he inhaled so sharply his collar nearly met his chin. There was a layer of grime around its edge. I wondered at his dress and demeanour in such a hoity-toity establishment.

'I think it's time to leave. Don't you?' His tone was ominously quiet.

Common sense told me to obey without cavil, but his haughty manner roused my anger. 'I don't see why. I've as much right to stay here and eat the food I've ordered as anyone else.'

He grabbed me by the arm, pulling me off the chair, jolting the tea he had so carefully poured into my cup just a moment ago. 'You're going.'

I gestured at the petits fours that would go to waste, only for him to snarl, 'Get your filthy fingers off them cakes,' even though I wasn't touching them. For a moment I felt incomprehension, then rage – how dare he speak to me like that? – and after that the instinctive warning not to react, not to struggle, not to strike back. This trio of emotions was all too familiar. I had to be sensible; the usual restraints men employed with women would not apply to me. Better to get out of there, fast. I picked up my meagre belongings and fled into the night, readjusting my veil on the way. The encounter had shaken me. What hurt most was that remarks like his rubbed off on me more than they should.

At a safe distance, on the other side of the street, I removed my right-hand glove. Although it was still only autumn, cold air hit the skin. I put my hand before my eyes and spread out the fingers, and for a moment I could not stop myself perceiving them as he did: filthy, tainted, unworthy. *His opinion has no value*, I told myself. *These hands have done worthy things.*

The effort of repeating these reassurances exhausted me. I feared that someday I would stop believing them. After all, there was nowhere on the planet, not Jamaica, not England, not Scotland, not France, where I could escape this struggle. Maybe in a country where no white people lived, but those were far away and impossible to get to . . . Slipping the glove back on, I laced my fingers together, feeling the cracked leather rub and creak. Oh, I was so weary, but I needed to press on! Even though my heart still pounded with rage and affront, my mind was clear. I was here to see Domi, not to rage against waiters.

The weather helped. Scotland made the rest of Britain feel like Jamaica. There are two seasons there: winter and winter. It was far colder than London, with a real blast of wind off the North Sea and the Firth of Clyde. I had telegraphed ahead to reserve accommodation in Jamaica Street, of all places. When I got there and greeted the concierge at the night desk, stating my (false) name and business, I was careful not to so much as twitch my veil, even though she had to ask me to speak up once or twice. She was much older than the waiter and better dressed. Her civility was such a contrast to his rudeness that, had I not known better, I might have thought her kinder by nature. But chances were that had she seen my true self she would have turned me out into the blisteringly cold night without a second thought.

At any rate, my disguise held, and the concierge showed me to my room. The shared water closet was across the hall she told me before leaving me alone. Once the key was turned in the lock, it was a relief to strip off my 'mourning wear' – those clothes had chafed badly.

I had paid a little extra for a hot-water bottle, and the bed covers were heavy and knitted. Given that my slumber on the train had been fitful and unsatisfactory, it was time for sleep. I dreamed of nothing. Not even Domi.

The following morning, I was roused by the raucous call of 'Housekeeping!' accompanied by a bell rung up and down the corridor. I yawned, stretched and trod barefoot to the vanity stand with its spotty, grotty mirror where I had left my watch.

I had slept in quite late: it was already five to nine. My skin was dry, so I rubbed some sweet almond and orange-blossom oil onto my face, neck and hands. The small bottle was a gift my mother had given me, for the wedding that had never gone ahead. Like most folk with my background, my hair was a bit corkscrewy, so I shook some more of the oil onto my fingers and ran it through my plaits.

The routine reminded me of the countless times Merry and I had done the same in front of our shared vanity stand at home in Cinnamon Hill, and I remembered with great sadness that my mother and I were still estranged. Since that day in 1915 she had not answered a single one of my letters. Eventually, just before I set sail to France, Meredith had written to tell me not to write any more, and I swear my heart felt nearly broke, which surprised me because I never thought she meant that much to me.

I had to pull mighty hard on the ends to settle them down before dragging my hairnet over my head. It was necessary to have that contraption under the veil to subdue my curls! Muttering prayers under my breath, I gathered my things, locked up behind me and, darting cautiously down the corridor, used the water closet. Then I pulled on the gloves. Time to go.

Past nine on a Monday morning, things were quiet on Jamaica Street. Wan sunlight cast a yolkish glow, and breakfast smells wafted from the working men's cafés, but the thought of greasy sausages turned my stomach. I was too nervous to be hungry. Perhaps a cup of tea later. I had carefully marked the address Mr Manning gave me on a city map of Glasgow I purchased at the station, but map or no map, a more instinctive guide was directing me because I continued down Jamaica Street all the way to the river.

Even as I told myself 'Turn around!' I felt the Clyde's pull like a magnet. I remembered that smell, of oil and steel and sewage. I remembered the taste. I remembered how my body had felt that day too: raw below the waist, still bleeding and dizzy . . . Everywhere I turned, under the railway bridge, along the north bank, past the water bus, memories assaulted me.

The ferry went across to Hutchesonstown. How could I forget the name of the place where the captain of the tugboat *Mariette*, who found me nearly drowned in the Clyde's waters and rescued me, had brought me? The screech of steel and welding mixed up with the howl of the wind that came off the river. It barrelled straight in from the Atlantic and chilled me through and through, even though I pulled my cloak tight. The few people around and about walked quickly, their heads down.

'I hate Glasgow,' Robin Mackenzie had once declared to a roomful of nurses. 'It's colder than a witch's tit.' At the time, I had cringed at his vulgarity, but I was to learn exactly what he meant. I leaned over the river wall and looked at those black swirling waters.

Why had I compromised myself so? I asked myself for the hundredth time. Why had I lain down with Robin Mackenzie?

Why was I so reckless, so incautious, when I knew the risks? White men and scorpions, my father had told me. Steer clear of them both. So where, then, was my self-respect? Where was my common sense?

The answer is war. War crazed me. War in my blood and veins, more potent than proof rum, sweeter than red wine, turning my head, making time short. War sharpened every colour, shrieked at the end of every note, made taste sweeter, made the need for human contact more important. War made us need each other, Robin and me, made us need life. We clung to flesh because we might be cleaved from the body tomorrow. When Robin and I came together, he cried, 'Save me, Lucia.' But I could not. Nor could he me.

The first Bangarang, just like the next one (as I suspect you know all too well), had no heroes in it, only villains of various moral degrees. We could not save each other. Neither could we part with each other. And believe me, we both tried.

13

AUGUST–SEPTEMBER 1916

I finally tackled Robin about it one sunny evening after we had dressed and were on our way back to the field hospital from our secret space along the foreshore. As I stumbled past the marshes by the tracks, I said, 'You do know we shouldn't keep meeting like this?'

'Meeting' being one way of putting it.

'I know, lassie, but it's such a nice coincidence.' He was ahead of me, and when he glanced back his grin was lopsided and sweet.

I was frustrated at his refusal to see the problems that lay ahead. Thing was, I liked him very much. Something in him sparked me and made me laugh. I could talk to him too, in a way I couldn't with anyone else. My English was no longer airless and correct around him, as it was with others. Yet he was still white, as well as – no matter what else, just that he was white. That was the beginning and end of it.

When I told him, a few weeks before that, about my dreams of being a musician, he just smiled in that thin Scottish way of his, remarking out of the side of his mouth, 'Thought you already were.'

'I mean singing on the stage. Going to masterclasses. The Royal Albert Hall.' I felt bold even saying it, but he just laughed, declaring, 'Lucy. You don't need that blather to be a musician. You just sing.' I hated when he called me Lucy. I disliked it when close family like Reginald took the liberty, so it irked even more from him.

'Cha, don't start with that rubbish. You think I'm willing to settle for singing in a backyard outside some rhaatid training camp, with chickens for an audience? Had I so little ambition I could have stayed at home.'

He regarded me in a slow, careful way. 'Aye, you're right. You're very talented, as I don't need to tell you. You should have your name in lights.' Oddly enough, even after we had lain down together, I found such examples of open tenderness a little embarrassing. That time I squirmed away from the arm he put around my shoulders.

Now, on the marshes, with sandpipers beginning to arrive in small clusters and poke at the sludge with their long beaks, I was the one to catch up with him and tug at his shirtsleeve. 'Robin. This is important. You know we can't be together. You're wasting your own time and mine.'

At that he went beetroot red. 'Who are you to tell me I'm wasting my time?'

I knew he was annoyed, but I kept on going. 'Me. The person who has the most to lose, that's who.' We were both standing front to front, panting from walking fast. 'You know we can't marry, Robin. So, I must be easy pickings. A coloured girl, here on her own, without a soul to call a friend.' I had meant to keep this conversation cool but could not suppress my mounting anger. 'Do you joke about me at the officers' mess? Were there bets, maybe, on how long it would take?' I was burning now, all my fears out in the open.

Silence. A pair of geese flew overhead, their wingspan wide. The sun was dropping in the sky, half obscured by a cloud. Robin took in a deep breath. I didn't dare look at him. When he answered, it was in a tone that was barely controlled. 'I don't speak of you to anyone.'

'Of course not,' I laughed nastily. 'I'm your dirty little secret, nuh?'

'Jesus Christ,' he swore under his breath. 'How could you say something like that? You think so little of me that you imagine this . . . is all for fun?' The hurt in his voice surprised me. Wasn't that supposed to be how it worked, between the races? Acquisition, use, disposal – what room was there for feeling, on any side? And yet feelings there were.

'What else can it be, Robin? Because you surely aren't serious.'

'Not serious, aye? You,' he burst out, his accent deepening, 'are the most serious thing that's ever happened to me. You, Lucia Percival, have me in serious fuckin' trouble.'

I clutched at my skirts, furious at him for swearing now, of all times. 'Do you hear what you just said? You would never speak that way to Amelia Hall, or Norah Smeaton, or any other white woman. You wouldn't even say "damn" without a thousand apologies. But with me? Nah, it's fine, just use whatever filth you like, it doesn't matter, does it?'

'No!' It was a shout. 'No, no, a thousand times no. Will you get that nonsense out of your head? I know I shouldn't swear in front of you. I keep tellin' myself. But I get so comfortable around you, it's like talking to another lad, you know? I never thought a man could talk to a woman like I do with you. You're the best friend I never had' – here there were tears in his eyes – 'but at the same time I can't keep my eyes off you. Not since you sang for Willie Loder.'

'Or your hands either,' I retorted, not wanting him to soften me up too much, though his words were working on me somewhat.

'Do you think I haven't worried about this?' He gestured a semicircle in the air. 'You say you're unsuitable, well I couldn't agree more, hen. Do you know Milly Hall? Nice girl, isn't she? Polite and charming?'

I made a face like sour milk. Amelia Hall was a particularly painful subject right at that moment. Just the previous night, after a long day's work, I'd finally plopped down on the bed, head in my hands, too tired to undress, too tired to move. I'd been facing away from the door and hadn't heard anyone come in when I felt the shock of cold steel against the back of my neck and a loud satisfied snip of a pair of surgical scissors. I whirled around in a fury to see Amelia standing there with that gap-toothed smile that so many of the men found attractive. 'Finally. That's been annoying me for months,' she announced, then put her hand to her mouth and giggled before quickly retreating.

'Oh, I know her all right,' I said through my teeth.

'Well, you'd put her in your front parlour and she'd hand out cups o' tea half full of milk with five cubes of sugar in 'em.' His words, unlike the hypothetical tea, were undiluted in their contempt. 'I could bring her or any number of girls home who would please that bi—, I mean my mother. But I have to be stuck on *you*! What in God's name is wrong with me?'

He counted on his fingers: 'You're black, you stitch left-handed, and you can't make a cup of tea to save your life – but I'm bewitched by you. Completely.' He put his hand on his heart. 'Honest to God, Lucia. This all took me by surprise. Wonderful bloody inconvenient surprise. I didn't have any nefarious plan to take advantage. Didn't have any plan at all.'

'You see, that's the difference between us,' I said gravely. 'I can't afford not to plan. Not when I'm trying to navigate through a world that's not made for people like me. I have to think of my future.'

'Fair point.' He was standing still then, obviously thinking. A briny odour came from the limp seaweed on the foreshore, carried to us on a cool, coastal breeze. It was strong, but not unpleasant. Distantly I saw female figures scrambling on the rocks near the beach, lifting their skirts, as the sun began to drop a little in the sky and flood the sands with light. VADs. The sight of them quickened my pulse a little.

He frowned. 'They didn't see us, did they?'

'No, but doesn't this show you why we can't go on?' The loss of his career, and my total future, hovered in the background. The endless, exhausting secrecy. I let him work it out, there in the cooling air.

'Yes,' he said seriously. 'It does.'

'Then can we shake hands and agree to part friends?'

'Shake hands and . . . what? What nonsense is this?' He shook his head at my extended hand. 'You want to go back to shaking hands, aye?'

'Aye,' I mimicked him. The wind was blowing at his shirt. It had been warm earlier, so he'd had the sleeves rolled up, but now his skin looked goose-pimpled and pale as chicken meat. Still he did not shiver.

'All right.' He thrust that pale arm towards me. 'Friends it is, and I'll respect that.' He added, *sotto voce*, 'though it'll damn well nearly kill me.' When we did shake on it, his grip was firm and warm and real. 'As for my feelings, I'll keep my own counsel.' He half turned away, then added, 'Will you be all right to go back alone?'

I assented, and Robin then broke into a faster pace, heading off up the well-worn path to the officers' block. I waited until he had disappeared before I made my way up the same path, taking the left fork rather than the right. That was what we had always done. And now it would be for the last time.

Decision made, I felt lighter of heart, if a little saddened. The sentiment had not been all on his side. I, too, felt the comfort of having someone to talk to honestly about life – something I had not experienced since taking that night bus to Kingston in 1915.

While I reminded myself that a white man could never be a friend, Robin Mackenzie had expressed more genuine curiosity about my ideas and my dreams than anyone since my father. I knew the names of the sandpipers and the oystercatchers because we would lie on our backs and he would point them out as they flew over us. He loved birdwatching and kept Bewick's *History of British Birds* in his hut.

He was crude, yes, but he had his sensitive side, if you troubled to enquire about it. I would miss his closeness during passionate moments – and his otherness, the odd, alien smell of his skin, the harsh accent like cut tin, the way his moustache brushed off my upper lip when we kissed, the unfamiliar masculine shape of him. It was only his race that prevented me from missing these aspects of him even more – and even that sometimes felt as nothing.

All the same, it couldn't go on, Robin and me. It was just too dangerous. Don't trouble trouble, I told myself, belatedly remembering the old Jamaican proverb. Yes, life would be a little more boring. Practising was sometimes boring too, which didn't mean I could stop doing it. From now on, I would concentrate on my music.

But it was already too late for these fine sentiments. A seed had been planted, and not just in my mind.

I did not become aware something was amiss until early September, several weeks into our uneasy new rapport. Every time Robin and I came together on those hot days of July and August 1916, he promised he would pull out in time. While I was a virgin when I met him, I possessed sufficient knowledge to know what he meant, and as far as I could tell he did not break his promise. At any rate, he had no great motive to. I knew only too well that the iron grip of Laura-Jane Mackenzie was more powerful than my claim on his heart. He would never dare risk incurring her wrath.

But that month, just a few days after that baleful visit from McCrum, the whispered misgivings in my mind started to sound more like a loud oratorio. On my lunch break that day, a consignment of oranges came in from the supposed-to-be-neutral Americans. The cooks' assistants had cut them into quarters and left them out on a tray. Oh, the last time I had drunk orange juice! Reggie and I had been mere pickneys, fooling about in a neighbour's orchard, sampling the fruit. Would it taste as good here in France, as tart-yet-sweet and fresh?

Unable to wait, I bit my teeth into the stringy pulp and sucked out all the juice. I was all at once possessed by a raging thirst that I could not allay. Cu yu, I drained that quarter dry. I let the juice dribble down my chin, then wiped it with my finger and sucked it. And on to the next one . . . I could have eaten the whole box. Several oranges later, I was forced out of my reverie. There, surrounding me, was a troupe of white-clad VADs with one blue-cloaked Sister in the middle, like the High Priest of the Sanhedrin with his minor Pharisees.

'What is the meaning of this?' the Sister shouted.

'I . . . er . . .' There I stood, like a half-eedjiat, an orange quarter still in my hand, dribbling between my thumb and fingers, drenching my palm. Six down! I never knew I had eaten them so fast! She barked at me to clean up the mess. When I was done, one of the VADs leaned over and said to me in a sour-breathed whisper, 'That's one of the first signs, you know. Craving fruit.' She sniggered, along with her confrères, and the oranges began to repeat on me and feel metallic on my tongue. I had to hurry off to be sick.

A few days later, while practising my early morning scales, I noticed that my breath did not sustain as many notes as usual, nor could I complete legato phrases. So on to an arpeggio, where I was confident of my range – and I could not hit the high note. *Macca, what was this?* I tried again: same.

Then a sensation I had never felt before: tension near my diaphragm, a shower of angry sparks under my skin. By now I was quite alarmed, being unacquainted with this new symptom and its implications. During the dog days of the Somme, I practised not only to improve my craft but also to process the noxious rubbish dump of emotions caused by war and pain. Just one long, sustained note – nothing more – could give me physical release. To be inhibited from this ability to self-heal was a serious mishap for me.

It turned out to be the second sign. The third was confirmed through the simple passage of time. It was advancing into October, and I hadn't seen blood since early August. As time went on, and the truth became more apparent every day, I was truly downcast. I was really in a fix.

14

24 SEPTEMBER 1917

In a fix then, and in a very different fix a year later! As the cold Glasgow wind blew through my veil and onto my face, I fled the cruel river, turned back northward and followed the route inland to the Great Western Road, being seemingly arbitrary in my ducking and diving yet striving to avoid a certain place that was not marked on the map but whose location I knew all too intimately.

The streets narrowed inward, and amid the turns and bends I got lost again – until I saw a high wall rise up in front of me, black and turreted, with one wooden door, now firmly locked. Morpethswade. Trying my hardest to avoid the place I had run straight into it. That solitary entrance like a prison gate, the stone placard with the lie 'Convalescent Home' inscribed upon it, the walls so high one would think the people walled in there were murderous men not vulnerable young girls.

'A terrible place.' I heard a voice behind me and turned around, to behold a man in a tam-o'-shanter and loose, brown trousers, somewhere in the wilderness of late middle age. His cheeks were flushed red, his eyes sinking into their sockets. I could smell alcohol on him. 'My auntie used to work there. The women . . . some of them never came out. Some of them are still in there. And the bairns . . .' He trailed off. For some reason, my teeth started chattering. 'I knew a girl there,' he continued. 'Got in the family way. They put her to work making beads. But she was slow. They beat her a lot. An innocent wee girl, a bit simple, you know?'

I swear my heart skipped a beat. 'Yes. I knew her.' Honestly, I didn't know whom exactly he was talking about, but I was thinking of Marianne. The memories returned with the force of an ungovernable flood. The windows up near the vaulted ceiling, frosted, too high for any of us to see life outside. What miserly shards of light they condescended to let in! Long rough-pine tables arranged in the shape of a cross, we penitents sitting at them on low benches, our backs killing us as we worked in silence, slipping rosary beads onto wiry strings.

And there she was, her face imprinted as vividly in my mind as if we were both at that table once more, her stubby fingers working clumsily: Marianne McGillivray. Wide face, heavy ruddy cheeks, upturned eyes that moved slowly, an opaque look on the blue irises. Pregnant by her own father, a Free Presbyterian Church of Scotland minister who broke with his sect and founded his own splinter group, ranting fire and brimstone by day in his tiny dark rain-lashed church, defiling his daughter by night. Everyone knew, a girl called Elsa whispered to me in the stone corridor one day, but nobody said. That was the culture of Morpethswade, run by the Sisters of Notre Dame, and though they were Catholic, they would do business with any other confession that was willing to enforce the same secrecy.

All together in this Romish hellhole, Irish and Scottish girls and me, we were nothing more than glorified prisoners. No money, no papers, no freedom, no rights. We did not even own the long colourless smocks the nuns forced us to wear to denote our shame. Marianne's fitted badly, her fingers barely visible over the ends of the wide, unflattering sleeves. When she ate, the edges constantly dipped in her porridge, or thick gravy, or semolina pudding, earning her a cuff of reproach from whichever black-clad Sister was passing by. I ached for her at those moments, and the times when she stumbled at her task: she was unable to hold onto the beads or apply the fine focus to get them on the string. I tried to pick up the slack, not wanting to see her whipped. It didn't matter; they whipped her anyway.

Oh, Marianne, that last night you spent in the huge unfriendly dormitory during the freezing Glasgow winter of 1916! There were about thirty of us, three rows of ten beds. We were allowed to lie on our backs only, keeping our hands above the covers, a position agonisingly uncomfortable when you are heavily pregnant and your every instinct is to turn onto your left side and draw the covers up. But none of us could do it for fear of being made to kneel on the stone floor all night.

Deep into the small hours, well before dawn prayers, I heard a deep wail the like I'd never heard before, even in that benighted place. Starting low, then rising in pitch and desperation until it surely must have been heard in the sergeants' billets behind the trenches far south-east of us, across the black torpedo-filled sea. The noise came from Marianne. She was rocking back and forth, screaming 'Baby! Baby!' and then, breaking my heart, 'Mammy!' Her own mother had died having her. I could only presume that she had been used as brutally by her husband as he used his own daughter afterwards.

'Wh'appen? Did they take it away?' I whispered to Elsa, in the next bed.

'Shhhh,' she warned as a nun charged past. The foul-smelling black-winged creature pulled Marianne out of bed and dragged her along the aisle of beds into the corridor, as Marianne bawled and screamed for her mother. I saw the nun raise her arm and bring a paddle down on Marianne, whose bellows turned to screams. The beating went on and on.

I brought my arms around my belly and my head to my chest. 'Deh nuttin mi kyaan do,' I whispered to myself. 'Mi kyaan save 'er.' But I hated myself for it. Then it stopped. Silence. And from that day to this, I have no idea what became of Marianne McGillivray. I only know I did nothing to stop it happening.

'Are you cryin', miss?' The man looked at my veiled figure with its shaking shoulders in surprise and, for a moment, compassion. Then his face clouded over again, and he stumbled away. He could not comfort me; he was hurting too much himself. I knew that once he was round the corner and out of my sight he would start to drink again. He had some sort of connection to this awful, awful building. If not Marianne, then someone like her. How many were there?

I hastened away myself. I wanted that vile place out of my sight. How on earth could Robin have let me be taken away to that dreadful place? And yet there were harder things. Morpethswade was a hellish prison, it was true, but a thousand times worse than that prison was being set free – alone.

At midday, after two more hours of walking, I finally reached the Great Western Road. At Woodlands Gate I found myself wandering around a concentric maze of Victorian sandstone buildings and small greens. By the time the interminable rabbit warren began to make sense, I was feeling slightly faint since I hadn't eaten or drunk anything all morning. Time for some chocolate. I'd brought a bar of Fry's Peppermint for general sustenance and broke off a square. The chocolate and fondant tasted rich and sweet on my tongue and the sugar galvanised me. It took all my self-control not to yam the whole lot. But I might need it for later. There wasn't much in the way of eating out here.

I took out the map and checked it again: Park Circus Avenue. A block of terraced sandstone houses looking out over a strip of lime trees uniformly planted a few feet apart. Despite the proximity of the city, all I could hear was the rustle of the trees in the wind and a bit of songbird chatter. I made a slow, careful circuit around the little green – and there it was: No. 45. The front door was flanked on each side with a painted wooden pot. The windows were three-sided bays, clean as still water. I could look straight in, allowing the perfect family scene to unfold in front of me.

The mother at her sewing, her chin dipped perhaps in a secret smile, paying scant attention to the father in the armchair opposite. He wore a knitted Fair Isle sleeveless jumper over a white shirt and held his newspaper at arm's length, a pair of spectacles on the table beside him. Was he a vain fool, I wondered, to refuse to wear his reading glasses? A figure scurried past them both: a scullery maid with a bucket of coal. She unloaded the coal lumps onto the glowing grate with a small shovel.

And then – my heart nearly stopped it was beating so hard in my chest – then I saw the pickney, sitting on a circular rug between the two chairs, wearing a white pinafore tunic with a lacy-looking bib at the front. Like most six-month-olds, a bit unfamiliar with his ability to sit, he swayed slightly as if about to fall over – but he did not. He was chewing at some sort of India-rubber toy, gripping it with his tiny hands.

Then, as if sensitive to my presence, he turned his head to the outside world, and I stepped a foot closer to see him, pushing up my veil a moment. His pout was deadly serious, his eyes fixing on mine, huge and wide and brown. *I know you*, they seemed to say. *I see you.*

The man and woman were ignoring him! That dullard, cha,

reading his paper; that doltish gyal, fixing on her needle and taking no notice. Ignorant fools! They did not deserve a child so beautiful, with his liquid, questioning eyes. They didn't deserve his time or attention. Whatever money had changed hands, they were no parents – neither by blood nor heart. That honour fell to me. Because I was sure I was looking at my son, Dominic Justus Percival, born just last April, taken from me a week later. Without my consent.

And I was so glad to see him! Those – Oh! He was stretching his hands out of those ridiculous frilly sleeves, waiting to be picked up, and nobody even noticed! He did not cry, the little fellow, no. He was crawling instead, right towards me, with a deeply serious expression on his little face. That got the attention of the Mr and Mrs; she half turned, then picked up a little bell on the round table beside her where her materials lay. A moment later, a black-clad figure rushed in and picked the baby up. She must have been the nanny. Some conversation followed, and then the little creature was bundled out of the room. Imagine that? The first show of life and they have him taken away?

Somewhere behind the door, I heard a nasty little bark: yapyapyap yapyapyap yapyapYAPYAPYAP! I hate most dogs, so it was time to retreat. I scooted down the closest laneway and leaned against the wall, panting hard even though I hadn't run that far. I could hear all manner of things going on around me in the houses: arguments, pots and pans, flushing lavatories. All the while the cold east wind flowed moaning through the narrow channel of air between the house walls.

I felt a little sick: a horrible tension in my bowels as if I were about to void them. My clothes weighed heavily but could not keep me warm.

So.

I had seen Domi. He was alive and healthy. That was what I had come for. That was enough.

Mi Gad, wha' mi a did say? Enough? How could it ever be enough? Seeing my little baby just for a few seconds was like sweet poison. Sweet because he was near; poison because he 'belonged' to someone else. I needed him near, with all the blood in my veins. I admitted it: I needed more.

What to do? How would I manage it? I would need to find some pretext to enter their house. I gathered my wits and thought for a while, then returned to No. 45. All was silent. The windows winked blankly at me. If I wanted to see the baby again, I had no choice but to go in. With a shaking, gloved finger, I pressed the doorbell hard. It was wired to some bells that chimed a low chord in B. Mi – doh.

Immediately another fusillade of YAPyapyapyapYAPs bombarded my ears, followed by shouts of 'Rusty! Down!' The door shuddered open with an angry creak, its jamb dragging on the red-tiled floor of the vestibule. The scullery maid I had seen earlier glowered out at me. Just behind her yapped Rusty. 'Yarse?' she barked at me, almost as if she too were a dog.

I launched into my genteel beggar's preamble with not a trace of inflection. 'verysorrytotroubleyou ... poorwidow ... thewar ... parched with thirst. Could I sit down a moment and have a glass of water?'

The girl looked at me sourly. 'Does t'master know you?'

I tried not to bristle. I have never liked the term 'master', for reasons I need not elaborate upon. 'I don't believe so. Please, could you help me?' I affected a slight quiver.

'If the master doesn't know you, I can't let you in,' she said, barely audible above the dog's wheeling, barking and yapping. And then, I had a brainwave. Carefully, without letting on that was what I was doing, I rummaged in my bag for some of the remaining Fry's Peppermint. Thank God I'd been smart enough not to eat the lot earlier! Meanwhile, I reassured the suspicious servant. 'I can wait here.'

She nodded and was about to close the door in my face when I tossed the sugary lump behind me. The dog spotted it immediately and ran out, barking and wheeling. Then he escaped onto the road. *Thank you, Rusty.*

The maid uttered a curse and ran out, while I scampered in. Now, I knew I would have limited time so I ran up the carpeted stairs as fast as I could. On the landing, I paused and then heard a soft coo. There he was! There wasn't much light in the hallway, so I pushed the veil off my face and made my way to the half-open nursery door.

The blinds in the little room were fully drawn, and an ornate paraffin lamp in the corner threw soft light and shadow over the cerise flower-patterned wallpaper. In the centre stood a white wooden cot, and behind it were pink upholstered armchairs and a window seat. A white deal table stood against the opposite wall, covered with a lace-edged muslin tablecloth and a changing mat.

The scent in the room was cloyingly sweetish-sharp, some sort of jasmine-scented fragrance masking a more elemental smell. The source was soon clear: on the mat, the baby – *my baby* – was getting his nappy changed. A new cloth lay folded at the side of the mat. With one hand, the nanny spread it out underneath him while with the other she held his ankles and lifted his little botty in the air. As she tucked the edges in, she chanted, 'Dance for your daddy, my little laddie, dance for your daddy, my little man' while the baby babbled a little, then wiggled, then let out a fat joyful little laugh that lit up his whole face.

The nanny handed him a painted wooden rattle, and he was nearly beside himself with shrieks of laughter as his fat little hand grasped and shook it. Then she sang back smilingly and said something like, 'Oh be good for your mummy.' I cannot remember what else she did. I was so angry I couldn't think straight. That happy little innocent laugh. I had missed his first laugh. His first smile. His first tooth – because I could see he had one or two. The first time he sat up by himself.

It had all been missed.

No, not missed.

STOLEN.

They rassclaat thief it from mi, the same way they stole everything else. They couldn't help themselves. No better than scorpions that couldn't help but sting.

I had the first feed, that was true. Laura-Jane Mackenzie and her accomplices could not take that away from me. I remembered that for days afterward the milk had built up inside me, with nowhere to go. The agonising heaviness in my breasts as I wandered the streets, my institution frock soaked at the front. My body was ready to give sustenance but denied the chance. Against my will.

I stood in the doorway, listening to my own son laughing and cooing, being handled by a stranger. My poor little boy, illegally owned and sold, the very fate my ancestors had striven to escape! So yes, seeing that happy baby filled me with rage against everyone who had severed me from him. But the rage, powerful as it was, was only a messenger sent by the other emotion hard on its heels: a longing more powerful and intense than anything I had felt in my life. A longing I had not experienced when I first held my baby as I didn't know I was about to lose him.

I missed little Domi: the sourish-sleepy smell of his hair, the warm spot he left on my chest, his comical frown when being winded, the way it creased up half his face. I missed him more than life. I needed to have him in my arms. Now.

'Hello, little Milk,' I whispered, too soft for anyone to hear, 'milk' being the nickname I gave him when I was feeding him because he wanted so much of it.

The nurse finished up with the nappy, deftly folding it and securing the front with a pin – something that always made me flinch, cu yuh – and set Domi down in the cot. He uttered a token protest then settled very quickly. She straightened up with a soft groan, her hand on her lower back.

Before she could see me, I beetled down the hall into one of the bedrooms. It was quiet and cold and filled with men's para- phernalia and scents. Outside I could hear Rusty yapping and Mr Pullman yelling at him to 'leave the other dog alone'. When I was sure the coast was clear, I tiptoed back into the nursery and stood over Domi's cot, my veil raised.

I could see myself in him, though he was much paler. 'Yu favah me,' I whispered. His eyes were tightly closed, his mouth in the intense frown of infant sleep, dark hair in a curl at the top. His hands rested behind his head in a posture of repose. Too big now to be swaddled, he was covered in a thick knitted blanket with a pattern of ships on waves.

I worried it was not enough to keep out the Glasgow cold; I worried it would be uncomfortable on his bare legs; oh, I worried about every little thing! He didn't belong in a prim little nursery in Glasgow with flowers on the walls and itchy woollen blankets and strangers changing his nappy. He belonged with me.

Very gently, I scooped him up. His eyes opened, startled, but he did not cry, just kicked a little. He felt soft and clean. Sometimes babies are afraid of strangers, but not this one. Or perhaps he knew I was no stranger. 'Ah-oo,' he said quietly.

'Hello,' I said in a reverent whisper. 'Hello, star.' I bent down my cheek to brush against his warm round one, just as I had done when he was born. He reached out a hand and swept it over my face, as if glazing my skin. Then he atchoo'ed at me. His little sneezy face, all scrunched up, was the most adorable thing I had ever seen. 'Excuse you,' I whispered, laughing softly.

Through the doorway I could hear a commotion downstairs.

'What, Millie? Did you let her in?' An irritated male voice, presumably Mr Pullman.

'I didnae mean to, sir. I got all caught up with the dog.'

'Never mind, Millie. Check upstairs – she's probably after Elsie's jewellery.'

I pulled the baby closer. Was there a way out of here? The back-bedroom door opened with a loud creak as the husband charged in. I slipped the veil back down over my face. The little fellow stared at me in pure astonishment and started pulling at it, bless him! 'No, star. Leave it now.' I cradled his head with my hand and tiptoed towards the landing. There was no way of escape apart from the stairs. I could hear drawers being opened in the bedroom, the soft fall of discarded clothing, the rattle of a jewellery box. Shouting and swearing.

He was in my arms. I could take him now, or lose him for ever. Decision made, I flew down the stairs as if the hounds of hell were behind me. Well, one hound, wheeling and barking, in front of me rather than behind. Thank you, Rusty, you canine reprobate.

As I ran for the door, Domi reached out his hand and knocked over a vase of chrysanthemums on the hall table. The whole thing crashed to the floor and shattered to pieces, water flowing on the tiles, flowers scattered everywhere. The baby stiffened, then cried, his cheeks flexed against my chest. I paused, briefly, fatally. Long enough for a strong pair of hands to grab me from behind and pull me back.

'What in heaven's name—!' Mr Pullman shouted.

I kept a tight grip on Domi and kicked Mr Pullman in the shins.

'Bitch!' he hissed, and I could smell his eggy breath and the foul sweat on his skin. I could not shake his grip. The wool of his jumper scratched my neck, his breath was hot on my skin, and above its sourness I could smell the sharp vetiver and cedarwood tang of his shaving cream. A wave of revulsion broke across me, and in one surge I broke free from him, still holding on to Domi, and ran to the door.

I had reckoned without the maid. She blocked me at the entrance, her mouth twisted with horror. Of course, to her I was a hostile presence in black, making off with the baby with God knows what in mind. No wonder the look on her freckled face was hard as marble. Grabbing Domi under the shoulders, she yanked him out of my embrace. His fussing turned into a full-on roar of panic. I lunged at her to take him back, but Mr Pullman dragged me away, keeping one arm around my waist, his free hand ripping at my veil until it came off. I felt the sudden rush of cool air on my scalp as the maid looked at me in shocked surprise.

'It's a ni—!'

At that, I saw Mrs Pullman appear at the top of the stairs, her eyes round with pure horror as they met mine. Horror, I noted, that bore no trace of surprise. She knew who I was. She must have been there when the money changed hands. She most likely had brokered the deal. Millie's crude announcement told her exactly who I was, and what I wanted.

'Don't take my Archie! Don't take my little boy!' Her voice was high-pitched, pleading.

'His name is Domi.' My voice rang out, 'and he is mine.'

Mr Pullman turned me round and slapped me hard across the face. But I was angry enough to hardly feel it. 'He mine, and you stole him, you bakra, you rassclaat, you—'

That pitched him into such a rage he attacked me, pushing me to the floor then kicking my back, my head, my buttocks. His wife screamed and shouted at him to stop, while Domi howled in distress, and Millie grabbed the telephone to call the police. There was pain, and there was screaming, and bloody spit on the carpet, but I was disconnecting, floating up into the sky, and even my baby's cries were fading.

'Domi,' I opened my mouth to say, but all I could taste was blood. Then I felt a *thunk* on the side of my head like heavy glass and knew nothing more.

I came to in the back seat of a motor car with a uniformed driver and two men flanking me. The windows had dark glass, so I could not tell if it were night or day. The Pullmans were gone. Domi was gone. I felt the emptiness hit me like a wave. My head was thumping, and I was tasting blood again. I ran my tongue around my teeth to check they were all there. 'Who are you?' I asked warily and none too politely either.

'City of Glasgow Police,' was the brusque answer. 'We're bringing you back with us to Turnbull Street.' They didn't say what Turnbull Street meant but not wanting to appear a complete fool I imagined it was a police station.

'Am I under arrest?'

The other man only smirked at me. 'What do you think?'

I said nothing in response. The motor was chugging and vibrating, and I thought I would throw up so I asked one of the men to wind down his window. Past the Great Western Road, we took a turn towards the river, then immediately back inland. I spied a little Presbyterian church, grey and nondescript. My stomach began to heave. 'Please . . . sir, I feel sick.'

The driver must have heard because he pulled in smartly enough. 'Take her out. I don't want the car to stink.' I flew out the opened door, one of the men keeping a hold on my arm to stop me fleeing altogether. He needn't have worried. Freedom was no use to me now.

I grasped the railings – the paint flaked off in my hands, prick-

ling my palms – and looked skyward. The cold damp air was a
relief, and for a moment I steadied, but then my head throbbed
and I threw up violently. I had eaten almost nothing that day so all
that came up was bile streaked with chocolate, and my innards
constricted with pain.

'Finished?' my captor asked, as I stood up and wiped my
mouth with my sleeve. I hated having to do that, but they had
taken away my purse with the two cotton handkerchiefs I could
have used. Before I staggered back into the car and we drove off, I
took a last, unloving look at that church. I tell you, I'd had good
reason to feel sick.

After Domi was born, they allowed me three days with him.
That was all I had with my baby. I had been hopeful, in spite of my
treatment to that point, that once the baby was born and by their
standards deemed unsaleable, we would be released together. The
more I thought about it, the more I was convinced this would be
the case.

I had become friendly with Father Dominic, the priest to
whom we inmates of Morpethswade made our weekly confessions, which to me was hilarious, given my father's strict
Methodism and my even rather more lax variety. As it turned out, I
was this priest's favourite, and the other inmates resented our
friendship somewhat – but I am used to having other women
resent me so did not worry too much about it. Father Dominic told
me that even here, in this outpost of the United Kingdom, the
phenomenon of dark-skinned children showing up in the mother
and baby homes was not unknown, but if they were too dark they
languished in the orphanages, unclaimed, until they eventually
became inmates themselves.

This, although uncomplimentary, was music to my ears. If my
child was of value only to me, then there was no reason I could not
leave with him. I told the priest to explain to the Sisters of

Morpethswade that I had no intention of troubling anyone, nor did I want any money. And I certainly did not intend to go next, nigh or near the Mackenzies.

Father Dominic listened, then said after a long pause, 'I will do as you ask, Lucia, but I cannot guarantee they will listen.' I should have listened to the pause rather than the promise, but the priest's gentle tone, his warmth and optimism had me convinced there was nothing more to fear. We shared a special bond, he and I: his great secret, revealed to me – a Methodist! – in the confessional box, was that he was of mixed blood himself, having been born Oswin Latus in a poor part of Spanish Town to a son of a freed slave and a French Creole woman. Even though he lived as a European, he was delighted to meet a fellow Islander, and we became fast friends.

There were some moments, even with his vows and my advancing pregnancy, when I could not help wondering if he might have wanted more. But his hopes, such as they were, never materialised. I hear he is an archbishop now. They still don't know his background.

What happened was this. On the 2nd of April 1917, after a brief and painful labour, my Domi was born – in the middle of a freak snowstorm. Even this far north, snow in late spring was very much the exception to the rule, and the nurses bustling in and out talked of little else. Presuming, correctly for once, that I had never seen snow before, they regaled me with stories as they wiped the slush off their boots. Three foot deep, an English sister pronounced, and all trains and motor traffic suspended.

'Farmhouses cut off for days,' one heavyset girl with a bob told me, 'and the poor wee lambs freezing to death in the fields. Lucky the coal vans got through this mornin', or we'd be in a right guid pickle. Never mind the snow, our hospital furnace needs a week's worth of coal for an ordinary winter!'

A porter wheeling a pile of sheets on a squeaking trolley stopped and muttered in a conspiratorial tone, 'My guess is they were more afeared of those nuns than twenty-five degrees o' the mercury!'

I did not respond to any of this. In the first hours of Domi's life, the last thing on my mind was the weather. The entirety of my attention, my existence, revolved around him. Cu yuh, I was obsessed, utterly, gripped by an infatuation so high, so sweet, so concentrated, that everything else was seen through blurred vision, heard as noise.

It was only the next day, during those daylight hours when Domi was sleeping – I never knew babies slept so much! – that my curiosity about the snow awoke. Once or twice I put on my slippers and shuffled to the window, a little unsteady on my feet. I stood up on my tiptoes, rested my chin on the windowsill with its flaking green paint, and pressed my forehead against the frost-covered pane, feeling the contrast of the bitter cold of the glass to the warm hospital air.

With a curiosity as newborn as Domi, I watched the swirling flakes descend from a uniform grey sky, blown thither and about. I wanted to catch them, feel them brush against my fingers. What a fool I was. Had I known what was about to happen, I would not have wasted any time on snow. I would not have left Domi's side for a minute. Because on the morning of April 5th, after the snows began to melt in the spring sun, they came and took him away.

I had been woken a little earlier by him crying in his bassinet. Newborns cry for just one thing – milk – and I limped across to pick him up. On the way, I lit the wick of the paraffin lamp by the bed. Then, whispering an apology for taking so long, I lifted him up and set him to my breast. For once, all was reasonably quiet: I could pretend it was just me and Mr Milk in the entire universe, having the last feed before morning.

I remember the corridor light through the glass panel above the door, girls around me shushing their babies, the wails of the infants who had been taken to the nursery while their mothers slept, the smell of borax and prepared hot milk, the agitated chirrup of a starling on the windowsill (God help the little bird, in the freezing cold he would surely fall off), the wet tickle of Domi suckling, his eyes open, his feed steady, his grip strong, almost hydraulic. I breathed in the peace. *Baby have a little feed . . .*

Then, suddenly, men and nuns charging in, shoulders first, arms demanding, insisting, compelling, ordering, tearing him off my breast without apology. Oh, I remember it so clearly, how I dripped milk onto my drab smock and bled from my nether regions, weak and tired, while they were strong and powerful. How I begged and pleaded, that I would take care of him, that I would be no trouble to his father, none at all.

One of the nuns struck me across the mouth. 'This way he has a chance not to be reared among savages.' In the middle of all the chaos, it impressed on my memory that she pronounced it 'rared'. Then Domi and the nun who held him vanished between double doors, my cries redoubling to screams. *Domi, Domi!* The Irish nun and her helpers pinned me down and shoved a mask on my face, the smell of the chloroform nearly choking me.

I came to with a headache like a spear in my forehead, my breasts still leaking milk, bleeding all over a shabby armchair in a green, drab parlour, with that same Irish nun staring me in the face. I was to be set free, with a fistful of dirty pound notes to buy my silence and the extra condition that I was to leave the city, never to return or make any claim on the child.

Yes, I took the money. I had no choice. I was destitute, and half mad. Savage, indeed, because they made me one, those people who threw me out on the street. For hours afterwards I wandered around, dazed and disoriented. Only a few hours before I'd had a baby – and now I had nothing. How could the little pickney be taken from my plentiful, loving body, so ready to nourish him? Losing him, my own life was surely over.

On that harshly bright April morning, I passed that very church we had just stopped outside for me to be sick. The door was open so I slipped in. Might as well be there as anywhere else. I sat on a wooden pew and felt the blood that flows after childbirth leach out of me onto the knotted pine bench, which was seasoned and smooth from all the worshippers who had sat there before me. I asked forgiveness for that too, though it wasn't my fault. The air smelled of wood and a slight tang of cleaning solution. Nothing more. The simplicity of the place quietened my anguish for a moment.

And then out of nowhere, I heard the most sublime music that I have ever experienced. Starting on a lone A, as pure as if someone had struck a tuning fork. The note coming from the choir stalls behind the altar but seeming to radiate before and behind, all about. Alto. Then, from the other side of the altar, a soprano on the higher fifth. Brief counterpoint between the two, then tenors and middle altos bringing richness to bare harmonies. Before the baritones can join in, I am in the midst of it.

No boundary exists between those voices and me; they seep in through my skin. Is it my disordered body? Am I hallucinating? Or do they suddenly multiply, by their own number – four to sixteen, sixteen to thirty-two and beyond? The sun reaches in through the nave, no stained glass, no portraits of saints. Dust motes dance as the singers multiply, golden heads everywhere, robed, faceless, nameless.

They sang in Latin. Why, in a Presbyterian church? I can hear them now, oh Jesu save me! I did not know what the words meant. But I did hear the piece again some years later in the dressing room of a concert hall in northern Italy. Someone had put on a record to calm their nerves – and shattered mine. I learned that it was composed by an Englishman, Thomas Tallis, and was called *Spem in alium*. 'Hope I have never had in anyone but you, O God of Israel.' How could this strange, coldly beautiful song be about hope?

Because there, in God's house, hearing this Latin sung for His adoration and pleasure, I knew then how much He hated me. The Bible says that to be a sinner is to estrange oneself from God. Well, I had sinned, and He had turned his back on me by taking Domi away. In cruel exchange He had given me the gift of musicianship and had turned it into a curse.

Even in my wretched state I could follow most of the melodic lines of that piece, those impersonal detached lines of a High Renaissance choral motet that spoke nothing to my culture or my background. Cold and beautiful and delicate and relentless as the snow that fell on my little boy's birthday. Yes, if God took my son away from me, then I must have mortally offended Him, because surely He knows more than anyone what it means to lose an only son. I tried once again to imagine Domi, but then an image flashed through my mind: scissors cutting the air, severing the sustaining cord while the music, supernal, continued. I was rooted to my seat, the shaft of sunlight avoiding me entirely, lapping gently over the sturdy church pews right to the organ at the back, bouncing off the pipes, sending bright squares up to the vaulted roof.

Understand one thing. Lucia Percival died that day, and though she walks and talks and breathes and sings, even so, the woman you see today is not her but a talking shadow.

When the music ended, I staggered out, faint with thirst and exhaustion. At the entrance of the church was a large font full of holy water. I dipped my tongue into the brackish stuff and lapped greedily. Why care about the detritus of parishioners' dutty fingers? When hope is taken away, what is left is no more than a farm animal, to be fed, reared and slaughtered.

I headed for the river. At the edge of every city riverbed there is a spot – if you have ever been in dire straits, you will know it, and I need say no more – a spot where people go to slip in quietly and disappear, unnoticed, bobbing along face down until the merciful sea catches up and sweeps them out of reach of human cruelty for ever. There is one such on the River Clyde. And I hope never to see it again.

How I made my way from the church to that dutty bank I can no longer recall. I was gone – an empty cave, singing nonsense. The shipyards were not far away. I could hear industry: dockers coming on shift and unloading all the produce that had made it through another barrage of U-boats. Still wearing my shoes, leaving my bag on the bank – I had no more need of material things – I stepped into the dark motionless sludge.

Suppressing the urge to retch, I walked in further until I was up to my shoulders. Teeth chattering. So cold, so cold. The city was clothed in fog, but as I sank I saw the lights of a ship emerging from the dockyard. Newborn, just like Domi emerging from me. The last thing I would ever see. Then I lost my footing; the fast-flowing river carried me out to a place beyond my depth. I felt the slick of machine oil on my cheeks, and my arms struggled to move in the soup of it.

My clothes started to pull me down, and now I was sinking in earnest. I kicked out with my legs, which were pretty useless, being weighed down with boots and skirts, and struggled with my arms. There is no book out there that can tell a person how to drown. Some ungovernable instinct had me splashing and struggling instead of calmly sinking into the water. My weight pulled me further down, water poured into my mouth, and I could barely keep above the surface long enough to breathe air. I could not speak, or shout. Then I could not breathe at all. My chest squeezed tightly as my head jerked up and down, and my lungs screamed for air. Pain, panic. Fear came too, but from a long way away.

As I began to drown in earnest, all I felt was dullness. Voices, internal. Speaking in a babble. So this was how it happened.

A credit to your race . . .

He has a chance not to be reared among savages...

The trouble with you, Lucia, is that you can do anything you want . . . I fear for you more than I do the others...

And then, ringing in my ears with the surging water, an unearthly, pathetic cry, a baby's weak sob. A vision of little Domi, starving for my milk, lying unfed and unnoticed. Desperate and weak with thirst, his legs kicking in the water, crying and crying, untended – and I could do nothing – couldn't reach him – I . . . could . . . not . . . breathe . . . Then the crying stopped. Everything stopped. Blessed, hellish calm. Bright, grey, airless, silent. White. White. White.

Surely by then I was beyond all hope of rescue? But as you can see, I was rescued.

The *Mariette*, a tug that towed the warships out past Port Glasgow and Greenock into the wastes of the North Atlantic, steamed past me on its way back to the dock in Govan. At considerable risk to his own safety, Captain Kenneth Reid hauled himself down over the side to rescue me. What can I say only the Lord must have sent him? Sometimes, I look at my life and wonder about the *Mariette* being there that night, and the captain spotting me. It could so easily have gone the other way. My life could have ended then and there. I was surely ready to go. And yet, while I would not say my life has been joyful since – how could it be? – it has been interesting. I've done things, and been places. I'm a curious person, you know, and have never lost interest in the world.

I joked with Eva that Kenneth Reid fell in love with me, but in my heart I think he was moved by simple kindness towards one's fellow man. He brought me to his own home in Hutchesonstown, and, with his wife, gave me the gift of simple human kindness, a bowl of soup and a safe night's sleep. I slept on my side, my belly still huge as if I carried anything other than emptiness. I hope he did not think I had tried to drown Domi with me, still in utero, but I never got the opportunity to explain.

His first mate, whose name I forget, retrieved my bag, with the money inside it, which I had left on the bank. I spent the money on a large meal in a dockside café and on a train ticket south, in an attempt to move on with my life.

WHEN WE REACHED TURNBULL STREET, I was formally arrested and charged with trespass and kidnapping. I wanted to tell them it was impossible to kidnap your own child, but a deep exhaustion from the past few hours of pain and fighting and the whole venture had set in, so I didn't say a word.

I was ushered into an interview room on the ground floor with no windows to the street and a solitary flyblown lightbulb. According to the large clock displayed above the duty sergeant's head, I was questioned for three hours – this when I could have told them all I knew in less than one minute.

They were an improvement on the nuns, I grant you: a woman constable did offer me refreshments of tea and fruitcake. I was handcuffed to the chair all the while – a waste of time, I was no flight risk – but allowed one free hand to eat and drink, which I did with enthusiasm. I related my tale and responded to their enquiries, trying not to talk with my mouth full, and I think I saw the senior detective flinch when I mentioned the name

Mackenzie. Apart from that, their faces were impassive and bland.

They brought me down to the cells and, without telling me how long I would be there, left me there overnight.

When I was a young girl, I sometimes attended the district court in Mandeville where my father was magistrate. I loved the ceremony of it all: the banging of the gavel, the witnesses attending the stand. But the crimes were often petty, and I felt sad for the young burglars and hawkers, lounging awkwardly in their Sunday best on a weekday, collars too high in their blazers, stuck in that boiling-hot place of justice before being led down into the even hotter remand cells to bake in misery. I certainly never imagined I would ever be among their number.

Once imprisoned, an ancestral horror filled me, and I banged on the door like a madwoman. It was made of steel seven inches thick, so I only hurt my own fist. What scared me was not that I was confined, though that was bad. It was the lack of a given time. In my fevered state, I feared I would be immured forever. Then mi fi go mad like Mrs Rochester Number One. Eventually I fell into an exhausted, unsatisfying sleep, waking occasionally from the cold. Morning dawned, and some light came through the tiny ceiling window. Shortly after that, the warden opened the flap and yelled, 'Lucia Percival! You're free to go. I'll take you up now.'

'You mean they're not charging me?' I shouted back through the same aperture.

'Seems so.'

'Wh'happen?' I asked when he opened the door. The man said nothing, just fumbled in his pockets, took out a crumpled piece of paper and handed it to me. 'I was asked to give you this.'

I opened the note. It simply said, 'Know when the game is over. *Zugzwang.*'

Robin. Couldn't be anyone else. 'The gentleman who wrote

this – is he here?' Without waiting for an answer, I dashed back up that drab corridor, with its limescale on the walls and eerie dripping sound, holding my ransom note in my hand. Up the stairs and through the entrance hall, then out the door. And there he was: across the street, in a long trench coat, tweed cap pulled down over his eyes. Hide himself he might, but I had been side by side with that man in battle: I knew his form intimately.

'Robin.' I had forgotten to collect my coat, and the wind went through me. I feared he wouldn't hear me above its noise. But he turned his head and pushed up his cap. For a moment we stood on opposite sides of the street, staring at each other.

Black move first. But no, not this time. I held Robin's gaze until he broke and crossed the street. Within seconds he was at my side. 'Hello, Lucy,' he muttered, pulling at his pigskin gloves. He smelled heavily of cigarettes.

'I've told you before, I hate it when you call me that.' A spark of amusement lit his eyes, and he winked at me, as if the intervening year had never happened. But then he said, more harshly, 'I can't be seen here. Not with you.'

'Spies everywhere, nuh?'

'You were only meant to read the bloody – I mean, you were only meant to read the note. We weren't supposed to meet like this.' He scuffed his foot against the path and dug his hands into his pockets. 'I shouldnae have hung about, but . . . it's been a long time since I've seen you.'

That wind was brutal, winnowing its way under my skirt and blouse. I wondered if I should go back into the station to collect my coat and belongings. But Robin, seemingly unaware of my discomfort, gestured me to follow him around the corner. Two minutes later, we were sitting in the welcome heat of a café not unlike the ones I had passed on Jamaica Street the previous morning. The place smelled of fried bacon, grease and smoke, but it was warm, and the cup of tea Robin put in front of me had a scalding comfort, though it was a little too milky for my taste.

Looking at the hands holding his own cup, I noticed an emerald solitaire on a silver band around his wedding finger. He saw that I saw, and looked askance.

'It has been a long time,' I agreed.

Robin took a sip at his tea. 'I don't think I saw you after that day with Professor Haldane.'

'Oh my God.' I giggled. 'That was so strange.'

He laughed too, and it was as if we had never broken our conversation. That my baby had never been gone, that I had never been banged up in a police station after trying to get him back. That Robin had never got married. That both our wars were over. The film spooled backwards, and we were in the camp once more, at the entrance of that strange lab Robin had urged me to have a look at.

'Professor Haldane's a hoot,' he had told me, 'and Scottish too.'

I was unenthusiastic. By then, as October approached, I knew for sure I was pregnant and was mustering up the courage to tell Robin. The last thing I needed was to be dragged off to see some wacky professor. 'Scottish, nuh?' I commented sardonically. 'What more is there to say? I must meet him without delay.'

'Don't be sarky, Lucy, it doesnae suit you.' I thought it suited me rather well, but he was off, leading me down towards the forbidden buildings where the male officers lived, ate and slept. I had my heart in my mouth for fear I would be caught when he finally stopped at a small hut with a notice affixed to the door: CHEMICAL WARFARE LABORATORY. He knocked, and, for sure, a clearly Scottish accent told him to come on in.

'Is it safe?' Robin shouted.

'Oh yes,' the voice called back through the door, 'I've just finished with the first lot, and I'm due to start the next batch at four o'clock. Must say the last one was disagreeable. I believe at full strength it burns out the bronchioles entirely and you die an agonisingly slow death. So, I'm lucky I'm still here, I suppose.'

Robin swung the door open. The room was small and square, its solitary window taped up with canvas, a smell of sulphur in the air. A blue gas cylinder stood in the corner with OXYGEN painted on it in white lettering. And in the middle of it all, there was the professor himself, perched on an odd metal throne that had various gas masks hanging off the back. He turned around, and I'll always remember the benign glance he bestowed on me: his middle-aged countenance, with piercing blue eyes and grey, frizzy, out-of-control moustache.

When he offered me his hand, his shake was moist and brisk. He smelled of mints, and I could see his mouth moving as he chewed on one. As I told him my name, a sudden wave of tiredness overwhelmed me. All I wanted to do was curl up in a sweet little corner outside with the vetch and celandine and the long grass and the wind blowing. I swayed and reached my hand out to steady myself. Professor Haldane clasped it immediately. 'Sorry, sir. Just took a little turn.'

'I'd say you did, my darling. Are you all right?' He was watching me closely now. 'Perhaps you should go outside. This room isn't the place for you. Not now.' That last was meaningful, and aimed at Robin, who understood, went chalk white, and more or less strong-armed me out the door, muttering apologies to Professor Haldane.

That was the first and last I saw of the man. Robin mentioning him now brought back a lot of painful thoughts.

'John Haldane and his box o' tricks,' Robin said thoughtfully. 'That was a crazy time.'

A crazy time? He thought so, did he? I took a deep breath, about to tell him exactly what *I* thought but thankfully was prevented by the arrival of two plates of black pudding and eggy toast. An incipient stare from the woman who served us was headed off by an answering glare from Robin. She retreated, and I was glad not to repeat my experience with the Grand Central Hotel and the petits fours.

Hungry again, I ploughed my way through the watery egg, stolid bread and dry black pudding. 'How did you find out about me?' I asked, after the tea was drained and my plate almost clear.

He put down his cup. 'Kept an eye, didn't I? Ever since the adoption went through.' He paused, weighing up his words. 'The mother – Mrs Pullman. She wanted it. She said she didn't mind that the bairn would be a . . . Anyway. The Sisters of Notre Dame were in communication with my mother all the time. Probably before I even knew about it.' He wiped his mouth with the back of his sleeve, making me wince.

'Did someone at the camp tell on me?' He said nothing. 'Who?' 'It doesn't matter.'

'Who? Amelia Hall? Norah? A matron?'

'Doesnae matter who.' He shook his head. 'It was always going to get out.' But I had seen the way he winced when I mentioned Amelia.

'Why are you trying to protect them?' Wrath filled me. I wanted to find Amelia – if it were her – and shake her so hard her teeth would fall out. Then the answer came to me in a flash. He had made some agreement, somewhere up the line, not to say anything. 'So you stood to one side and let your mother do all this? You selfish coward.'

'Selfish coward, aye.' Robin was bitter. 'Had to lie to my wife to tell her where the bail money was going to get you out of there, that's the selfish coward I am.'

'I was going to ask you about that little detail' – I gestured at the ring. 'That your mother's idea too? Planned when you were yea high?' His slumped shoulders confirmed my suspicions. 'I wish you every good fortune and happiness.' Said in the nastiest tone I could muster.

His face crumpled, and he cradled his mug again, bending his head so I could see the roots of his hair, and the small balding patch on his scalp. Then he spoke, still not meeting my eye. 'You know, everything I said . . . about going with you, back to Jamaica, all that. I really meant it. I would have made my life with you.'

I laughed, lightly and with scorn. He'd talked about going to Jamaica that afternoon, after we parted from Professor Haldane and had it out about the pregnancy. I'd told him no, that I wanted to return alone, to try and mend fences with my mother. How would she have reacted? Hard to say. She would have been angry, true-true, and yet she had a practical streak. The unfair reality was that a mulatto, even one born under the bar sinister, would have much better opportunities in life.

The thought of Robin barging in with no understanding of this delicate, unwritten code was too much. He'd never have had the fortitude for island life: the heat, the stigma, the isolation of marrying out of one's own kind, being surrounded by descendants of slaves. He would either have returned to Scotland within a year or taken to the drink.

Once the Jamaica idea had been shot down, he had turned threatening. He tried to talk me into getting an abortion, something I told him I absolutely wouldn't do. I'd helped many girls procure that service, and Eva was the one I remembered most. Her wretchedness, her pale face and shaking limbs, how she had clung to me the night before and begged me not to go, when I had no choice. How much pain she was in the morning after. The furtiveness, the horror of it. And cu yuh, I am talking about Eva, who never felt guilty about what she was doing. She swore she never willingly bedded her husband in all their miserable time together and that nothing conceived from rape needed to be given life. At the time I made sympathetic noises, but inside I disapproved, being convinced I could never do what she had done. I was, as the English say, a bit of a prig back then.

'You'll do as I say,' Robin had said through gritted teeth. 'I'm warning you.' His fingers encircled my wrist, tightly.

I wrenched them free. 'You think you can tell me what to do? Yu nuh get the memo? Slavery abolished fram 1833. Mi free to do what mi want.'

At that he had inhaled deeply, his cheeks sinking inwards and his face going very pale. I got the sense of a volcano just before an eruption. 'This isn't easy for me, you know. I can't make you – *this* – respectable.' The insult hit me like a slap.

Over the next half hour, he paced up and down a patch of grass, still arguing, while I tried to answer him, all the while looking out for roving matrons or military police. It was a wonder he didn't wear the ground smooth. He certainly got through a lot of cigarettes. (Come to think of it, he was lighting up now, in a café already submerged in a fug of smoke.) Finally, he declared he was in no fit state to discuss the matter further. 'We'll talk more tomorrow,' he told me, before striding off into the safe world of men, leaving me standing there like a half-eedjiat.

That was the last I'd seen of him until now, face to face across this table with its stained oilcloth, its dirty cutlery and its Notice for Dietary Restrictions in Wartime affixed to the wall opposite. I could not help wondering briefly if their peacetime menu tasted any better than what I had sampled. I doubted it.

'I'm sorry about what happened to you.' His sigh was heavy enough to blow his unsecured tea doily into my lap. While I retrieved it and put it back on the table, he continued, lamenting, 'I was frantic trying to find out where you had gone. On the blower with Divisional Headquarters in Rouen. Telegrams to Her Back Home. I was out of my mind.'

'I'm sure.' The past two winters in the British Isles had brought me an acquaintance with frost, and I hoped those two words contained enough of it to shut him up. I was infuriated beyond belief at his self-justifying whine.

What happened was that late on a rainy night in October 1916, I was summoned by a Sister I didn't know, hauled in front of the Matron, and within ten minutes my career in the Voluntary Aid Detachment, Mile End section, was over.

I remember standing in that small square office, my coat on over my thin nightclothes and dressing gown, shivering, my insides somersaulting. Two silent, heavyset women in late middle age flanked the Matron. I learned later that they worked for Mrs Mackenzie. 'I thought you would be a credit to your race,' the Matron said, with a disappointed sigh.

What a ridiculous comment! 'What about Jack the Ripper, or Kaiser Wilhelm II? Are they a "credit to their race", ma'am?'

'Shut up, you,' one of the women barked, in an accent that could cut through gristle. 'Yer in disgrace.'

Then they took my passport from me and bundled me into a car. I am not joking. The Matron just sat there while these red-faced ham hocks abducted me in plain sight. I struggled under the pincer grip of their meaty fingers in the softness of my upper arms. Tried with all my might to break free, yelled at them to be careful of the baby. But those pigs did not care.

'How can you let them get away with this?' I shouted at the Matron as they dragged me off.

To that she answered, 'It's more than my job's worth to get involved.' The last I saw of her, she was at the small sink, vigorously soaping up her hands like Pontius Pilate.

I could have told Robin all of this. Could have told him about every indignity I had endured since then. Could have crucified him in real time, my every accusation a nail being driven into his hand or foot. Morpethswade. A nail. Losing Domi. Another nail. Nearly drowning myself in the Clyde. Another. Nail after nail after nail. I could have hoisted him up on that cross and watched him suffer as I hammered them in myself.

But then I felt the warmth of his palm against mine, as our fingers interlaced. I was taken aback by how pleasant it still felt, how my ill will drained away, replaced by . . . I wasn't quite sure what. When he slid his hand back, I felt almost disappointment. When he spoke, he sounded disappointed too. 'I didn't come here to fight about the past. I came to save your life.'

'My . . . ?'

'Lucia. If my mother knew you were out and free again, she'd have you put in the Clyde with a rock tied to your neck. You need to get out of Glasgow right quick.'

To my ears, this sounded preposterous. 'I know in your eyes she's all-powerful,' I said wearily, 'but mercy, even white folk cannot go about murdering whoever they please.'

'You don't understand,' Robin said. 'I need to tell you a story. My father is a renowned psychiatrist, a handsome man. Always has been, though the drink is fraying him now. But his family were on hard times, so he married for money. If you saw my ma . . . Look, she's built like a brick shithouse – Sorry, I mean—'

'Never mind.' Swearing was the least of my problems right then.

'He had a mania for younger women, my father; you couldn't leave him in a room with any young girl for any length of time, not even my cousins once they came of age . . . The one thing that kept our family together was Mama's money.' Here Robin cleared his throat repeatedly. 'And then one day my pa fell for one of them. Her name was Tabitha Lewes. She was a patient of his with a neurasthenic complaint, so I heard. And all the gold and silver on the planet earth couldn't hold him back. He was going to leave us for her. Planned to start a new life. On what, I don't know. He couldn't keep money from one month to the next.'

He started rearranging the saucers and cups. 'I remember him leaving. I was fifteen, and saw him at the door, all stiff and proper with his hat and suitcases. And then a week later he came back. A broken man.' For a long moment, Robin said nothing. Then he added, in a harsh whisper, 'I overheard the servants talking. Tabitha Lewes was found dead and she eight months' pregnant with my dad's baby. They say she was murdered, but there wasn't a mark on her. No one was ever charged, and a blind eye was turned. A fast girl in an embarrassing position, a girl who didn't know her place.'

He turned and motioned as if to spit, then seemed to recall he was in the middle of a café, stopped mid-gesture, and turned back around. His eyes were milky where they were usually clear.

'Your mother did that?' I said in slow horror, my hands reaching for my empty cup, something to fiddle with to stop my hands shaking. I focused on that wartime recipe notice as if it were the Bible it own self.

'Not directly.' Robin's smile was unpleasantly thin. 'But she knew who to turn to for help. And who to bribe to cover it up.'

I shook my head. 'And all that for . . . I know he's your father, but cha, he is worthless, surely? She could make her own life, with her house and pickney dem and all that family money?'

'You'd think, wouldn't you?' Robin took out another cigarette but left it unlit on the oilcloth. 'Sorry. Been smoking away and forgot you don't like 'em. My mother never fell out of love with my pa, that's the trouble. She always hoped for just a crumb of his affection – if only he'd a given her a crumb! Then he mightn't have created such a monster.' The last was delivered with a sigh that would have blown the leaves off the tree outside our window. 'I signed up and went to France to get away from her, to be honest. And then . . . well, you know the rest. She's got me married to Sarah Morrison, whose pappy owns half the shipyards on the Clyde.'

A waitress cleared away our plates and said in a loud, not-looking-at-anyone-in-particular voice, if she could get the gentleman anything else. 'No, nor the lady,' Robin firmly responded, and for a moment I felt almost fond of him. Raindrops began to fall on the café window, and outside a woman in a long black coat with a fur collar battled the intricate settings of her umbrella.

'So now you know what she's capable of,' Robin concluded, 'can you understand why I wrote that you're in *Zugzwang*, my love? This is the last I can do for you. Even now I'm risking quite a bit.' He glanced around, then out at the woman in black, who had paused in her struggles to stare at me – I suspected for the usual reason.

No move without loss. If I went near Domi again, I would lose at minimum my freedom. Possibly more. But if I did as Robin advised . . . well, I would lose Domi. Robin saw my hesitation and grasped my forearms. 'Go back to London, Lucia. Make your life there. Find a good man.' He twisted his wedding ring around his finger. It looked as if it didn't fit.

'I can make my life in London,' I said gently, allowing myself to touch his cheek. He closed his eyes. 'I *can* find a good man—'

'You mean you've already found one,' he interrupted sharply, then inhaled. 'I'm sorry. It's none of my bizney. I've got a cheek, really, to resent it.'

I tried to think of Arthur and Robin in the same room, holding a conversation. Arthur: artistic, courteous, restrained, a snappy dresser. And, well, Robin. What would they talk about? I couldn't imagine. Then I thought of the life Robin had made for himself in

Glasgow – or, the one that had been made for him. Like his father, he'd married into money, and I suspected that, like for his father, it would be a disaster.

'Just be careful, all right, Lucia?' I realised that Robin had no idea that my new suitor – if I could even presume to describe Arthur in those terms – was black. 'You deserve better than me.' The most irritating line a man can utter to a woman – and in Robin Mackenzie's case and mine, the truest. What could I do but agree?

'I'll be careful, Robin Mackenzie,' I said, 'but you must promise me something in return.' He put his head to one side and looked wary. We both knew he was in a poor position to promise anything. 'You know where my little boy is. So . . . keep an eye out for him? Please?' At that point, my composure broke slightly, and I fervently wished I had my handkerchief with me rather than in a bag of effects in a police-station cloakroom. I grabbed the mimeo-graphed menu with its egg stains, turned it over, and retrieved a pen from the windowsill. Thankfully, there was ink in it. I wrote my address, leaving out my name and the name of the city, to avoid a trail. Folding it into quarters, I passed it back to Robin, who put it into his breast pocket, all the while watching me intently. What was going on with this miserable fellow?

Then he muttered, 'If you had a quarter of the love you have for that child for me . . .'

I felt such overpowering rage that I was nearly overtaken by a desire to turn over the table and leave all the dishes and scraps chaka-chaka on the floor, like Jesus turning over the tables in the Temple. What a selfish, demanding, privileged . . .

He must have seen my reaction because he pulled up short, mumbling shamefacedly, 'Of course I'll keep my eye out for the bairn. But you know I can't interfere with his life, any more than you can. Sarah's hoping . . .' He turned his dirty fork over and over between his fingers. I guessed that Sarah's hopes were that they would have children. Domi's siblings, if only they – or he – knew it.

Poor Robin! I pitied him. If only he'd had the courage to stand up to his mother. Now he'd made a noose for himself, and everything he did only seemed to tighten it. *Zugzwang*, indeed.

'I love you,' he said. 'D'you believe me?'

'You're married, Robin,' I said, as gently as I could. 'Thank you for the meal, and for helping – within your limits.' Thereupon, without looking at him, I got up and made my way out to the grey skies and the police station on Turnbull Street to collect my belongings.

I looked back once. Just once, from the other side of that rain-flecked window. Robin was still sitting where I had left him, his face contorted with anguish, as if he were frozen mid-weep. It was a shock to me, seeing him like that. Then my heart hardened against him, and I turned away. To my dying day, I'll never say I didn't have feelings for Robin Mackenzie – something about him made my heart go a-flutter even then – but I loved Domi so, so much more. His words showed me that he did not understand, and never would. I was sure I'd never see him again from that day on – oh, would to God that were true!

15

LONDON, 27 SEPTEMBER 1917

H arrow Road, London
    27 September 1917, 8 p.m.

MY DEAR MISS PERCIVAL,

I must confess to being very disappointed after arriving at the
Royal Academy at the agreed time and date, then waiting a considerable interval for you to appear, only to give up after an hour in
the freezing cold and trudge home again to my solitary rooms. It
makes me feel a little ill used to have put aside a piece of my time I
could have spent composing standing on the sidewalk of a London
street getting the usual panoply of dirty looks and whistles from
passing vagrants – and so-called respectable people too!

That said, I will put aside my offence, for perhaps in a way it is
for the best. Lately, I have found myself pulled in many directions
with staging *Symphonia* and composing my second work, *Atlantica*.
The orchestra sure is fractious, and perpetually short of money,

not to mention people. Freddie Corder says he is in despair of them ever speaking to each other, let alone getting as far as the performance. You know what we musicians are like, vain as all get out!

But all this is by the by. The real purpose of this letter is to let you know that I'm packing up here and going back to the States to train as an officer and enlist in the war effort. There's a new Negro officer-training college set up in Fort Des Moines, Iowa, quite a distance away from my home town, and I've enrolled as a cadet. Do you not think, Lucia, that we black folk deserve the opportunity to serve our country and excel in the fight? Of course, your brother is already in the thick of it – such a pity being an officer isn't open to him. Yet another petty injustice I wish I could rectify.

Anyways, I can't commit to a return date to London yet – unless Fritz wants to commit to surrendering – but wished to let you know that, recent annoyances notwithstanding, I will retain the memory of our brief, strange and enlightening acquaintance and, should our paths cross again, hope to be able to re-establish it.

Yours in musicianship and conversation,

Arthur Rosewell

IT WAS a full day before I even saw that letter, let alone read it. When I did, I scanned it quickly and threw it on the floor with a bleak cackle. So much for my suitor.

The journey from Glasgow Central back to that shabby room off Fulham Road had taken all day. I shoved the key in the door late that evening, exhausted after a long and hostile journey – hostile since I no longer had the disguise of Mrs Herminia to protect me. Too exhausted to try and cook anything, not to mention too low on coins for the meter, I dug out some ancient sticks of liquorice Eva had left at the bottom of a tin and chewed on the sticky aniseed strands.

Further rifling unearthed the rear end of a lump of cheddar. It didn't smell too rank, so I scraped off the mould and ate it almost to the rind with two McVitie's digestive biscuits. I don't usually eat much dairy, but my state of mind was not so dire as to render me immune from hunger, and there was little else left.

I didn't leave the house for three days. For much of the time I slept, drank water, gobbled down crackers – Eva's emergency stash – then slept some more, not even bothering to move the scores I left scattered chaka-chaka around my pillow. I drooled over a page of Mozart and curled up next to one from Puccini. I didn't sing a note. After I had said goodbye to Robin that morning, I thought my throat had closed over and that I would never be able to sing again.

Nobody from the outside world troubled me during that time; no telephone could connect the irate Major Carroll from Roehampton to me, and no word came from Audrey, who would presumably be puzzled and annoyed at the disappearance of her possessions. Even the odious Mrs Baxter didn't intrude.

It dimly occurred to me that my prolonged absence meant I would surely lose my job, and that would deprive me of any means of paying future rent. I would be out on the street, and Eva too if she ever returned from tending to her Germans. I felt oddly indifferent to the prospect. My sole concern was what I had nearly gained, and then completely lost.

Like a Pathé reel, I played back the scenes where I had held little Domi in my arms but added colour to his face, the heat of his skin, and the scent of cream on it, the way his arms moved, how his little head bobbed against mine. His cry, soft at first, then loud and distressed as the maid and Mr Pullman chased me and pinned me down. Again and again I played that little film of every memory I possessed of Dominic. I gained no satisfaction from it.

Eva's words rang in my head: a voice would not be enough, I would want all of him. She was speaking of a different desire, but the intensity was the same. Eventually I realised I could not go on like this. Confined to that stale room, never going out of doors, going slowly mad like poor Mrs Rochester Number One. I needed to make like poor Bertha and start a fire – even if only in my heart. But, oh, in that grey-brown, gloopish London, in a lonely, comfortless room, grieving my little boy for a second time, it was hard.

'You shall never see him again,' I told myself as I put out the light and settled down for the evening. 'You shall never see him again,' I reminded myself when I woke the following morning, crumpled and stiff, my stomach doubling up from the crackers and liquorice. 'You shall never see him again,' I chanted under my breath as I made my way to the water closet. 'You shall never see him again,' as I headed around the corner and down Fulham Road with headscarf and shawl wrapped tight. It was good that I said it so often. Because when a singer repeats the same phrase often enough, it is practice, and practice makes the unbearable seem normal.

That brisk cold morning, dashing for the train and the job I had no doubt lost, dodging elbows, a melody unwound in my mind: Handel's 'Dove sei, amato bene?' from *Rodelinda*. 'Sono oppresso da' tormenti, ed i crudeli miei lamenti,' I sang quietly in that rackety old carriage, which smelled of rain, feet and rationed misery. Warm tears sprung from the corners of my eyes as the train emerged into the light and made its way over the brown Thames.

Back in 1913, Mr Garfield had placed the score to that piece on the music desk of the piano so we could read the Italian together. We sat awkwardly side by side on the piano bench, our knees almost touching: mine bare, their backs sweating against the padded green leather of the seat, his clad with the lightest of grey cottons. I suspected it was no coincidence that his brushed mine so frequently as he recited the beautiful foreign syllables.

It almost felt nice, like a cooling breeze in the heat, or little prickles down my spine. It was unfortunate, then, when I felt his squashy fingers creeping at the back of my neck, stretching down to that soft part we call the cubbitch-hole, pressing gently. Ugh. Why men haffi ruin a good moment by taking things too far? Although I did not fall in love with Mr Garfield as a result of such foolery, I did fall deeply for the song, whose flowing, sustained notes were a pleasure to sing. I do like the baroque stuff, so free of fluff, bel-canto theatrics and all that labba-labba.

That day on the train I let myself sing it very softly, very unob-trusively, taking it up to G as the original key was just that little bit contralto for me. I was so glad to feel my voice come back after such a sad few days that I quite forgot to worry whether anyone could hear me. And then I felt a tap on the shoulder.

'Miss?'

I recognised the long-faced man with his short moustache and trailing light-brown sidelocks. When I say recognised, I didn't know him from Adam, but we had shared this train every morning for the past few months, so I had long managed to avoid his eye, and he mine. His coat was a long tweed one that looked like it had seen better days. A civilian coat but with a wound stripe tied around it near his left shoulder, which meant he had been invalided out of battle. He wore a battered fedora.

'Miss?' he said again. I didn't conceal my surprise; white men rarely address me so nicely.

'Yes?'

'I was wondering, miss. The singing. Could you . . . ?'

'Oh. I'm so sorry, sir. I didn't mean to disturb you.'

He cleared his throat. 'No. I jus' meant . . . could you sing a little louder? We was enjoying it.' To my even greater surprise, I heard a ripple of agreement from the rest of the carriage.

'Life gets very boring right now, with all the war going on,' a woman in a servant's skirt piped up. 'And it's been a few months now since my best boy—' She broke off, sobbing into a handkerchief, waving an incoherent apology.

Their kindness moved my heart, so I sang for them, there on the train, just as I had sung for the soldiers in Étaples. It was one of those rare moments when white and black did not matter, when in our sorrow and humanity we were all as one.

Thanks to Mr Garfield, I knew every syllable of that Handel aria off by heart and became so absorbed in it that I forgot to get off at my stop, and I did not care. When I finished, the whole carriage applauded. This in spite of my not having a high opinion of my performance; to my mind, my vocal was a little thin and cracked from nearly a week's disuse never mind yelling to be let out of a Glasgow remand cell.

The train pulled into the next station, and I stepped off, waving goodbye to my new friends. I realised that I sorely missed Arthur, who would have provided a pleasant accompaniment. Miss Slade too. I dreaded seeing her again. Since I had missed that Wednesday's lesson without notice, the very sight of me would make her vex, and explaining that I had been detained by the City of Glasgow Police would not help matters one bit.

My sorrow had so overwhelmed me that I had been unable to think much of Arthur's letter, but now the reality of his journey sobered me. He could not have reached America yet so was probably still travelling over the treacherous Atlantic. As I walked across the gardens at Roehampton, the briefest of prayers escaped my lips: may he escape the terror of the U-boats! The Germans had started their unrestricted warfare again, and everyone was petrified. Although Arthur had skipped the country and left me without an important friend and ally – not to mention a handsome companion – I cherished him and did not wish him any harm. Once enough time had elapsed, I might even consider replying to his letter.

My song on the train had made me late, but my instinct told me it didn't matter, and my instinct was right. As I reached the entrance and clocked in, my way was soon blocked by a supervisor who escorted me up to Major Carroll's office. I was told to leave the premises with immediate effect and collect the remainder of my pay on the way out. The major was in too much pain to even get the words out – I had to infer them between his gasps and grunts.

There it was. Another rotten job had come to its inevitable end. If you have a musician's soul, my friend, you know the pain of the day job. Perhaps it was because music had always been my true vocation and I resented labouring at anything else. After everything I had endured, I could not bring myself to care about losing my position, much less the people I was leaving behind: the grimacing major, the unspeakable Cath, and, of course, Audrey Partridge, who could not resist casting on me a look of reproach as I passed her on my way out. So what if she didn't get her rhaatid cloak and gloves back? Wear an armband and be done with it! This endless grieving for nothing was wearing me out. This war was wearing me out, full stop.

I wandered awhile, making a long route towards Putney Hill, looking out for a bus home. Again, I missed Arthur: a walk like this would have been a good time to converse. Precious few people of his understanding and intelligence were available to me now. It was a pity he had upped and gone off to America like that. What a foolish fellow, wasting his energies on a white man's war instead of concentrating on his music.

At first, I could not comprehend his actions, but reading his letter again, a thought came to mind. That Arthur Rosewell was too much of a perfectionist. That he was waiting for the perfect moment, the perfect melody, the perfect *society*, before he let himself become closer to me. Whatever about the moment or the melody, the society would be a long time coming, and we both knew it.

In the end, never mind society, even the damn bus never turned up after twenty minutes' waiting. I took a very long walk home, past the reservoirs where the Thames took a loop at Richmond, then making my way back to Fulham and the little room I would surely soon lose.

I briefly entered the building to collect the large pink canvas grocery bag Eva used to buy things, then, plucking up my courage, made my way to Woodcock's, a local grocer's which she often patronised. She had told me that Mr Woodcock had a son in Mesopotamia, so I used my brain and charm, mentioned that I was a housemate of Miss Downey's and that I hoped his son was safe.

He brightened instantly, suspicion vanishing, and he took a halfpenny off the price of the bread and fruit I bought. When he enquired about renewing our milk subscription, I assured him I had no need of it with Eva gone, and he scratched his head and declared I was a rum 'un for sure. Back then, nobody had heard of the saying 'you are what you eat,' but I couldn't help but notice that English people did drink a lot of milk.

As I made my way back, the bag swinging against my legs and jabbing me in the calf, my thoughts turned again to what had happened that morning in the train and how it might help me continue my life without Domi. I realised that in future music must be my mainstay. *Mark every day with melody and practice*, an inner voice instructed me, *turn every sadness into song.* A creative excitement that I had forgotten existed began to beat its little wings against the bars of its cage. None of this would be wasted. Out of caca, I could make gold. I vowed it.

But what of my little boy? Could I just forget him? I recalled a poem Eva used to recite when she was thinking of Christopher. On learning that the poet was the sister of the woman who had created the ghastly Mr Rochester, I had dismissed the lines without ceremony, but now they bubbled back up in my mind: 'Then did I learn how existence could be cherished / Strengthened, and fed without the aid of joy.'

I went into the park at Parson's Green and sat down on a bench. I would speak to Domi's – well, not his ghost, since thank God he was alive and well, but his spirit, which would surely hear my voice as I willed it to him with all my might. I let the bag of groceries sag at my feet then started talking to Domi, occasionally breaking into song.

My sole audience that winter afternoon was a small fox that burst through the undergrowth, sat stock still and stared at me for a moment. I told the fox, and the empty air, that I missed my little boy, that he had been taken from me against my will, that I loved him more than I had ever loved anyone in my life, and that I hoped someday he would know how hard I had striven for him. 'I fought for you, little one,' I said, my voice low and tear-choked. 'I fought my very hardest for you, just like the pawns in the battle your father and I patched up. No other woman can understand or feel about you how I do. I would have broken every commandment for you, little boy.'

Just then I heard the bush rustle. My fox friend had long since scarpered, so I jumped up and stared into the undergrowth, beating at the bushes with my gloved hands. But whatever it was had vanished, and once again I had only my own thoughts to keep me company.

ÉTAPLES FIELD HOSPITAL, **France**
6 November 1917

MY DEAR LUCIA,

I was glad to receive your last and know that you are well. Though I was surprised to hear of Mr Rosewell gone just like that, and you all debonair about it. Your last job 'coming to an end'? And your new one? Has Mr Rosewell weighed in on that or did he leave before you secured it? Does he think you are betraying the sacred principles of opera by singing the new jazz? I won't lie: I have a lot of questions!

I just worry and hope you are all right. I know how betrayed you felt when I left so suddenly, and it's been on my conscience, along with all the usual depressing stuff I won't bore you with. Sybil hasn't written at all. I'm still in the doghouse with her and imagine I will be for some time. Could you do me a favour and look in on her from time to time? I know relations are a bit frosty between you, but you and she are the only true friends I have left.

Apologies, also, for not having written in a while, and before then only brief notes: I've been absolutely run off my feet. The POWs are piling up, and there is never enough room. For obvious reasons we are last on the list for beds and equipment. We have some German orderlies to help out, but I have been working thirteen hours a day for the past month, and I am utterly bunched. It doesn't help that a new push has started at _____, barely weeks after the last one ended.

The Sister on the ward I work on is pleasant, if distant. She and I are the only non-German staff who speak the language, though I believe an informal trade in cigarettes has helped overcome the communications barrier for most. I must go now because they have brought in a new load in the ambulance, and there is one Fritz howling his head off. I think he must be in need of morphine – must dash.

Following day

I am going to include this letter with the last one as I was so busy I never got time to stamp it for the post. Oh my, Lucia, I am so tired I feel as if there are corkscrews jabbing at me inside my head! I've had about four? five? hours' sleep between yesterday and today. Alfrecht the POW orderly made me some hastily improvised coffee, bless him. I've no idea where he got it from, but he swears to me in dreadful English that it was powder and he just poured boiling water on it without even putting it in a pot. I've never in my life heard of such a monstrous idea, but it tasted quite good.

So, what are the Germans like? The Prussians are all a bit obnoxious, it is true, but the rest are quite friendly. In general, they are better read than the Tommies. You know that I learned German in school? Well, when I was struggling with all the noun cases, I remember Mlle Hautbois reprimanding me for saying 'hilf mich' instead of 'hilf mir,' which is the dative rather than accusative. (Sorry, Lu. I forget most people don't care about this sort of thing. I can't talk to the one person who did any more, so you get to hear all about it.)

Anyway, I had cause to remember it, because of the howling man I told you about in the last instalment. The minute he saw me, he stared, grabbed my arm so hard it hurt, and repeated over and over, 'hilf mir, hilf mir,' until his eyes went dull and blank. He dropped the polite pronoun, that's how bad a way he was in. 'I will try,' I said to him in the same language, though I'm not sure he heard.

Miraculously he stabilised and made it through the night, and soon he was well enough to be able to talk. I found out his name and rank from his army book: Stefan Badura, second lieutenant in the Third Division of the Prussian Guards. He is just seven years older than I, so was still in the middle of his degree in Breslau when the recruitment started. He hoped to become an engineer. They thought it would all be over soon, you know?

Later again

Over the past day or two, my Hun has grown quite attached to me and quite content to be informal in his own language. Once he looked at me and said, 'Bist Du ein Engel?' which means 'Are you an angel?' and, oh Lucia! I said, 'Nein, nicht ein Engel, aber eine Verräterin.' That means, 'I'm not an angel, I am a traitor.' Which really was not the wisest thing to say in that room. It caused a bit of a stir among the prisoners.

The funny thing is, this wretched Fritz is now trying to play counsellor to my woes. After I made that remark, he answered instantly, 'Tell me, why are you so harsh on yourself? Whom you betray? You seem wery sad.'

I told him it was a painful subject, hard to talk about even with close friends, and hoped that would deter him, but if there is one thing I have learned about Germans it's that they won't get the hint. They don't know what a hint *is*. He said, 'Also, you cannot talk to your friends. So. You tell the enemy. It is simple. Today, we talk; tomorrow maybe we fight and die. No judgement. You tell the enemy, and he listen.'

Oh Lucia, I don't know what it was that made me tell him. Maybe it was being aware of that anniversary coming up – the 16th – oh, I am dreading it – or perhaps just the kindness and simplicity of his words. But last night, I just did: the whole sad story from start to finish. (There were bits I had to tell him in English because there was no equivalent in German for a white feather of cowardice, for example.) I confess I was quite undignified, crying with my nose running, but he was patient and listened intently, and when I had finished, the stony thing in me that was stronger than hunger and sleep, that kept me nervy and exhausted, it all rolled gently off my back.

When I took to my bed that night, just for once the air smelled of sweet jasmine and was not unfriendly. Just for once I woke in the morning without my first thought being 'I want to die.' It didn't last, mind you, but while it did it was precious.

Best love,

Eva.

16

NOVEMBER 1917

D *aily Herald*, 15 November 1917

Negro Musicians, East End Concert To-Morrow
REAL RAGTIMES BY REAL DARKIES!
People's Palace, Mile End Road, London
ADMISSION FREE! Doors 8 p.m.

YOU SEE THAT? What sort of notice in a newspaper is that, you may ask? I'll tell you: it was my first engagement with my new job. Yes, that was what Eva was asking about in the letter I just showed you. Poor Eva. That was painful to read again. I had forgotten how much she suffered, that she needed a German to comfort her.

To return to this advertisement: the 'real darkies' were the Southern Syncopated Orchestra, a group of musicians to whom I would be lending my vocal. We met through the efforts of Gwen and Dr Alcindor, who kept a weather eye out for me after Arthur's departure. I did not tell them the circumstances of my losing my last job, but they did not stint on helping me, and for that I was deeply grateful.

The men of the Southern Syncopated Orchestra were very famous indeed. Black, but not American; many of them from the West Indies. Most were long settled in London. Some of them had even married white Englishwomen, and this was regarded as nothing scandalous. It made me wonder from time to time how my future would have worked out if Robin had been willing to take courage and step up, but since that part of my life was over, I did not dwell on it too long.

Arthur would not have approved. He was a strict classicist and couldn't stand the new 'jazz' craze that had crossed the Atlantic and was now sweeping London. He told me he feared its effect on my voice if I ever tried to sing it. That first night, Friday, 16th November, I would find out if he were right.

I arrived early, going in via the tradesmen's entrance with the other musicians. Arthur used to complain that whenever he went to a social gathering someone would mistake him for a musician and direct him in the wrong door!

I slipped into the small dressing room I shared with Evelyn Sparrow, the girl I was to duet with. She was a strikingly beautiful woman of West African descent with a close bob and a small forehead. She was a little cold with me, but not actively obstructive. Later she confided in me the reason for her stand-offish behaviour: at the time I joined the band, her brother was at the second Passchendaele offensive during the thick of the battle there. That partly explained her distance; the rest was natural competitiveness, which I returned.

I learned the jazz style of singing by listening to her – often there was not even a score. It was much different from classical, with more independence of rhythm and the vocal more in the head and chest. I used to follow her vocal line in close harmony and often found that I picked up the music faster than the lyrics.

As the orchestra began to tune up, I concentrated on my make-up. I always liked to brighten myself up with a bit of lipstick and rouge, especially throughout those miserable war years. Face powder was my nemesis since in the entire city of London I could never find the right shade. Evelyn had managed to get some, brought over from America, and while it was a bit lighter than I would have liked, there was little enough difference between it and my skin tone that I could safely pat it on my cheeks and nose and look quite presentable.

I browsed the eyeshadow palette and selected what would become my favourite shade, a glistening turquoise, then a lipstick called Dark Plum. I saw my face in the mirror and the face pleased me. And why should I not admit it? Evelyn cast me another look of sly resentment. There was only room for one star in this place, apparently. But the fellows in the band seemed to like their new girl fine, if not quite as much as they did Evelyn Sparrow, so I didn't mind.

I hoped the crowd that night would be reasonable. I'd heard stories from Evelyn and Frank Bates, the male vocalist, that sometimes they could get a bit rowdy and shout insults at the performers. Evelyn and I were directed to practise torch songs such as 'I'm Always Chasing Rainbows' and 'After You've Gone.' When the band played those numbers, Evelyn told me, the men and women in the audience would pair off into couples and intertwine themselves so deeply it was almost obscene.

I asked her why they would do such a thing, and she shrugged as she arranged a delicate, almost transparent, Chinese shawl over her narrow shoulders, which looked more naked draped with the material than they had without. For once she was kind. 'They're dancing away the war, hon. They forget we're here. They just need us to be invisible, like wallpaper, y'know?' It was a strange contrast from my usual situation, where I longed for invisibility when I walked into a room but could not get it for love or money! But I understood what she meant.

The manager, Mr Lattimore, a lyrically beautiful man with bright eyes and a strict hair parting, preferred us to play film music and more serious compositions. He had hopes of entertaining royalty, hopes which were frustrated by Mr Bates's preferences, and the 'vulgar nature of the audience.'

The rehearsal went fine, and the night started well. We came out to riotous applause before we had even struck a note. I loved the male musicians' outfits: they wore white shirts with top collars buttoned and no neckties under black dinner jackets with lapels that shone in the stage lights. The audience, for their part, were tickled at getting access to black musicians since our jazz was more 'authentic' than the white imitators who were springing up everywhere. (One did not mention the Original Dixieland Jazz Band in Frank Bates's presence; those pretenders drove him wild more than anything.)

Frank, as he insisted I call him, got us started on an upbeat number, 'Tiger Rag', which was so fast and syncopated it shocked the punters into life: they could not stay in their seats. Sidney Bechet played the saxophone with such virtuosity and perfect embouchure that I wanted to kiss his feet. Fiah fi all the people who said this wasn't music!

Later on, when Evelyn Sparrow's sad, melting-toffee voice sang the line 'Waiting to find a little bluebird in vain', with me in close accompaniment, several people got out their handkerchiefs and, inevitably, danced the way Evelyn had warned me they would. I didn't mind. I was caught up in the ecstasy of public performance. Classical singing had not given me many opportunities, but now

...! And then, as I looked away from Evelyn and at the audience – the briefest of glances – my heart leapt so far into my mouth that the ability to sing was temporarily removed from me.

There was the old woman again, second row in the centre, on the far right, her hand tapping the rhythm of the music on the armrest, hair in an up-do that even from a distance I could tell was inappropriately loose for her age. Thankfully she wasn't dancing. She appeared to be alone. But her gaze was not on the orchestra, or on Miss Sparrow, resplendent in a long ivory dress with a single sequin-dotted panel at the front, the kind of dress that only looks good on darker skin. She was not looking at the stocky conductor, his elbows moving in a lather of fuss, the back of his neck creasing. No. Her gaze was entirely fixed on me. Oh mi Gad, why could these people not leave me alone? Had that vile Laura-Jane Mackenzie decided that even after Robin's warning I must be done away with and had put a mark on me to determine my movements? Would I never be free until I were dead?

It was all I could do not to bound down from the stage there and then, pull this woman out of her seat and demand to know who she was and what she thought she was doing. But Evelyn was looking daggers at me for dropping a note – only a note, for God's sake! – and we were moving on to a new piece. So, with the old woman sitting staring at me, I continued singing, but there was a hard, angry edge to my voice, and during the interval Mr Lattimore chided me for sounding too aggressive. 'You're singing to a lost generation,' he told me. 'From us they need comfort. Never forget that.'

Be like wallpaper. Yes, I got the message. But right at that moment comfort was far from my mind. I endured the second half with burning impatience. My one ambition, as pointed and singular as an arrowhead, was to pounce on that woman before she left the auditorium. Eventually – after *three* encores – the conductor brought the baton down, the house lights went up, and the musicians all walked off. Except me. I jumped down off that stage, nearly turning the heel of my shoe and spraining my ankle. A blond young man in a fawn jacket exclaimed, 'Oh I say!'

The old woman had left her seat immediately after the encore and was heading to the double doors. Now that she had her back to me, I saw her hair was even wilder than I thought, a long ponytail of dark-silver strands falling down her back. A woman her age not even bothering to put her hair up properly! What sort of creature was she, to neglect the basics like that?

You're not getting away this time. I charged up that aisle and followed as she slipped through the doors and out into the night. Then I reached out for that ponytail and pulled her back with all my might. I could have just grabbed her by the shoulder, but I wanted to have her secure in my grip. I wanted to make her squirm. She reacted with a loud, unmusical cry.

Now! Time to see what I had fished up! I spun her round. Her face was deathly white, and I could see the blue veins in her neck; her chin was so sharp, her cheekbones so razor-thin, that the whole face looked like the end of a V. Her eyes were pointedly blue, her lips thin and red. In another context, I might have described her as having had beauty in her youth, and still being quite striking in old age. But now? Nah.

I gave it to her with both barrels. 'You vulture! You have to keep watching me? Well, here I am. Go tell on me. There's nothing more your people can do to me.'

'Are you all right madam? Is this person bothering you?' – a woman constable, younger than the one in Glasgow. She was, of course, addressing the old woman, not me. Why on earth did they have police officers at the venue? Did they think we'd start a riot? Then I began to wonder if the woman officer and the woman spy were in cahoots. My experience with the Mackenzies had taught me that authority could be bought very easily. I had already been persecuted, imprisoned and warned off. I was not sure how much more I could take.

But my prey recovered herself remarkably well, fixing a withering look on the uniformed female. '*You're* bothering me. Please, go away. I've had enough of the State to last a lifetime.' Her voice was dry, cultured, very English. Alto, at a guess.

'Very good, ma'am,' the constable said in a hurt voice, withdrawing.

I was surprised at her willingness to send the policewoman away. 'Thank you,' I said, somewhat reluctantly. 'I have already been arrested this year. Twice might be one time too many.'

She raised an eyebrow, her forehead wrinkling further on that side. 'Really? You make me feel like an amateur.'

The cheek of her! 'I don't make a habit of it. Other people's wickedness is not my fault. But you know all this: the Mackenzies are *your* paymasters.'

She frowned at me then and tilted her head back. 'You mistake me, I'm afraid,' she said, fussing with her worn chamois gloves. I wanted to slap her hands down.

'I don't think I've made any mistake. You've been following me for months. Obviously they pay you. Probably his mother organise it all.' My composure began to slip away, along with my King's English grammar, but the woman was unmoved.

'You're labouring under a delusion. I've no idea what or whom you're talking about.'

'You lie!' I cried out in rage.

'It's the God's honest truth.' Now, at last, some indignation. 'Nobody is paying me a farthing. I don't know any Mackenzies.'

'You were there at Euston when I took the train to Glasgow. You must have been spying for them then.'

Her shoulders sagged. 'I never saw you at Euston station. That must have been a coincidence. I would have been taking a connecting train to go back to Kent, where I live.'

I gaped at her. This was getting weirder by the minute. 'So . . . then, why?'

She sighed and looked wretched. 'It wasn't you I wanted to talk to at first. It was your friend. I saw the two of you go about together a few months back and remembered you. Since then I've come into the city from time to time, hoping to speak to her. Then, finally, I got my chance, and I made a mess of it.'

'My friend?' For a preposterous moment, I thought she was talking about Arthur Rosewell. No, wait: 'her'. That couldn't be right. 'You mean *Eva*?'

She nodded. 'Last time I saw her was in a department store. She was at the counter, waiting to pay. I think she was buying a hat.'

Wait a minute . . .

'She wasn't expecting to see me, and oh! the look on her face. She was horrified, I could tell. All the colour drained from her, and she fled. I wish she had waited. All I wanted to do was apologise. You see, I said something terrible about her. I said—'

'You said, "God is unjust if she dies a quiet death,"' I finished for her. 'That was pretty terrible, all right.' It was her. Christopher's mother. Obeah woman. Lilian the Witch. And the same woman I had seen trotting after Brigadier McCrum that night in Euston Square!

'Tonight is a bad night for you, nah? Your son a year dead. And you running after the man who sent him back to battle? Yes, I saw you, last August! Why are you coming to shows like mine? Why you sniffing around McCrum? Acting like the Virgin Mary getting licky-licky with Pontius Pilate? You should mourn decently, at home.'

'*Decently?*' She almost spat the word. 'Perhaps I've had enough of decency. Of having bricks thrown in my window. Of being cut dead in the street. Of having bakers and fishmongers in my village refuse to serve me because "your boy's a conchie." Why should I be decent? How can I grieve when according to them my son didn't die in the correct manner? Might as well go out.' She looked down at her hands. 'As for McCrum,' she added in a lower voice, 'I have my reasons.'

Crowds were beginning to spill out of the doors, drunk, manically cheerful. As they passed us by, they blocked the light and obscured Lilian Shandlin's face. The wind got up and blew their coats about.

'"Conchie"? I thought he enlisted?' I was confused.

'Eventually, yes, but try telling *them* that,' she responded bitterly. 'Try telling them to ease up after he's actually dead. Try telling them you're not apologising for his non-combatant role. Try complaining to the authorities about the transfer that killed him, then being told to stop wasting their time. Because you're "egregious". Because you ought to shut up and smile. I'd already lost my elder son in the South African War, and now this.' The light suddenly returned, bathing her face in a gloomy yellow. Her eyes looked bruised, but dry. Discreetly, I looked around for Frank Bates. He had promised to hail a taxi to take Miss Sparrow and me home, but there was no sign of him. I wished he'd come. I did not want to be sucked into this woman's misery.

'I have to go,' I said.

'I know about your boy too.'

That pulled me up sharp. 'What do you know about him?'

She jerked her head at the gate. 'You're leaving, yes? I have a cab waiting. Get in and I'll tell you.'

I quickly declined. Even knowing her true identity, I still wasn't convinced that I wouldn't be exchanging a watery grave in the Clyde for one in the Thames.

'All right. Tomorrow, then.' Mi Gad, this woman was like a limpet. 'Shall we say Brompton Cemetery at half past four?'

A cemetery? I was about to refuse even more firmly, but then, almost in a whisper, she added, 'I promise I'll make it worth your while.' I swear she saw me waver. 'Entirely up to you, of course. I'll wait an hour. It was a pleasure to hear you sing, Miss Percival.'

'How do you know my—'

She smiled slightly. 'Programme. We all got one on entry. Goodbye.' She stalked off, presumably to her car. As the night swallowed her up, I heard a flapping of coat, a rustle of keys that indicated Frank Bates had found me at last. Hot on his heels followed Miss Sparrow, none too amused. I recalled that my belongings were still in the building. She'd like that even less.

'Where were you?' she demanded, 'and who was that?' Mrs Shandlin's car was moving off.

'I have a small idea of who she is,' I said, watching the head-lights curve away, 'but I think I'm about to find out more.'

THE FOLLOWING AFTERNOON, in spite of the groaning and pleading of my better instincts, I made my way to Kensington, and from there to Brompton Cemetery. I fervently wished Lilian Shandlin had picked somewhere else; Jamaicans don't have much truck with cemeteries. Too many duppies, too much bad air. When we were pickney dem, Merry warned me never to point at a grave, or the offending finger would rot and fall off. The only remedy was to bite it straightaway.

My friend, you can imagine I had many thoughts about this woman and what she might want of me. Life experience had told me that people like Lilian Shandlin do not generally give away something for nothing. But the old tug had set itself under my heart, and the siren words *I promise to make it worth your while* drove me forward.

I came in by the South Lodge entrance and immediately got lost. I found myself alone in a place the like of which I had feared all my life, with dusk beginning to fall. I wandered along the paths with great foreboding, staying clear of the graves because the thought of raising those spirits with my clodhopper feet gave me the shivers. I resolved that if I didn't clap eyes on Mrs Shandlin within the next five minutes, I would go home. But just as I had that thought, I found her, in the cemetery's military section.

She was standing by the railings, a wisp of cigarette smoke rising from her hand and what looked like a small case at her feet. Apart from the two of us, there wasn't a soul to be seen. The monuments to officers from past conflicts were far larger and grander than the new war graves: curlicues of vanity, moss-covered crosses and mausoleums boasting of faraway conquests. Nevertheless, their battles and reputations had been forgotten in the wake of more recent horrors, and they were left largely to nature and the occasional attention of the groundskeeper.

Mrs Shandlin must have heard my step because she raised her non-smoking hand in acknowledgement. As I drew closer, I could see she was agitated. Every inch of her stood tense and untranquil, like a wild deer waiting for a predator to emerge.

'I'm glad you came,' she said. 'I thought you mightn't.'

'So did I,' was my honest reply, earning a short laugh before she directed me to sit down beside her on a stone bench, laying her coat down so I could sit comfortably. 'Won't you be cold?' I asked her. A brief shake of the head. 'I'm never cold. Since both my boys were murdered by this lying State, I have enough rage to set the whole of London on fire.'

Lard a mercy. I sat down, kissing my teeth in dismay. Teetotaller that I mostly was, I wanted a drink all of a sudden. Sybil's little flask of gin would have come in handy.

Mrs Shandlin unfastened the locks of the case and handed me a slim file, along with a small torch with a spring-loaded button that reminded me of my time among the military.

'What's this?'

'Just open it.' I noticed she had an odd way of sitting. Both her knees were bent at a slight angle, ankles and feet lifted off the floor. And she stank of cigarette smoke. She was a strange mixture of social confidence and personal diffidence, old age and youthful mannerisms. I could not fathom her.

The manila cover had only a series of letters and numbers on the top right-hand corner: KV-2-2154. I flipped it open. The first page was a mimeographed document barely readable in the fading light, so I brought the torch close and squinted, then read aloud: '"15th August 1914, meeting in 78 Gordon Square, London, along with Ottoline Morrell, Lytton Strachey and others" – what's this about?'

'Keep going.' Her voice was deep and gravelly.

Cha, I was curious, so I read on: '"Subject spoke at length on Kitchener, detailing his wish that the Field Marshal perish. Subject's brother fought in South African War and spread misinformation about Kitchener's actions there" . . . can't read this bit . . . "Mr Strachey urged 'tone it down', said that organising a petition would be enough."' I handed her back the file and switched off the torch. 'Your Christopher was under surveillance?'

'Yes. From MI5. Standard enough for anti-war activism. Given who was in the room, the agent probably did a job lot on the files.' The old woman chuckled. 'Lytton Strachey refused to enlist. They asked him what he would do if a German soldier assaulted his sister. He said he'd come between them.'

I was silent.

'You're shocked at my saying things like that?' She lit up another cigarette, gesturing to me to indicate I could have one. I shook my head. 'You're right,' she said. 'It's rather a disgusting habit for ladies, isn't it? I used to be a such a nice, compliant old woman myself. Then McCrum and his henchmen did for my son and I got mean. Besides,' she looked at me sidelong, 'a predilection is not a perversion, is it? Strachey is a man who likes men, that's all. McCrum, now, he—'

I put up a hand. 'You don't have to tell me. I've met him, in the field hospital in France. We had to rescue a boy from his clutches.' Robin's pale face swam before me again. *He's a cunt.* He certainly repelled *me*; how on earth could this woman bear to be around him? The file did not explain it.

'Interesting, that he was so brazen that time.' Mrs Shandlin took a deep drag from her cigarette. 'It's an open secret, but he's got a lot to hide. Anyone who threatens his secrecy is in trouble. And if there's a file on record, so much the better to discredit them.'

The dusk deepened around us. I thought I heard a ship hooting a long, mournful, low D, but I must have been imagining things; ships didn't venture that far upstream, did they? The acoustic unnerved me: I did not understand it, or trust my own ears any more.

'We had a nickname for you,' I said. 'Eva and I.'

A sharp intake of breath. 'Really? What was it?'

'Because you put obeah – a curse – on her, we called you Lilian the Witch.'

For a second there was dead silence, then she chuckled softly. 'Really? Dear God. You flatter me if you think I have that kind of power.' She took another drag of her cigarette. 'There was no magic getting hold of that file. I was rather naïve, in fact. Wrote several letters to McCrum's office and then when I got no response, presented myself at Whitehall where he works.'

'He in the secret service?' I swallowed back a cough. This air was damp.

'Yes. Although they don't call it that. Security branch, something like that, quite high up. Not because he's any good, mind you.' She leaned over to me and dropped her voice to a whisper. 'They promote each other, you understand? There's a whole ring of them. McCrum is their pimp. He procures the boys, and the rest ...' Her voice trailed off. 'The rest indulge their pleasures once the boys are captured and brought to fine rooms all over London. They're poor, of course: foundlings, homeless boys, orphans. They're careful to pick the ones that won't be missed.'

That had me sucking in my breath and kissing my teeth again, hard. I remembered how McCrum had thought the French pickney was an orphan. How Robin had been so scared of him. 'If so many people know this, why does he not get caught?'

'His associates are too powerful. They need him to shield them. Men in Cabinet. Judges. High-ranking military. Secret Service. Even ... ' She stopped herself. 'Just look up his old prep-school class. They know each other from way back. Nobody dares cross them. Lieutenant Commander Magnanti in the Bureau tried once. He was in the Navy, so McCrum got him transferred to second-in-command of a paddle steamer bringing supplies to prisoners at Kut-al-Amara.'

If it were true, I was darkly impressed by McCrum's inventive spite.

'The Turks sank it, and McCrum destroyed the file Magnanti had on him. That's what they do. Send people back into war, just like they did with Christopher. Deploy them to a fatal mission. Destroy the evidence. Keep some oily solicitor on retainer to sue for libel if talk spreads.' She sighed deeply. 'Power protects power. My poor boy. He didn't have a clue.'

'If he didn't know, why did they go after him?'

'Because he was very mouthy at his tribunal.' *I wonder where he got that from?* 'Looked straight across at McCrum and said, "I know exactly what you are." He didn't, but McCrum thought he did, and so his fate was sealed. I was there, you see.' For the first time since our meeting her voice broke slightly. 'I was there.'

What a dreadful story! I thought of Eva, of the long hours she had spent writing *her* account of things, trying to make sense of such a senseless event. Then I thought of Reginald, who I had warned about not going down the same road. He was vulnerable enough out there with the white Englishmen he served under. Imagine him in the middle of that den of vipers!

I felt suffocated by horror. This elderly creature beside me, enveloped in fug in the middle of these moss-covered gravestones – why, she seemed only half real. Her tale read like some lurid story rejected from *The Union Jack*, not a sober recounting of loss during wartime. Spies, perverts, ha'penny drama. *The woman is sick*, I told myself. Look at her hollow cheeks, the rings around her eyes.

Then I recalled my own meeting with McCrum, the one I had just spoken of. When I did, suddenly nothing of Lilian Shandlin's account felt strange.

'Who told you all this?'

'The man who destroyed Lieutenant Commander Magnanti's file. A junior adjutant called Tulloch. When I went to the War Office, I got turned away by another of McCrum's men. Oh, I was a disgrace to British motherhood, how dare I dishonour the real heroes, how egregious. The usual.' She coughed. 'I'm afraid I did respond to their shaming. I was quite discomposed, and in public.

I didn't think the tears of an old lady roused pity in the hearts of men, but Mr Tulloch was passing, and, well it worked.'

I said nothing. *My* tears, rarely shed, had never aroused pity in a single man in England, and possibly only one in Scotland. I didn't believe a word of her story. I guessed she'd bribed him.

'He'd heard me mention Christopher and guessed who I was. Ushered me into his office once the coast was clear. He's terrified himself, you see. McCrum's gotten a position as a supervising commander in the Homeland 6th Division, so that he can supervise the sea-scout patrols on the coastline. Guess whose son is in the sea scouts? That's the unwritten bargain. Commit crimes for me, and I leave your son untouched.' Mrs Shandlin stretched out her hand. 'Tulloch trusts me, for some odd reason. Perhaps because I'm so powerless, he knows I can't get him in trouble. Hence the file. Cigarette?' Again? I pointed to my throat. 'Ah, yes. Your voice. Very rich and full. I'm dreadfully unmusical, but I would have thought from your tone that you were an opera singer.'

'I hope to be. But, *as you know*, I've had some problems.'

'Indeed.' Her voice was softer now. 'As I know.' For once she abandoned her own cigarette and busied herself looking at her fingernails. 'Overheard you.' Her words were barely distinct over the ringing of a bell. The cemetery and gardens would close soon.

'When?'

'You were sitting on a bench in Parson's Green, talking to . . . Dominic? Is that his name? Him or his ghost, since you were alone. While I, well, I was crouching in the bushes like a vagrant. Even after I knew you weren't the person I wanted, I got into the habit of following you. Pathetic, I know. Creeping around the edges of other people's lives.'

I remembered the rustling, how I'd mistaken it for a fox.

'What struck me was hearing you say you'd break commandments for your little boy. That was the first thing I'd heard in a year that made any sense to me.'

A wave of anger prickled across my skin. Could nothing I cherished not be taken and cheapened by these people? How dared she! 'You had no right.' I managed eventually. 'That was private.'

'In a public park?'

'You knew it was not for your ears! And no, you shouldn't be following me. I have every right to press charges. Your business is with Eva, not me.' That was bravado, of course. Lilian Shandlin might see herself as powerless, but she was several degrees of power above me. Our encounter with the woman police constable had made that clear enough.

'I can't talk to Eva. If you saw the look she gave me! The whole thing's broken. I can't fix it. God help me, I wouldn't know where to start,' Mrs Shandlin declared, with real anguish. 'You're right. It's a terrible curse. I was upset, but that's no excuse.'

The bell started ringing again, and soon I saw the watchman himself, his instrument in one hand, a gas lantern in the other, face obscured by his hat and upturned coat collar as he passed us on the gravel path. *Crunch crunch crunch* went his boots on the stones. All around the cemetery that man would ring his one-note bell, sending the duppies back to their homes and the mortal beings back to theirs.

'I told you I could help you get your boy back. I wasn't lying.'

I turned to her once more. 'Thank you, but I'm not sure it's a good idea.' She waved away that one. 'Nonsense. Why else are you here?'

She had a point.

'We'll have to leave this place soon. Why don't you walk with me?' She offered me her elbow, which amused me, given my relative youth, but I accepted. We left Brompton Cemetery and walked east to Redcliffe Square Gardens, past Federau's pawnshop, where the WE ARE RUSSIANS sign had been recently repainted. Eva knew the area and had once told me that Old Man Federau had put it up to stop the locals thinking his was a German business and smashing it in. It was just about visible in the dark, but Mrs Shandlin didn't comment on it. Of course, just because Eva and she had *one* shared obsession didn't mean they shared all of them.

I shouldn't be here, I told myself. *I swore I would move on.* And yet here I was, taking this woman's arm, jumping like a trained dog when offered a biscuit. Where was my resolve, my character? In what universe could I trust Lilian Shandlin, with her misery, her file, her torch, her cigarettes? Still, I wanted to hear what she had to say.

'I met a woman when I was in the Mothers' Union – back when I was still eligible for membership.' *Now* some wit for sure, but cha, so bitter! 'A Mrs Gunning. Irish. A perfectly respectable retired head housekeeper in Poplar. Except that for years she's been rescuing children from institutions after the State removes them from their families. I could engage her to find him for you, you know. I have ample means.'

'My son was not removed by the State,' I interjected, feeling some bitterness of my own, 'but by family intrigue.'

She stopped dead in the street and turned me to face her. 'Was it wickedly done?'

Something of her rage must have infected me; what was ice in her blood turned to fire in mine. 'Yes! A thousand times yes.'

'Then you have no choice but to retrieve him.' She was stern. 'If he is alive, you cannot ignore this chance. You are his mother.'

'It's not as simple as that.' My finger traced my coat collar. 'My life is in danger if I try. I've been told by multiple people to move on.'

'And have you?' There were few street lights and the moon such a tiny sliver it was barely more than new, but somehow I could see every lineament of her face as her eyes bored into me. 'Have you?' she repeated, her voice harsh as splinters.

I didn't have to say no. My silence told her everything. She placed both her hands on my shoulders. 'Listen to me, Miss Percival – Lucia, if you permit.' She cleared her throat. 'If you have borne a child, heard their first cry, fed them, held them, loved them – you'll never "move on" a day in your life if you lose them. What a thoughtless, contemptible phrase. Dreamed up by a government salesman. You may grieve as long as you please, in whatever manner you please. Anyone who tells you to forget that child is more witless than a turnip. Now.' She released me. 'Are you in, or are you out?'

'Am I . . . what?' I was bewildered.

'Oh, I'm ahead of myself, I do apologise. Your problem can be solved, but I will be asking a favour in return.'

Of course.

'It concerns McCrum. You'll wonder why I've been following him around all this time.' And for the first time she seemed awkward, tugging at the edge of one glove with the other hand. As if I were her sweetheart and she a little coy in my presence, trying to convince me of her motives. Then – 'I need you to help me kill him.'

What? I staggered backwards. *Mad obeah woman fi tru'!*

'Please, hear me out. I've planned it all reasonably well. A lonely old woman with no hope and plenty of money, don't you know.' She resumed walking, the crazy woman, as if she'd just made a comment on the weather! I told myself that she was cracked, that I could humour her, that we were not so far from the nearest Tube station. 'I did consider the alternatives. But Tulloch did a good job warning me off. No reporter will touch this. There was one young fellow tried, and McCrum threatened to sue his newspaper. Then the proprietor got untraceable telephone calls late at night, and the young man vanished. No. Nothing can dislodge McCrum. He has his poisonous finger everywhere. So, I've cultivated a pseudonym, changed my hair and appearance slightly, and made myself his adoring factotum. Honestly didn't think it would work, and the first time I approached him looking for him to cut the ribbon at a Women's Institute meeting, I nearly wanted to vomit. He's a vain man, and he thinks old women are stupid, so he fell for it.'

'You have to give me a moment,' I declared. 'You suck up to the man who more or less killed your son, sacrifice your pride, your dignity . . . all so you can kill him in return?' I saw a passer-by approach, and dropped my voice.

'Exactly,' Lilian Shandlin replied, not dropping hers at all, 'but I can't do it alone. I need someone to help. Provide lookout, moral support. You've been in my situation. Well, as the Romish folk say, purgatory for you, limbo for me. Your soul is saved, mine is lost.' She chuckled, in that same dark fashion as with her earlier joke about the Mothers' Union. 'Understand that one way or the other, this *will* happen.' She leaned in again, and in the dim light her expression was so satanic I almost fled up the street in horror. Her voice now was barely above a whisper.

'If you believe nothing else I tell you, believe this: I want that man to die like a dog for what he did to my son.'

17

ROYAL ACADEMY OF MUSIC, NOVEMBER 1917

'Miss Percival, can you concentrate please? That intonation was way off.'

All right, Miss Slade, just one minute...

'You need to pay attention. Your phrasing is all over the place today.'

I was tired out from a poor night's sleep, had been dousing my parched throat all day with water, and now here I was in the Royal Academy with Miss Slade in a worse humour than ever.

'The Schubert!' she roared, in the tone one might say, 'The hanging!' and launched into those relentless right-hand triplets that signal the approach of the Erl-King. Her fingers could barely sustain the octaves she was playing them at such speed, and she was gasping nearly as hard as if she were the vocalist.

Miss Slade once told me that Schubert had been a choirboy and possessed a wonderful understanding of the human voice. I would wager that Schubert had never had to stay up late singing torch songs in a grotty smoky club then practise late at night in a dismal shed, rushing through that last diminished seventh before running back inside.

Miss Slade needn't have worried about me though. After the night I'd had with that creature Lilian Shandlin, I was well in the mood for the Erl-King that day. The father riding through the dark wood, clutching his son. The boy, the high end of my range, pleading with him for protection from the Erl-King. That nyaamps of a father ignoring him! Then the Erl-King's wheedling. He was a spirit who would take your pickney away or replace him with a changeling. Just like McCrum, who took children away and defiled them.

I want that man to die like a dog . . .

The sweet sickly evil of the Erl-King poured into my vocal as I tried to entice the frightened little boy with flowers, games, dancing daughters. I was like a woman possessed. And so was Miss Slade. Those octave triplets were no longer hers but the soft pounding of hooves in a wintry forest, pines laden with snow, the father urging the beast forward with his crop. I no longer sang the song: I *was* the song. Disregarding the rules Miss Slade had set me – hands by your *sides*, Miss Percival! – I let them fly free, paced the floorboards, felt the icy wind on my cheeks as I drew deep breaths from my core. I voiced them all: father, son, spirit – cha, what an unholy trinity!

When it came to the Erl-King's threat to the helpless pickney – I love you, I'll have you, if not willingly, then by force – I rendered the line with such an unmusical snarl that my teeth clenched. The anger that came from my throat must have shocked Miss Slade, because her piano dropped for nearly half a bar. *The horse's hooves are tripping up, Domi! Come on, man, we gwaan get out of here!* The last line was marked on my score as 'recitative'. I half sang it, biting off each note: 'In his arms the child – was – dead.' Too late. All done.

After the last chord, Miss Slade said nothing for fifteen seconds, just massaged her knuckles. I was shaky and nauseated, and the colour was draining out of the walls, piano and even Miss Slade's mauve cardigan. I wanted to know her thoughts, but my mouth had dried up. The power that passed through me singing that dreadful song had burned me. I could barely fix my gaze on her.

'Miss Percival.' Her voice felt like it was coming from ten thousand miles away. 'That gave me the willies.'

'Miss Slade . . .'

She wasn't listening. In a harsh, crowlike voice she ripped me up for breaking the rules. For moving my hands. For being too expressive. Even in my unsteady state, I could hear an undertone of fear in it all. 'For God's sake,' she concluded, her voice sounding to my ears as if she were shouting through a tin can, 'I'm telling you this for your own good!'

'No, you're not,' I said, my tongue thick as a whale in my mouth. 'You're telling me because you want to own me. Put a choke chain around my neck. You're just the same as the rest of them.' I barely got the last sentence out before the corkscrews in my head intensified and my legs would no longer bear my weight.

My fall seemed slow, but the hand on my elbow came quickly. She crossed the room seemingly without a sound. 'Breathe. Head over your knees.' She smelled of Pears Soap.

She put me in a sitting position, pushing my head forward, slipping her hand onto my belly. Then the command came. 'Remember your exercises. Inhale' – I tried to breathe deep into my belly while she pressed her hand down on it. 'Exhale' – I pursed my lips, letting the air out as slowly as I could, her hand rigid. It was not easy; my lips were trembling. Again, she said, 'Inhale,' and I did; then 'Exhale' – and so on. It took a few more cycles of this before my breathing came back to normal.

When I came to properly, and was sitting on the piano stool and sipping water from a chipped glass, Miss Slade regarded me sternly, her arms folded. 'I pushed you too hard. Something happened, I could tell, and I pushed you regardless. I had this crazy idea that given the right piece you could subsume whatever pain you were feeling into your art. That you could be a conductor for my pain too. But now, look at you.' She shook her head. 'I thought I could get you back on track for the Associated Board exam. But no, we're losing you. To the jazz bands, yes, but it's not only that, is it?'

I clung to that glass of water as if it were a lifebelt. I couldn't tell Miss Slade about last night. About that woman and her stories. How she had smiled and once again put a gloved hand on my shoulder, murmured, 'I'll write to you, my dear,' then disappeared into the night, just outside my gate. How my sleep had been disturbed in the hours since then, how all the dreams about Domi had returned, coupled with Robin, McCrum, even Christopher, whom I had never seen. All because of a woman whose silhouette I could have sworn I saw disappear before she got to the end of the road. 'Lilian the Witch' — for sure!

'We'll drop that piece from the repertoire,' Miss Slade said, then, looking away, 'I will never again use your voice to earth my own pain like that. I'm ashamed of myself. You had every right to chastise me.' After the energy of the accompaniment she had played, her body was slumped and tired. She moved like a woman twice her age. Again I thought of Lilian Shandlin, who really *was* an old woman but who moved with a deftness and lightness entirely absent from this woman thirty years her junior. The rage that kept *her* warm absolutely exhausted the rest of us.

Damn Eva to hell for bringing that woman into my life!

'I had plenty of electricity of my own, Miss Slade. Lightning bolts of it,' I said without rancour. None of this mess was her fault, after all.

'Haven't we all, my dear?' she said, with a wry smile that made her look older and nicer at the same time. Her kindness made me feel almost a little guilty for going straight from my lesson at the Royal Academy to the devilish activity she had warned me against, my jazz scores concealed in one of the classical books.

When I arrived – late – at the Albert Rooms, Evelyn Sparrow shot me a look of disapproval – 'The President of Liberia is already here!' I ran down to the dressing rooms to get changed and apply my eyeshadow and lipstick. The musicians' rooms were scented with men's cedarwood hair oils and the most exotic ladies' perfumes. Having not eaten, I felt as if I were drunk breathing them all in. Then, out of nowhere, jarring and uninvited, that voice: *You will never move on a single day of your life.*

Never mind the President of Liberia, or lipstick. I needed some air. I needed to forget that woman.

I escaped down the hallway to a quiet bathroom, plain enough for staff or servants, a row of water-worn but clean enamel sinks to one side, but no mirror. Closing my eyes, I pressed the lids hard with my fingers, until I saw feverish white-red splotches of light. Then I turned on the tap at full force and splashed my face again and again, until the cold woke me up and I felt less exhausted and more human.

Once back in the dressing room, with my face dry and lipstick on, and the long dress with its diamanté detail shimmying down my body, I put on my most dazzling smile, pulled a fake gardenia out of a vase and put it behind my ear, and made my way on stage beside Evelyn and the musicians. I was happy to see an audience that was at least fifty per cent African, and I didn't miss a note.

The evening was a roaring success; the aforementioned President of Liberia even got up and danced to 'At the Jazz Band Ball.'

Nobody would have known that even as I sang in close harmony with Evelyn, I heard that Schubert in my brain and had to concentrate hard to tamp down those hammering triplets.

During the interval, I stared blankly at my reflection in the dressing room's mirror while several people asked me if I were all right. 'I am well,' I responded mechanically to their enquiries, until they went away shaking their heads and frowning. Even Evelyn Sparrow looked a little concerned. 'You're trying to do too much,' she said, leaning over the counter as I played idly with the eyeshadow compact and lipstick holder. 'Arthur told me he's worried about you.'

Blouse and skirt! So Arthur Rosewell wanted to fas inna mi business but didn't want to walk out with me any more? He could get lost as far as I was concerned. 'He could have told me that himself' was all I allowed myself to say.

'Don't blame him, hon. I was the one who told him you were overdoing it. I was worried.' She put her hand on my shoulder. I clasped it briefly but said nothing. Many times, I was grateful to our small community for its support, but sometimes the feeling of being watched and monitored felt suffocating. My family was scattered, but I seemed to have found a new one in its place, with all its blessings and constraints.

I thanked her, although I was annoyed, not to mention a little jealous that she and Arthur were in communication. Not that I could fault her for that. She was trying in her own way to help. But I needed a bit of peace in my life. Not this jumble of semi-coherent thoughts with their sharp edges.

When I got back to the flat, I was beyond tired, but sleep evaded me. I had the sudden desire to make myself a cup of tea. Maybe I had finally 'gone native', I laughed to myself. So, I made a fist of it and drank the watery stuff. Then I read the Bible. Following that, I muttered chromatic scales under my breath.

Following that, I recited the Lord's Prayer several times. When even that failed, I got up and paced around the room. (It hardly took four steps to get from one end to the other.) Then I (mentally) sang a round of arpeggios, major, minor, diminished seventh. Augh! Still no good.

I remembered when I was only a pickney and had bad dreams at night, my mother would come into my room, her skin warm beneath her nightgown, her body smelling of verbena and musk, and would sing to me, softly so my father wouldn't hear. He hated when she used dialect.

'Chi chi a bud oh,' she would sing.

'Some a dem a holla, some a bawl,' I would answer.

Then she would name a bird, and I would sing the chorus again. She would list through the whole sequence of birds, me echoing the same response: 'Some a blue foot . . . a tintin . . . a black bud . . . a chickman chick . . . a pea dove . . . a cling-cling . . .' I always fell asleep before she finished listing all the birds.

This time was different: my mother was not there, and I was a grown woman. I would have to remember them myself, and perhaps even add a few new ones, for even in this barbarous dirty city, birds were known to sing. Each line bubbled out of my memory: my mother's and my own, mine and Domi's. The discipline needed to recall each verse calmed my mind, chased away that fiendish Erl-King and banished Lilian the Witch's siren song from my mind.

Finally, those awful banging triplets stopped pounding in my head, and sleep came over me like lapping waves, just as it had done when my mother sang to me as a child. I forgot that my mother and I no longer spoke and once again became as innocent as a child.

I must have drifted off soon afterwards because when I next woke it was morning, bitterly cold, and real birds were singing in the bare branches of the trees. I clambered out of bed and onto my knees and said my prayers. The floorboards dug into my bare knees and left ridges on my skin.

I resolved to live as Christian a life as I could under the circumstances I had been given. To ignore the Devil's voice inviting me to indulge in memories that would only break me and the pathetic revenge fantasies of a broken old woman who was nobody's mother now, and who would never sing lullabies to anyone again. In my prayers, I could leave her to God's mercy and comfort. What became of her would have nothing to do with me.

PART II

PART II

18

LONDON, 1950

I can't believe you're back for more, my friend. After last night, when I apologised for keeping you so late, you were barely able to reply. I was worried about you: you seemed very drunk, or dazed. My story is a heavy one to tell, true. It weighed on me so that while I was drinking my third ... fourth ... fifth glass – all right, thank you – I just had to kick off my shoes and put my poor tired feet up. You raised your eyebrows, but let me tell you, if you tried to speak your life story wearing ladies shoes that itch your heels and give you bunions, you would soon follow suit! You don't know what it is like, a woman's life.

Augh, that stuff though. Scotch. Named after Scotland, as if I hadn't had enough of that country. It burns the tongue and scorches the insides. A woman as cultured as myself should not be barefoot and drinking whisky. Rum is what we should drink tonight. Have you some? Oh, you are a resourceful fellow.

About what you heard: it is a heavy story, yes, and no lighter for the listener to hear. But you listened, and made notes, and here you are again with your notebook and pen, ready to scribble down some more. I admire your stamina. After we left off last night, I was fit for nothing. I spread heagle pon di bed sheets and pass out till morning just so! I don't regret it though. Talking to you took the edge off my great anguish.

Did you know I went to rehearsal today? I wasn't going to, as you know. But after yesterday – the shock of my bad news, then you pouring me whiskies and getting me to talk – I felt a little softer around the edges. I thought of that old conductor. Couldn't bear him looking at me so sadly. So I went and made a good fist of Mr Strauss. My voice was fine; it just didn't belong to me. But I'm a professional so nobody noticed.

You look like you have something important to say. A lot of young men think that. They're usually mistaken. But since you are here, and want to hear the rest of my story, you had better sit down. Let's start with the Armistice . . .

19

LONDON, 11 NOVEMBER 1918

The examiner, Mr Charles Kirby, a tall grey-bearded man, had been putting me through my paces since half past nine. I had sung my way through the entire range of scales, from A below C to two octaves above, then a defiantly English catalogue of Dowland, Purcell and Thomas Arne. No Schubert, thankfully. I was not worried about what grade Mr Kirby put on my card: I had prepared well and had given him my best. I could do no more.

Miss Slade had decided to defer the exam for a year to allow my voice, and spirits, recover. Over the course of that year I was able to abandon my jazz singing, and my voice regained its former suppleness of range, timbre and dynamic. At first it had felt strange, as if I were a straying husband returning to a cold wife after a red-hot year with a beautiful mistress, but after a while that whole world felt so very distant. From time to time I've wondered what would have happened if I had continued on down that road – I suspect I would have got on quite well – but I do not believe it was what God intended for me and so I am content with my choice.

As a result of my vocal prowess, I managed to secure a few engagements, mostly with fellow students. The previous Christmas I joined a small chamber choir and sang carols with them, with the promise of a solo the following year. At a 'Promising Debuts' concert in St Giles-without-Cripplegate, I sang two Handel mezzo arias in Italian.

Events had put matters in sad perspective. That past spring, the Spanish flu had torn through our little community of musicians. Mozart's *Gran Partita* serenade no longer floated out the windows: the boys in the wind ensemble, who stayed in the same boarding house in Muswell Hill, had all been found one morning by their distressed landlady, their bodies stiff and almost frozen in the winter cold. They had died within hours of each other. A young pianist who occasionally accompanied me when Miss Slade was indisposed suffered the same fate just two weeks later. The obituary pages now had more civilians than war dead. Soldiers dying overseas, that we were all used to by now, but young lads, clarinettists, people to whom we had cheerfully said good morning only days before? It felt wrong, and frightening.

Eva had requested that I look out for Sybil, and just before the epidemic established itself I decided I should do as asked. We fashioned a loose arrangement that had me calling to Moscow Road once a month or so. The first few occasions were polite and stiff, then one day I called without giving advance notice. To my great shock, Sybil's butler, Mr Wilson, answered the door wearing a sanitary mask, and Jessie, her maid, appeared declaring that Miss Roma had 'taken a turn' and that Sybil was with her. 'She's not expected to survive the night, my lady tells me. And I'm frightened my lady will fall sick too.' She too was wearing a mask; 'my lady' had insisted on it, she sighed, to the point of rudeness.

I left Moscow Road greatly agitated. Much as I had never warmed to Sybil, I could not wish such a fate on her or her companion, Roma (as I was now instructed to call her.) As it happened (thank God!), she did not succumb to the illness, and Roma survived. A week later, I learned the whole story. When Roma realised her symptoms, she took a room in a nearby hotel, pinned a note to her door saying, 'Please do not disturb,' locked herself in, and then, 'ever the *bloody* journalist', started to take notes on her deteriorating condition.

'The goose thought it would be a great last feature! "My Flu Diary!"' Sybil later told me. 'She cared more about that than surviving.'

Sybil found out where Roma had gone and, with Mr Wilson in tow, thundered up the stairs past a shouting concierge, ripped the paper off the door and had Mr Wilson break the door down. She found that lady supine in bed, accompanied by a notebook covered in scribbles, marked by date and time. The earliest ones were quite readable, but the ones noted in later days had trailed off into nonsense, then terminated altogether.

Roma had gazed at Sybil, 'like a stricken deer, my poor love,' and begged her to file the copy. Sybil, anguished at being unable to rush to her beloved's side for fear of contagion, shouted, 'Don't be such an idiot. Nobody's going to touch that paper. They'll burn it first.'

Even as ambulance men, masked and gloved, took her away on a stretcher, and cleaners moved in to disinfect the room, Roma continued to plead, the last thing she said before the ambulance doors closed being, 'But the story . . . my notes . . .!'

'And I said, "Hang the bloody notes!"' Sybil concluded over tea in china cups. The drink had gone too, I noticed. No more flasks. 'Another biscuit?'

'Thank you, I'll pass,' I said. 'I'm glad she made it, Sybil.'

To my surprise, her eyes filled with tears. She reached over and pressed my hand. 'You don't know how much it means to hear that. I've been so worried. She could so easily have died. And on top of all that black-book nonsense we had to go through with that horrible little man Pemberton Billing. I think that's why Roma got the flu. She hadn't been sleeping because she was terrified we would end up in court, and she didn't wear her bloody mask the way I told her to. I'm usually the one who's cavalier about these things, but I had to be the sensible person this time.'

'Oh, you mean the Cult of the . . .' I had heard about all this in the newspapers but couldn't quite bring myself to say the word.

'Clitoris. Good golly, I always knew what it was, but now I know what it's *called*.'

Noel Pemberton Billing was the proprietor of a rag called *Vigilante* that had alleged forty-seven thousand 'perverts of Sodom and Lesbia' were being blackmailed by the Germans to undermine the war effort. I know, I know, you shake your head. The hysteria in those days . . . He wrote an article about a Canadian exotic dancer named Maud Allan, a friend of Mrs Asquith, saying she was in bed with the Germans too, and called it 'The Cult of the Clitoris'. When she sued him, he won! That was what had terrified Roma.

I generally paid little attention to scandal and gossip, but even I had heard of it. It all made me wonder if those who loved others of the same sex were more the victims of society's ills than the instigators. Seeing Sybil and Roma so persecuted and afraid made me feel differently about the whole thing than I had before.

'I'm glad to say, Miss Percival,' Mr Charles Kirby said warmly, bringing me back to the present moment, 'that your ordeal is over. Well done.'

'How did I do, sir?' I ventured.

'I'm pleased to say you have passed with distinction. Your tone is exceptional, and I can tell you put the work in. What a lovely end to this long and terrible war, thanks to your beautiful voice.'

Tremulous joy filled me. I had always known I was good, but that is not the same as having it confirmed by a dispassionate observer. But . . . was what he said true? I gestured at the window, where a racket outside was growing. 'Is it really over, Mr Kirby?'

'It really is.' He rose and handed me my sheet.

'Thank God,' I said, taking it and scanning it briefly. I gasped at the mark. It was a full score of 150. I looked up at him. 'Full marks? You really mean this?'

'Be quiet, or he'll change his mind,' Miss Slade cut in. 'He's the toughest marker we've ever had.'

'This is the toughest war we've ever had,' I exclaimed. 'I earned every point!'

'Percival!' Miss Slade exclaimed. But Mr Kirby roared with laughter and declared that I certainly had.

'It's a pleasure for me to acknowledge real talent, Miss Percival, and you have that in spades. You deserve to go far, and I hope you do.'

'I have no doubt of it,' chimed in a familiar voice from the doorway.

'Arthur!'

There he was, leaning on the door jamb. He sported a brown single-breasted blazer with the bottom button open, a yellow and blue tie and a flat cap on his head. Nobody, but nobody, would have gotten away with that ensemble but him.

'What you doin' here?' I demanded.

'Just passing,' said he, the cheeky buoy.

'Mr Rosewell,' Mr Kirby shook his hand. Everybody here knew him, it seemed. 'What a delight to see you again. Thought we'd lost you to the war effort.'

'Only for a little while,' Arthur said, avoiding my eye. 'I was kept in reserve long enough that I missed my chance altogether.'

'A little while? More like a year.' That sounded more bitter than I meant it.

'I certainly do owe explanations for my absence. Which I will provide.' Arthur pulled back and leaned against the wall. 'I was thinking, given the happy circumstances, that I could bring you all out to tea.'

Mr Kirby and Miss Slade thanked him but pleaded off, disappearing very dexterously into the corridors of the building and conspiring to leave us two alone. More examinations were due to be held, though from the banging and whistling of the maroon rockets that floated up from the river bank, I doubted that anyone would be in the mood. I did not know what to think or feel about the news and wished for silence and time alone to take it all in.

When Arthur offered his arm, I could not see any way of refusing without causing awkwardness, so I took it, and we ventured out. We walked all the way to the Chelsea Embankment and then towards the bridge. As we approached the river, the crowds were so thick and surged so fast that we were dragged back and forth and Arthur had to pull me close not to lose me. No care about the flu now! We tried conversation and soon abandoned it. There was just too much noise.

The crowds were everywhere: troops on leave kissing their girlfriends, omnibuses full of passengers leaning out the windows and cheering, even patients from Millbank Hospital who had discharged themselves and were limping down the road on crutches. And the rhaatid bugles! They blared ceaselessly, in one long drone. I almost missed Ernie Cuthbert's tuba, which at least had a variety of notes. The river reflected the hellish glow like a puddle. 'I thought this was meant to be peace,' I hollered in Arthur's ear, 'but it's never been so noisy.'

'WHAT?' Arthur hadn't heard a word I'd said.

I looked up. Even though it was still only morning, the clouds were low and the gas lamps switched on – it was a dull day – creating a sky of greyish tea and brown dishwater. Seagulls flocked overhead while fireworks rent the sky. In the daytime, they were surprisingly colourful. I saw a girl feet away from me get swallowed up by two enthusiastic men in uniform. She was whooping and screaming – from fear of the men or joy at the Armistice I couldn't tell. On the river bank, a few bewildered Indians, also in uniform, some turbanned, stood together, arms linked as if they were a little island. Sensible fellows. Hawkers shouted the news, waving the papers in case anyone had somehow missed it: Armistice! Armistice!

Just beyond the bridge I saw a commotion with a motor car and the crumpled, black-clothed body of an old woman half hanging off the front bumper. The familiar white cape of a VAD was bending over her and checking her pulse before shaking her head and standing up once more. A tentative shift in the daylight showed the dead woman's face: soft and blank. The peace had just claimed its first victim.

'Let's get out of here.' Arthur escorted me away from the riverbank, towards Trafalgar Square. There we were confronted by American troops passing by in trucks, waving the Stars and Stripes. Across the upper floors of the Grand Hotel, the banner 'DO YOUR PART WITH WILLING HEART' still hung down. But the willing hearts had a new focus: the Americans. The girls around me went wild at the sight of them, jumping up and down as the GIs blew kisses.

Arthur sucked in his breath, and the arm he linked with mine was tense. He did not cheer, and neither did I. I had heard too many stories about how black people were treated in the States. Not allowed to sit next to a white person on a bus, or use the same restaurant, or even the same bathroom. Arthur told me about sundown towns, where any coloured person present after sunset would be whipped and driven off. How his father lived in fear of the Ku Klux Klan burning his house down and patrolled the perimeters with a shotgun every night. And if a man like Arthur should own a bit of land, or drive a nice car, or look at a white woman in a way a white man imagined he didn't like, the Southerners would tie a noose around his neck and hang him from a tree, cheering as he died. In the merry faces of the American soldiers, I saw too the lynched men's blue lips, knotted tongues, bulging dead eyes. No, I would not cheer them on. Nor could I understand how Arthur ever wanted to be among their number, even in a Negro division. But it was not my place to judge. I had some idea of what it had cost him to get as far as he had socially.

A truckful of GIs veered close. Someone sent a bouquet of pink roses flying up towards them, and the petals exploded on the soldiers' caps and epaulettes. They laughed and threw their caps in the air. Next thing, a pair of bloomers flew over, and the crowd hooted.

I felt Arthur's hand in mine. It was warm and firm. I was glad he was there. Alone among that mob, he understood what I was feeling, as I understood him. Everyone else looked to have lost their mind. Land girl or VAD, shopgirl or society woman, kitchen maid or Lady Muck, it made no difference: they all abandoned propriety and openly, passionately, kissed any man in uniform they could get their hands on. The men's hands roamed everywhere, squeezing breasts and buttocks, devouring necks. Arthur made no verbal comment, but he did wink at me. And retained my hand.

We kept walking until we were out of the din. Somewhere in the chaos of Trafalgar Square my hat had been knocked off my head, and I knew that if my hair got wet it would defy gravity afterwards. Arthur immediately offered me his: a grey wool trilby whose brim fell over my forehead. I kept having to push it up, and nearly didn't hear Arthur enquiring, 'I hear you're working for Dr Alcindor?'

'Yes, at the Infirmary.'

One evening, I confided to my Coterie friends how hard the late-night jazz sessions were on my voice, and Dr Alcindor had offered me a position as an assistant nurse. The pay was eleven shillings a week, a severe reduction on my previous wage even though the work was far harder and more skilled, but he could not spare any more. Nor would I have dreamed of asking.

'He tells me they're full to the brim with flu patients,' Arthur said grimly. 'I hope you're being careful, Lucia.'

'Dr Alcindor would not allow carelessness,' I said. 'We don fresh masks and gowns every time we go on the ward and spray our hands with alcohol solution at the door. He's a stickler.'

'It must be terrible for you, seeing all those sick folk.' He pressed my hand. I wanted to cling on to him and never let go.

'It is. The Spanish flu is a horrible disease. The way they die . . .' I shivered. I didn't want to tell Arthur what I had witnessed in the past three months working for the good doctor. It was somehow worse than what I had seen alongside Robin Mackenzie: the blood that poured out of every orifice, white bodies turning black from lack of oxygen, victims drowned from fluid in their lungs. Nor did I feel able to tell him about the time neighbours broke down the door of a family of six in Crouch End and found them all in one bed, unconscious, the husband already cold. The baby's comforter had been dipped in cough mixture and set in its mouth, as if that might somehow save the little thing. They were all brought to the Infirmary, but we could not rescue any of them.

That one particularly brought me low. The night following that day, and every night for a week after I cried for them. And for little Dominic too. How could I forget him, when illness brought so many dying children to my door? Imagine if my Domi, with his beautiful eyes and his fat little laugh . . . imagine if he were lying on a bed somewhere, surrounded by corpses, in soiled and wet cloths, shivering, dying himself, a drug-soaked comforter in his mouth – and I could not tend to him?

But I could not make inquiries. Robin had made that very clear. At best, I would be arrested. At worst . . . I would be in the Clyde again, at the bottom this time, and not of my own volition. When Lilian Shandlin had taken her leave, she had slipped a card into my hand, detailing her name and address, even as she promised she would write me. It was still on my shelf, slipped in between the pages of *The Care and Feeding of Children*. Every time I had sworn I would throw it away, that it was bad magic, that Eva might see it, never mind that she was away in France – something had always stopped me.

Several times, brought low by that cruel epidemic, I picked up my pen to request her help, then put it down once more. I knew in my heart her promises were like the Erl-King's: empty and dangerous. On the other hand, I was distraught enough to return to Edgar Manning's office in Soho, but after several minutes ringing the doorbell I was informed by a neighbour in a hairnet and dressing gown (at three in the afternoon!) that he had done a 'moonlight flit'. The Metropolitan Police were looking for him in relation to his kneecapping three criminal acquaintances in broad daylight.

She looked a little wistful. 'He was ever so polite, always paid his rent on time. And so well spoken for a coloured man.' She smiled, it never occurring to her that I might take offence. Seeing my disappointment, she added, misapprehending the reason, 'He was a gentleman too. Always considerate to the ladies.' That might have been because he was paying them, I thought uncharitably, but not wanting to put a brother's private business in the street I just thanked her and trudged home.

Now, on the night of the Armistice, Arthur was wise enough not to press me; he merely squeezed my hand again and said, 'You are so brave, Lucia, risking your own health to save lives. I often thought of you when I was in training. I wondered if my cowardice in leaving England – and you – was greater than the cowardice involved in not enlisting.'

'I've come to the conclusion,' I said, briefly thinking of Christopher Shandlin, 'that refusing to enlist takes great courage, but it's courage that goes against the tide so it's not praised.' *They threw a brick in my window. Cut me dead in the street. Called me 'egregious'.*

'That's a good point,' Arthur said. 'I thought I was a coward for not doing my bit, but that was just indoctrination, frankly. I was bored as all-get-out during my officer training. I just wanted to hang out with the brass band. I heard nothing from you, but Freddie Corder kept writing to tell me he missed me.' He looked at me wistfully. 'But I cared more about *you* missing me than Freddie Corder.'

'Then perhaps you could have let me know in person rather than writing a letter and running away?'

'You're absolutely right!' He threw up his hands, releasing mine. 'My trouble is I think too much about giving the right impression and end up doing the wrong thing. Lucia, pull up that hat – I can hardly see you.'

I handed it back to him, willing to chance the weather. 'I haven't seen you for a long time, Arthur. Perhaps we are getting ahead of ourselves.' And yet it had felt right when he took my hand. And he smelled good: a comforting mixture of pipe tobacco and lavender, cedarwood and soap. I liked that he was fastidious. I was drawn to his clean soul, his safety, his natural understanding of me. But for all that, I did not want him to think he could just waltz back in and claim me.

'Perhaps,' he said, recognising my game and pulling back in turn. 'Much has happened, clearly. Freddie mentioned you frequently by the way. Told me Miss Slade quite raves about you.'

'Not to my face, she doesn't.'

He laughed. 'That would be Venetia.'

Keeping up my practice had been hard but worthwhile; throughout the grimness of the work, with all my grief for the flu victims, music was the one thing that kept me sane. Miss Slade drove me as if she were Cleopatra and I a lower-ranking Egyptian, but I was perfectly happy for her to do so. I would have carried that woman all the way from Alexandria to Rome because she liberated me from my own mind. The more she pushed me, the more all other thoughts were consigned into exhausted oblivion.

I finally found out what happened to her fiancé. During the musical performance in St Giles-without-Cripplegate church I mentioned, I was sitting behind three fellow students who had their heads together all the way through the concert, gossiping and whispering. When Miss Slade arrived late and slipped into the second row, one of them exclaimed, 'I say, there's old Vinnie.'

'Isn't she the one that goes about with the new ... protégée?'

'You mean the piccaninny? "Mi sing so good Missis Slade."' The speaker lapsed into sing-song, and they collapsed into snorts and giggles. I balled my fingers into fists and dug my nails into my palm – I would be on stage after the interval, and I had to keep calm. 'You'll have to work a hundred times harder and be fifty times better than everyone else to even win basic respect,' Miss Slade had warned me once. White as she was, she wasn't wrong.

'She's such a joke. I mean, the holes in her stockings.'

'The piccaninny?'

'No, you idiot. Miss Slade. Did you hear what happened to her best boy? It was so disgusting.'

'No! What?'

'Well he was out in . . . Egypt? Tunisia? They're all the same, these coon places. And this tribe of wogs did for him and his company, didn't they? Only they didn't leave it at that . . .' She paused dramatically, and the other two gathered closer still, close enough to kiss. I guessed that the 'tribe of wogs' were the Senussi, who, I knew, were fighting with the Ottomans against the Western Frontier Force.

'They were *shot dead*,' the first girl declared in a dramatic whisper, as if shooting your enemy dead were not a regrettably common custom, 'and then . . .' – she put her programme to her mouth – '. . . their heads were chopped off. Then the natives *cut off* their private parts and stuffed them in their mouths . . .'

'Ugh,' one of her companions exclaimed with distasteful relish.

'. . . and their heads were just *dumped* in the middle of the road. Can you *imagine*? Filthy people.' A gasp, then a round of incredulous titters.

I was disgusted listening to them but could not tear myself away from the horror of it. Mi Gad, to have the man you loved subjected to such indignities, even if he were already dead.

'Are you sure?' one of them had asked after a while. 'It sounds a bit gruesome.'

'I swear by all that's holy. It's in the War Office file. My mother is friends with Freddie Corder's wife and she knows it all. Miss Slade insisted on hearing about it. The "shot in the head" explanation didn't really wash.' Then, getting bored, 'I say, did you hear the latest about Venetia Stanley? Carrying on with Lord Beaverbrook. I mean what do you expect? She married a Jew after all. It was never going to work . . .'

I drifted away from the conversation. I'd had enough of their poison for one evening. So now I knew why the poor woman was so angry all the time. Poor Miss Slade.

Then Arthur turned to me and spoke more urgently. 'Hospital work is eating away at you. You shouldn't have to strive so hard.' He put his hand on my chin, turning my face to his. 'I've been negligent, leaving you here.'

'You don't owe me anything,' I said. The yellow glow of the lamp gave a livid appearance to his cheeks, and his eyes looked as if they were burning.

'That's not how it should be, sweetheart.' He traced the outline of my jaw with his finger. 'When you meet a girl, and it's going well, there are . . . expectations. Especially when the girl's got no family to speak of. A gentleman doesn't just run off and leave her to fend for herself.'

I laughed lightly, though my heart was beating like a drum. 'You make me sound like one of your projects, nah. I can look after myself.'

'Why don't I become your manager?'

'Manager? Of what?'

'Of your career, honey. I could advance you a business loan – so you don't have to wear yourself to the bone working in that hospital any more – and you could pay me back from your earnings.' He sighed. 'I'd give you the money outright, but I know you're not that kind of girl.'

Then he bent down, took hold of my chin again and kissed me. His lips were taut and urgent, and as I tilted my head back I felt as if I were drinking him in. His hands held my upper arms as his lips stayed glued to mine, slightly open. After a long moment, he released me and let my head fall on that soft space just below the shoulder and above his lapel, so the button pressed against my cheek. He had a warm smell about him, as if I had just opened the kitchen door to my mother's and Rose's cooking.

'Happy Armistice Day, Lucia Percival,' he whispered. 'I hope we have many more peaceful years ahead of us.' I said nothing, just melted into his embrace and allowed myself to linger. The wind blew all about me, but I felt protected – as if I had taken shelter under a thick redwood. So transported was I that I almost missed his murmured words: 'Swear to God, I'm going to make you my girl, and make you the musician you were always meant to be.'

Chelsea

12 November 1918, 8 p.m.

MY DEAREST LUCIA,

I know it has been barely twenty-four hours, but just a quick note from my modest hotel room to say how much I enjoyed spending yesterday with you. Rambling about town was real special, and I loved discussing ideas and music (at first, anyways!).

I realise that I was overly forward yesterday, and I apologise for that (not for the intentions behind it, which are absolutely genuine). It must be said you did not object to all my churlish behaviour, much to my happy relief. May we do this again soon?

I am looking forward to meeting your friends, as well as your brother. I want him to know that my intentions towards you are honourable to the hilt, and, devil take it, I intend to make them formal as soon as is appropriate.

Yours very affectionately

Arthur

. . .

20 NOVEMBER 1918, 9 a.m.

Dear Arthur,

Thank you for your kind note. We might schedule a repeat ramble. As for my friends and brother, don't worry. They've never heard of you.

Lucia

ÉTAPLES, France

21 November 1918

MY DEAR LUCIA,

Hurrah! I am so glad Mr Rosewell is back! Of course I remember him – why do you think I wouldn't? My demobilisation is stuck in the queue, so I'm still here and may be until after Christmas. I'm well past having had enough now. My last leave was in June, and with the war over I just want out. That said, I didn't resign until I was sure they wouldn't dock a chunk of my salary for leaving early. Can you believe they only changed that rule now? You would think THE WAR ENDING would be grounds for early termination of a contract with the WAR Office, but there you go.

There's fellow VADs been summoned back to look after demanding parents and live the life of the old maid. The advantage of being on the outs with my entire surviving family is that I'm spared that fate, thank heaven above.

The prisoners are all going back to Germany under supervision from the Army of Occupation. Most of them are not too dejected; they're just happy they don't have to fight any more. As for me, I've had enough of it. Since Herr Leutnant Badura's discharge last spring, I've met nobody on the ward half as congenial, British, French OR German.

I am glad you had a good time celebrating the Armistice. It fell a bit flat for me, I'm afraid, but you know November is never a good month. I fall increasingly dejected as the anniversary date approaches and nothing can rouse me from my gloom. All the girls were celebrating, and Matron Campbell organised a party with liquorice sweets. Supposedly a luxury, but they felt like cardboard in my mouth. I just think about everything CS will never know and the time that was robbed from us. I miss his dry asides on so much of the nonsense that's been going on the past few years. Sometimes I 'script' what his responses would be in my head. But that's all from myself and returns to myself. Barren and useless.

I tried writing to his mother again, but I just tore it up. Why torment her any further? For all that I find your superstitions a little on the melodramatic side, Lucia, something of what you said stays with me. I feel as if under a curse and that she put it there. The worst thing is, I deserve every bit of it.

My stepsister Grace keeps writing to me, and had I burned all the letters she's sent me I could have heated the hospital for a month. She's turned Fenian now, and last I heard she was wanted by the authorities for sedition. If they catch her, good riddance, frankly. She's nothing to me.

But never mind all that. Let's talk about a cheery subject, namely your beau! I remember him from the séance, and I was struck by his aura of self-possession. He seems to have common sense and intelligence in spades, even though he is an American. Hopefully he will not be silly enough to leave you again. You have suffered so much, Lucia, it is really only fair that you have some peace, and whatever happiness you can find.

Yours affec.,
Eva

TARANTO, Italy
    23 November 1918
    Via green envelope

MY DEAR SISTER LUCIA,

I read your letter with great Pleasure, especially to hear that
your Friend has returned and you have an understanding with
him. I don't know Mr Rosewell from Adam, and I'm not sure how a
Musician makes his living, but hope I will meet him soon and
learn his Intentions. This might be some time because they are
keeping us back here for the foreseeable future. We all want to go
home so Mutiny is brewing in the ranks. (Don't worry. I heed your
Warning and I keep out of it.)

At least there is no more need for Trenches, so no more back-
breaking digging. Though even that would be better than being
shipped to Egypt. You told me you heard bad things from there
and I'm not surprised. Some of the other West Indian Soldiers in
Egypt have had a lot of Problems. I'm glad Major General Chaytor
who commands the whole Regiment has let our Battalion stay in
Italy, even though I would much rather still go home. The idea
was to Fend off the Turks, though the only ships I ever saw were
ours – Royal Navy ones – and sometimes a Bottle-Nosed Dolphin
swimming around the smaller craft. I don't think the Dolphin
cared if it were Allies or Axis.

Rumpelstiltskin has now come to join me while I write you
this Letter: he is our resident camp Squirrel Monkey and our
battalion are his minders and feeders. He is very affectionate, and

we have endless fun with him. One fellow even dressed him up and put a pair of underpants on his head. We take our own Amusement as we can find it out here, my dear Sister. On a more serious note, the English Officers are very sometimeish. They still abuse us at length and give us pointless Tasks to do. They make me so vex, Lucia! I had to write this whole letter in a green Envelope to avoid the Censor but there is still the Risk of the letter ending up at HQ in a random sample and of me getting Court-Martialled as a result. The one comfort I have is Rumpelstiltskin as he does not Read private letters nor care for the orders of Englishmen. All he cares about is getting enough Hazelnuts.

I trust you have written to our Mother? It is not right that you should still be at Loggerheads, for I have no doubt she will be very Relieved to hear you have gotten through this Dreadful War. I have not yet written, as I am not so good with words and don't know what to say to her, but do let her know I am well and have escaped unscathed. Now all I have to do is survive the Peace.

God willing I will see you in London soon, and your Intended. I am glad that you are now Respectable, after your earlier Mistake, which you can thankfully now Forget.

Your Brother,
Reginald Percival

20

DECEMBER 1918

Within a fortnight of his return to England, Arthur procured for me two auditions: the first, a minor chorus part in a performance of *Madama Butterfly*, would have been to tour the major opera houses in Europe and the United States. The second was a British offshoot of the Victor Light Opera Company, which sang favourites from Gilbert and Sullivan as well as opera standards. I could choose my own aria, and I already had my eye on 'È strano! . . . Ah, fors'è lui' from *La Traviata*. Its virtuoso parts pushed well into the coloratura and I could show off my voice quite nicely.

The 'business loan' was also transferred. I didn't have a bank account – the process of a single woman opening a bank account being such a three-act opera I had never attempted it. Rather than have me fret about storing a large amount of money on my person, Arthur arranged to pay me a set amount weekly, and while I worried that I would not earn enough to pay him back, it was a relief to hand in my notice.

Dr Alcindor had already spoken to Arthur, and my resignation was fully anticipated by him. It was hard not to feel that these brothers and fathers of the community were deciding my fate, but it was not disagreeable to relax a while and not worry where my next meal was coming from.

Arthur paid me as much personal as professional attention, courting me with breakneck speed and calling on me several times at Fulham Road, though he was strict about never entering the flat. I spent very little time there anyway, except to sleep and pick up post – mostly letters from Eva about how her demobilisation process was dragging on. There was something off about the tone of her letters: I got the feeling that she wasn't telling me everything, but I didn't really care, so caught up was I with Arthur.

We walked the London parks, him taking my arm and occasionally pausing to kiss me, but never for too long. We hired a box at the Royal Opera House in Covent Garden for three weeks, and he introduced me to a queue of musicians, including a stammering youth called Giovanni Barbirolli. Only eighteen when I met him, he would become one of Britain's most eminent cellists. In 1918, he was complaining about Mr Corder for not letting him play a Ravel string quartet. 'What should I do?' he implored, looking at me for some reason.

'What sort of fool-fool question is that?' I laughed. 'Get your friends together, play the Ravel and ignore him.' Arthur nodded approvingly. He was very keen on modern music, rather too much so for my taste.

Then there was the night I finally told Arthur about my past and we made things official. We were at the Dorchester along with some Coterie folk and the Southern Syncopated Orchestra, at yet another end-of-war party. Arthur knew more than half of them already and was fully aware I had been singing with them all along, even though I hadn't mentioned it in my letters. Evelyn Sparrow had presumably filled him in.

That was the night I had my first taste of absinthe, which was legal in Britain but banned everywhere else – and I soon learned why. We were brought two glasses with a green liquid that smelled strongly of aniseed and two teaspoons of crystallised sugar. Then the waiter returned with a glass jug of iced water. The cubes clinked as he walked. The man had calluses on his fingers, a sign of holding a bayonet for long periods, and his accent was French. Which hellhole had he survived? Verdun? Artois I, II or III?

As for me, once the sugar had dissolved (which took a while) and the drink was ready, I downed the small glass in one. And why not—? *Aaaaaaaaaaaagggggghhhhhhhhffffffffffffoooooooooooooo!* My throat! My brain! My eyeballs! My tongue! The roof of my mouth! Blood fiah in my belly! The taste was like inhaling fire – no, more like swallowing burning rubber. I breathed fast to try and cool my mouth down, but my entire face throbbed, and my skin tingled and felt numb, although even that could not cancel out the rank bitterness of the woodworm.

The walls loomed and retreated. They were a tepid shade of pink with white braid detailing, and the colours blurred together so the whole thing looked like a wobbling blancmange. I swayed, reaching out for someone to catch me the way Miss Slade had done when I sang the Erl-King. A hand firmly grasped my arm, then another encircled my shoulder, leading me out into the shock of cold air. I recalled little except that the hand on my arm was dark brown and felt protective and safe.

Arthur told me later that I giggled like a loon, then started crying and calling out nonsense. By the time I had recovered and checked my watch, I was shocked to notice an hour had elapsed. Someone had put my coat on; Arthur and I were alone. We were sitting on a low wall that curved around a small stone fountain, where four crazy-paved paths met. There were palm trees – poor stunted things, confused in such a miserable climate, not unlike myself.

He held me steady and asked, 'Lucia, I need to ask you something. Who is Domi? You kept saying his name. Is he someone important to you?'

My heart stopped pounding, and cold air hit me like a wave. The realisation that I would have to tell my story was sobering me up fast. *Best get it over with*, I thought, and started talking. Arthur got an abridged version: the bit about ending up in prison and talking to Robin afterwards I entirely omitted. Lord knows I was presenting myself in an unflattering enough light already without illuminating those kinds of details. When I finished, he said nothing for half a minute. I was beginning to feel the cold, my coat once again proving altogether inadequate. I had just told Arthur Rosewell I'd thrown away my virtue to a white man and had fallen into disgrace. That I'd had a son of mixed blood. All I could do now was listen to the fountain trickle prettily into its bowl and wait for his response.

Eventually, he exhaled softly. 'I knew there was something.' Then, 'That schmuck,' he muttered, so quietly I barely heard him above the fountain.

'That ... who?'

'I'm not going to dignify him with a name,' Arthur declared. 'How dare he take advantage of you like that? He destroyed your life.'

Oh. He meant Robin. 'It wasn't quite like that—'

'Don't defend him,' Arthur interrupted. 'He can't see – *won't* see – you're worth so much more than the way he treated you. Hiding behind his mother. Leading you on with promises he never meant to keep.' On those points I could only agree. Robin *had* known all along that our affair was a pipe dream, even if he'd denied it to himself. 'If I ever meet that fellow ... I couldn't answer for what I'd do.' Arthur turned to me, and I saw an entirely different cast to his eyes than the usual sharp merry brown. His pupils filled his eyes, and his handsome countenance was marred by a deep frown that quite broke up his face. He saw I was dismayed, and looked away, bundling his fingers into fists then flexing them. When his eyes met mine again, the fury in them had died down.

He put his finger under my chin. 'None of this was your fault, Lucia. D'y'hear me? It grieves me to know how much you have endured. Without a friend in the world to support you.' I felt warmed by his fervour and kindness – was even feeling a little tearful myself.

'You probably feel differently about me now,' I ventured, a little shakily.

'For sure, yes.' *Oh God* . . . 'I love you even more than I already did.'

'What?'

His arm around my shoulders was a warm shelter. 'Listening to your story, my heart ached for you. How you persisted through terrible odds. Don't be sorry you told me, 'cause I'm glad. You made a mistake, sure, like real human beings do. And of course you loved that little boy. Why wouldn't you?'

My friend, I was astonished and delighted. Most men of Arthur's calibre would have run like the wind, but here he was showing such wisdom and understanding. His kindness was extraordinary, and I told him so.

'Though you do know he's lost to you now, don't you, Lucia?' He said it gently, but it was like a knife right through the heart.

'Yes,' I whispered. A dry cold breeze played with the hem of my dress and rippled my coat sleeves. I closed my eyes for a long time, conjuring my Domi's little face, then opened them again. And there was only the night around us, the city sounds and smells, the drunk aristocrats singing nearby. And Arthur, regarding me compassionately.

'What happened was wrong,' he pronounced, 'but, in the end, how could you have cared for him? You had neither the means nor the ability. You would have had to give him up anyway. He would be somewhere worse than where he is now, and still lost to you.'

I had never thought of it that way before, but Arthur was right. How could I have kept a howling baby in that stuffy little room, with Eva complaining, as she surely would have done? The land-lady barely tolerated my presence as it was. We would have both been out on the street, and then the workhouse.

'You need to put away that episode of your life – no, not because I wish it, don't think that,' he held up his palm, 'but because it is over, Lucia.' He was firm, and his authoritative manner should have been a relief. Yet – my treacherous heart! – even now I could not quite forget Lilian Shandlin's words: *You'll never 'move on' a day in your life.* Words spoken, I sternly reminded myself, by a broken woman whose infernal stories seemed like the stuff of nightmares. Not like this man, solid before me, both ambitious yet pragmatic, his hand on mine, his cedarwood cologne sweet and refreshing. Besides, who needs permission from a white woman for anything?

'Forgive me if I spoke out of turn' – Arthur sounded anxious – 'I did not mean to be harsh, just realistic.' When I assured him no forgiveness was required, he responded, 'I was going to wait for the right moment, but—' He fiddled in his pockets, then dropped elegantly and swiftly to one knee, brandishing a small velvet-covered box. 'Will you marry me, Lucia?' He added with a wink, 'Please?'

Oh, believe me, I said yes. I jumped up and down my yes. I sang my yes to the stars. I said yes to the little sparrow that tottered under a holly bush nearby. I said yes and pulled Arthur to his feet and put my arms around his neck, and he lifted me into the air, leaning back so hard that his derby hat fell off his head and landed springily on a bunch of cyclamen. Lord Drunkenham and Lady Tiddlychampagne, who had vacated the function to 'get some aih', cheered so loudly that the doorman threatened to move us all on for causing a public nuisance.

I had not realised until then that I would feel such relief as I did. It was like I had been holding my breath all that time. I felt lucky beyond my dreams.

'Are you happy?' he murmured in my ear later, as we danced inside, cheered on by our friends in the Coterie and serenaded by the band.

'Never been happier in my life.' He kissed me for almost a minute, in the middle of the hotel ballroom, provoking whistles and applause.

Later, he took me home in a horse-drawn cab. My mind was a whirl: full of Dr Alcindor's warm congratulations, his wife wreathed in smiles as she hugged me repeatedly, Mr Tandoh's brief handshake followed by the warm and wry observation that if he had to stand aside for anyone Mr Rosewell was a worthy contender. This was a great surprise for I had never suspected Mr Tandoh to have had designs on me.

And here, now, by my side, Arthur squeezed my thigh and muttered in my ear, 'Ain't gonna 'pologise for being a little naughty,' with a laugh that was as dark as rum.

'I hate leaving you here,' he said, as we reached the flat and he helped me out, fingers laced in mine, 'but please God it won't be for much longer.'

'I certainly won't miss this place,' I agreed, 'but I can wait a little while – for you to be considerably naughtier.' He kissed my gloved fingers and clambered back into the cab, waving at me one last time with his handkerchief. The horses picked up speed and trotted off.

I made my way inside. All the lights were off, and the hall was cold and unlit, with its usual melange of antisocial smells. I could hear the creak of a man pacing back and forth upstairs. Every now and then, a female voice remonstrated with him, and sometimes I heard banging and shouting. Another demobbed officer fallen on hard times, one of the many men the Bangarang had eaten up and spat out. Not for the first time I sadly contemplated that Eva had dodged a bullet.

Then I saw the postcard on the mat. It was unsigned, but the post was marked Eastling, Kent. It could only have come from one person. The message read, 'Apologies for long delay in writing. I will be at the Aerated Bread Company café on 233, The Strand, Westminster, every afternoon next week from 4.30 p.m.'

21

THE STRAND, FRIDAY, 6 DECEMBER 1918

I knew that even as I ignored the note Monday, Tuesday, Wednesday and Thursday, I would give in. Sure enough, come Friday afternoon I cut my practice short and made my way to the café Lilian Shandlin had mentioned.

December had been a miserable month. Barely a week in, and all it could do was rain. Even the politicians seeking votes in the general election looked dejected. A stream of people flowed past the AERATED BREAD CAFÉ sign painted in white capitals at the top of the curved window, and traffic rattled by.

Inside, the windows were covered with gaudy gold-paper decorations which had been put up the day before to mark the first Christmas of peace. It felt unconvincing, as if people still could not quite believe the war was over. The place was almost empty. The witch herself was sitting at a table, wearing her silver-bird headscarf and belted serge winter coat, a carpet bag stuffed with papers at her feet.

She was better dressed than when I had last seen her. Her cheeks were fully rouged, and, when her eyes caught mine, there was a bright dangerous look in them that unnerved me. I hoped she would not take too long: I had an extra rehearsal with Miss Slade at seven o'clock, deliberately arranged so I would have an excuse not to linger.

When I took the seat opposite, Mrs Shandlin raised her hand to summon the waitress, who immediately darted over, licking her finger as she turned the page of her orders notebook. She ordered afternoon tea for two while I removed my gloves. As soon as the waitress left, her eyes immediately darted to my left hand.

'Nice ring.'

'Thank you. I recently became engaged.'

'Congratulations.' When I was silent, she added, 'Thank you for coming. I didn't presume you would.'

I didn't tell her that I had dreamed of Domi every single night since the day her card arrived. That my dreams had been vivid and terrible, and that I woke from them feeling as if I'd had no rest. 'I'm here.'

'After we spoke last year . . .' she said, fiddling with her coat, 'I fell into a depression. Didn't leave the house for months. Milk piling up on the doorstep, that sort of thing. Thought I was over the worst of it, but evidently not.'

That made sense. There had been a false euphoria about her when we had last spoken, and her energy had been febrile and strange. No wonder her front had all collapsed.

'I'm sorry to hear that, Mrs Shandlin.' I said gently, because I was.

'Well. You should call me Lilian, since you already do behind my back.' She took out a handkerchief and unfolded it on her lap. 'I've done a bit of digging.' She paused again, significantly. 'If you recall, I told you about Mrs Gunning. I've asked her to investigate your case, and she's been on it this past month, at my expense.'

'Afternoon tea, ma'am.' The waitress set down a three-tiered pink ceramic stand, each tier holding a selection of slices of battenberg and chocolate cake. Lilian gestured at me to help myself, but I couldn't stomach a thing, not after what she had just told me. She had no such constraint and tucked into a chocolate fancy with an appetite that banished all hope that she was a duppy of my imagination. How on earth did someone so thin eat like that?

'And?' I said, my voice hoarse. 'Is he alive?'

Her response was swift. 'Yes.'

I put my fingers to my temples. 'Mi Gad. I was scared the flu had taken him.'

'It still might,' Lilian said darkly. 'Anyway, she believes the rescue can be done.'

I felt as if someone had put a rock in my throat. 'Did she say how he is?'

Lilian shook her head. 'You need to talk to her.'

The café began to fill up: clerks from the offices in Westminster were coming in now – their working day ended early on a Friday. Many of them were women, still young, who might have hoped for a more traditional life of marriage. Now, I presumed, they would never see their 'best boys' again. Their future was torn up.

Outside the window, a group of schoolboys in long coats gathered in a crescent. The path was too narrow for them all, so the little ensemble spilled onto the road. Then the sheets of music came out in a flurry. Mercy, were we going to be subjected to Christmas carols this early? I recognised their conductor, Mr Gethins, who had studied alongside me in the Royal Academy and was now a professional tenor. Like many musicians, he supplemented his income by teaching, and these boys presumably comprised one of his classes.

Not wanting him to recognise me, I pulled down my hat and

turned away from the window. Out came the tuning fork, then a series of unbroken voices chanting reedily, 'In the bleak midwinter . . .'

I tried to filter them out. 'This is hard, Lilian,' I said slowly. 'This . . . I wasn't expecting it. He must be' – I counted on my fingers – 'eighteen months? He won't know me. And—' The plain silver engagement ring she had earlier complimented lay heavy on my finger. 'Arthur – my fiancé – he has plans for me. My music career is beginning to do quite well.'

The carol singers moved on to a new verse, the boys mounting a semi-harmonious hum while Mr Gethins sang above them, in a crooning style, with too much vibrato and not enough support. The words he sang he could not quite ruin, for they were simple and searingly beautiful:

Enough for Him, whom cherubim, worship night and day,
A breastful of milk, and a mangerful of hay;
Enough for him whom angels fall down before . . .

Domi and I had *had* enough, and they had taken it away. I couldn't bear to listen to these carols, all about babies and their mothers' milk. It was too much. I put my fingers in my ears.

'Lucia,' Lilian reached over and touched my arm. When I didn't respond, she yanked my hands away from my ears and gave me a stern look. 'I need your answer. Shall I pursue this? Just say the word.' I sighed hard. The boys went on singing, and the girls in the café nursed their cooling tea and continued to look wistfully at Mr Gethins.

'Do it.'

Lilian closed her eyes a moment. Her brilliant peacock blue-black eyeshadow creased into her wrinkled eyelids. 'Are you sure?'

'Yes.'

She licked her lips. Her eyes were cold fire, her nails dark red and her eyes a boundless abyss. 'You know what I need you to do in return.' I had been expecting this, but a cold chill settled on my heart all the same. Lilian lifted a slice of cake on my plate and smiled, 'I'm very impressed by their battenberg. They're very difficult to make. Nine panels in one small slice.'

'I'm having trouble keeping up. One minute you hint at cold-blooded murder, the next you're making chit-chat about cake?'

'Oh no.' Lilian set to work on the other slice of battenberg. 'I'm still talking about murder. By cake.'

This would be comical, if it weren't so crazy. 'And how will you do that?'

Lilian looked offended. 'I'll have you know I'm an excellent baker. Eva very much enjoyed my cake when I met her on the Isle of Wight.'

She didn't enjoy you cursing her out later, I didn't say out loud. After mentioning the Isle of Wight, a shadow had crossed over Lilian's features, and I guessed she was thinking about her son. I felt a pang of pity for her, one that didn't quite rise to the level of fellow-feeling, but enough for me to keep my mouth shut.

She recollected herself and continued. 'I can make the cake with a much thicker layer of icing, which would be ideal in this case. Thankfully, Mr Fillmore stocked up on sugar for me, because I'd never have had enough if I relied on rations. He's a good friend from the village,' Lilian explained, swallowing back some of her slice. 'Always been there for me. Offered to do my errands when I couldn't face it myself. A few months ago, I got thrown out of the Links school reunion in Eastbourne, for being the mother of a conchie who got an F minus in dying discreetly for the war effort. Mr Fillmore was waiting for me outside the gates, even though I'd told him not to when he dropped me there earlier.'

She was not looking at me while speaking. If she had, she

would have seen a face of stone. I was not interested. I was insulted. The hell with Mr Fillmore. How much of my time did this woman think she could waste? There she was, rambling on: '. . . So I need to be careful when I put it in the oven that it doesn't all sink to the bottom. If it's concentrated it will taste too bitter, and I need him to eat at least one slice. Plenty in the icing because that's the bit he likes best.' She rambled away as if she were reciting a page from *Mrs Humphrey's Cookbook.*

'What's "*it*"?'

'Oh! Strychnine.' Lilian drained her cup and set it down with a decisive clink.

Blouse and skirt! Strychnine?! Once my father took us to the Castleton Botanical Gardens just outside Kingston and showed us the plant – *Nux vomica* – and its citrus-like nut. He told us how lethal it was. That people used it as common rat poison. Now Lilian was going to upend a docker's meal of it into a cake and feed it to another human being. 'I can't, Lilian. Not even for Domi. Unna people might feel differently, but Commandment Number Five is not a breakable rule for me.'

'Well, you've changed your tune.' She lit a cigarette. 'Look, all I'm asking is that you keep lookout. We'll go to the War Office in Whitehall, enter through different doors, and you find the office and keep guard. I can get you in as one of the cleaning staff. No problem now it's peacetime.'

I shook my head. 'Look at me, nah. They'd recognise me fast. I'd swing from a rope,' I hissed at her, 'right beside you.'

She put her elbow on the table, and I watched the smoke drift from the cigarette holder held between her two fingers. 'That won't happen. But let's say we *were* caught, and the case went to trial, and I were free to speak in open court.' She paused, letting me think for a moment.

'You mean . . . you'd bring them all down with you? All di topanoris dem?'

That last part evidently needed no translation because she responded with a wide, wolfish smile. 'Pre-cise-ly. McCrum's . . . *associates* won't want to take the risk. They won't even want a murder enquiry. A brief note of his death on page four of *The Times* with heavy hints of suicide. That'll be it.'

'You have this all planned so neat and tidy,' I said. 'The cake. The outcome. I'm sure you even have a map of his office.'

Lilian frowned. 'Why, of course I do. I made two: one for me and one for you.' She looked down at the table, her fingers doing a little dance. 'What I need is backup – support – if things go wrong.' To my incredulous look, she responded, 'I mean moral support. I don't want to do this alone. This whole nightmare these past two years, I've had to go through it alone. It's been very hard. Besides' – her mouth twisted, and she looked altogether ugly – 'you'll need to keep watch because I don't plan on leaving in a hurry. I want to see that man die at my personal leisure.' Again she flashed me that satanic look that had scared me so much that night in Kensington.

The carol singers had switched to 'O Little Town of Bethlehem', and people were beginning to drop coins into their box. Mr Gethins sang with his eyes closed, swaying from side to side – and putting himself in the way of passing traffic, the pretentious, self-regarding h'eedjiat! But the harmonies were nice and easy. I listened closely to hear them, even Mr Gethins' warbling, to drive away the hate and rage I had just witnessed.

'Why me?' I asked, after another pause.

'Because you're desperate.' The reply was like a slap; I was too shocked to respond. She waved at the waitress, and through a series of nods and gestures indicated she wanted the bill. 'Oh, don't look at me like that,' she said. 'I heard it all, remember? You would break commandments for your boy. You said so yourself. Don't get me wrong: from everything I've heard, Eva would have been the same. For different reasons.'

I gazed on her in fascinated horror. 'You are a vulture.'

She regarded me seriously. 'Then ask yourself what made me that way.' She clasped my hands. 'Listen, just listen to me. We are war mothers. A cruel power took our boys away from us. Neither of us can leave that behind, no matter how much we're told to. You went back to Glasgow, didn't you? We are both vultures. Returning to the same place, picking at the same bones.'

I released my hands from hers and put my head in them. Her words were hypnotic and affected me deeply. What was I thinking, going on with my life and career as if nothing had happened? I could no more leave Domi behind than cut out my own heart and throw it over Beachy Head. Only he, sweet pickney, could arouse pure love in my soul. Lilian Shandlin was right: I *was* desperate. If I could have him while I was in this world, no matter how briefly, I'd take perdition in the next.

Seeing me buckle, Lilian moved in for the kill. 'Tell me,' she said gently, as the waitress cleared away the tea things, 'hand on heart: if anyone caused harm to Dominic, would you not feel the same towards them as I do, now, towards McCrum?'

That creature! She had me there, and she knew it. Vulture.

Her next set of instructions were clear. That Sunday, I was to take the Dover train and get off at Teynham. She would meet me, and from there we would drive to her home in Eastling, where Mrs Gunning would be waiting for us. She would answer any questions I might have about Domi and how he would be returned to me. As for the deed, it was planned for the day before the general election, Friday the thirteenth. When I reminded Lilian of the significance, she laughed lightly. 'His unlucky day, yes.'

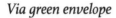

Via green envelope

   Taranto, December 1, 1918

   My dear Sister Lucia,

   Once again I must Resort to the green Envelope, which explains the delay, since we are only allowed them once a Month. Our quartermaster was extremely Sometimeish when I requested it, demanding to know if I had anything to Hide. I explained that it was about family Matters, but I think the idea of Coloured People having privacy is in his eyes a form of Insubordination.

   Anyway, we are now almost a Month into the Armistice, but nobody seems to have any Plan to send Caribbean soldiers home. Lucia, the situation here is truly terrible and there has already been a Bloodbath. The Straw that broke the Camel's back was when our Company Sergeant told us to clean the dirty Latrines the Italians had used. My fellow Soldiers felt ill-used at being told to scrub White men's lavatories, and they Mutinied. The Englishmen got in the Worcestershires with Machine Guns and killed two of our NCOs.

   Now you see why I insisted on the Green Envelope! I cannot speak to anyone.

   Everything is crazy: the only Sane living creature here is Rumpelstiltskin and he is a great comfort. I took your Advice, Lucia, much as it hurt my Pride, and laid low. I do not want to end up in that Ditch you warned me about and break our Mother's heart, like the other man's mother's was surely broken. I am low in spirit though, because the White men we fought alongside shot us with Machine-gun fire. I thought there was Honour in battle. I was wrong.

   I hope Mr Rosewell is treating you Kindly and please Pray for your distressed Brother and hope that the transport ships Arrive soon before I lose my cool Altogether,

Affectionately,

Reginald

THE SUNDAY MORNING train to Dover was packed with grim-eyed veterans, many on crutches; with women, flat with exhaustion; and with children, coughing and fretting. I found some standing room by the door of a third-class compartment, where the mist leaked in through half-open panes. I thought of all the children I had seen sicken in Dr Alcindor's hospital, how they looked, breathed, smelled. I couldn't forget that baby from Crouch End with its pathetic little comforter soaked in cough mixture. And my thoughts turned to Domi, too, yes.

Worrying about Reginald, which I had done constantly since receiving his letter, was almost a distraction from the grim turn of my thoughts on that train. I hoped he could keep his promise and hold on. I knew how hard it must be to be forced to smile and bear it when those over you treated you like dirt. And Reggie, as I knew only too well, did not have a strong character. He had, however, expressed the desire not to put our mother through what Lilian had endured, which was a relief.

The train's rhythm was an echoing, sad heartbeat. When it stopped at Teynham, I was the only person who alighted. I saw through the window that Lilian was alone on the platform, rigid and poised as usual. After brief greetings, we were soon in the legendary Mr Fillmore's pony and trap, heading towards Eastling village boundary.

Lilian made little conversation during the journey, and most of that she directed towards Mr Fillmore, who would reply with slow thoughtfulness, as if he were chewing on a piece of gristle. I knew, from what she had told me, that they had a long and close acquaintance, but throughout the short journey they called each other 'Mrs Shandlin' and 'Mr Fillmore', and I scratched my head about that. I will never understand the English, not if I live to be a hundred.

Lilian drew her shawl around her shoulders and shivered, at which Mr Fillmore leaned over and asked very solicitously if Mrs Shandlin was all right, to which she responded, 'Yes, thank you, Mr Fillmore,' and pulled her glove sleeve over her wrist. Kiss mi neck!

The countryside was wintry and silent. Up a road called Kettle Hill, we passed a school and emerged into rolling countryside. A few of the fields had been dug up during the war, presumably by land girls, and were being allowed to go fallow again. The beds were frozen and covered in weeds. Mr Fillmore pulled sharply on the reins to turn left, and we trotted up a country lane, bouncing around and rocking from side to side.

The pony and trap came to a halt outside a low wrought-iron gate, painted white. By the moss-covered gate post, a small letterbox read 'Calcutta' in faded black capitals. Mr Fillmore helped Lilian down, and I leapt off myself, grabbing my skirts as I landed heels first in the frozen mud. Mr Fillmore politely said good day to me, tipping his hat as he moved off, stirring the horse gently with his whip.

I followed Lilian up a short gravel path to a low, L-shaped bungalow, feeling quite odd at the thought of entering her house. Eva had much more of a right to be there than I but had never, to my knowledge, set foot in it. We went through a modest hall into a large parlour with a bay window at the far end that looked out onto a hillocky garden. Cabinets lined one side, laden with crystal jars and trophies; other shelves held photographs, most of two young men – one fair and smiling, the other dark and looking as if he would rather be anywhere else than in front of a camera. Not difficult to guess which was which. There were one or two family portraits with a younger, unsmiling Lilian and the boys as children. Photographs. That was all that was left of that family.

There was an emptiness in the air that not even the crackling fire in the grate could dispel. I kept expecting the other people to come in. But no one did. It felt as dark and lonely as Purgatory.

Mrs Gunning was sitting on a sofa near the window, sipping tea from a plain white mug. She was a woman in late middle age, heavyset, curly-haired, with an odd yellow scar on her cheek. Lilian introduced us, and we exchanged greetings.

'Can I get you tea?' Lilian asked me.

'No, thanks. Let's get to business.'

'Of course.' There was an awkward silence. It struck me then that Mrs Gunning had not been enlightened about my part of the bargain with Lilian. Probably just as well.

'How are you going to do this?' I blurted out. I knew I was being rude but couldn't help myself. This place was a house of death, and being here made me kraa-kraa – clumsy and nervous. Mrs Gunning was more than happy to enlighten me. In a harsh voice, she elaborated how she had stalked the local park on the Western Road for a month, spying on his parents. Domi's father was cold towards him, and the mother, 'as is', overcompensated. 'Fusses over him something terrible,' Mrs Gunning commented, adding, 'There's a look in his eyes – 'tis one I've seen on infants before, in them mother and baby homes. 'Tis a withdrawn look. Not to alarm you, miss, but he doesn't look happy in himself.'

My heart lurched and turned over in anguish. Lilian put her hand on my knee. I angrily pushed it off. What was she doing only using my pain to get me to help her perverted scheme? She didn't give a damn about Domi.

'Don't you fret,' Mrs Gunning told me. 'I'm just waitin' for the right time to get him for you. 'Tis a delicate operation you see. It takes months to build up enough trust before I can get access to the child for long enough to be able to sneak him away. Funny,' she added. 'Not being previous, but he's not very mixed looking. You wouldn't take him for a half-caste at all. Just a little sallow lookin'. I'd say it was a shock for them to find out.'

I greeted this comment with silence.

'Don't you worry,' Mrs Gunning went on. 'I'll see you right. You see that scar there?' She pointed at her cheek. 'Got that when a prison officer hit me in the face with his big bunch of keys. They put me in for stealing bread off a van. I did it because I had three younger brothers. We were starving. Things were desperate. So I'm not afraid of nattin' any more. I've rescued twenty childer and never had a hand laid on me.' I softened towards her. She was a bit rough, a true dat, but she'd obviously had a hellish life. 'I never saw my brothers again, y'know. They got took away and all died young.'

'Hush!' I exclaimed without thinking.

'Thank you,' Mrs Gunning replied. Then, seeing my surprise, 'I used to live in Liverpool, down near the docks. I met a lot of sailors.' She set the mug down on an ormolu coffee table and glanced at Lilian. 'It's very good of Mrs Shandlin to pay for it. Takes a lot of work, what I do.'

'We are mothers,' Lilian answered, strong, firm, unwavering.

I am, I thought, *but you're not any more*. But I'd never say that out loud. For all that I was angry with her still, I couldn't be that cruel. And she was financing this, I couldn't deny that.

The afternoon quickly turned to evening, and the two older women turned to more general conversation while I wished I had requested that cup of tea after all, if only to be able to hold onto the cup, to keep myself from fidgeting. Mr Fillmore eventually

returned with his pony and trap – did that man have anything else
to do? – to bring Mrs Gunning back to the station. After they left,
Lilian switched on the lamps one by one. Standing on various
bureaux, side tables and mantelpieces, they all had pretty lamp-
shades, with tassels and brocade and were in warm colours like
tea rose and butter yellow. But even when they were all lit they
only seemed to accentuate the retreating light and the darkness
that was looming.

It was time to stop beating around the bush. 'This lookout I do
for you. How does it work?'

'You find some way of bringing any intruder to my attention.'
Lilian placed some timber on the fire and it crackled and roared
back to life.

'I gathered as much. How, though?'

'Any way you please, as long as I can hear you.' She sat down in
the spot Mrs Gunning had lately vacated. 'I've very little in the way
of food, I'm afraid: some cured ham and preserves and water
biscuits, that's all.'

'Never mind the food. You need a better plan. You're telling me
we're just going to waltz into the War Office and do this? These
people won't just let us in. They aren't half-eedjiats.'

At that Lilian raised an eyebrow. 'Lucia. You were involved in
the war. You know full well they're *complete* idiots.'

Yu favah im, I was going to say, thinking of Christopher and
what Eva had told me about his sharp tongue – then realised I had
it backwards. While still living, *he* would have favoured *her*. And
still would have done, if it weren't for that war getting everything
backasswards, as Arthur would have put it in a profane moment.

'There is a back entrance the cleaning staff use, halfway up a
narrow laneway called Whitehall Court, just off Horse Guards
Avenue. That is the one you will use.'

'And how do I find you?'

'I will be on the second floor, Room 7 on the south side, over-looking the Quadrangle. That's McCrum's office. Make sure you find the right room. There are seven miles of corridors, so if you get lost, you'll have trouble finding me.'

She took a piece of paper from a bureau drawer and handed it to me. It was a carefully drawn map of the building. 'I owe thanks to Mr Tulloch for this. He'd normally be at his desk but has kindly decided to take the day off as sick leave. He plans to telegram the news last minute, mind you, so they'll struggle to find a replace-ment and McCrum and I will be alone. Tulloch thinks I'm just going to tell him who I really am. He thinks I'm doomed.' She smiled. 'But if I get this right, his own problem will be solved. His boy Teddy will be safe.'

'Would it not make more sense for him to help you out, then?' *And get me off the hook you've put me on?*

'It would,' Lilian admitted, 'but I didn't have the courage to ask him to be a co-conspirator. His loyalty to McCrum is embedded. He could turn on us any minute, out of self-preservation.'

'What time are you going to meet . . .' I couldn't get his name out. To me, hearing Lilian's certainty, he was already dead; naming him would be a curse.

'McCrum? My appointment is at twelve. He told me to make it quick,' Lilian chuckled, 'because he only has half an hour in his diary.'

'And how long do you expect it to take?'

'About thirty minutes, I would imagine. I'd hardly want to keep him from his next appointment, would I?'

I shook my head. 'I can't believe I'm doing this. I don't think I want to, now.'

She got angry then. 'We do it my way or we don't do it at all. And I think you know what the consequences of that will be.' No

Domi. I had to weigh the balance: if we were caught, and sentenced, I'd never see him again anyway.

Was I afraid of death? The grim reaper was no stranger to me. I'd walked straight into the River Clyde and his waiting arms without fear. But that was just after they took my baby away from me. Then, I had nothing to live for. Death, as another Purcell aria I sang put it, was a welcome guest. Now I had more to lose. And so, more to risk.

I looked out at the gathering dark. 'All right. I have all the information. I'll meet you at Horse Guards Avenue at half past eleven to give you time to organise yourself. I should probably go back to London now. When is the last train?'

'It's gone, I'm afraid. Mrs Gunning was on it.'

Now I was cross. 'Did you not think of mentioning that before? How am I supposed to get home?'

'Why don't you stay here? I have food, and a bottle of wine that's not too ancient.' When I shook my head violently, she laughed. 'Don't worry, I shan't poison you.'

'I needed to check,' I said, earning a smile and a shake of the head from Lilian.

It had begun to rain, in that dismal wintry fashion, and the wind started a low G with eerie harmonic overtones that gave me the creeps. I realised that she'd done it deliberately, that she didn't want to be alone. And, heaven knows why, I pitied her and her pathetic attempt to prevent me leaving her house. 'All right. I'll stay. But I won't have any wine. And I won't sleep in any of *their* rooms.'

Her expression was unreadable. 'As you wish. I'll fetch blankets for the couch.'

In spite of my request, she returned with two wine glasses and a full carafe, followed by a cheeseboard and a selection of cold meats. Not an appealing selection for a stomach like mine, but I was hungry all the same. As she set the carafe down by the fire and its flicker caught the colour of the liquid, I was distracted by the thought that McCrum's blood was surely the same hue.

'Elderberry. Made it myself,' Lilian remarked, 'so it might be a little strong. I find it distracts me from the cold. You can try some if you want.' My friend, you see a pattern! I held out a glass, and she poured. Her eyes were on me as I tasted the wine and set the glass down on the table.

'What do you think?'

'Not bad. A little bitter at first, then sweet in the aftertaste.'

'Like our mission.' Lilian closed her eyes and sipped. I wanted to tell her sharply that I'd like less of the 'our' business, thank you very much.

She set her glass down then cut a small bit of cheddar and ate it without a plate, the crumbs falling in her lap. I had to admire her. She really didn't care about anything. A woman who eats without a plate could easily commit murder!

For my part, I took the plate.

'It must be lonely for you.' For a moment I thought I had misheard her, but she repeated her statement, adding, 'Every gathering you enter, you are alone. Constantly having to negotiate people's attention while being deprived of their comradeship.'

'That's not altogether true,' I said, sipping more wine. 'I'm lucky enough to have friends of my own race here. Respectable, cultured people.' I told her about the Coterie and how I met Arthur, Gwen and Dr Alcindor. Lilian listened in that characteristic position of hers, head cocked slightly to one side, knees drawn up sideways, cradling her glass of wine.

She was interested enough not even to bother reaching for a cigarette – an open case was balanced on the arm of the sofa. 'I'm so pleased,' she said at last, cunningly topping up my glass. 'Because there is nothing lonelier than living among the English when you are not of their race.' It was my turn to give her a questioning look (as well as to take another 'sip' of that rather nice home-made wine). 'My husband was Anglo-Indian.'

Macca! That was a turn-up for the books.

'My father-in-law spent time out at a tea plantation in Singampatti, and even though he had a wife at home in England, he started up a liaison with the daughter of the foreman. She was thirteen.'

'So young,' I whispered.

'Yes. Quite shocking. The family didn't object because he was rich by their standards. The girl died three years later. Cholera. By then James had been born, and his father decided to take him home and "adopt" him.' She wiggled her fingers in a quote gesture. 'Of course, my mother-in-law – his wife, I should say – soon guessed the truth. You can imagine what James's early childhood was like.'

I could, all too well. The story she had just told me, with small variations, was the story of hundreds of people I knew back in Jamaica.

'James was quite a wretched man. So ashamed of his origins. It was something disgraceful, never to be talked about. If you knew, it was obvious enough looking at him. To strangers, we passed him off as having southern European heritage, even pretending his birth records were destroyed in a fire. He made me swear never to tell the boys, and I obeyed. "Don't make their lives harder than they need to be," that's what he always told me. It helped that Francis at least was very fair.'

I took a big gulp of wine and looked her inna she h'eye. 'Were *you* ashamed of him, once you knew?'

'Never.' Almost a shout. 'But I could not break through the shame he had of himself, no matter how I tried. It killed him, through drink, violence, despair. I had to protect myself and shield the children.'

Those children, who were all gone now. Poor Lilian! It would take a heart stonier than mine not to take pity on her. She was looking down and away from me now, a look I recognised from the times I feared I'd confided too much in someone.

'Shall I put away the wine?' she said, picking up the carafe, which was still almost three-quarters full.

I pulled it from her and set it down on the table. 'You will do no such thing. Pour me another glass. And don't stint on it.' And so we had another glass each . . . and another . . . and another. At some stage we emptied the carafe, and Lilian staggered to the kitchen to fill it up a second time. I might have slurred that I didn't want to put an old lady to such trouble, to which she told me, in equally slurred tones, to shut up and light her a cigarette if I were so concerned for her welfare.

I took one of the long slim cigarettes and held it to the fire but nearly lost my balance and singed a loose lock of my hair. I was aware of being very inebriated, but still didn't refuse the glass Lilian offered on her return. Our conversation continued, though of necessity it grew ever more rambling and inconsequential.

I do remember I told her about Amelia Hall, and she looked serious for a while. When I had finished, she said, 'Well. I've plenty more of that strychnine lying around. It would be a shame for it to go to waste,' and for some reason we both thought that was the funniest thing ever and went into a round of giggles.

Then Lilian expressed some curiosity about Jamaican dialect. I attempted to explain, but honestly? That whole conversation can be safely forgotten. We talked about Eva, then about my mother. Lilian was shocked to hear she wouldn't speak to me, hissing 'stupid woman', under her breath but loud enough for me to hear. In my haze I recalled Lilian saying sometime after that, 'Well, I told the Parish Council they needed to stop mowing the village green lawn, and that horrible new rector, Mr Glynn, just laughed at me and said, "Oh, you're being silly, Mrs Shandlin, we won't be running out of bees any time soon." I wrote to Christopher about it at the time, and he told me' – she hiccupped – 'he told me, "Pipe down, Ma, you really need to pick your battles."' She broke into a fit of the giggles. 'I mean, the cheek of *him* telling me that!'

Tears of laughter streamed from her eyes, and I couldn't help joining in. We laughed for a good while, and then the laughter faded into an air cold enough that even fire and wine couldn't quite keep at bay.

'I miss him every day, you know. I miss them both.'

'I know.' I put my hand on hers. 'I miss Domi every day too.'

'Oh well,' she said, with a prolonged, inebriated yawn, 'maybe we should sing a song. Before I fall asleep.'

I was too drunk to sing but too drunk to refuse. 'What sorta song you want?'

'Shleepy shong.' Lilian's head lolled on my shoulder. She was nearly out of it. And Lord help me but the first song that came to mind was the very one my mother had sung me. I explained to Lilian that she needed to chant the refrain and felt a slight nod of her head.

'Chi chi a bud oh,' I began, then nudged the inanimate lump beside me, who responded with a drunken, accented but clear, 'Some a dem a holla, some a bawl.' I did two more, using English birds instead of our own – blackbird, starling, pigeon – but by the third the only response I got was a snore. Not wanting to go one step beyond the living room, I stood to my feet, swayed awhile, then grasped Lilian by the shoulders and gently dragged her into an armchair. I covered her with one of the three blankets she had brought for me, propping up her lolling head with a cushion. Then I took off her shoes.

I stayed on the couch with all the lights blazing just in case the ghosts of Christopher and Francis might decide to chase me out of their mother's home. But in my heart I knew that would not happen. Neither spirit lingered. There was nothing but absence and the wind in the eaves. Our tame carousing had warded off the emptiness for a while, but it would descend once more, given time.

I woke on several occasions, the final time just after dawn, when the winter sun was coming in through the smaller east window. The armchair was empty, the blanket gone. Lilian must have woken up and gone to her own room. She had left her shoes, no longer scattered any which way but neatly placed side by side at the foot of the chair.

The remains of our well-past-midnight feast littered the table – one glass was on its side on the carpet. The sun made me blink. It shot right through the room onto a glass cabinet door and a photograph of Christopher I had seen earlier. Turning my face from the light, I could not miss his. He was standing in a field bordered by trees in the background. It looked to be summer. He wore a rumpled, loosely buttoned jacket and an open-collared shirt. His face was pale and narrow, the forehead high. His hair was jet black, his eyes dark and resentful.

Eva once told me that Christopher looked odd whenever he smiled. It occurred to me that the same was true of Lilian. Meeting his eye, I saw for myself what Eva still loved about him, so far beyond distraction that she had tried to take her own life when she lost him. Furthermore, his eyes and hair might have been his Anglo-Indian heritage, so brutally suppressed, but the shape of his face, those hollow cheeks and high forehead? Pure Lilian. She loved him enough to kill for him.

Tentatively, I put my hand to the photo. All this was about him; it seemed only right to acknowledge him somehow. And if any part of Christopher Shandlin were brown, be it twelve per cent, or twenty-five, or...who knows? that percentage was what made him stand up and say no to The Man. I was sure of it.

'Hello, brother,' I said. 'I'm sorry I never got to know you. But I've heard good things.' Nothing happened. The air temperature didn't change. His frown did not soften into even a hint of a smile. But the burden on my shoulders felt lighter, and I padded back to the couch and the last stage of sleep with peace in my heart.

CALAIS, 10 December 1918

DEAR LUCIA,

Just a quick note to let you know that after interminable delays I am finally coming home! We leave on the morrow, taking a P&O ferry to Dover and the train up to London, so we should be all in by Wednesday night. It would be wonderful if you were at home, as after all the upheaval I have mislaid my keys. If not, I will try to persuade Mrs Baxter to let me in.

Thank you so much for keeping everything together in my absence – I am looking forward to meeting Mr Rosewell once again, not to mention the soon-to-be Mrs Rosewell. I have been thinking of you and Sybil so much, Lucia, and how things will be on my return, for in truth a lot has happened, and when I do arrive, well, let's say things might not be as expected. I think it is probably better to explain some things in person.

Affectionately,

Eva

22

11 DECEMBER 1918

The high B flat floated out, sweet as honey, powerful as ammunition. I was told later that many gasped, and some wept. I couldn't tell; I had my eyes closed. It was Wednesday night: two weeks before Christmas, two days before the general election. Not a soul in the whole of the United Kingdom could take that B flat away from me. For just that one night, I had respite.

Brass chandeliers gleamed against the panelled ceiling of Clapton's Round Chapel, and around the chancel a circle of tall, plain wax candles in bronze holders danced and flickered. In front of the small orchestra, facing the congregation, was the singer's stand, from which I faced a surprised audience – even in cosmopolitan London a black carol singer was out of the ordinary those days.

Directly in front of me, the reassuring stumpy figure of Freddie Corder wielded his baton. At the start of the piece, the massive organ at the back of the nave had played the familiar triplets that marked the introduction to 'O Holy Night.' So much nicer than those other triplets . . .

Miss Slade had enquired whether I had fears about managing the high B flat. I knew her well by now and was sure she was winding me up. Cu yu, I could sing that B flat in my sleep. But I did feel oppressed: that coming Friday loomed over everything. It took all my singing power to forget about it for a moment. From my stand, I banished doubt, proclaimed Our Lord's power and glory, peace on earth and goodwill to all men. Were these now shallow words?

Soon after my final B flat, the choir and soloists rose and sang 'Hark! The Herald Angels Sing' in unison. Then the lights went up, allowing me to see the audience. There was Arthur, along with several members of the Coterie, in the second row, smiling proudly; Miss Slade just behind, not smiling outright but her eyes were shining; and a few rows back from there a surprising flash of brilliant vermilion – Sybil Faugharne was adjusting her hair under her hat. I had invited her but hadn't expected her to attend. That she had touched me very deeply. She was alone; Roma was still too fragile to be out.

I made to join Arthur and Miss Slade, when—

'Not so fast, piccaninny.'

The three witches I had sat behind at St Giles-without-Cripplegate as they gossiped about Venetia Slade flanked me now, disapproving stares plastered on their plaster faces. Standing next to them was my favourite VAD, Amelia Hall. Bax cova! How on earth had she materialised? Was she studying music now too?

'Well!' The one with the freckles wrinkled her snub nose. 'You've got an opinion of yourself, don't you?'

'Excuse me,' I murmured, attempting to push past them.

'Don't think we don't all know why you got picked.' Amelia put her hand on my shoulder and gave me a shining smile. 'They feel

sorry for you. Next year they'll have real singers.' She frowned
sulkily and flicked her finger under my chin. 'There's no such
thing as a black flower, you know. Nature doesn't like it.'

During my years away from Jamaica, I had built up a store of
retorts for white people's ignorant remarks, but this one left me
wordless. Because it wasn't ignorant. It was spiteful and clever, and
I had no answer for it. Her friends could see it too; they swarmed
closer.

'Really? "Nature doesn't like it," eh?' Sybil had materialised,
red in tooth and claw – and hair, which she had somehow
managed to unfasten again since I'd last seen her. Scandalously,
she wore a pair of tweed britches and a tailored matching jacket,
although I had to admit she looked rather smart. She towered over
the trio.

'Who are you?' Amelia could not hide her annoyance.

'Me? Viscountess Clive Faugharne, previously Lady
Destouches. My friend' – here she indicated me – 'calls me Sybil.
You may call me "Lady Faugharne".'

Amelia sniggered like a piglet. 'Don't you know it's vulgar to
flash your peerage around?'

'Well, let's see. My peerage is about, oh, a thousand years old,
chum. Whereas your daddy bought a baronetcy from Maundy
Gregory for forty thou. Didn't your mother work in the Deepdene
Hotel? And I mean "worked".' I had no idea what Sybil was talking
about, but Amelia Hall evidently *did* know since she blushed a
deep pink. 'I doubt she saw many flowers then, or daylight,' Sybil
added breezily. 'Oh, and didn't Beaverbrook help hush up the
rumours about Lord Hall? How he was married with two small
daughters when you prised him away from his wife?' Her voice
was loud enough now that people turned around.

'How dare you—' Amelia began, but Sybil cut in. 'Listen,
darling, I eat little parvenues like you for breakfast. If I were

serious about destroying you, your name would be ruined in all of London. Now, I wouldn't know a viola from a jew's harp, but even I can tell that my friend Lucia here has the voice of a generation. Whereas you elf-helpers are a bunch of frogs.' She clicked her fingers. 'Now, scoot!'

For a moment the quartet stared slack-jawed at Sybil, then they slowly melted away. Amelia shot Sybil one last glare, but Sybil's answering look had her quailing and flouncing.

I heard clapping – the sharp echoes bouncing over the hum of the crowd. 'Bravo, ma'am, bravo!' Arthur strode over, applauding her as he walked. He and Sybil were the same height and made rather an imposing duo. 'Thank you for standing up for my fiancée,' he added, putting an arm around my shoulders. 'It hasn't been easy for her.'

'My pleasure, Mr ... Rosewell, isn't it? Delighted to meet you at last. Sybil Faugharne.' They shook hands like two men. 'I'm sure I don't know what came over me just now. I'm normally nice as pie. Just ask Lucia.' She winked at me.

'Whatever it was, it was mighty impressive.'

'Not as impressive as the singing,' Sybil indicated to me. 'Roma will be sorry to have missed it. She sends her apologies and good wishes.'

Arthur hugged me tighter. 'Lucia is a project, for sure. I think she will go on to great things. Starting already.'

Did I imagine it, or did Sybil raise an eyebrow? If she did, it was so fast I fancied I didn't see it. Turning to me, she said, 'I always knew Amelia Hall was a nasty little tart, but what she said to you there was quite breathtakingly cruel. I've no idea how you put up with it.'

'We're used to it, ma'am.' Arthur was tense beside me, debating how much to tell.

'I see it as like paying tax,' I chimed in. 'On my existence.'

'Tax on one's existence,' Sybil said thoughtfully, tapping her chin. 'Now there's a rum idea.' After a pause, she added, 'Come to think of it, I was pretty nasty to you too. Outside that bloody museum. Not in that league, thank God no, but I'm not proud of what I said.'

I made polite noises. God bless her for trying, but I was tired of laying bare my pain for ignorant strangers to ask questions and learn their lessons. As was she, I was sure. I knew that part of her anger at me that day was because she knew of my disapproval of her romantic life. Yes, I remembered what she said to me, but I would rather simply forget it than go through the upheaval of forgiveness.

Sybil, I knew, was highly socially aware, and I think she understood me because she changed the subject, agreeing with Arthur that I was sublime. After a few more pleasantries, she declared she had a party to go to. 'Oh, do come along! My companions are enlightened people, not Amelia Halls. And there's decent champagne. I've no idea how it was sourced with all these blasted shortages, but I'm not asking questions.'

'I think not, thank you.' Arthur was polite but firm. 'I do hope we get a chance to meet again.' He shook Sybil's hand, putting the conversation to an end. I had wanted it to continue a while and felt a little resentful. Was he my manager in life as well as in music, rejecting invitations on my behalf? We put on our coats and hats, and he steered me out into the dirty December sleet. 'Did you notice that gentleman with the thick moustache over by the pillar? The one who barely spoke?' he asked.

I said that I had: a tall, severe man in his fifties with a thick head of dark hair and a sharply levelled moustache. He had glanced over at me occasionally.

'That's M. Japrisot, the French impresario. He singled you out for particular praise, Lucia. Said your mastery was "quite remar-rrrkable".' Arthur was ebullient.

I laughed. 'Your French accent is terrible.'

'I know! Who cares?' Arthur declared gaily. 'He wants you to join the spring season performance of *Aida* at the Paris National Opera! It's the chorus, yes, but also to understudy for Nehebka.'

'Without an audition?' I was incredulous.

'He said that after hearing you tonight none was needed. Oh, and about the part. He was quite apologetic about that but said there weren't any other parts available.' It was clear to both of us that M. Japrisot's apology was based on Nehebka being a 'Nubian slave,' but frankly I couldn't have cared less. I clapped my gloved hands and jumped in the air, Arthur laughingly telling me to steady on.

We walked to Clapton Square where Arthur flagged us a motor cab, thankfully without incident. I settled into the leather seat and tucked my coat over my calves, and he dived in beside me. 'So, we're going to Paris?' I said.

'Right after we get married, honey. Straight on the boat to Dover.'

Then it hit me like a blast of sleet. I might not be on that boat. I might be in prison because Lilian's plan had fallen apart.

'Are you OK? You look a bit ill.'

My heart was cold and heavy. The whole thing with Lilian seemed little more than a feverish dream, and yet I knew I would meet her on Friday all the same. The two parts of me – musician versus mother, public versus private – were separating out so rapidly and so completely there seemed to be no way of reconciling the two.

I turned a beseeching gaze to Arthur, but he wasn't looking at me and could not know what I was going through. The cab lurched through the busy streets, the driver humming 'Jingle Bells' under his breath. I was sick of Christmas already.

Arthur stroked my cheek. 'Lucia. I only want you to be happy.' *No*, a new voice spoke up in my head, *you want me to be your puppet. 'Your project', that was what you called me.* I shut it down. It was unfair on Arthur to think like that. He had only ever helped me, why should I be ungrateful?

'Arthur,' I sighed, 'I am delighted, of course. I just feel as if – as if I am leaving little Domi behind.' And with that, tears sprang from my eyes.

Arthur did not tell me to wipe them away as I thought he might. Instead he gave me a worried look. 'Lucia.' He was grave. 'You cannot let future jewels be stolen from you by past sadness.' One of the tears rolled down my cheek. If Arthur couldn't tolerate such a basic expression of regret, how could I tell him even the half of it?

'It's not past,' was all I could choke out. 'It never is.'

At that he grew quite stern indeed. 'Well you must make it past. You need to let go.'

'I'll never let go. I'll always wait for him. You need to understand that.' He would never realise how much courage I had to muster to say that.

He replied with an unenthusiastic 'I do understand.' Then, 'Here's you. I'll see you to your door, then I need to go home.' He kissed my hand as he took me down from the taxi, but his lips on my knuckles felt more like a reproof. We walked to my door in silence. I expected us to part then and there, politely at odds. But then I saw two people in the doorway and heard Mrs Baxter shouting.

'If I've told you once, I've told you ten times: we don't want your kind here.' Her voice was husky and raw around the edges: 'I lost my son at Cambrai. You've a brass neck calling round 'ere!'

I recognised Eva, but not her companion: a tall, fair-haired man with a round face and snub nose. He was wearing a long, shabby coat. From the look he gave me and Arthur, I could tell he was unused to seeing people of colour. Something in his height, his bearing, the intensity of his blue eyes, set a warning instinct tingling. And then I understood. In the past, I found it hard to tell one white man from another at six yards. But this man's type I recognised instantly. So that was why Eva had been so reticent in her letters. And why, now, she wouldn't look us in the eye.

'Everyone, this is Mr Badura. My husband.'

To say there was chaos would be an understatement. In the middle of that cold night, Mrs Baxter made it clear, loudly and repeatedly, that neither Eva nor her new husband – 'as she calls him. I would say he's a filthy Hun' – would be welcome in her house. Coloured folks were fine, she added, waving at myself and Arthur, who, having met her on several occasions previous, could not hide his amusement at her volte-face.

'Guess we've been promoted,' was his comment while Eva and the Hun stood there, staring like bumblepuppies, with hardly three suitcases between them. I was glad Arthur was there because I couldn't bring myself to say a word to her. All that labba-labba about her delayed demobilisation was to put us off the scent. She had married a German.

After Bo Destouches being bayonetted to shreds and Sybil drinking herself insensible for two years afterwards. After Robin Mackenzie's anguish as the barely living pieces of raw meat had wailed and howled their death agony on his operating table. After the passionate obsession she had carried for Christopher all this time. *She had married a German.* I couldn't get over it. Couldn't look at him. Couldn't imagine how she could touch him.

Somewhere in the background she was wittering on about taking a slow train through the bombed-out countryside and crossing the border to Saarbrücken to find him, tracking him down in a hospital ward – and the rest being history. Said with a smile while I cringed with disgust.

Arthur, by contrast, redeemed himself. With nobody knowing what to do next, he effortlessly took charge. 'Sir,' he addressed Eva's husband, 'may I introduce myself? Arthur Rosewell. I can take care of this. But I must request that you say nothing for the next half hour. And I mean nothing.'

'Ja, I do dat now—' the fellow began (an unexpectedly melodic baritone).

'Did you hear me?' Arthur hissed. 'Say nothing. Do. Not. Open. Your. Mouth. Now' – to Eva – 'shall we proceed?'

'By all means, Mr Rosewell.' The girl had the cheek to look flirty at him!

We escorted Eva and the German – I could not bring myself to say his name – to a guesthouse for commercial travellers down by Chelsea Harbour. The place was all shuttered up; Arthur had to wake up the concierge by banging on the window. If that gentleman in his nightgown was confused at the sight of a black man doing all the talking while a silent hulking white fellow lingered several steps behind, he didn't bring it up.

Arthur managed to get Eva and the German a room. Eva profusely thanked him, while, all through the exchange, the German did as he was told and kept his mouth shut. Phew! She did try to talk to me just as we were leaving, asking, all pathetic, 'Do you hate me, Lucia?'

'Never mind what I feel about you,' I returned. 'Wait until Sybil learns of this.'

Eva already looked haggard and green in that entrance hall, but when I mentioned Sybil her face collapsed. 'She'll be furious, I know. Oh, does nobody here understand? These past few years have been so hard. Do I not deserve a little comfort and peace?'

In the arms of the enemy? 'What about your dreams? To go to . . . Summerplace? To write books? Is that all gone? You were going to be a proper bluestocking, just like . . .' I trailed off.

Eva answered me quickly. 'Stefan knows all about Christopher. D'you remember, I told him everything that first week he came in at death's door?'

'Ja, the Eva save me—'

'Shhhhhh!' we all hissed at him.

'Sorry,' he mouthed. I felt a sudden urge to giggle. It was all too ridiculous for words. But then Eva began to cry. 'I can't hold on to those dreams. I haven't a penny to my name. Neither does Stefan. Maybe some day I'll go to Oxford. But I've been fighting so long. Surviving so long alone.' She put her hands to her eyes. 'I need to rest.'

I could see that it was true by looking at her. She had bruised, greenish rings around her eyes, her cheeks were dragged down, and she looked far older than her twenty-two years. I held my arms out. 'Come here, sweetheart. I'm not gwaan turn away from you.' At that moment, I knew I had done the right thing by not telling her about Lilian's appearance in my life. She was in no state to hear about that, especially since I suspected she was in a fragile place, hadn't really got over Christopher, and never would. In marrying this Badura, she wanted to hurt and shock the world that had destroyed her first love.

'Thank you,' Eva sniffled a little. 'And please thank your Mr Rosewell for his kindness.' Arthur was waiting outside, at a discreet distance.

'I'll tell him,' I said. I was re-warming to Arthur myself.

We said our goodbyes, with promises to talk more later, then he and I left the 'newlyweds' and returned to Fulham Road.

'Did you pay for the room?' I asked, once out of earshot.

Arthur's loud laughter made me feel all was right with the

world again. 'You gotta be joking. I'm a tolerant man, as you know.' I suppressed a snort. 'But I ain't gonna pay for a Boche.'

'I'm glad to hear it, Mr Rosewell,' I said, reaching up to kiss him goodnight and receiving a long embrace. The adventure of Eva and her German had had the paradoxical effect of putting us to rights again. I felt a fiery gratitude to him. And then I remembered what I had to do. This could be your last moment of happiness, I thought, so make the most of it. I let him enter into a kiss so prolonged that when he pulled away he exclaimed, 'Phew!'

After he was gone, and I was inside and alone, all gaiety drained away. The gas was out again so I could not even light the ring for its meagre heat, and I shivered in my blankets. I wished more than anything that my father was still alive. I missed his wisdom, his advice, his cigar and rum smell. 'The trouble with you, Lucia, is that you can do anything.' Turned out my father was right, just not in the way he meant. I was capable of doing anything.

23

FRIDAY, 13 DECEMBER 1918

s the winter dawn eased its light over London, I made my way to Victoria Station's buffet and waited there for some time, perched on a three-legged stool, watching the trains arrive and depart. *It's not too late to leave*, I told myself, but after each train pulled out, I was still there, rooted on that bockety stool. A paralysis had seized me. Eva used to talk about Fate and the Ancient Greeks and all that labba-labba. Now I understood what she meant.

The train from Kent arrived, belching smoke, brakes screeching. I hoped Lilian would not be on it, but no: there she was, scarved head bent, fumbling her way down the carriage steps. Again, she looked smarter than the last time I'd seen her; the closer we got to McCrum's hopeful demise, the better she looked. Nobody rushed chivalrously to the old woman's side. And nor did I. She had told me to meet her outside the Grosvenor Hotel, near the bridge that was struck by an anti-aircraft shell, but I decided to stay where I was. Let her find me. My goodwill, brought on by such quantities of her home-made wine, had somewhat seeped away over the intervening days.

The station was less crowded than when twelve boat trains left every day, each packed to the roof with soldiers. Nevertheless, I was impressed by how quickly Lilian spotted me. She waved, strode over and plonked down in a rattan chair opposite me, dropping a patchwork bag with tortoiseshell handles in a bundle at her feet. I noticed a cake tin peeping out. Presumably inside that was her murder weapon. 'Ready to go?'

'I'll say this one more time, so we're clear—' I began.

'You're doing this for one reason only. I know. I am confident you will see him again.'

'I wish I could share your optimism,' I replied sourly.

Lilian was sharp. 'Get up. We have no time to waste.'

We walked the mile from Victoria Station to Horse Guards Avenue in silence. All around us there were signs of electioneering having its last gasp: posters up on lamp posts, while newsboys screamed headlines praising whichever politician their papers were supporting. I cared nothing for Lloyd George or Bonar Law, Liberal or Conservative. Who was there for me? The Irish had their own party, it was true, but there was nothing for coloured people, even though we had fought the war for the British. As far as the government were concerned, we didn't count.

A COUNTRY FIT FOR HEROES, one poster screamed, with Lloyd George's head underneath. *The ones left after you've killed half of them and broken the rest*, I thought. On this point at least, Lilian and I were of one mind. Among her drunken confessions to me the previous Sunday night was that as a woman of property aged over thirty she had gained the vote. 'Couldn't care less about it,' she'd told me. 'Am I supposed to be grateful or something?'

We were early, but Lilian did not slow down her pace, going forward with the grim determination of a subaltern headed over the top at the Somme. We reached the odd-looking Cádiz Memorial, which seemed to show a cannon sticking out of the backside of a dragon, and, right across from it, the War Office. Five storeys high and grim as thunder.

'Here is where we part company,' Lilian said, clutching the bag to her chest. 'Have you got the map?'

'Yes.'

She frowned. 'Show me.'

Blouse and skirt! What a martinet. I took it out of my purse and unfolded it for her to see. When she saw I was irritated, she smirked. 'I was the same with Christopher, always checking his bags. It annoyed him too. Spoil-the-party Lilian, he called me.'

La la la, as if I cared.

Seeing my indifference, her smile faded. 'Go to where it's marked,' she told me. 'You know what to do from there.'

We parted without another word. I found the staff entrance relatively quickly: a set of double doors with a ramp attached for trolleys. There appeared to be no checks on anyone entering the building. Of course, with the Bangarang over, even someone like that German Eva had incomprehensibly married could probably stroll in, and nobody would be bothered.

The doors opened into a surprisingly airy corridor, with stone floors, wide internal windows framed with light timber and red-painted glass-panelled doors every couple of yards. There was an odd floral fragrance – some cleaning solution I hadn't yet come across: citronella and ammonia. The musician in me yearned to toss a few notes and hear them bounce off the walls, but I knew what I was there for, and the absurdity of such a thought made me want to laugh. Or cry. And I was in no position to do either.

A quick look at the map soon established that I needed to head right to get to the heart of the building: the Quadrangle. The corridor passed high-ceilinged rooms where men worked away at comptometers, heads bent over the arrays of keys as they tap-tap-tapped and made notes. So absorbed were they that I was able to walk straight past them without being observed.

I found a wooden swing door marked CLEANING STAFF ONLY and tentatively pushed it open – then immediately darted back. Two girls were inside, bickering about soap. They must not see me under any circumstance. Heart thudding, I flattened myself behind another set of double doors and waited until the girls emerged and departed in the other direction. Praying the room was now empty, I slid through the doors into a room filled with lockers.

Most of them were padlocked, but one or two were unlocked. I rifled through the first looking for a uniform. A long, blue corduroy skirt, a blouse . . . no good, those were street clothes. In the next one I found, beautifully folded, a maid's cap, a starched pinafore dress and a plain, worn pair of pumps. Relief! I folded my own clothes and put them carefully behind a stack of lockers. On my way out the door I spotted a duster on a small trolley and took it with me. If anyone were to enquire after my business, I could wave it in their faces.

The corridors were all numbered in an ordered structure, like bars in a stave marked common time, but it still took a while to get to McCrum's office. Every time I heard somebody coming, I ducked into an alcove or a stairwell, and when I could not avoid passing them, I was careful to dip my head and wave the duster so that all they saw was the cloth.

I reached the Quadrangle corridor, second floor, office No. 7. The walls were fancier here, panelled in oak. The door to No. 7 was firmly shut, and I had no idea whether McCrum or Lilian were inside. My stomach dropped with nerves, and I imagined the scratching feeling of rope on the tender skin under my throat. Then the tightening. Then the drop—

I pressed my ear to the door. I could make out a male voice: a barking baritone. That would be the bakra McCrum. Listening further, I could hear Lilian, her voice higher than usual, crooning, supplicating, gasping with gullible wonder. Mezzo-soprano. Not her usual cigarette-addled contralto at all. She was putting it on for the brigadier big time.

'You know you can still get out of this mess?' I whispered fiercely to myself. 'You can turn around and walk right out of here. Worry about the uniform later. Just go.' I walked back to the nearest corner. But then I remembered what Mrs Gunning had told me about Domi: 'He doesn't look happy in himself,' and the anguish I had felt then returned as fresh as a new day. The way she had said it, her face composed and serious, I knew it wasn't a line Lilian had fed her. No, I would not retreat. I would stay and see this out.

Pressing my ear to the door again, I heard Lilian say, in that same unnatural croon, 'Do have some cake, sir.'

'Thank you, I shall . . . Oh, that is rather excellent.'

A strange relief filled me. The conductor had raised his baton, the performance was in train. There was no going back now.

'Delicious!' McCrum again. I hoped Lilian had got the balance of strychnine right so that McCrum would eat enough to fell him without detecting the aftertaste.

'Have another, dear sir. It gives me such pleasure to see you enjoy my humble offering.'

Haha! I bet it did. I wondered if she had laid it on a little thick. The obsequiousness, that is, not the strychnine. The more of that the better, to hurry things up.

Then I heard the echoing clatter of footsteps. Someone was coming! I fled my position and started pretend-dusting the far wall. No point poking my nose out until I had to. In the end, I didn't have to: the man disappeared into an office along the corridor. I wondered at Lilian's desire to have me there. She seemed to be handling things well herself. How could I provide moral support from the other side of a closed door?

All was quiet once more, apart from the voices in McCrum's office, which still had the timbre and cadence of normal conversation. I stayed close to the door, compelled to listen. I must admit to you, my friend, I was utterly enthralled. I am an opera singer, and drama is my natural home.

McCrum was talking again – or rather it sounded like a rant. I heard 'malingerers' and 'bloody well shot'. Then, mid-sentence, he was suddenly cut off. There was a loud thud, as if he had hit the floor, and quiet footsteps, followed by a quick firm click of the lock. I guessed what had happened. The poison was taking effect, and Lilian had locked the door and put the key out of McCrum's reach.

I knew something of the effects of strychnine poisoning from a story my father had told me about a murder back home in Jamaica. The Lockharts were an old plantation family who continued to live in their home, Martin's Hill, near Mile Gully Church, after emancipation went through. One windy day in 1841, the sole remaining house servant entered the master bedroom to see Mrs Lockhart sprawled out on the bed, her body jerking in spasms, jaw locked, agony in her eyes. On the bedside table stood a half-drunk glass of strychnine tonic, taken in those days as a stimulant like coffee, but this glass contained about a hundred times the normal dose.

Upon her death, Mr Lockhart was arrested, though he swore one of the field men had done it. The family left Jamaica, and nobody went near the plantation again. Even the church at Mile Gully was abandoned as the locals swore it was haunted by Mrs Lockhart's ghost.

Lilian Shandlin had told me she wanted to see McCrum die

like a dog. If the Lockhart murder was any indication, she would get her wish. But how long would it take? It had been ten minutes, fifteen, twenty! since McCrum ate the cake. From time to time, I could still hear his anger rise before being quenched by another wave of the poison working its malign magic on his body. Part of me could not help being impressed. He would surely die, but still he fought it like a tiger. And it was probably the closest he'd ever been to fighting anything, despite all his medals and dinky badges on his military uniform.

Thirty-five minutes. This was going on for far too long. The first movement of Beethoven's fifth is just over seven minutes long. This was five times longer and still no sign of reaching the coda! The light was shifting in the panes from midday to afternoon. It would soon start its long retreat across the stone floors. Again I considered fleeing.

Dusting. Forty minutes. Banging in the office again. Now Lilian talking, in her own voice now, more confident. Then another interruption, this time from outside in the corridor.

Two men carrying files and discussing something with each other were walking towards me. 'You see, if we bring it to his attention now, it might be premature.'

'Yes, but . . .' Mumble.

Whose attention? Were they talking about McCrum? I couldn't know, but they were getting closer, and there was no time to waste. Lilian had said to bring interlopers to her attention by any means necessary. So I backed away around the bend in the corridor and began to sing. Loud and sweet, like the clanging bells at St Giles-without-Cripplegate. The acoustics in the War Office corridor were not quite on point, echoes all over the damn place, but I did my best.

The two men stopped talking, presumably in wonder at the sudden sound of a soprano so unreasonably brightening their dull day, but having taken advantage of the building's curve, I was just beyond their vision. Would it work, though? Yes. I heard the key turn in the lock and the door opening. Lilian put her head out and said, 'Are you looking for the brigadier? He's asked not to be disturbed.'

A muffled roar from said brigadier made it clear that he would like to be disturbed, thank you very much, but his meaning did not translate itself to the men waiting outside, who must have presumed he was in a mood and didn't want to see them. They shuffled uncomfortably for a moment, being English and not wanting to get involved in any fuss-fuss. 'I . . . think it can wait,' one of them finally said.

'Yes, we'll come back.'

Still they stood there, looking awkward.

'Where's Tulloch?' one of them enquired. 'Isn't he normally McCrum's man?'

Mi Gad, would yu gweh, I silently begged.

Lilian sweetly informed them Mr Tulloch was indisposed that day and shut the door again. Finally they walked off, clearly not satisfied. I could tell they would be back soon. Lilian might have been sure that McCrum's death would not elicit a prosecution; I was not inclined to be as optimistic. Not to mention the man wasn't even dead yet!

I knocked smartly on the door. No response. I banged and shouted until Lilian unlocked the door. She looked a bit flustered as she hissed at me to shut it quickly. The room was chaka-chaka, in utter chaos. A huge teak desk with a green leather top stood in the far corner near the Quadrangle windows. The lamp on it was knocked over, and fragments of glass from the bulb littered the desk and the deep pile carpet. Papers and files were strewn all over the place, and there was a sharp scent of spilled gin. Perfectly intact, however, was the plate that still held two-thirds of the Cake of Death. The fireplace implements were scattered on the floor – I guessed that somebody had tried to use them as weapons.

Smack bang in the middle of the room, on a red and grey Turkish rug, lay McCrum, supine, purple-faced, legs in the air as if waiting for an adult nappy change. His jaw was stiff, and he gasped for air even though the windows were open and a wet breeze rolled in. His eyes were turned up towards the back of his head so I could only see the whites, while his military jacket was ripped open, buttons scattered around him. He was making some sort of snorting sound, trying to speak but his jaw was too tight. It was a horrible sight. Lilian had surely got her wish. She was not happy though – more panicked.

'It's taking so long. He ate one slice, and I tried to get him to eat another one, but he refused—'

'Stop babbling. We need to get out of here.' I grabbed her arm, but she shook me off.

'We can't. He hasn't ingested enough. He could take another hour to lose consciousness at this rate. And between spasms he may be able to speak. We need to wait until he's—'

I heard a roar behind me. Cha, he was trying to get up! McCrum fixed on me a malevolent glare, and I nearly quailed. The purple on his cheeks had cleared, his breathing had returned to normal, and there was something frightening about his even tan and the pallor beneath it, his pouting lips, the contemptuous expression beneath his moustache, even at such an extreme moment in his life.

Lilian, quick as a flash, had her hand on the fire iron and struck at his arms as he raised himself up. Confused, he fell back on the floor while she stood above him, brandishing her weapon. I saw that she had bruises on her face and neck. He must have tried to tackle her before.

'You need to finish him off with that poker.' I said. My friend, when I think of it now, I cannot believe the words that came out of my own mouth. McCrum evidently could, though, because he fixed me with one of his glares, first of general racial disgust, then of particular, enraged recognition. He remembered me all right: as the associate of the surgeon Robin Mackenzie who had interfered with his plans for the injured French boy. Now mine was one of the last faces he would see. But even dying as he was, he was far stronger than myself and Lilian put together. He would surely overpower us.

Lilian appeared paralysed, as if she had administered poison to herself as well as to her victim. Her plan was not working, and she didn't have the mental flexibility to come up with a new one. That was a problem because there was every chance that when the men I'd distracted came back, a still-living McCrum would have time to tell them what had happened to him. He was now wrenching himself free of Lilian, pulling and dragging himself back to the desk, while she just stood there with that poker, useless, her face drained. Macca! This was a disaster. We were the worst murderers on earth.

Right there and then, something someone once told me rushed into my mind, clearing out all other thoughts. A grating, familiar Scots accent. *King Solomon's Mines.* Two African tribes having a fierce battle. The medicine men opening a major artery when the casualty was a lost cause and letting them die.

I had said to Robin, outraged, 'That would be murder!'

'Och, how though? When the poor chavie is already half dead?' he had answered. Then he'd said...mi Gad, what?

Help me, Robin. What do I do?

I could not remember. Fear was beginning to cloud my judgement. 'How did you do it, Robin?' I said aloud. 'I need you to tell me.' And as if he stood before me, something clicked, and Robin's instructions poured calmly and dispassionately into my brain. *I concluded the easiest option was to cut the left carotid, just below the sinus bulb.*

My mind had entered the eye of the tornado, and I was unnaturally calm. Ready to do what was needed. How do I cut that artery, at that point? How do I even get to it?

McCrum was behind his desk. Now I saw what he was looking for: the letter-opener sitting in its holder on the far left-hand side from where I was standing. His hand was reaching for it . . . If I could get there before him, that was my weapon. Carefully, as if I had hours to think about it, I contemplated the pattern of serration, the turn of the blade. The slight angling of the handle's edges. How it would fit in my hand. How I would have to inflect my wrist. All calculations I used every day, whenever I took up a pen, or a cup, or anything involving my dominant hand.

But this was different. My mind was never clearer, or freer of disruptive thought, like a still pool of water. No joy, anguish, anticipation or regret. Just an arc of careful sight-reading followed by pure action. A scattering of semiquavers. Miss Slade slamming into the 'Exsultate, jubilate.' Sing the fast notes slowly, first, to savour each one. Then, knowing the music, a little faster each time until it no longer hurts to sing them with precision as well as speed. This is the score. These are the notes. Read, breathe and read again.

Robin's voice again, firm and encouraging. *He's a cunt, Lucy. Go get him.*

Right there and then, there was nobody else in that room, in the whole universe, except me and that man, and the knife on the desk between us.

24

DECEMBER 1918–MARCH 1919

Well, my friend, what is there to say? You sit across the table from an unapprehended murderer. The incident didn't hit the news-stands until two days later, and even then it was reported in a surprisingly subdued manner: on the bottom of page three of the *Daily Mail*, page four of *The Times*. Each article contained just a few paragraphs, divulging only the victim's rank and not his name, adding that 'police are regarding his death as a tragedy' – a phrase that prompted much feverish decoding on my part. Did tragedy mean they had decided to ignore that it was murder? I had sung enough arias to know that the tragic hero in an opera normally dispatched themselves. Was that what the reporter was hinting at?

Either way, I was on tenterhooks for a good long time. Every time a policeman looked at me for more than a second, I imagined that rather than being briefly curious about the colour of my skin he was intently interested in the colour of my guilt.

'Why the sudden interest in the news?' Arthur laughed, as I bought a copy of each paper at a corner stall after leaving Covent

Garden one night. I dodged his question and, once home, folded them out on the floor to have a good read. I wanted to be sure that there wasn't something I had missed, something that would indicate the officers of the law were hot on my trail. Because for all that Lilian Shandlin had delivered a lethal dose of strychnine in that cake she baked, for all that he was doomed after two mouthfuls, she had not ended the life of Lionel Anthony McCrum.

I had.

To this day I find it difficult to recall the sequence of events. It all happened so fast, and my mind was so detached from normal time that I recall it in flashes. The run for the desk. The leap I made with almost superhuman strength. My hand battling his for possession of the knife handle, and quickly winning. He had not expected a left-handed onslaught. The bright December sun filtered through the panelled windows, glinting off the blade edge. Making quick, cold calculations: where to aim for the sinus bulge in the artery, whether to flick up or down, when the next spasm would bring him to me. The moment my eyes met his. My face as close to his as if we were about to kiss. The balefulness in his eyes as the life drained out of them, the pupils dilating. I held his gaze until he could gaze no more. I wanted to say, 'I know your type,' whispering Christopher Shandlin's words into his ear like a lover would, but I was so locked in that gaze, in every pore of his unlovely, dying face, in the strange odour from his skin, that I quite forgot.

And then, finish. Down like a tree. Head on the desk. My friend, I beg you not to be shocked at this point, but I must tell you of the mild exultation. It was like applause after a testing but well-delivered musical performance. It felt as if I had done something creative rather than destructive. I didn't feel a whit of guilt. I still don't.

Later on that day, in harsh early-afternoon brightness, I sat next to Lilian on the stone lip of the fountain at Trafalgar Square. We were both breathing heavily: I had dragged her out of the War Office and down Whitehall Court at top speed, pausing barely two minutes to change into my street clothes, Lilian standing there like a ghost while I struggled into them and stuffed the stained clothing into her patchwork bag. I remember the grip I kept on it, pressing so tightly on the handles that my skin was white around my nails. In that bag were the maid's dress, the pinny stained with dark, arterial blood, the remains of the poisoned cake.

Nearby, a man was juggling what looked like burning sticks. A crowd had gathered around him. I watched for a while, inhaling, exhaling. Lilian's eyes were hooded and dull, her face more cavernous than ever. On this busy day full of Christmas shoppers and street carols, of new life and hope, she looked like a ship-wreck. Then she turned and looked at me, with those frozen blue eyes turned black. 'You know,' she murmured, 'I wonder if his death was somewhat intentional.'

'Blouse and skirt, woman! Of course, it was intentional. *You* intended it.'

'I don't mean McCrum's,' she said distantly. 'I was thinking of Christopher's.'

'Oh?' I was cold. The euphoria I'd felt earlier was wearing off.

'Christopher was so . . . *defiant* during that tribunal. It was almost as if he wanted it all to happen. You know, he once told me about an officer he'd met who had bayonetted a Boche in the face. The officer's own face was in a perpetual rictus, Christopher said, so that he could make himself suffer what he'd inflicted on the German. That's the kind of memory those men were dealing with. Perhaps he couldn't handle it anymore. Perhaps he was looking for McCrum to give him an honourable way out . . . At least it's broken up the ring. Though there'll be another McCrum. As long as men are men, and men are dangerous.'

I felt exhausted and bleak. Suddenly I wanted nothing more to do with this woman. She'd brought me nothing but trouble, and made me vex. I still worried about those two men passing by McCrum's office. We might see each other again – as co-defendants in court. 'I can't help you there, Lilian. I don't think your son would have wanted this.' I rose. 'Please tell me when there's news of Domi.'

Turning away from her, I walked towards the juggler, not looking back. Higher and higher the flames went, and yet still he surely caught the objects by their handles, to applause and whoops every time. He was only a few feet from me as I walked past the crowd, but the flames didn't give off any heat.

Half an hour later, at the back of a used-goods yard near our flat, I found another fire burning. The air around it was dark and noxious, and I could see tyres on the heap of burning rubbish. But on that cold afternoon the heat was welcome, and a few vagrants sat around it, warming their hands. I threw in the bag and watched the flames slowly consume the patchwork patterns, the blood, the apron, the cake. 'Burning the evidence,' I told the down-and-outs, pretending I was joking. They, cheeks blue from the cold, merely grinned at my supposed joke and enjoyed the surge of heat. I stood and watched until there was no trace of any of it left.

While I did not wish to hear from Lilian again, I still hoped that I might be brought news of Domi, via the Irishwoman. When weeks and months passed, the furore about McCrum died down and I heard nothing, I realised I had been had. When would I learn the lesson my father had taught me about white people? They always want something. They always welsh on their promises. All Lilian's drunken confidences, her attempts to identify with me because of her injudicious marriage – it was all just to get what she needed. Just like Robin and the rest of them.

It was time to try and get my life back to normal.

The more time I spent with Arthur, making plans and formal-
ising dreams, the more the whole horror of McCrum seemed like
a dream, as if someone else had administered that final blow. But
at night when I tried to pray I was reminded of the madness still
somewhere within me. The hands Arthur kissed had held the
knife. The eyes that looked into his with love had looked into
McCrum's with cool control. The musician's pleasure felt the same
as the murderer's. Lilian had forced that discovery on me too. Bad
cess to her, as Eva would say.

You say so little, my friend. You don't look shocked – that's
something. That smile of yours . . . If your conscience does bother
you, there is a building around the corner, untouched by the Luft-
waffe, which contains the Metropolitan Police. You are welcome to
denounce me to them for the murder of Brigadier Lionel
McCrum. However, I suspect that the legacy of his infamous deeds
casts long enough a shadow that even now the good officers would
be unwilling to prosecute.

I didn't tell anyone else about what I'd done. Either I did not
trust them enough to keep this secret or I valued them too highly
as people to have them know something like that about me. And
the more I edited it out of my interactions with anyone else the
more it seemed implausible that I had ever committed such an act,
that I had raised a weapon against another human being in a state
of – I should say *anger* but that was the furthest emotion from my
mind that day. The one person who might have understood was
Eva. I know she was capable of deep implacable hatred. But her
marriage had alienated us, and she was preoccupied with the
problems her impulsive gesture had caused.

Stefan Badura had not fared well since his arrival in
England. The morning after Arthur and I booked him into the
hotel on Chelsea Embankment, the proprietor heard one word

out of his mouth and immediately called the police. Barely half an hour after that they arrived at his rooms and packed him off to an internment camp on the Isle of Man, amid much protesting from Eva. What on earth was she expecting? That a Hun would be let off by an arresting officer who had probably lost many friends in the war? I couldn't sympathise with her. At least we were still talking. From Sybil, there was utter, contemptuous silence.

He wrote every day, Eva reported with pride. I merely humphed, being disinclined to praise him for frequent letter-writing, since a man in his situation usually has little else to do. He was preparing to apply for employment too, she told me. I tried to explain to Eva that given I had been unable to hold down any job that did not involve using my vocal cords, what earthly hope did he have? 'You'd be better off divorcing him,' I said, not bothering to mince my words.

It did no good. She was obdurate, deciding to remain in London and wait for his release. Mrs Baxter's antagonism had forced her to move to shabbier rooms in the East End. On the other hand, Eva's treachery had induced a slight change in that lady's temperament towards me. When we passed in the hall, she would even give me an occasional 'good morning', and one time she said to me in a whisper, 'You've got any friends looking for a room, you just tell 'em to ask for Mrs Baxter, and I'll do 'em a deal. As long as they're well-behaved like you.' I murmured my thanks and quickly moved on. I had no reason to believe she wouldn't turn on me again whenever it suited her.

Eva, meanwhile, stayed in the East End, pounding away on her newly filched Noiseless Typewriter, possibly the most comically misnamed product on the planet. The men had snatched back all the clerical jobs, so for a brief while she worked in a backroom in the same department in Liberty's where she had encountered

Lilian the Witch, fetching hatboxes for wealthy customers, a job she detested.

The tenement she lived in was truly grotty, to the point where drunks would vomit on the landing outside her attic room. I feared for her safety during those months. Arthur more than once counselled me not to go there, but from time to time I would make the trek out to visit. Eva would coax the little gas flame into life and make tea, and we would argue gently about the Irish Question. I thought that Eva's race had every right to self-determination and cited the great slave rebellions of the previous century in Jamaica, not to mention my own mother's Maroon ancestors proudly rising up too. To my surprise, she was staunchly unionist in her sympathies. Or rather, I suspected, she was staunchly opposed to her stepsister's beliefs, which tended towards the Fenian.

We also talked about Arthur's and my engagement. Eva praised Arthur to the rafters, as well she might, and added meaningfully that she was glad I could move on. That was as much talk as she would allow of little Dominic, and since that subject reminded me of others, I was happy to let it go. We discussed at length her unresolved quarrel with Sybil, who from the moment she learned of Eva's marriage had vowed to have nothing further to do with her friend. This grieved Eva very much, and she often asked me how to make amends.

In Eva's dealings with me, particularly in her defensiveness around Mr Badura, I detected some of the same unnaturally high energy I had witnessed in the woman who might have been her mother-in-law. Eva spoke about Christopher less often now, and I did not encourage her to do so. To be frank, I'd had enough of that entire rhaatid family to last several lifetimes. I just wanted to forget about anything to do with them.

While Eva knew nothing of my experiences with Lilian – I did not wish to cause her pain, or complicate her life – sometimes when the light of evening was wan and half baked and she was talking about some poem, or a piece of music, or anything that took her out of the daily path and into a place of sublimity, a veil of sadness would drop over her eyes and I knew she was thinking of Christopher. Or when she started on about some terrible poem by some ex-Tommy she'd read in the paper. (There were a lot of those.) At those times I knew Mr Badura's volatile, sometimeish predecessor was still on her mind.

I *did* want to talk to her about McCrum's death so I could get practised at sounding smooth about it. One day I tentatively brought it up.

'Yes. I saw it in the paper.' She didn't seem very excited. 'Suicide, eh? That's what they're hinting at, though I wouldn't be surprised if someone killed him and they covered it up.'

'Can't imagine who.' I kept my voice calm, though my thumbs were pressing into my palms and my heart was racing. I hadn't expected her to get that close to the truth. No more than I was telling her the truth in return, cu yu. I didn't have to imagine.

Thankfully, Eva seemed to have no interest in pursuing that line of thought. 'Either way, I'm glad he's gone,' she said distantly, casting her eye over at the Noiseless Typewriter that dwarfed the miserable bureau upon which it was precariously placed. 'It means he can't sue.' She then admitted that she had finally submitted her article to *Blackwood's*. 'Once I mentioned McCrum, Mr St Leger, the editor, told me it could never get published. I said I would change the name and rank, but they still said no. He sues everybody, apparently, and the very threat of it is enough to make people back down. Now at least we don't have that obstacle.'

When I asked her what her husband thought, she said, 'Stefan's been very kind and understanding, but he doesn't really get it. I've tried to explain the white-feather thing to him several times, and he still doesn't understand.'

'Really? What did they do in Germany when a man didn't want to fight?'

'Brought him along anyway, I gather. Happened with the Quakers. Not having a weapon meant he wouldn't last very long.'

I whistled. 'Brutal. But honest, I suppose.'

Eva hugged the book in her arms. I noticed the title said *Schiller: Poems* and was glad her German engineer was not completely uncultured. 'One of the camp guards has a brother who works as a quantity surveyor, and they think there might be work for him. But we would have to move to Liverpool.' So, no scholarship, no Summerplace, no Oxford. Everything Christopher had wanted for her was over.

I asked her then did she ever miss him, and she gave me a look. 'What do you think? Half of me continues, at best. Maybe a quarter. The rest died with him. Have mercy, Lucia. Don't ask me again.' I pressed her hand and said nothing. After a brief but full silence, I told her that I was going to see Sybil the following morning about my wedding dress and I would try and bring about a rapprochement then.

Eva rewarded me with a big grin. 'She's making a dress for you? She did that for me once.'

'When?'

'Our first dance at school.' Eva was dreamy. 'Our class went to a fancy ballroom near Winchester, and we all had dance cards and had to wait to be asked to dance by suitable men. I couldn't afford the dress I wanted, so Sybil made it for me.' Now her face was lit up, her memory no longer sad. 'The most *un*-suitable man was watching from afar as we boarded the coaches. Later, we danced on the lawn.'

At that moment, we were brought back to a simpler time: Eva

in her fine dress, she and Christopher dancing. Before the big Bangarang. Before everything was destroyed. Then I wished I hadn't said anything because Eva suddenly put her hands to her face and began to sob. 'Poor boy. He didn't deserve this.' All I could do was put my arms around her and agree. None of us had deserved any of it.

25

MARCH 1919

My wedding day dawned fine and sunny and continued in that fashion until the evening. The horses that brought me to chapel that morning were fine black shires, their manes edged with white, bells tinkling as they trotted down the road. The driver even offered me the reins, and, wary as I was of dirtying my bridal attire, I couldn't resist. So, as we travelled towards the City Temple church on Holborn Viaduct, where my bridegroom awaited me, I was in the driving seat.

I felt the pleasurable chafe of the rough side of the leather on my fingers and palms and the gentle tug of the well-trained horses at my fingertips, and I contemplated joyfully that I would be seeing my brother Reginald again, too. His battalion had been broken up and – finally! – discharged from Taranto, and he had taken a steamer to Southampton. He would delay his outward journey to the West Indies for long enough to celebrate my nuptials. Thank God he had held his peace. His future could have been so much grimmer.

Reginald would not be giving me away, even though he was my only close male relative. Arthur and I had agreed that duty could only be given to the kind, generous Dr Alcindor. When I asked him, he was so astonished I feared he might refuse but then he enveloped me in a bear hug and told me that my request had brought him to tears and he would be delighted to do the honours.

Meredith had written a letter of warm congratulations from Mandeville. Mr Willis had rebuilt his shop at last and (reading between the lines) was doing indifferently with it. She was pregnant with her third child and feeling a little sick. My mother sent nothing. I tried not to be hurt, knowing she was angry that I had not gone along with her plan to marry Mr Paul Dakins of the United Fruit Company back in 1915, but how long could anyone hold a grudge?

Of course, the root cause was that my father had cherished me and not her. She would never forgive me for that, and it hurt now that he was gone and I so badly needed her guiding hand. But wishing would not make it so. Some dem a holla, some a bawl . . .

And my father . . . I wished he were there too. I wished he could take my hand and tell me I had done him proud. Then again, was he proud of me when I lay with Robin? When I tried to drown myself in the Clyde? When I buried that paper knife in McCrum's neck? Perhaps it was just as well if his spirit did not linger too long.

I had slept well, having spent my last night as a single woman in a guest room in Sybil's apartment. 'I'm not having you stuck by yourself in that miserable dump,' she had ordered. That she and Roma shared a bed along the corridor . . . well, I confess that didn't bother me so much any more. Considering.

Sybil took over planning for my wedding with the same military determination that had got her decorated during the war. She made me a gift of my wedding dress, one among the many unworn ones in her wardrobe, and had cranked up her sewing machine to trim and adjust it. It was lovely to look at and touch: canary yellow with a lace flounce peplum. Flimsier in material and further up the calf than I would have liked, cu yu, but she and Roma were both adamant. It suited me very well, certainly better than it would ever have suited Sybil.

'Clive got it for me,' she had explained, making a face when mentioning her ex-husband, 'and I swear he must have been drunk. Can you imagine me wearing it?' I admitted I could not. And it did suit me very well.

Ten minutes before we were due to leave, I got a bit faasty and picked a huge bloom off a potted orchid in one of the windows, fastening it to the dress with a brooch. I nodded at my reflection in the hall mirror of Sybil's building. 'Nice,' I said, and Mirror Lucia nodded back at me.

Sybil and Eva were both invited to the wedding, which was a bit difficult since Eva had stoutly told me she would go nowhere without her new husband and Sybil refused to go near either of them. It took considerable pleading from me, and some gentle reproof from Roma, to persuade her to promise not start a fight, or leave, but she wasn't all that happy about it.

Stefan Badura had been released from the camp on the Isle of Man in late February and had immediately made his way to London to be with Eva. Once his nationality was discovered by her new landlord, Eva, along with her husband and her Noiseless Typewriter, was forced to move *again*. I wondered sometimes why she stuck it out with him but understood that it was her way of rebellion. Let her take up with a loyal, loving enemy since her own state had turned her into a traitor against her first love. A depressing sort of logic, but it made sense.

He and I had little to say to each other at first. He was no more used to black people than I was used to Germans. We eyed each other like duelling fighters. He warmed up to me a little when he learned I was an accomplished musician whose repertoire included Bach, Mozart, and, well, *some* Schubert.

Eva was also at pains to bring us together through our shared left-handedness. 'I'm sure it's very inconvenient for you both,' she declared, hoping desperately for some common ground to unite us. It was a touchy topic, though. I was trying to forget that all too recently my left-handedness had served me extremely well. Mr Badura, too, was reticent, just raising his wide blue eyes.

But then he looked my way, and something happened.

A series of flashes, like the ones I experienced with Major Loder. A grey rainy sky, where the drops feel dirty on your cheek and hair. An advance dugout, for snipers, guarded by a painted iron tree, so carefully fashioned that you only know it is fake when you knock on the trunk and hear its metallic ring. The heft and grasp of a sniper's rifle, that wrong feeling when you hold a right-handed object. Then another flash, a bayonet charge, the feeling of feet trying to run through mud, heavy boots, once more the wrongness of the handle. The same wrongness I had felt when . . . Mi Gad, he was smiling now, this German. Did this intuition go both ways? When I saw those images of war – had he seen me working that paper knife on McCrum?

It was clear that Eva was unaware of this exchange. She went out to make tea. While she was in the tiny, filthy shared kitchen, the roar of the water hitting the tin sink as she washed the cups, Mr Badura gestured in her direction and said in his rather sonorous baritone, 'The right hand does not know . . . '

He knows. I put my finger to my lips, and he grinned broadly. A fly buzzed at the window; he paced across the small room and opened the sash. It knocked about the glass for a while until he muttered something and it flew right out.

'Must be a German fly,' he said with a wink. 'It knows it's not supposed to be here.'

'And yet here we both are.' I made a buzzing noise, and he laughed. He had a nice laugh.

'Oh good,' Eva declared, re-entering, the tension gone from her face and limbs, 'I'm so glad you're having a conversation!'

That had been a few weeks ago. On another visit, I'd cornered him and said, 'Look, you know my wedding's coming up. Just to make life easy, can't you pretend to be a Pole?'

He looked at me with incomprehension. 'I am German.'

'Yes, I'm aware of that. That's the problem. So, if you are intro-duced, can we say you're Polish?'

He frowned, more deeply this time. 'That would be a lie.'

I struck my forehead. 'Cha, it would be a social convenience. To make life easier for everyone. Please? Your grandfather was Polish, Eva said. After all, we don't have to reveal everything we know, do we?' I held up my ringed left hand with a meaningful look. He smiled just as meaningfully and nodded. Apart from the Coterie, there are few private organisations that have had me as a member. The Left-Handed Killers Club would not have been my first choice, but beggars cannot be choosers.

'I am Polish now. Stefan Badura. *Polnisch, ja.*' He nodded his head and stamped his heel in decidedly un-Polish fashion. 'The Fräulein Percival – Frau Rosewell soon! – is wery vise.'

'The Herr Badura better believe it.'

'I go mend my shirt for my *Polnisch* wedding.' He excused himself. It was hard to believe that this beaming man had once carefully stared down a rifle's scope, once bayonet-charged some luckless Englishman.

Dr Alcindor was waiting at the church door. He wore a long, light-grey morning coat teamed with a matching fedora and was beaming from ear to ear. 'Ready, Mrs Rosewell-to-be?' He extended his arm and hooked it into mine. Gwen Coleridge-Taylor, at my side, handed me a bouquet and fixed my headpiece.

'Ready.' I smiled, entering the gloom. As my foot crossed the threshold, the organ blared into life, and the building vibrated. Up in the gallery I saw Miss Slade's familiar head, bobbing up and down as her feet bounced along the organ pedals, blurring some of the sounds but generally doing brilliantly for someone who hadn't played the organ in almost a decade. The chords of the aria from *Aida* were a fitting valediction of my past and a doorway to my future. Speed your journey, my thoughts and my longings.

Oh inspire us, Jehovah, with courage
So that we may endure to the last . . .

Miss Slade's playing the organ had not been planned. One day, while taking me through my paces with the Purcell song from *The Indian Queen*, she queried the engagement ring on my finger. 'Is that from Mr Rosewell?'

'Yes. It is.'

'I'm so glad to hear it. It's well beyond time. He's a fine man, and you make a beautiful couple.' I swear I nearly wept.

'I am sorry about what happened to your fiancé.' I didn't tell her I knew the details.

She played a low F, *piano ma sostenuto*. 'Ah yes. But today is about your happiness.' She broke into the fast part of Brahms *Hungarian Dance No. 1*, but I did not dance, not being very light on my feet. Still, I was very happy.

That was the point at which Venetia Slade and I moved beyond being teacher and pupil and became genuine friends. She was the oddest of women, but my Lord, I was sorry to say goodbye to her. We corresponded for a decade afterwards, until she sadly died from cancer in 1930. She left me her spinet, which had been given to her by her fiancé all those years ago. I must collect it one of these days . . .

But now we are almost at the top of the aisle, Dr Alcindor and I, so these memories must be left aside. Sybil had done such a fine job organising bunches of freshly cut lilies and yellow crocuses to be placed throughout the church, and I was so moved to see all the friendly faces in the congregation, black and white, wishing me well. Seeing Reginald among them, bronze and unassumingly handsome even in his plain demob suit, made my heart soar. I hoped there would be time at the wedding breakfast to have a long, proper chat.

At the altar stood Reverend Green, Arthur's great friend and a well-known black pastor, and by his side Miss Maude Royden, the great female preacher, who would read the Gospel that day. And with them, most importantly, Arthur – my Arthur! – in his fine black morning suit. My heart did a little fillip as I glided up the aisle, borne up by Dr Alcindor's supporting grip.

As he melted away, and Arthur and I stood face to face, a light hit the gable window and illuminated his features. I felt such love for him then, such happiness, at the beauty surrounding me.

Even Stefan Badura, that well-known Polish gentleman, did not cause trouble. During Miss Royden's sermon, he bowed his head – and well he might, since she mentioned the Bangarang and the toll it had taken while acknowledging that this day's purpose was a happy one. Then Reverend Green started reciting the words of the marriage ceremony, Arthur clasping my hands all the while. 'We had better say for good measure,' the Reverend joked, 'that should anyone here present know of any reason why this couple should not be joined in holy matrimony, speak now or forever hold your peace.'

I was so engrossed in Arthur I barely took into account a slight darkening at the door. Then, out of the corner of my eye I saw the shadowy shape of an old woman with a bundle – and presumed it was a beggar. The ushers would take care of them. But then a strangled cry from Eva rent the air, followed by a blasphemous 'Oh hell, what's *she* doing here?' from Sybil.

'Who is dat?' Stefan Badura, in a not-very-Polish accent.

'Is everything all right back there?' Reverend Green called out.

The light that had illuminated my future husband now danced and shifted until it alighted on the interloper – and I immediately saw why Eva and Sybil were horrified.

'Oh, don't mind me,' Lilian Shandlin said. 'Keep going.'

But everyone, including Reverend Green, was open-mouthed as her small companion pulled at her hand, fussing and complaining.

Reginald broke the silence. 'What the hell fool-fool business is this? Apologies, Reverend.'

'It's not fool-fool business,' I shot back. I'd forgotten how much it annoyed me when my brother took over like that.

Lilian spoke up. 'We went to the house, but your landlady told me you were not there. I thought about waiting, but I need to catch a train. Look, he wants to walk the rest of the way.' She was laughing softly, transformed into gentleness. 'He's tired of being carried all this distance. Come on little fellow. Walk, walk.'

'Wook,' echoed Domi, toddling along at his own pace, clasping Lilian's hand as she led him up the aisle.

To me. His mother.

26

DOVER, SAME DAY, 8 P.M.

'Show mi yu motion, tra la la la, Im look lakka sugar and a plum – plum plum! Ah no, ickle buoy, nuh cry, nuh cry!' I was pacing the room, singing the song over and over – with frequent interruptions – all to try and soothe the little fellow. I had carried him around for half an hour, jiggling him and kissing his teary cheek, begging him to shush, but I could not comfort the little pickney at all. Not milk, not kisses, not even a bit of mashed potato I had ordered in the hotel restaurant. Nothing helped. He just pushed my offerings away with a face.

And he weighed a ton. And how strong his feet were as they kicked at my pretty yellow dress! He cried and he cried, as the rain beat steadily on the window, and my spirits, so high that morning, steadily flagged.

'Shhhhh,' I murmured. 'Shhhhhhh.' I buried my face in his neck and did another circuit of the room, avoiding Arthur's eye. Domi's skin felt warm and clammy against mine, his arms linked around my neck.

He smelled of sweet salt and a slightly wet nappy. Anxiously I reckoned how many more there were in the holdall. Five more? Oh if he would only quiet down and stop kicking at me!

I hoiked up him up once more and faced the dirty, rain-speckled window that looked westwards out to the country we would soon be leaving, hopefully for good. Yes, 'we.' To his credit, Arthur had not brought the wedding to a halt. Briefly, after rings and vows were exchanged, he *had* hissed at me, 'This is unforgivable,' and my blood had run to ice. Now he was hardly speaking to me, and the more Domi howled, the colder Arthur became.

There was not much of a view from our nondescript lodgings on the Marine Parade, even in broad daylight. When writing to make the reservation, weeks before, Arthur had requested a sea-facing room, but he made the cardinal error of failing to mention we were black. One look at us when we turned up at reception and suddenly the room was no longer available. The eager-to-please-by-post concierge turned hostile and grim.

We were shunted off to a cold grubby cubicle just under the attic that had a tide mark around the sink and virulent yellow walls. When the vents were closed, the place smelled renk of cabbage; when open, the cold would freeze a brass monkey's proverbials. To cap it all, a solitary green towel, hanging lopsided on the rail as if it had been tossed there, was speckled with blood. Thankfully Arthur, ever-punctilious, had packed his own. It was an unpleasant coda to my years in the British Isles – one last poke in the eye, one last snide effort.

It had been a difficult day, to put it mildly. Eva, naturally, lost her composure upon seeing Lilian. Stefan Badura made himself surprisingly useful, fanning Eva with her own hat as she slumped in her pew. Reverend Green was nonplussed for a moment, but when Mrs Shandlin sat down with her small charge and indicated she was not, in fact, objecting to our marriage, he falteringly resumed where he had left off.

Arthur guessed Domi's identity immediately and turned towards me with no love or affection in his eyes. Oh, when Mr Tandoh handed him the ring, he put it on my finger all right, but he did not look at me, and he made his responses in such a flat, resentful tone that when he said, 'I do,' Reverend Green asked him, in a low voice, 'Are you sure?'

'Yes!' Arthur snapped back, and we got on with it, though the clergyman quailed at his look.

Miss Slade must have slipped on the organ keys, because a ghastly discord reverberated through the building for a full three seconds, making everyone jump. When Reverend Green started saying, 'You may kiss—', Arthur gave him a long look before bending down and barely pressing his lips on mine. What a change from the happy embraces we had exchanged in the months beforehand, embraces that had grown ever more lingering as the day drew closer. I had been pleased with myself that I'd decided to wait, unlike with Robin in the midst of battle. Now I might be waiting forever.

So the deed was done and the papers signed at the back of the vestry: my signature in clear, large handwriting, Arthur's a sulky, barely legible scribble. The congregation had picked up that something was wrong and sat in gloomy silence. Lilian, meanwhile, was impassive, occasionally craning her neck to look over at the pew opposite, where Eva was sitting. For the first time since I'd seen her, she was entirely clad in black.

As the ceremony concluded and Miss Slade banged out the Wedding March, loud enough to prevent conversation, Arthur stormed out ahead, barely hanging onto his hat he walked so fast. Mr Tandoh followed him, confused and sad. Gwen, sitting in the front row, her white-gloved fingers interlaced, looked straight ahead. I suspected she didn't want to approach me. Sybil's head was bent towards Roma's, and she was whispering furiously, gesticulating at Lilian. Reverend Green muttered his apologies and disappeared.

I stood there at that altar, utterly alone.

Then little Domi was at my feet, waving at me, as if he knew me. Lilian was close behind, dragging another of her holdalls and reading items off on her fingers: 'Nappies, cloths, nappy cream, two sets of dungarees and shirts, two pairs of socks, woolly hat and coat, some belladonna medicine for fever, oh and a passport.' She looked up. 'I'm sorry, Lucia. That was dreadful timing, but I looked for you everywhere. Sent you two telegrams in the past three days and you never responded.' Of course! I had been staying at Sybil's. 'I even went to the house, only to meet a very rude woman who told me you were getting married today in Holborn. Well, I knew it was on the cards, just not that it was this very day! I tore up here as fast as I could and tried every church in the neighbourhood, which at my age … you know.'

'Mama,' Domi interrupted, pointing at me, his soft dark eyes penetrating the hardened layers of my heart.

'Don't get too excited,' Lilian said. 'He's at the stage where he calls every woman that. Even me.' Said with a wintry smile. It had been wrong of me to think she had stopped being a mother the day her younger son had been blown up. That was not how it worked.

'Maybe one day he'll call me it for real.' I got down on my hunkers and took his little hand in mine. 'Hallo, sweetness,' I whispered, like he was the holiest thing in that church. 'Hallo, Little Milk. You've got so big now. Here, show mi yuh hand miggle.' I put my finger in the palm of his hand and pressed it gently. Domi curled his fingers around my index finger and gripped it as if I were about to cut him loose. But rather than speak to me, he stared at the ground.

Lilian stood behind, gently, unobtrusively protective. She

looked a lot less haunted than before. 'He'll be like that a while,' she said, 'till he gets to know you properly.'

I straightened up. It felt like a wrench to detach my gaze from his, pull his little finger away. A breeze blew in from the vestibule and rippled both my and Lilian's skirts. Domi was transfixed at the movement. 'I thought you had lied to me,' I said. 'I thought once the other thing was done you would abandon me—' Lilian shushed me with a genuine laugh, not the bitter jesting she'd done before. 'I knew you'd had enough of me by then, so I stayed away until we could find your little boy. Look, I'm wearing black – like a real witch.' She seemed happy about it. 'At last I can start to mourn. If people don't like it, I don't care.'

She seemed more at peace than any time I'd ever known her. Even if she had crashed my wedding, I thought of everything we had been through and my heart softened. 'Never mind what the people in the village say. Christopher was brave, Lilian. You should be proud of him.'

Her eyes glistened and went violet. 'I always have been.' Then, swiftly, she was brisk again. 'Most of the delay getting Domi to you was because other people wanted him. With most of Mrs Gunning's cases, the institutions don't fight too hard to retain their orphans. Domi – Archie, as he was called – was different. Mrs Gunning had a lot of work to do. You see, when it came to his surname – No, little one, don't open the bag. You'll only throw it all on the floor again.' Lilian bent and fussed as Domi prised the handle open. 'I've packed some milk as well. Just Cow & Gate powder. You'll have to boil water and mix it yourself. He should eat most foods. Nothing too salty or spicy.'

'Mah!' cried Domi, once again pulling at the bag. It took a minute or two to work out that he meant milk, by which point he was exclaiming the word more and more loudly.

'It's fine, Lilian. I know what I'm doing.' Lilian said nothing.

She must have known that when it came to looking after an almost two-year-old, I was a gyal dunce but was too polite to say so. 'Thank you,' I said to her, 'for all you've done. I can't believe he's here.'

'Yes, he is.' And then, a bare whisper. 'You're very lucky. Remember that.'

'Lilian,' a voice broke in from behind. It was Eva, her husband in her wake. She still looked a bit green around the gills, but I could see how Stefan's presence steadied her, helped her face the woman who should have been her mother-in-law but who was now her perceived adversary. He might not be her great love, but this shambling German was right for her. A shaft of unflattering light cast across Eva's wide, pale face. 'I have no idea what you're doing here, with that child, but we need to talk,' she said. I could tell she was probably digging her nails into her palms from sheer nerves.

'No,' Lilian said, in a harsh deep voice that sounded as if she had been crying, even though she had been happy a few moments before. 'I need to apologise. For what I said...'

I was interrupted by a hand on my arm. It was Dr Alcindor. He looked at me very tenderly, sadly. 'Are you bringing this little infant with you?'

I swallowed. 'Yes, I am. He's mine.'

To his credit, the good doctor did not have an apoplexy, just told me that Arthur and the rest of the wedding party had gone on ahead to the meal and perhaps I would like to follow them.

'Come on, star,' I whispered to my new little companion. 'Time to go.'

I left Lilian and Eva there together, Badura keeping a discreet but watchful distance, like the sniper he used to be.

The celebration meal was held in a little restaurant under the railway line up the road from the church. The proprietor was

Anglo-Indian, and we had made the arrangements in person, and far in advance, wanting to ensure that we and our friends were not going to be turned away on arrival. It was pretty, the way the cutlery was all laid out. Proper silver, polished and gleaming, spotless ivory damask tablecloths. The owner greeting us with a smile. If only the mood of the wedding party had matched.

But throughout the meal Arthur avoided my eye, while Reginald, sitting opposite me, looked daggers. So much for a new understanding between us! I was holding Domi in my lap. The little pickney squirmed, and when he was in the mood for it, wolfed down crusts of bread dipped in soup as I fed them to him. I beamed with pride as he fingered each morsel and scooped it into his mouth. When a familiar smell emerged, I braved the tiny, unsuitable water closet at the back of the restaurant and changed him deftly on the floor while he kicked and shouted.

Through all this, Arthur said hardly a word, except to order his food. Reginald was more than happy to make up for his silence. 'Why yu do dis, Lucia? You mad?' he hissed at me across the table.

'Reggie, people looking,' I said nervously.

'They looking, all right. But not at me. At you, dat a sketel.' He looked like he was about to spit on the table. As he might as well have done. He'd just called me a whore! 'Fadda muss e be hashamed a you now,' he added, for good measure.

'At least he die first,' I said with venom. 'He ashamed of you while you still alive.' It was depressing how fast the old hatred had returned. I do believe we would have both been on our feet within seconds had Arthur not intervened. 'Stop it. Both of you. This is a wedding, and we will be happy, no matter what.' A wedding, cha, he looked as if he were at a funeral.

Reginald pushed his chair back and declared he wouldn't stay a moment longer at this sham of a celebration. He hadn't fought in France and Italy all these years to be disappointed in me again like this. Patronising little bloodclaat brudda ah mine! He'd never fought in any of those places. (In my anger, I forgot he'd never been given the opportunity.)

He stormed out of the restaurant, his poached salmon left unfinished on the plate. I didn't go after him. By now the other diners were indeed giving us looks. I feared we might be ejected, but in the event nobody wanted to linger. Guest after guest made polite excuses and left. Not one of them acknowledged Domi.

'So,' I said to Arthur, who was disconsolately toying with his crème brûlée, 'what time is the train? We'll need a good space to get to Victoria in traffic.'

Arthur put down his dessert spoon. 'Lucia.' The way he looked, the way he trailed off . . . Fire rose in my blood.

'He is staying, Arthur.'

'And my consent is not requested?'

'I never lied to you. I told you I'd always want him back. You the one pretended not to hear me.'

Domi, ignorant of our conversation, was shredding the doilies on which our china cups rested. I tutted gently at him and pulled his hands away. He squawked discontentedly. 'Want cup!'

'All right, baby. Try this instead.' I handed him my doily and let him rip it to pieces.

'Really, Lucia? You would forsake your career and all that promise? You would deprive the world of your gift – for some two-year-old? Who has been illegally abducted from his parents?' Nothing could have been better calculated to drive me to fury than that comment.

'*I* am his parent. He was taken from me by force, Arthur. Stolen. *They* are the ones who broke the law, not I.'

'Keep. Your. Voice. Down,' Arthur hissed, as if I were Eva's German. 'You are incredibly naive, that's all I can say. You're his parent, huh? Where's his birth certificate?' Domi started to giggle, hoarse and happy, a soft chuckle that came all the way from his belly. He appeared to find Arthur's rage hilarious. I had to look away, tears filling my eyes as he played happily with the shreds of the doily, setting them on the air like little white insects. That sweet little innocent boy knew nothing about what he had been put through.

But Arthur had a point. Shortly after Domi was taken from me, I had begged for his birth certificate, only to be told, 'You needn't bother. Not with the family involved,' meaning the Mackenzies. My protests about it being illegal were laughed at.

'And you are aware he is a British citizen and you are not?' Arthur continued. 'You lost your citizenship the moment you signed to marry me. You are taking him away from his home country with no means of returning – because good luck persuading the American Embassy in Paris that you have any right to go back to Britain. Or Jamaica.'

I wanted to tell him that Lilian and Mrs Gunning had forged the passport but feared inviting further wrath on my head. At any rate, even the forged document stated that Domi was British. If only there had been more time to prepare for this! I could not help but wish Lilian had been able to give me advance warning. God bless her, though, she had tried hard enough.

Silence fell on our table. Even Domi was subdued, bending his head and sniffling, leaving a trace of snot on my hand. Arthur instinctively reached in his pocket for his handkerchief – then pulled his hand back, annoyed at himself for nearly committing a fatherly act. Instead, he fiddled with his cufflinks.

'It's all right, I'll get it.' I rummaged in the holdall for a muslin cloth and wiped Domi's nose with it, then scrunched it in a ball and put it back in the bag.

'Why on earth did she do it?' Arthur burst out. 'Turn up like that, with the kid?'

'Who, Lilian?'

'The dame in black, yeah.'

I put Domi down on the carpet. 'It's . . . complicated. Look, does it matter? All I know is that I lost him twice, and now he is here. And I will never let him go again.' I embraced him tightly and he giggled. 'I'm your mama, Domi. Never forget that.'

'Mama,' he echoed, as if talking about his rattle, the wall, or some piece of furniture.

Arthur sipped from a glass of water, still grim. 'I was a little worried, I admit, that you were so intense about the boy. But you're intense about everything, Lucia.' He rubbed his temples. 'God damn her to the pit of hell. She's ruined everything!' He banged the table with his fist. 'I'm so sick of this country. Of being treated like garbage. They're all the same, you know. Including that boy's father.' He jabbed a finger at Domi, who, startled, began to cry, a series of guttural gasps. 'He used you, and you let him.' I jiggled Domi and waved the rattle in his face. He batted it away, bored with such a simple toy at his age, but the play appeared to improve his mood. Unlike Arthur, whose anger and frustration I could not pay any attention to right then. Domi's demands were more urgent, wedding or no.

Reginald was back. 'That jacket still here?' He gestured at Domi with contempt. 'You should have left him behind.'

'You should have left your own self behind, in Jamaica,' I hissed at him. 'Yu wutless kyaan done.' His handsome bronze face reddened a little at that, and he started blustering about how he was head of the family and I should have consulted him before marrying Mr Rosewell.

He was stopped in the end not by me, but by Arthur. 'Shut up, you fool,' that gentleman instructed. Any sensible man would have got the message, but poor Reginald had consumed rather a lot of wine and continued to harangue us both. Eventually Arthur lost patience with him. 'If you continue to insult my wife in public, I will physically drag you out of this building.' Oh mi Gad, could you imagine the headlines? ROWDY BLACK MEN ARRESTED IN FIGHT! Thankfully, Reginald quickly divined that Arthur had every intention of carrying out his threat, and backed off.

'Hush,' he muttered, 'I didn't mean to spoil things for you, gyal. I just got angry. I'm angry all the time since Taranto.' He looked at his feet. 'It's the disrespect. It really gets to you.'

'I hear you, brother.' Arthur held out his hand for Reggie to shake.

'Thanks, man. I thought maybe they left you alone. On account of you being so well spoken and that.'

Arthur laughed softly, bitterly. 'Leave me alone? They hate me even more for it.' He brightened: 'I meant to thank you for your service. I enlisted, but it was too late, and it didn't work out.' Reggie sat back down, and the two men fell into conversation about the war while Domi reached for my forearm and stroked it with his small warm fingers. His touch was rhythmical and comforting. *Yu favah me, ickle buoy, you are a born musician!*

I broke into a smile just for him because the men were not looking at us. Arthur sounded calmer, though, and there was real fellow feeling in his conversation with Reginald. Maybe this day was not a complete write-off after all.

It was true that Domi did not look much like me, apart from the dark eyes and slightly frizzy hair. He was much paler, and his nose, while still of course a baby's nose, did not have the slight flare at the nostrils mine had. It was Robin's, all the way. I took his wooden cup and poured some water from the glass jug on the table. He drank some, spilled the rest and gave me a grin. 'De,' he declared, as if he were king of the world. I was so in love with him, and yet he moved too fast for me to dwell in the love.

The afternoon was getting on, and staff were clearing away the plates. The manager, Mr Ramires, appeared briefly at the restaurant kitchen entrance to see that all was well, then withdrew. At last Reginald took his leave for the second and last time, clasping Arthur's shoulder, and warning me, 'He's a good man, Lucia. You might want to think about what you're bringing to the table. Walk good, sister.' He bade us goodbye and pushed the door open, then was swallowed up by the London spring day.

Arthur stared at the bottom of his empty teacup. 'I love you, Lucia, truly I do. But I never signed up for this.'

'I know, Art.' Domi was tracing my palm, exclaiming in little high breathy sounds at its whiteness.

'But I do want to.' His hand gingerly touched my shoulder, as if stroking a hedgehog and trying to avoid pain. 'I'm not a boor, or a cad. It's just . . . I don't want this child.' Arthur was genuinely upset, even casting an apologetic glance at Domi.

'Can he at least come with us tonight?' I begged. I could work on him. Take it one day at a time.

Arthur sighed through his lips, so it sounded like a whistle. 'Well. All right, then. But this isn't over.'

That had been several hours ago. Now, here we were, waiting to leave England, at loggerheads, and instead of singing scales I was singing lullabies. Which weren't working.

'I can't take any more of this noise,' Arthur said and walked out, slamming the door behind him and leaving me alone on my wedding night, in a cold room, walking a little boy up and down.

At last my son and I were alone, just as we had been that bitterly cold but sweet April morning. Thinking of that made me sad, because the gap I had felt between newborn and six months was nothing on the gap between a six-month-old and a little boy. Domi was too big now to be carried around in slings or perambulators. He ran about and messed everything up. Earlier he got his fingers in my cold cream and spilled rosewater on the floor.

Another woman's hands had steered him, fed him, guided him. I had missed so much that I could never get back.

Then Domi turned to me and said the words that broke my heart: 'Mama. Ham. HAM.' He repeated it, getting steadily more upset as he did so, pointing in an indeterminate direction, waving his hand. He meant that he wanted his mama, and he wanted to go home.

And I had nothing to tell him.

Two long, exhausting hours later, Domi eventually stopped fretting and fell into a doze. There was still no sign of Arthur, and all was quiet, apart from the sound of the rain on the windowpane and the baby's snuffles, as well as the occasional gurgle of the pipes and roar of water whenever someone flushed a WC.

Half an hour later, Domi woke up, blinking and fretting. Among the holdall's treasures was a small tin full of sugar rusks. I took one out, and immediately he grabbed at it, his mouth open like a gaping fish. He ate messily, crumbs scattering over his clothes. I smiled at him: the little chap was as greedy now as he had been when he was hardly a scrap, feeding and feeding and feeding. The challenge now would be to make sure he ate properly.

'Who am I, Domi?' I said to him.

'Mama,' he replied readily. I remembered Lilian's warning.

'And who are you?'

'A-chie.' That blasted name! I had forgotten.

'You are Domi Rosewell, my little star.'

'De.' That was his answer for everything.

Soon afterwards he fell fast asleep in my arms, his curly head lolling back over the crook of my elbow, and I did not dare move for fear of disturbing him. I was forced to sit still, there in the middle of the floor, still wearing my wedding dress, the bright yellow looking a bit shabby now. I briefly wondered what Sybil would have thought of the whole affair. At least she wouldn't miss the dress. What a colour scheme, for a redhead!

My life was at rock bottom, my new husband possibly about to leave me, but I experienced a moment of pure contentment the like of which I had only felt before when Domi was in my arms. I had never understood the kind of complete love that Eva felt for Christopher, or Sybil for Roma, but this was the closest I'd ever come.

The hotel-room door creaked open, and Arthur reappeared, illuminated in a strange green glow by the gaslight that burned in the corridor. His hair was plastered on his head, his sodden hat in his free hand while with the other he held onto the door, swinging back and forth. For a moment I feared he had got himself drunk. 'Arthur! Were you out in that rain?'

He put his finger to his lips, pointing at Domi and shutting the door quietly behind him. Then he hunkered down and dragged a mattress out from under the bed. He scooped up the sleeping child and set him down on the mattress with quiet tenderness, then pulled the rough wool coverlet off the bed and covered him with it. Domi opened his eyes for one second then closed them again and rolled over, his thumb in his mouth. Once he was tucked in, Arthur sat beside me on the bed.

'I needed to think,' he said in a low whisper.

'You gwaan think yourself into bronchial pneumonia if you go out in weather like that with no coat.'

He ignored me and reached down to Domi, stroking the little boy's cheek with his knuckle. 'Let's all sleep for now,' he said – I liked that he included the three of us in that instruction – 'and we can talk in the morning.' He removed his shirt and trousers, carefully draping the latter over the chair, folding the former collar upwards. I admired the gleam of his naked torso in the light from the window, the limber way he lifted his arms over his head. He took one of his towels out of his valise and rubbed his hair until it stood on ends.

'Would have been handy to have a valet to do that,' he said jokingly.

'Cha, if you are so limp and lazy you cannot dry your own hair, then you have no business marrying any woman.'

He laughed. 'True-true,' he said, imitating my accent.

I in turn removed my clothes and put on a thin sateen night-gown. Then I joined him in bed, allowing myself the luxury of leaning back against those fine thighs, feeling the strength and support of him all around me. Oh, how I would love him . . . but his breathing had become very even now, even a little snorey, and I found a pleasant tiredness drape itself over me too. Before I knew it I was asleep.

We slept like that all night and were only woken at six o'clock the following morning when Domi clambered over us and demanded his 'mah'. I had made a spare bottle the night before, with the help of the night manager's kettle, so I just handed it over and rolled back to slumber next to Arthur's warm body while Domi suckled away at the rubber teat.

When I woke again, daylight was peeping in through the closed curtains. I felt exhausted, and my stomach was churning a little. But I could not think of my own needs now. I realised with a shock that having chosen Domi I could never think of my own needs first again. I cast my eye over him: his breathing light as a feather, his eyes tight shut and his mouth deeply serious. His left hand was curled in a little fist by his lips.

'Hello,' I whispered very softly, feeling the small glow of light on my face. 'Hello sleepybones.'

'Hello yourself.' Arthur's amused baritone, a little distance away. The space next to me in the bed was warm and vacant. He was not only awake but fully dressed, sitting on the battered pine chiffonier, the actual chair being too low for his height. On the desk were sheets of paper, and the familiar turn of his treble clef. He had kept the curtains closed for us while he composed, and worked by the light of a battered pink opaline lamp. I felt a great softening pull at the edges of my heart at the kindness.

'Aren't you going to say good morning?' He beckoned me over and gave me a slow and lingering kiss. I returned his kiss eagerly, until the little gentleman stirred, stretched out his hands in a comically exaggerated manner. Arthur grinned. 'I think it might be time for us to get some breakfast.' Then his face creased and he sniffed the air. 'Oh-oh.' He picked up Domi. 'Somebody is a bit smelly this morning.'

'Nappy,' agreed Domi, pulling at the layers of rough cloth.

'I'll do it,' I said. 'Hand him over.'

I was doing my best with a cold water tap and disposing the waste in the lavatory but had a vanishing number of clean muslin cloths and precious little opportunity to wash the nappies in plain cold water and soap, let alone boil them. We didn't have washing powder in those days, you see. By then, I had just one dry one left. We would have to get some more before our sailing.

Changing an almost two-year-old was a different proposition from changing a newborn. Quickly I folded the cloth around his bottom, but he squirmed and fought and got the dirt on his heels and his hands, and me wiping up frantically after him.

I began to hum under my breath as I finished up, patting the lotion on.

'"*Bella señora*",' Arthur noted approvingly.

Perhaps we could do this, I wondered, as I pinned the little fellow's nappy and put on his rompers, carefully fastening all the buttons while he wriggled in my grasp. Perhaps we could take care of the boy together, and I could still sing. We could hire a house-keeper or a maid to help.

I wanted that morning to never end and feared it ending, like someone keeping shattered glass together and cutting her fingers on the broken edges to do so.

'Come on, let's get packed. We board at midday.'

I checked my watch. 'Arthur, honey, we've plenty of time.'

He clapped his hands. 'Never too early. C'mon, little fella, put on your coat and be good for your mama.'

Domi smiled and scuttled over to my husband, wrapping his arms around his leg. His need for affection was heartbreaking – or maybe they were all like that when they were small. I wondered if Mr Pullman had been remote. These British, they were so cold, like their weather...

Arthur looked down at Domi with a broad smile. The cold, doubtful man of yesterday seemed to have vanished. 'Well, Lucia dear,' he said, Domi still hanging out of him, 'that was not the wedding night I expected, but we have many, many nights ahead of us, never fear. Let's give this thing a try, eh?'

My friend, I never loved Arthur Rosewell more than at that moment, and I was never to love him half that much again.

We went down to the dining room for early breakfast. In theory, Arthur and I breakfasted on tea and a small bread roll each while Domi had a bowl of warm milky porridge, but in practice he grabbed at our bread rolls, cried when he touched the hot ceramic teapot, for it had no cosy, and hardly touched his porridge at all, stirring it with such vigour that it slopped outside the edges and dribbled down the corner of the tablecloth.

On the bright side, he appeared unperturbed by the unfamiliar faces around him, interested only in causing as much chaos as possible. But the feeling wasn't mutual. I was so absorbed in helping him with his food that at first I did not notice that people were looking at us oddly. Now, we were not the only people of non-European descent breakfasting that day; a few tables down, a group of African men were conversing loudly in French. I guessed they were Senegalese, probably demobbed soldiers.

From time to time they raised their heads to look at the three of us, and one of them made a sucking sound with his tongue and teeth. It was insulting, and he knew I would understand the insult. I gave them the cut-eye, and looked back at Arthur to see if he had noticed. But he was oblivious, scribbling hemidemisemiquavers on a staff with one hand and drinking black tea with the other. Arthur had an uncanny ability to detach himself from his surroundings when he was in a state of concentration.

An English family passed us by, fully packed and ready to check out. I guessed they would be on the same ship as us. An ordinary family: husband, wife, two children, people you wouldn't notice in the street. The wife had an owlish, small-eyed stare, and she gave us the full benefit of it, not bothering to hide her distaste or afford us even rudimentary courtesy. And then she said it. 'What on earth are those people doing with a white child?'

Time slowed down. The room fell silent. All eyes were on us. My cheeks burned. Little Domi spooned his porridge and let it drop on the tablecloth. 'Hot,' he said softly, breathily, and stuck his spoon in again. Little innocent, unaware of a stranger's hate. But it was the change in Arthur's demeanour that had my blood run cold. He dropped his pencil and sat bolt upright. The gentle dreamy look playing on his face all morning had gone, and I saw, with terrible foreboding, that the earlier coldness had returned. His eyes were like black ice. I reached down to pick up his pencil, but he pushed away my arm.

The owlish woman had left. Her children had followed her into the lobby, and the husband had gone on ahead. So it was not at her that Arthur was glaring with resentment. It was at little Domi.

When he spoke, it was with a torment of sadness and anger.

'I'm sorry, Lucia, but I made a mistake entertaining this fantasy for so long. That boy is to be sent away before we leave this morning.'

Oh, we had such bitter argument after he said that! Arthur wouldn't let up, lecturing me even as we left the hotel and I stood in the middle of the street, crying. The rain had returned and was lashing at me and little Domi, who was howling, 'Ham! Ham!' meaning Glasgow, the poor mite.

Arthur set off down the street, dragging his valise. I stumbled and rushed to catch up, suitcase in one hand, Domi clasped to me with my other arm. I couldn't stop sobbing, while Domi roared, his fists pounding my shoulder, his legs kicking out, flailing desperately. I tried to calm down and make myself think, not an easy task with the state he was in.

Get in the queue for the ship. Buy a third ticket for Domi. Cajole Arthur until he returned to the good humour of this morning. He had been so tender with that little boy. Why should a passing insult from some dunce gyal stop him in his tracks like that? I finally caught up with him, and we started walking by his side. My shoulder was damp from Domi's snuffles and tears. Poor little scrap.

'Please, Arthur,' I said, once I had regained some control over my speech. 'Please don't separate us.'

He looked at me with great weariness. 'He doesn't belong to you, sweetheart.'

I wasn't going to give up. This argument could still be won. 'We were so happy earlier. And you were kind to us both. Why can it not always be like that?'

He took his time meeting my eye. 'Lucia. I was trying to let you down gently, that was all.' My heart raced with shock. How could he be so cruel? The message was cold and clear: if I stayed with the little fellow in my arms, I was on my own. With no money, no friends, no future. Arthur had never had any intention of letting me bring him with us. And I could not manage without him.

Dully, I replied, 'Lilian gave me Mrs Gunning's details so I could telegraph in case of urgency. Or if I changed my mind.'

'Good,' Arthur said, kissing me on the cheek. 'I know this will be hard, but let's do it as quickly and maturely as possible. There's a telegraph office on the main street. We'll have to postpone our sailing, but I'll wire Paris and tell them we will be delayed. Nothing is too much trouble, I assure you.'

I made to follow him, but my feet wouldn't move.

'Come on, my love. The sooner the better: for him and for us.' He tried to keep it light, but the threat in his tone was unmistakeable.

I'll never forget how happy and smart my Dominic looked that last half hour, in his little green serge coat and blue boots. 'Well, Mr Milk,' I said, in a shaky voice, 'it looks like I'm going to have to say goodbye after all.'

'Bye bye,' said Domi, waving his hand. 'Ni' ni'.'

'I hope you know I'm your mama, sweetie,' I whispered. 'I know I don't look much like it, but . . .' Domi reached a hand out and pulled at a strand of my hair.

'A'chie, bye bye.'

'That's not your name, star,' I whispered, enveloping him in my arms. He smelled of soap.

'Ag! Ag!' he exclaimed.

'Yes, I'm giving you a big hug, little one.'

My dress was very tight around the knees, and women aren't supposed to kneel in the street. But I knelt. 'You know I love you very much, don't you?'

He stared into my eyes. Those long lashes, the first thing I had noticed about him when he was born. Then he scratched the back of his neck with studied concentration.

'Lucia. Come on now,' Arthur said, with some emotion. 'Don't make me the villain in this. I like the little fella. He's sweet. But he's not like us. You can see it yourself.'

I thought of what Lilian had said about her husband: 'He made me swear never to tell the boys. "Don't make their lives harder than they need to be," that's what he always told me.' Maybe – and it was like a hot jab to my heart – Lilian had done the right thing. Maybe Domi would be better off with white parents, never knowing he was different. In this wicked society that shamed you for being black, he could 'pass' while neither Arthur nor I could. Of course neither of us wanted to, but this was not about what we wanted.

'Walk with me,' I told him. He trotted obediently, hand in my hand, as we made our way to the telegraph office. So trustful, when I was about to betray him. I felt my heart break a little more with each step.

27

APRIL–OCTOBER 1919

y friend, I should have loved Paris. You've been there, yes? The city was the most beautiful place I had ever seen, even barely six months after a horrible war. The spring days were warm, the paved banks of the Seine beautiful to walk along, under linden and horse-chestnut trees. If rations were grim and prices high, it was concealed to a tourist like me.

I watched pleasure boats travel up and down the wide dirty river while I ate sorbets from the Berthillon store and wandered along the narrow laneways of the Île Saint-Louis, sometimes alone, sometimes with Miss Julianne Evanti. A fellow opera singer, she lived in Nice but was in Paris for a season to sing in the same ensemble as me.

Miss Evanti was American, like my husband; coloured too, and she had grown up with similar restrictions on where she could go and what she could do. But Paris was different. She and I could buy croissants at a boulangerie without anyone batting much of an eyelid, and when Miss Evanti and I travelled together, we attracted next to no attention.

The Paris National Opera was in a building called the Palais Garnier which was gilded and exquisite, with painted ceilings and gold trickery and chandeliers with a thousand pieces. I felt as if I should stay silent within its walls, rather than sing, out of sheer reverence for the structure. Fortunately, M. Japrisot and his company did not share that sentiment, and as I sang with them, in that vast arena, propelled there by the strength of my own B flat the Christmas before, I felt as if I were a minor angelic minion in Heaven. Very soon my understudied Nehebka became useful, and I took over the role. At last one of the Nubians was being sung by someone who vaguely looked the part! A review at the time mentioned the 'up and coming Miss Percival, a coloured singer with considerable talent and mastery of range'. Paris, success, music. It was all beautiful: everything just falling at my feet.

But my marriage never recovered from that cold wet day in Dover. Since our wedding night, since letting Domi go, I had not allowed Arthur to share a room with me. The first time, he scolded me like a child and told me to behave. I told him to go away. He retreated, telling me I would see sense eventually. He was wrong. We never shared a bed again. During the day, we reached a modus vivendi. I resumed my practice and even let him coach me, to a degree, as long as he came nowhere near me at night.

I saw, too late, that he truly did love and cherish me. That he might have had some reason on his side when he parted me from my son. That the 'let me down gently' comment was untrue; he had not planned this at all but just panicked at the last minute. Knowing this made no difference to the hatred that surged through me whenever I saw his pleading face.

It frightened me, the depth of my feeling. I felt far less ill will towards Lionel McCrum, the man I had murdered in cold blood, than I did towards Arthur Rosewell. When Lilian Shandlin had said, *I want that man to die like a dog for what he did to my son*, I had been repelled by the ugliness of her rage. The impropriety of it. Now I felt it every time I looked at my own husband.

Arthur had made the error of thinking I was in any way controllable or manageable. He had never seen the living fury I had conjured when singing the Erl-King. Now, when you and I sit and talk about it, I can forgive the poor man. He grew up in a country where his ability to feel anything was stunted at every opportunity. How would I have fared if I had lived in such a hell-hole? Jim Crow, sundown towns, places where a spirit of intelligence and culture could never hope to thrive?

His fear of shame and disapproval was reflexive. I blamed him for so long when I should have blamed the society that made him that way for survival's sake. I hated myself too. How could I be so cruel that I could not find it in myself to give him a bit of comfort? He was an attractive man, you know, and had eyes only for me. That a love so hopeful, a union of intellect and heart, had broken down into this! We were broken by the system, after struggling so hard to escape that fate.

Then the run for *Aida* started. I put my domestic strain behind me and sang for my life. I earned so much money in the months afterwards that I no longer needed Arthur for anything and was able to leave him for good. Julianne and I moved into two rooms on a small laneway off the Boulevard Richard-Lenoir. There, I would sit at the window ledge and listen to the raucous sounds of the Saturday morning market, the smell of fish reminding me of similar days in Mandeville, while Julianne filled the cafetière with ground coffee and slowly poured in hot water so the whole place smelled of freshly brewed coffee.

My room was small and unassuming, but it had a piano, neatly stacked scores and a fold-out bed. I had my laundry washed twice weekly and a boulangerie just around the corner. Apart from Julianne, who understood a musician's life, I had nobody to answer to and could come and go as I pleased. It was not paradise, but it was nice.

As for Domi? Ah, I tell you ... All through my days in Paris, my many solitary, compulsive walks, I would imagine my little shadow tottering alongside me. I would take his hand and narrate all the pleasures and joys of the city: 'See, Domi! There is the Eiffel Tower. Some day we will go to the very top. Keep dreaming, little star.' I would even feel him jump up and down with excitement, his little hand in mine. Then I would remember: there was nobody there.

Nights alone in my bed were hell. During the day, in my more lucid moments, I would tell myself that he was with people who knew him and who would look after him. Then I remembered sitting in that dingy telegraph office, waiting for the telegram to be sent. Domi was being so good. I desperately wanted him to be naughty, to cry and kick and lay waste to everything. But he had calmed down by then, looking at me with those eyes – my eyes – as if he were drinking my soul, and in my deep shame I looked away.

Several hours later, we were back in the hotel lobby with Mrs Gunning, her mouth a thin line. So many explanations, so many apologies I wanted to give her, but I was exhausted from crying, and Arthur had already warned me not to prolong the moment. All she said when I wordlessly handed Domi back was, 'And to think of the great trouble Mrs Shandlin put herself to.'

'That woman has caused *us* a great deal of trouble,' Arthur said sternly. I wanted to tell him to go to hell and burn there for eternity, alive and in agony. Instead I started apologising for Domi's wet nappy, before feeling foolish and stopping myself. Arthur was right. Domi was no longer my responsibility. Three times I had failed him, like Peter failed Jesus, and the last by my own fault. There was no going back from that.

I kept the red blanket he constantly held on to, I admit. He didn't notice me taking it – he was too busy laughing at Mrs Gunning making faces at him. Another agonising reminder of how ignorant he was of my treachery to him.

Arthur and I divorced quickly enough. At the after-party for the last performance of *Aida*, drunk on champagne, I ran into a maampsy general with a bulging stomach like he had dropsy. He clasped my hand with his huge meaty one and told me I was *magnifique, mademoiselle* while breathing down my chest. I later learned that he was personally responsible for the loss of at least four hundred thousand of his own men.

'Dites-moi, s'il vous plait,' I replied, 'where I can find a cheap divorce lawyer in this town?'

He lifted his head from my décolletage and grinned broadly. 'You are to be a free woman? That is good news indeed. My friend Maître le Gallimard is not cheap, no, but he is very good.' He scribbled something down on a plain white card and handed it to me. I put it in my purse, and the general leaned in, about to say something else of a more suggestive nature, but I ducked away with a demure smile.

Arthur was at that party too, but I studiously avoided him. I never saw him again after that night.

The following morning, I went immediately to Maître le Gallimard's office on the Boulevard Saint-Michel, and in a mixture of English and appalling French insisted on an appointment. 'Tell him I'm a friend of the general,' I told his secretary, which speeded things up a lot, because five minutes later I was in a broad airy room that served as the Maître's office. When I asked him to start proceedings for a foreign divorce, he frowned and said, 'On what grounds? We may need to prove adultery.'

'No. That is not the reason.' I had no intention of procuring Arthur a suitable female with whom to be found in flagrante!

'Well, you might be in luck,' the lawyer said, in a bored tone. 'Since the war ended, divorce in Paris is proving to be rather popular among *les Américains. Les Noirs aussi comme les Blancs.* Much easier to do over here. People travel all the way from Iowa and Nebraska to Paris because the French judge is kinder and will give them their freedom. Not so religious, you understand? We may not need the adultery.'

Things moved swiftly after that. Within a year I had won my freedom from Arthur Rosewell. I heard of him intermittently over the years, through society columns and my friends in the Coterie. He went to live with Edmund Jenkins, who was also in Paris, but they too parted company. I never found out why – perhaps jealousy reared its ugly head. As my fortunes soared, his, from what I heard, diminished.

When Dr Alcindor told me that Arthur was in dire straits in a slum in Rome, I wired him some money. The wire was never cashed, but I hope he did receive it and knew that my last thoughts of him were kind. These past few years I've been arranging a retrospective of his work, and I hope I can bring it to a new audience. He wrote some beautiful pieces, and were I limber enough I would sing some of them, but, alas, I fear I cannot now.

The Coterie did not survive for long. For all Arthur's charm, Eddie Jenkins had been its centre, and once he left for Paris, shortly after we did, everyone else drifted apart. Dr Alcindor proved a faithful friend, writing to me at least three times a year. He never addressed what transpired between Arthur and me, though he must have heard about it. Shortly after I left England, he was awarded a Red Cross medal for his work with the war wounded in railway stations around London. He was a man of

Christ, and when his wife wrote to tell me of his death in 1924, I cried bitterly, for I had lost a true friend.

The others also faded away. Poor Eva Badura. How she suffered with her husband in the years after the war! She never made it to Summerplace – yes, I know now it is *Somerville* – but she did publish that article about Christopher and the white feather in *Blackwood's*, to much acclaim and notoriety, and then wrote some more and did well for herself for a while. It took a while to recover from the stigma of her marriage, though at least people usually thought Mr Badura was Polish. I lost track of her sometime after 1924 and never found her again. I should have tried harder to hold on to my friends. But those were busy years.

As for Lilian . . . Ah, what can I say about that faasty witch? I never heard from her again – directly. But shortly after my divorce came through I did get a letter from my own mother, the first in years. After the briefest and most ungracious apology for her silence, she launched into a jeremiad about some crazy English lady who had written her an abusive letter calling her a 'thoroughly stupid woman' for ignoring me and claiming that 'NOBODY CARES that your daughter failed to marry Paul Dakins from the United Fruit Company!'

'I was offended at her language,' my mother wrote, 'but she said one thing I couldn't get out of my mind. She told me to thank the Lord every day that I had daughters.' That sentence made it clear to me who the 'crazy English lady' was.

My mother and I were reconciled after that – something I was very grateful to Lilian for – and I made several attempts to pick up the pen and thank her. But recalling how she would have heard from Mrs Gunning that I had abandoned Domi I felt too guilty to continue past the first line. Just as Eva had done, I realised, with a wry smile.

The greatest guilt I felt over the years was towards Arthur.

Looking back, his objections were reasonable. What was any man supposed to do when his wedding and honeymoon were crashed by a small child his bride had borne for someone else? Had I been in his position, I would have objected too. Loudly.

Perhaps if I had not allowed myself to hate him so, if the fog of my grief weren't so thick, I might have had another child. As it was, when I eventually married again, to a black professor of humanities at Spelman College who reminded me very much of my father, I was too old to have any more. My second marriage was long and happy, but Domi was the only child I ever had.

And then yesterday I heard the terrible news.

28

LONDON, 1950

I spent the morning in the Royal Albert Hall with the orchestra, rehearsing the Strauss, and felt such excitement to be singing this brand new melody in front of an orchestra for the first time. That Mr Strauss had trusted me with his last melodies was a gift more special than I can describe. We broke for lunch, and I started walking back to the hotel. I had on a mink coat – this winter's cold enough, you know? – and I was glad of the fur because just as I left the Albert Hall it started to snow.

As I crossed the road to the Albert Memorial, I heard a harsh, scraping voice: 'Lucy! Lucy!' At first I thought I had misheard, that it was just some beggar and not someone calling me, and I ignored it. I dodged a black cab that nearly knocked me over – this new fashion in shoes does nothing for my walking pace – and as I righted myself I looked over at the low wall in front of the monument. I realised that the man hunched in front of it, calling my name incorrectly and barely able to stand upright, was Robin Mackenzie.

At the sight of him, my heart started beating at a hundred

miles an hour, as if a flock of hummingbirds were banging their wings against my ribcage. Despite the biting cold, beads of sweat broke out on my skin. He looked like a tramp: red-grey tufts of hair and beard, bilious face, roaming eyes. The neatly kept man, bright-eyed, with such compressed rage and intelligence – all that had gone. It was easy to figure out why: he smelled rank with liquor.

'Robin,' I said, with slow wonder. 'It's been a long time.'

'Oh, aye, it has,' he answered. A tuft of snow landed on his dirty sleeve. I brushed it off, and the flakes melted on my manicured nail. 'I've been looking for you, Lucy. Took me a long time to track you down.'

Looking for *me*? I was surprised he had the wherewithal to get out of bed in the morning, the state he was in. 'Well, here I am,' I replied, at a loss for anything else to say.

'Here you are, indeed,' said Robin. 'All Lady Muck now. Everyone all over the world knows you, but they don't know the wee darkie girl I once did.'

In all the time I had known Robin Mackenzie, after his first objectionable comment about the Dark Angel of Mons, he had never used language like that. He must have fallen low indeed. I decided to give him some tough love. 'Stop being offensive and go get yourself a wash, man. You smell rank.'

'Ah, you always were a bitch.' He closed his eyes and grinned. His teeth were rotting and several were missing. 'I loved that about you. Am I a ginger midget still?'

'Why are you here, Robin? Do you need money?' I did not mean it snidely. He was a wreck of a man, and I would help him if I could, but I did not want to tarry too long with him. Too many memories.

'Ah, no, darlin'.' He swayed forward again, snatching my arm, wheezing in my face. 'I might need a shilling or two, but I'm no' gonna beg for it. You won't have to sell your fancy coat to help me. Just bear in mind that once you weren't so fancy. I once knew a girl who got into a bit of trouble.'

My laugh cut the air in a vaporous cloud. 'Are you trying to blackmail me, Robin? Seriously? You look like you couldn't piss in a straight line, man.' He jumped at my vulgarity, sagged in on himself and started muttering. 'You think I'm ashamed of Domi – is that it? You're threatening to go the papers about him?'

Throughout my life I had never spoken about Domi to anyone, not even my late second husband. Yes, Lilian's gatecrashing my first wedding might have provoked some gossip. Maybe a few who were there still recalled the day with a rueful chuckle. But thirty years later, and another war . . . I had no illusions that anyone would remember Domi.

But Robin was one of those people who would surely always remember our son, so I could never be entirely hostile to him.

He gave me a rheumy glance. 'Domi? And who might that be?'

Macca! What a fool. 'Your son.' I snapped. 'You remember? *"Zugzwang"*?'

'Ah. Yes.'

The snow was falling in earnest now, about Robin's cheeks and trousers and boots and face. He had no gloves, and I noticed something else: his left hand was bare. 'Your wife gwaan left you, Robin?'

'Don't I wish? No, the old hag . . . she stayed with me purely to torture me. She was like my mother, had a bad nature. Then she died and I sold the ring. Good riddance to her.' And now he laughed, or rather rattled, the sound of mucus raw in his throat and lungs. 'Didn't take her long to find out I never got over you, Lucy.'

'Lucia.'

'Ah, tomayto, tomato.' For a moment he reminded me of

Arthur. 'She pushed out three bairns in three years and got me well trapped.'

'All by herself? That's impressive. Sounds like we had a genuine religious miracle in the city of Glasgow.' But I couldn't mock him for too long, even though he still seemed to enjoy it. It wouldn't be fair. We were so unequal now. The friendless young girl from Jamaica was long gone; so was the dashing doctor who faced down Lionel McCrum and nearly beat me at chess.

'What happened, Robin?' I said softly. 'Never mind this blackmail labba-labba. I'll help you straight if you want.'

He smiled and demurred. 'No, sweet Lucy. I'm beyond your help now. Everything that happened back then . . . I know it destroyed you. It ate me up too.' Tears filled his eyes. 'From time to time I hired an investigator to keep track of you. Told Sarah I spent the money on hoors.' His grin was gap-toothed and cruel. I shivered, glad not to have had a ringside seat on that marriage. He spat on the ground, a disgusting gob of phlegm. The snow could not fall fast enough to cover it up.

'And Domi?' I asked, my voice shaking a little. 'Did you keep track of him?'

Robin's silence seemed to last minutes. The wind began a slow moan as it rolled down from Hyde Park and funnelled through the white streets of South Kensington. People bent forward like stick figures, scarves around their necks. Then he clutched my hand. I recoiled at his grip. 'Ah, Lucia,' he said, his expression suddenly clear, all trace of drunkenness gone. 'I thought you knew.'

The November sky suddenly felt lower and greyer. A fist gathered around my heart and began to squeeze . . . 'He's dead, Lucy. Scarlet fever. A long time ago now, I would say 1920. Took me a long time to make enquiries with that bitch breathing down my neck, but I finally managed it. The father – I mean the adoptive one

– wasn't having any more of him after that time he got abducted by some mad Irishwoman then dumped back barely days later. Said he was having no more of that nonsense and sent the bairn off to the poorhouse at Govan Merryflats. The hygiene wasn't great, and there was a typhoid outbreak . . . I was well upset when I found out, I can tell you, and I couldn't even show it because of my wife.'

At his words, I sank down on my knees and put my face to the iron sky. Those snowflakes. How soft they are on my cheek, how relentlessly they fall. 'No. No, it's not true.'

'I'm afraid it is, Lucy.' The unpleasant, sweet-edged warmth of his breath on my neck as he bends down himself, putting his arm around my shoulders. 'I'm sorry.'

'No.' My hands on the ground. The coat covering me like an animal's hide. Shake it off. I don't need it any more. *I'm never cold.* 'No.' Raising my head to the sky, a confusion and flurry of whiteness. A black taxi, careening slowly on the icy road. A man in a greatcoat shoving at a heap of snow with a yard brush. A thrush flying over towards the Albert Memorial, not a bit of water on that golden folly that was not frozen solid.

I have enough rage to set the whole of London on fire.

A sound escaping me, the like of which I'd never heard before, from myself or anyone else. Howling as if I were a wolf, on my hands and knees, not caring about anyone around me, Robin included. Not enough room for my sorrow. It consumes me, the way great music does.

You see, my grief was new and horrific, like lightning going to earth, the fastest way possible. It gripped my very bones dem, it went through me like waves.

I had lost him. I had lost the love of my life. Forever.

I knew then how Lilian Shandlin must have felt. Twice over. And I wish to God I'd never been given that knowledge, by a drunk, derelict Robin Mackenzie, because it broke me all over again. And this time there can be no repair.

Now, do you understand why I cannot perform tomorrow?

You've been listening patiently all this time, in the shadows, but I need you to take note of this more than anything else you've been scribbling down these past two days.

I want to prove to you that I did love him. No. Stop talking. I asked you to listen. I won't allow Domi to be a secret, not any more. What hurt most about Robin Mackenzie's account was knowing that my little fellow died alone and unloved in a poorhouse. No, I said don't interrupt. I need this to be heard.

Because if I'd known, no corner of the earth would have been too far away for me to hasten to his side. Do you see this blanket? For months it had his smell, and even when that faded I couldn't bear to give it up. I still can't. That's what he means to me. More than any man. More than any performance. If I had been able to tend to him, even if he were dying, I would have done it. He would have been a bit old for milk, but it's one thing I could have given him: heated up with a bit of nutmeg and a crumbled rusk, maybe. If my pickney were still alive when I reached him, I would have fed him that last drink. Even if he couldn't swallow, perhaps even the taste on the lips would be a nice last memory? And if he were already gone? I would have wrapped it up inside the little blanket and put it in beside him. He would have gone to the other world with his last feed prepared and ready, like a Jamaican child.

Are you listening to me? Do you understand? And do you know what else is strange? On some deep, ghastly level, this news came as no surprise. In all my thoughts of Domi over the years, I never saw him as a boy, or a grown man making his way in the world. He was eternally a baby, those infant eyes wide, looking at me. It was as if I knew he would never be anything less pure, less elemental. His life would be so brief it would not be remembered, except by me.

Now you understand why I won't be singing tomorrow. You can tell them that and leave your rhaatid column blank.

I have told you the full story. Let me alone now to mourn my little boy. Please, I beg you. There is nothing on earth you can say to me now that would change my mind.

EPILOGUE

11 NOVEMBER 1950

D *raft of Evening Standard Column*
     M. D. Quinton, reviewer

MUSIC REVIEW: Lucia Percival at the Royal Albert Hall: *Four Last Songs* by Richard Strauss; Schubert; Wagner's *Wesendonck* song cycle.

FIRST: a warning that this will be a somewhat different review from my usual fare. I did attend Miss Percival's recital in which the singer, come out of early retirement in order to perform the Strauss directly at the late composer's request, delivered what was for her age a more than passable rendition of the above works. It was a pleasure for me to finally hear a recital of hers, given that I have followed her work and life for many decades, long past the point of obsession.

For those unfamiliar with her work, Lucia Percival was born in Mandeville, Manchester Parish, Jamaica in 1895 and made her debut in 1919, singing the part of Nehebka in Louis Japrisot's production of *Aida*, with the help of her then manager and husband, Mr Arthur J. Rosewell. This performance attracted further attention, and Miss Percival achieved a level of fame largely unknown to coloured singers but matched by her fellow musicians Marian Anderson and Julianne Evanti, who have similarly battled racial prejudice to excel.

Percival later graduated into a full dramatic soprano with coloratura range and a mixed Fach of dramatic and lyrical ability. Limited from performing full opera because of her race, she excelled in concert performances, and her recital of the 'Liebestod' from *Tristan und Isolde* regularly drew standing ovations.

But that is just the standard paragraph. There is more to know about this fascinating woman, and we are in discussions about an official biography. I conducted a long, intimate interview with Miss Percival in which she spoke to me about various details of her life. Even aficionados will probably not know that she was a servicewoman in the First World War, joining the Voluntary Aid Detachment with Mile End General in France, nor will they be aware of the long and tragic path she undertook to attain the level of eminence she now enjoys.

All this, and considerably more besides, makes it difficult for me, in my turn, to render a dispassionate review of her performance. But here it is. All round, I have heard better voices than Miss Percival's, but I have not heard better fifty-four-year-olds. And in spite of occasional infelicities and roughness around the edges, when her voice does slip free of its confines, such as in the long sostenutos of 'Im Abendrot', the quality is supreme in a way that a younger vocal has never managed to encompass. She more than does justice to the long, deceptively easy cadences of Mr Strauss's last work.

The Schubert was problematic in the descending fast quavers of 'An Silvia', a well-known trip-up which a singer as experienced as Miss Percival could have avoided by skipping the song. The Wagner, while rich and deep, perhaps missed the finesse required on the higher register. But the audience was forgiving that night, cheering her on. I am also inclined to forgive. For, and here we depart from our usual review format, Lucia Percival was told such devastating news two nights ago that with the recital imminent she seriously considered withdrawing.

Under normal circumstances I do not have any role in encouraging musicians to perform on the night. This critic, after all, is usually the first to eviscerate their performances the following morning. He also believes it a disservice to lie when not served with the best. So I do not fraternise. But Miss Percival performed last night specifically at my urging because I was unwilling to let her withdraw on the basis of a lie.

One might ask why did I push a deeply upset woman into continuing the show? The answer is simple: the dreadful news related to Miss Percival was a falsehood invented by the jealous wife of the man who told it to her. He was under the impression that his information was gained privately, but it transpired that his wife, riven by jealousy, had bribed the private investigator he had employed. Lucia Percival's mistaken impression was that a child – her child, born in 1917 – had sadly died in 1920. I had to repeat to her several times that this was not true before she fully understood:

That no such expiry had occurred. That the child was transferred out of the workhouse to another family shortly after his arrival. That he survives this very day, through privation and war, the middle initial of the byline a testimony to his first name. That he would be the first person to encourage her back on that stage to render the work of Richard Strauss as best she could. And that he would be willing to eviscerate her performance the following morning. If this compromises reviewer impartiality, so be it. Lucia Percival is the one musician in the world about whom I cannot be impartial.

She is my mother.

ENJOYED THIS BOOK?

If you would like more stories similar to *Lucia's War*, please consider this free short story *Unfortunate Stars*, a bittersweet tale of love and friendship between men across the barricades at wartime, and during a dangerous peace. This link is exclusive to readers of this book, as a gift of thanks.

ACKNOWLEDGMENTS

This book is the culmination of many years' effort and there are many people to thank. Firstly Liz Hudson, who so ably took the editorial helm for my previous novel, *White Feathers*. When I approached her for the sequel, without a publishing house, she did not bat an eyelid but said yes straightaway. Viewing how she refined each draft was a joy. Encouraging the best of me while firmly but kindly reining in the worst, she truly earns the title Eliot gave Pound: *il miglior fabbro*.

Lyeanne Beckford-Jones surveyed the manuscript to ensure it rang true to Lucia's background and culture. She corrected course with patience and good humour, even as I made crashing errors with some of my Jamaican expressions! Her insights regarding characters' motives and background were invaluable and working with her was both educational and fun. She truly "made Lucia more Lucia".

After Liz and Lyeanne's diligent work, any remaining errors, either cultural or typographical, are entirely my own.

The exquisite cover is the work of Richie Cumberlidge from

More Visual cover design. I love that it has Lucia, war and music all involved. Thank you, Richie, for your care and attention.

To those who believed in this novel's predecessor, *White Feathers*: Margaret Madden of Bleach House Library blog; Liz Nugent for her reassurance at a difficult time. Michael O'Brien, Svetlana Pironko, and everyone at O'Brien Press for their kindness. To my friends Mary Conroy and Orlaith Mannion for drinks and encouragement and to Tanya Monier for taking the book to her heart. To all those who told me how the book moved them, and how they cared about the characters, I hope Lucia's War will do the same.

The following acknowledgement is included for every novel I write during the Trump administration. Mueller She Wrote podcast and its successor, the Daily Beans, processed all the Trump stuff with humour and grace so I could get on with writing the book and not carry the psychic burden of that man on my shoulders. Also to all those who have showed courage and who walk in light, including Robert Mueller himself.

A book like this requires research, and I am grateful to those who chronicled the era in question. It was a vibrant time, one where the real people who populated the Coterie of Friends in early twentieth century London could and did thrive: decorated physician Dr John Alcindor, gifted and underrated composer Edmund Thornton Jenkins, Evelyn Dove (changed to Sparrow in this version) and the gentlemen of the Southern Syncopated Orchestra, many of whom sadly died en route to perform in Dublin in 1921 when their ship sank. Julianne Evanti is a fictional re-naming of Lillian Evanti, an American soprano who found living in Paris far more congenial and less racist than America. I hope in the coming years we can learn more about these wonderful people.

A non-exhaustive list of sources includes *Dope Girls: the Birth of* the British Drug Underground by Marek Kohn (Lawrence & Wishart, 1992), *Staying Power: the History of Black People in Britain* by Peter Fryer (University of Alberta, 1984) *Jamaican Women and the World Wars: On the Front Line of Change* by Dalea Bean (Palgrave Macmillan, 2018) and *Black Edwardians: Black People in Britain 1901-1914* by Jeffrey P. Green. Mr Green also has a website with details of some of the more interesting characters of the time, including Edgar Manning, who deserves a book of his own. The memories of William Dale, a private in the British West Indies Regiment during WWI, also informed much of Reginald's story, including Rumpelstiltskin the squirrel monkey. For Yeats's cameo and his marital intentions, I am indebted to the works of Ann Saddlemyer and the late Brenda Maddox, as well as more traditional biographies of the poet.

On a personal note, my thanks to the Lanigans for emotional Gatorade and encouragement, and a special shout-out to my mother-in-law, Lil O'Neill, for her steadfast belief in my books. To Jonathan, who lived with Lucia all this time and understood why I had to finish this one, publisher or no. To the wonderful staff at Hopscotch in Cobh, who provided the precious time to get it done.

And finally, Luca, without whom there would have been no book.

29 May, 2020

ABOUT THE AUTHOR

Susan Lanigan is the author of *White Feathers* (Brandon, 2014) a historical WWI novel shortlisted for the Romantic Novel of the Year Award in 2015, and *Unfortunate Stars* (2020) a short novella also set in that universe. She has been thrice shortlisted for the Hennessy New Irish Writing Award and is an Irish Writers' Centre Novel Fair winner.

She lives by the sea in County Cork, Ireland.

ALSO BY SUSAN LANIGAN

White Feathers

Unfortunate Stars